R.L. STINE

Goosebumps®

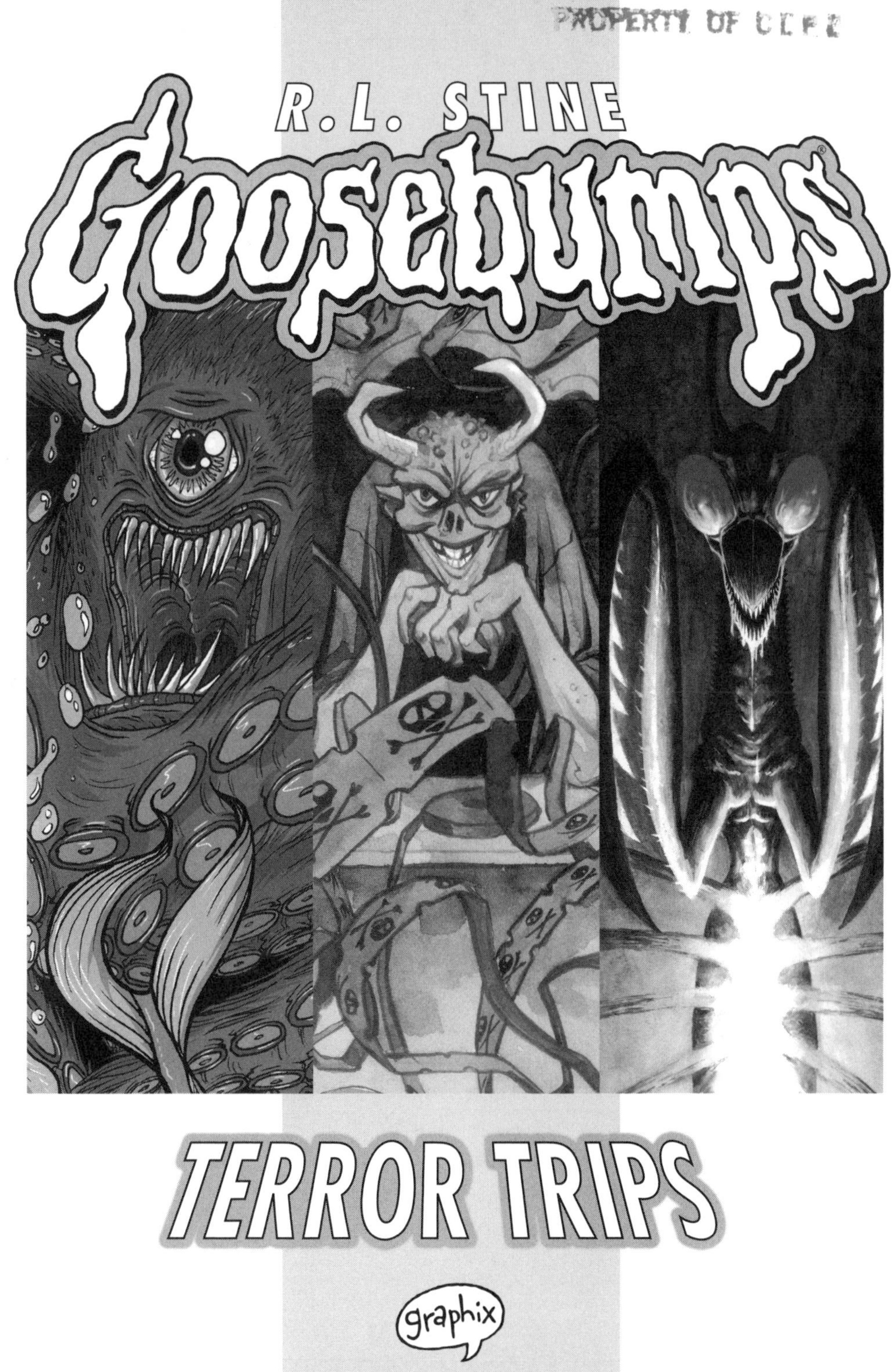

TERROR TRIPS

graphix

AN IMPRINT OF

SCHOLASTIC

NEW YORK TORONTO LONDON AUCKLAND SYDNEY MEXICO CITY NEW DELHI HONG KONG BUENOS AIRES

The Goosebumps book series created by Parachute Press, Inc.

Library of Congress Cataloging-in-Publication Data available

ISBN-13: 978-0-439-85777-2 / ISBN-10: 0-439-85777-5 (hardcover)

ISBN 0-439-85780-5 (paperback)

12 11 10 9 8 7 6 5 4 3 2 1 07 08 09 10 11

First edition, March 2007

Edited by Sheila Keenan

Book design by Richard Amari

Creative Director: David Saylor

Printed in the United States of America 23

ONE DAY AT HORRORLAND

adapted and illustrated by
Jill Thompson

ONE DAY AT HORRORLAND

adapted and illustrated by
Jill Thompson 5

A SHOCKER ON SHOCK STREET

adapted and illustrated by
Jamie Tolagson 47

DEEP TROUBLE

adapted and illustrated by
Amy Kim Ganter 89

Meet the Artists 137

ONE DAY AT HORRORLAND

ADAPTED AND ILLUSTRATED BY

Jill Thompson

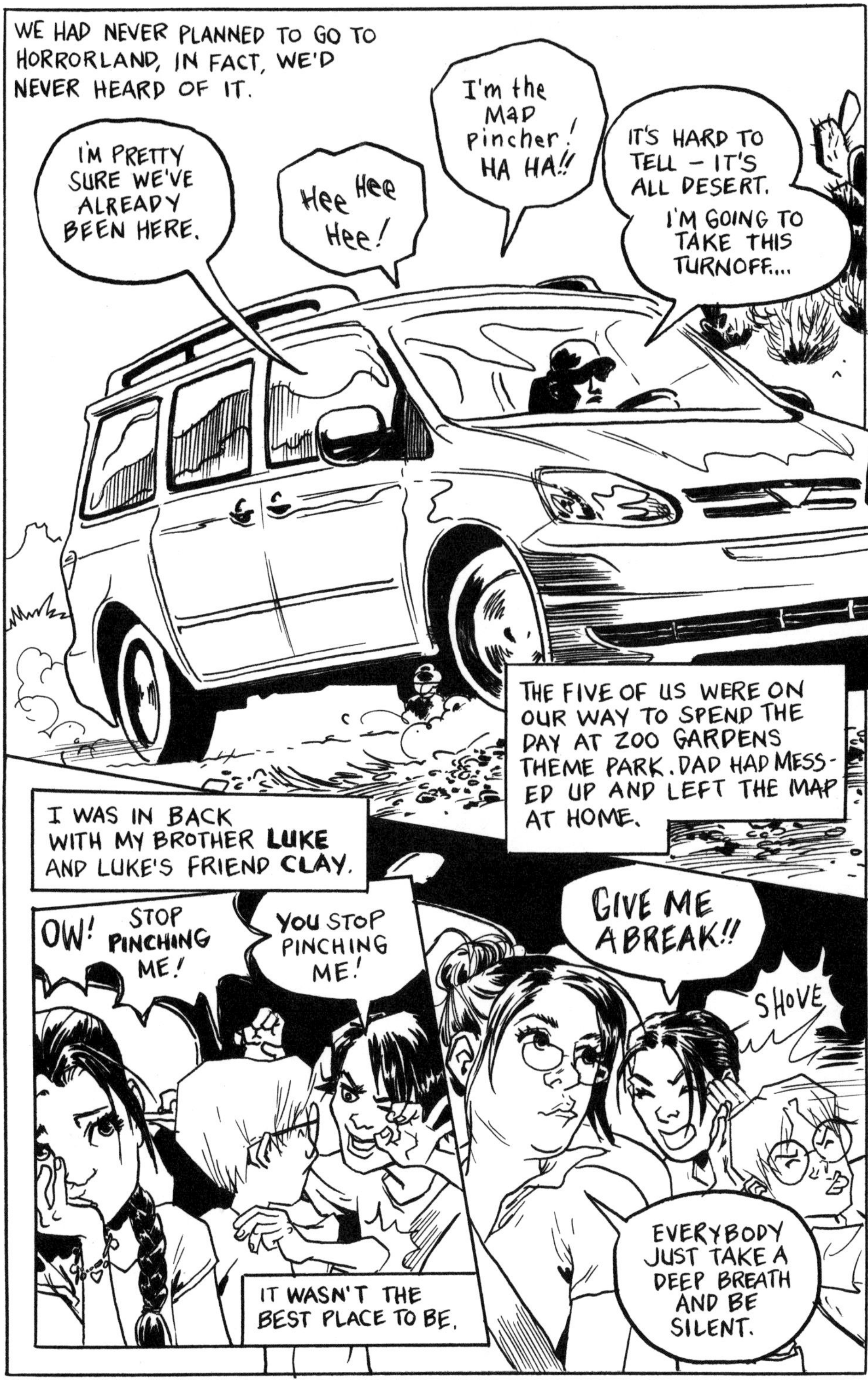
WE HAD NEVER PLANNED TO GO TO HORRORLAND, IN FACT, WE'D NEVER HEARD OF IT.
I'M PRETTY SURE WE'VE ALREADY BEEN HERE.
Hee Hee Hee!
I'm the Map pincher! HA HA!!
IT'S HARD TO TELL – IT'S ALL DESERT.
I'M GOING TO TAKE THIS TURNOFF....
THE FIVE OF US WERE ON OUR WAY TO SPEND THE DAY AT ZOO GARDENS THEME PARK. DAD HAD MESS-ED UP AND LEFT THE MAP AT HOME.
I WAS IN BACK WITH MY BROTHER LUKE AND LUKE'S FRIEND CLAY.
OW! STOP PINCHING ME!
YOU STOP PINCHING ME!
IT WASN'T THE BEST PLACE TO BE.
GIVE ME A BREAK!!
SHOVE
EVERYBODY JUST TAKE A DEEP BREATH AND BE SILENT.

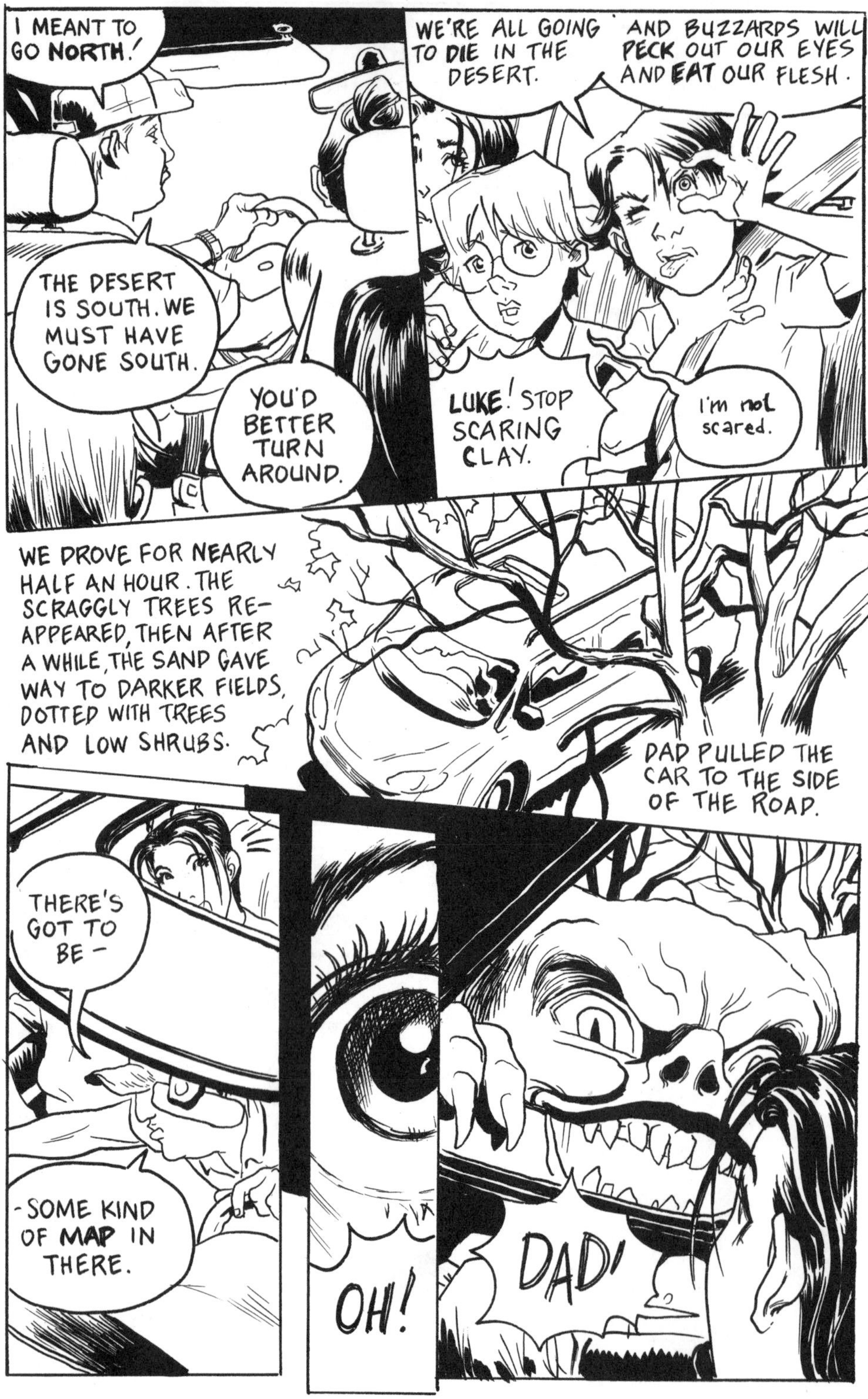
I MEANT TO GO NORTH!
THE DESERT IS SOUTH. WE MUST HAVE GONE SOUTH.
YOU'D BETTER TURN AROUND.
WE'RE ALL GOING TO DIE IN THE DESERT.
AND BUZZARDS WILL PECK OUT OUR EYES AND EAT OUR FLESH.
LUKE! STOP SCARING CLAY.
I'm not scared.
WE DROVE FOR NEARLY HALF AN HOUR. THE SCRAGGLY TREES RE-APPEARED, THEN AFTER A WHILE, THE SAND GAVE WAY TO DARKER FIELDS, DOTTED WITH TREES AND LOW SHRUBS.
DAD PULLED THE CAR TO THE SIDE OF THE ROAD.
THERE'S GOT TO BE -
- SOME KIND OF MAP IN THERE.
OH!
DAD!

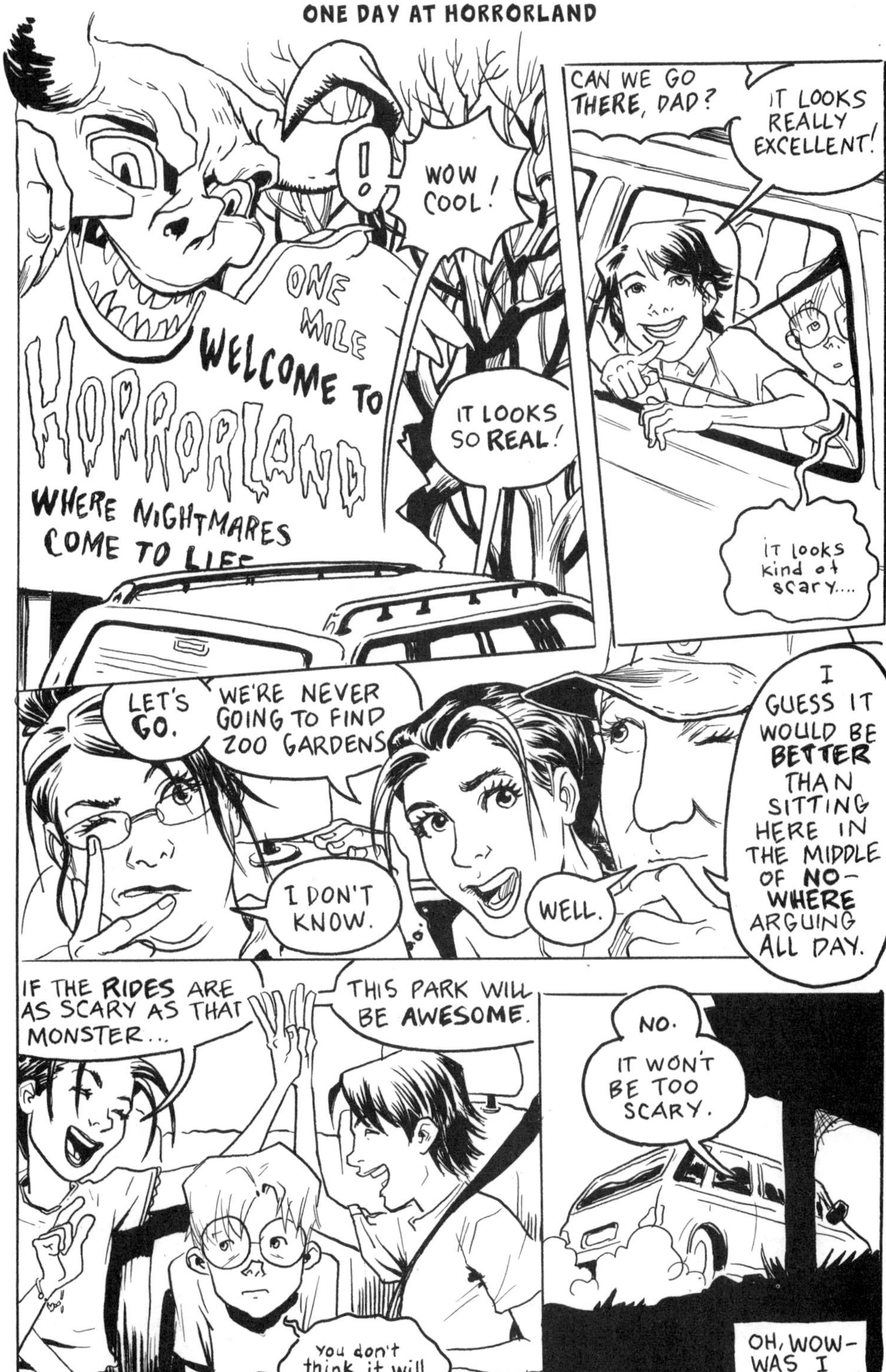
!
WOW COOL!
ONE MILE
WELCOME TO HORRORLAND
WHERE NIGHTMARES COME TO LIF
IT LOOKS SO REAL!
CAN WE GO THERE, DAD?
IT LOOKS REALLY EXCELLENT!
it looks kind of scary....
LET'S GO.
WE'RE NEVER GOING TO FIND ZOO GARDENS.
I DON'T KNOW.
WELL.
I GUESS IT WOULD BE BETTER THAN SITTING HERE IN THE MIDDLE OF NO-WHERE ARGUING ALL DAY.
IF THE RIDES ARE AS SCARY AS THAT MONSTER...
THIS PARK WILL BE AWESOME.
You don't think it will be TOO scary do you?
NO. IT WON'T BE TOO SCARY.
OH, WOW- WAS I WRONG!

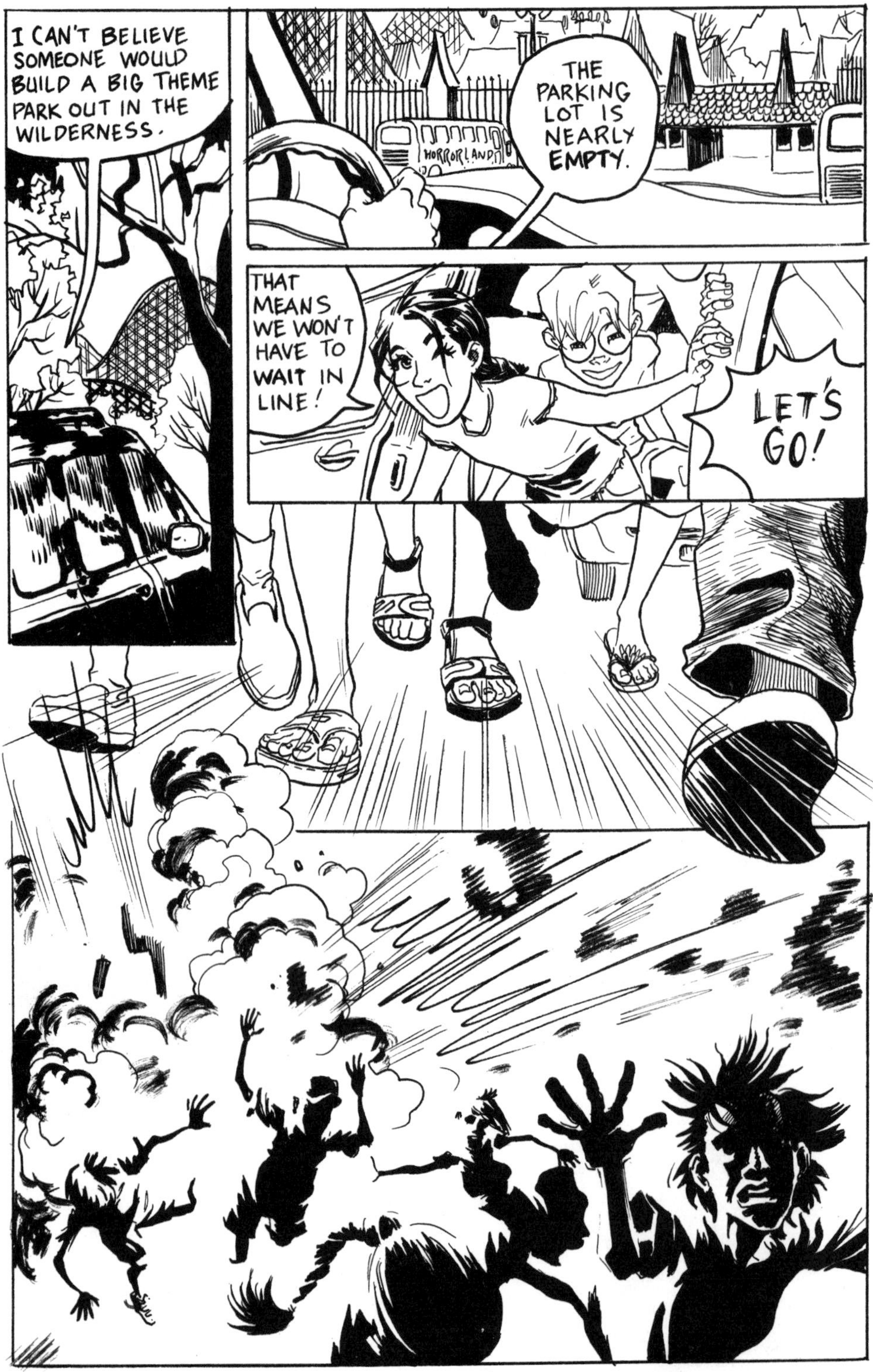
I CAN'T BELIEVE SOMEONE WOULD BUILD A BIG THEME PARK OUT IN THE WILDERNESS.
HORRORLAND
THE PARKING LOT IS NEARLY EMPTY.
THAT MEANS WE WON'T HAVE TO WAIT IN LINE!
LET'S GO!

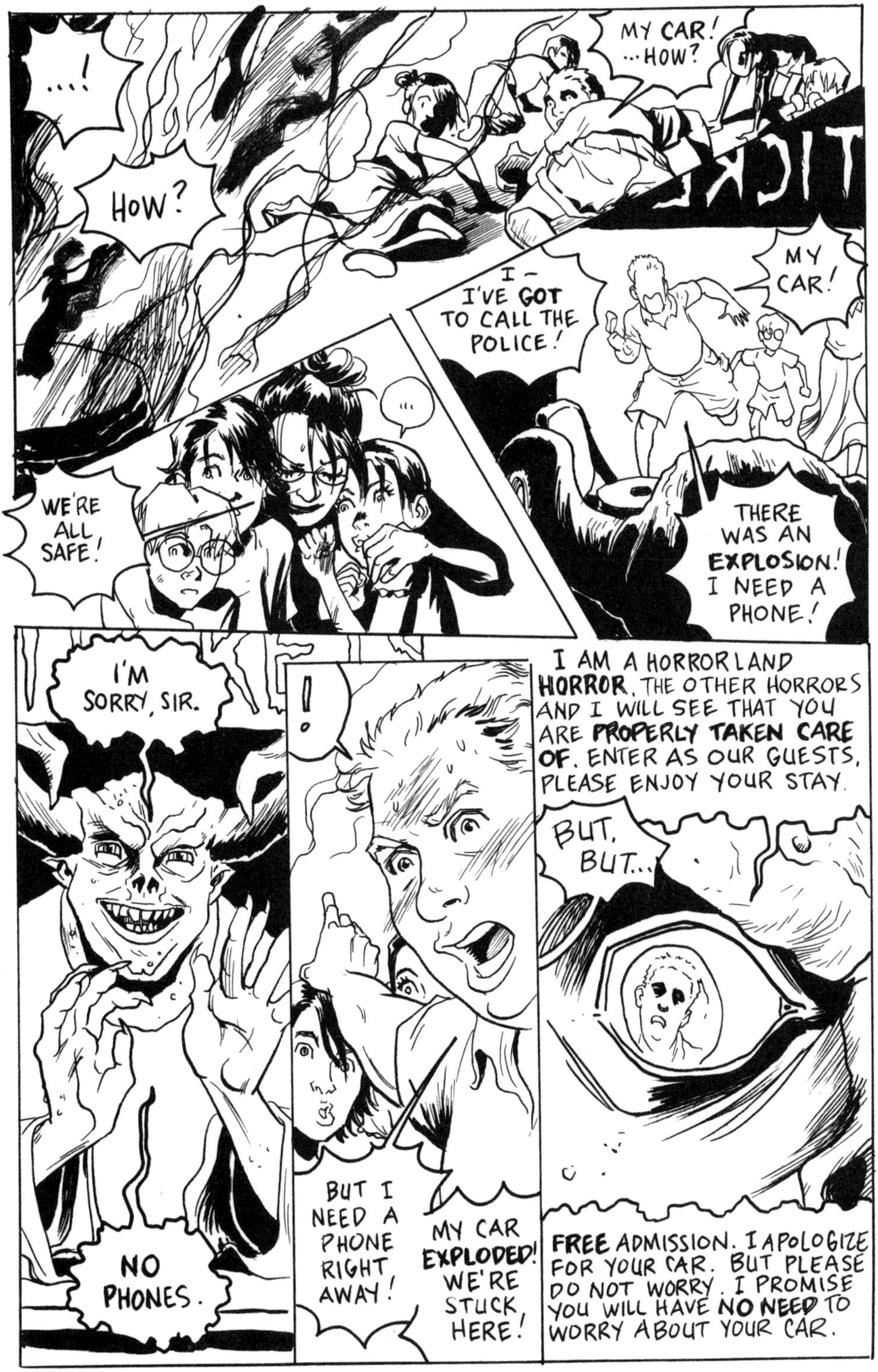
...!
HOW?
MY CAR! ...HOW?
WE'RE ALL SAFE!
...
I— I'VE GOT TO CALL THE POLICE!
MY CAR!
THERE WAS AN EXPLOSION! I NEED A PHONE!
I'M SORRY, SIR.
NO PHONES.
!
BUT I NEED A PHONE RIGHT AWAY!
MY CAR EXPLODED! WE'RE STUCK HERE!
I AM A HORRORLAND HORROR. THE OTHER HORRORS AND I WILL SEE THAT YOU ARE PROPERLY TAKEN CARE OF. ENTER AS OUR GUESTS. PLEASE ENJOY YOUR STAY.
BUT, BUT...
FREE ADMISSION. I APOLOGIZE FOR YOUR CAR. BUT PLEASE DO NOT WORRY. I PROMISE YOU WILL HAVE NO NEED TO WORRY ABOUT YOUR CAR.

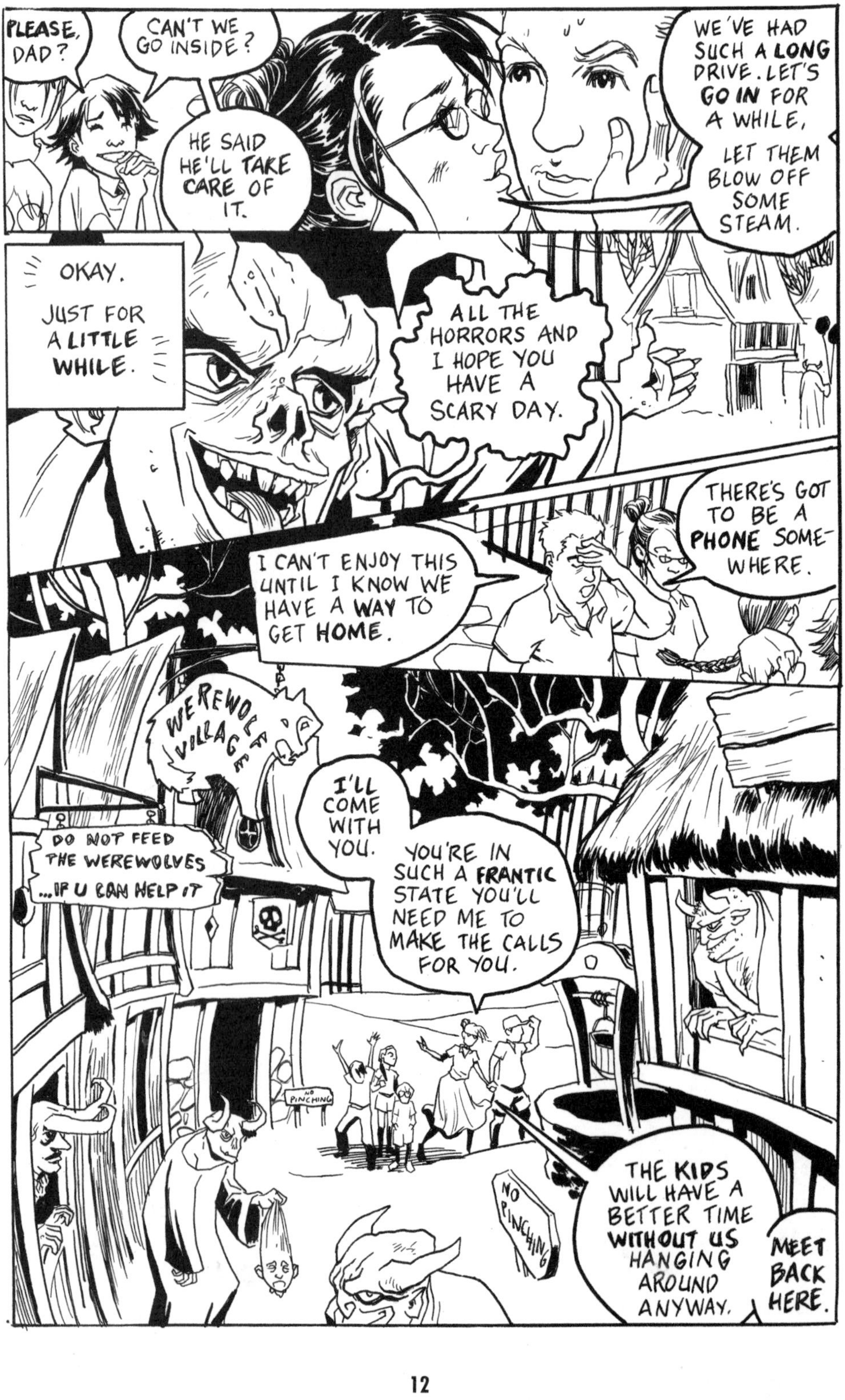
PLEASE, DAD?
CAN'T WE GO INSIDE?
HE SAID HE'LL TAKE CARE OF IT.
WE'VE HAD SUCH A LONG DRIVE. LET'S GO IN FOR A WHILE,
LET THEM BLOW OFF SOME STEAM.
OKAY.
JUST FOR A LITTLE WHILE.
ALL THE HORRORS AND I HOPE YOU HAVE A SCARY DAY.
I CAN'T ENJOY THIS UNTIL I KNOW WE HAVE A WAY TO GET HOME.
THERE'S GOT TO BE A PHONE SOMEWHERE.
WEREWOLF VILLAGE
DO NOT FEED THE WEREWOLVES ...IF U CAN HELP IT
I'LL COME WITH YOU.
YOU'RE IN SUCH A FRANTIC STATE YOU'LL NEED ME TO MAKE THE CALLS FOR YOU.
NO PINCHING
NO PINCHING
THE KIDS WILL HAVE A BETTER TIME WITHOUT US HANGING AROUND ANYWAY.
MEET BACK HERE.

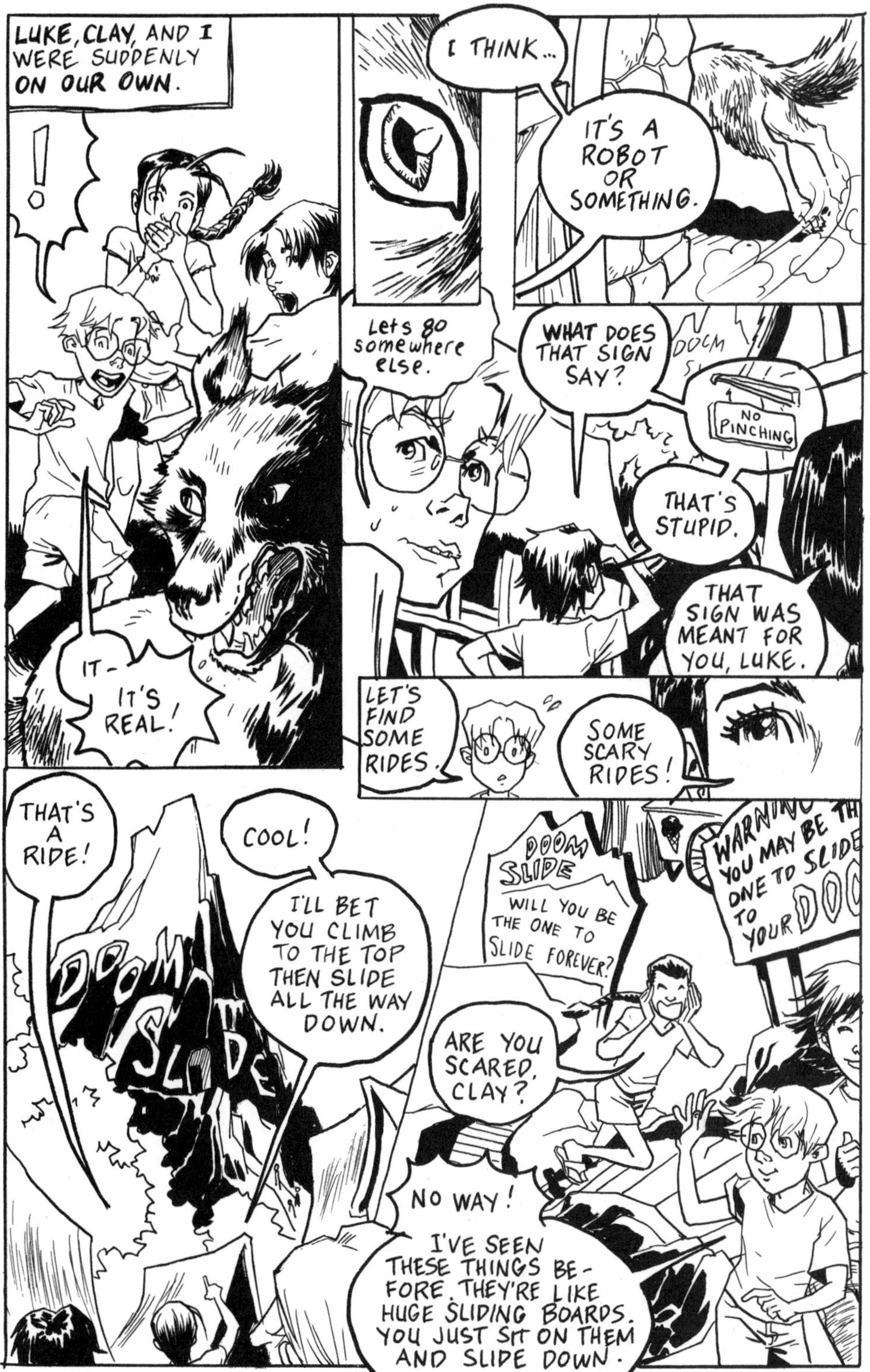
LUKE, CLAY, AND I WERE SUDDENLY ON OUR OWN.
!
IT-
IT'S REAL!
I THINK...
IT'S A ROBOT OR SOMETHING.
Lets go somewhere else.
WHAT DOES THAT SIGN SAY?
DOOM
NO PINCHING
THAT'S STUPID.
THAT SIGN WAS MEANT FOR YOU, LUKE.
LET'S FIND SOME RIDES.
SOME SCARY RIDES!
THAT'S A RIDE!
COOL!
I'LL BET YOU CLIMB TO THE TOP THEN SLIDE ALL THE WAY DOWN.
DOOM SLIDE
DOOM SLIDE
WILL YOU BE THE ONE TO SLIDE FOREVER?
ARE YOU SCARED, CLAY?
NO WAY!
I'VE SEEN THESE THINGS BE-FORE. THEY'RE LIKE HUGE SLIDING BOARDS. YOU JUST SIT ON THEM AND SLIDE DOWN.

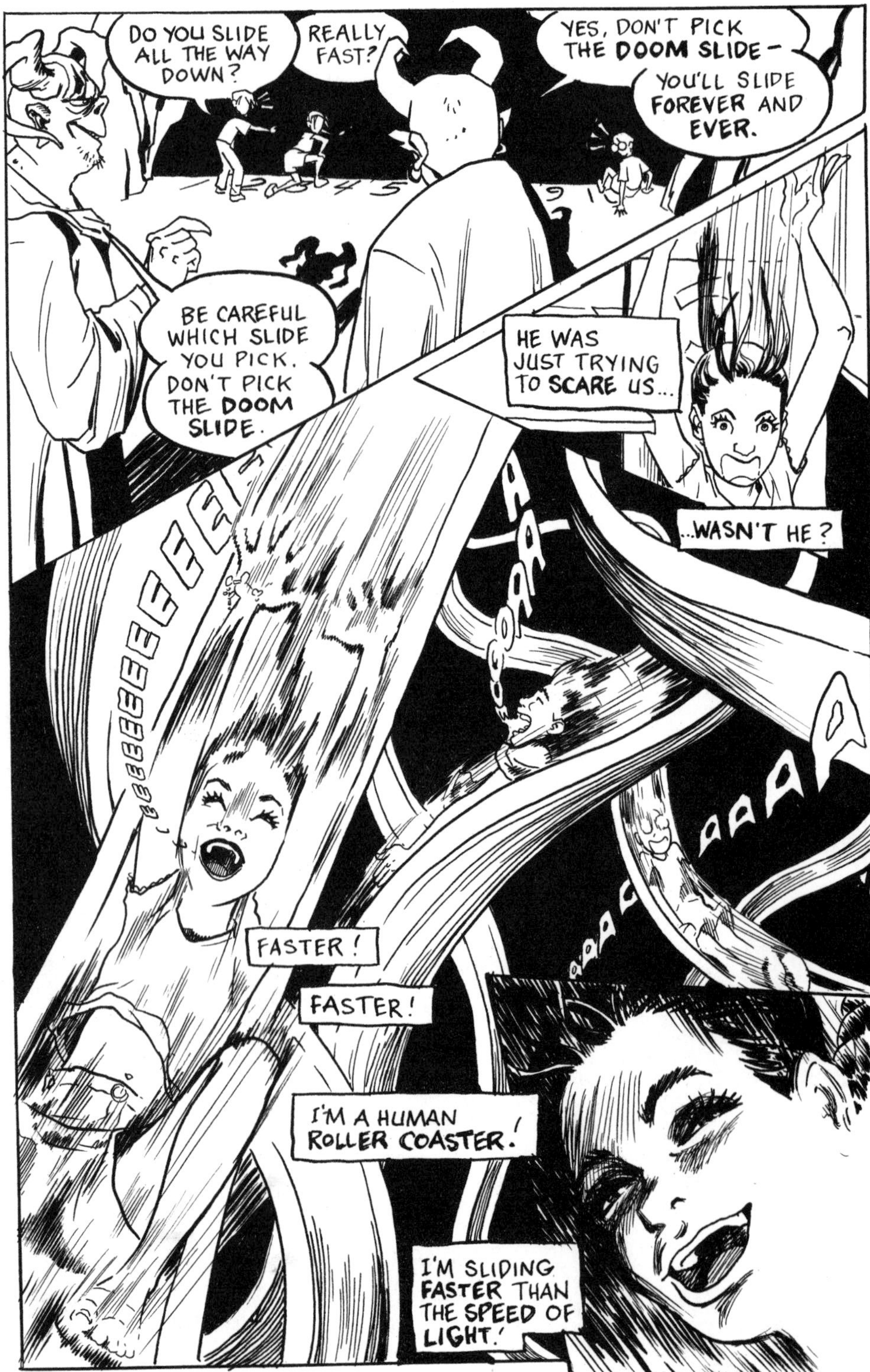
DO YOU SLIDE ALL THE WAY DOWN?
REALLY FAST?
YES, DON'T PICK THE DOOM SLIDE -
YOU'LL SLIDE FOREVER AND EVER.
BE CAREFUL WHICH SLIDE YOU PICK. DON'T PICK THE DOOM SLIDE.
HE WAS JUST TRYING TO SCARE US...
...WASN'T HE?
EEEEEEEEEEEEEEE
AAAAAAA
AAAAAAAAAA
FASTER!
FASTER!
I'M A HUMAN ROLLER COASTER!
I'M SLIDING FASTER THAN THE SPEED OF LIGHT!

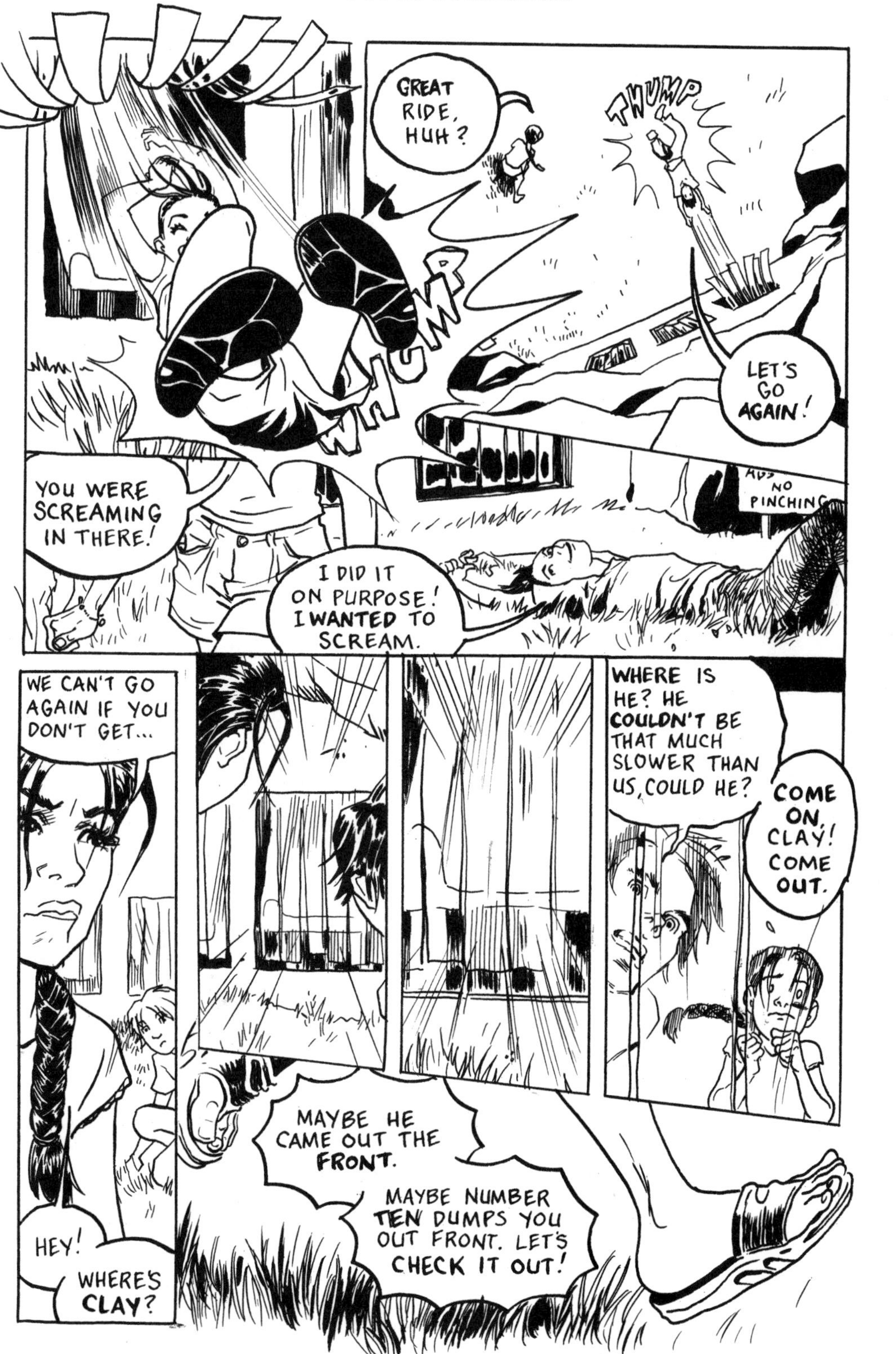
WHUMP
GREAT RIDE, HUH?
THUMP
LET'S GO AGAIN!
YOU WERE SCREAMING IN THERE!
NO PINCHING
I DID IT ON PURPOSE! I WANTED TO SCREAM.
WE CAN'T GO AGAIN IF YOU DON'T GET...
HEY!
WHERE'S CLAY?
WHERE IS HE? HE COULDN'T BE THAT MUCH SLOWER THAN US, COULD HE?
COME ON, CLAY! COME OUT.
MAYBE HE CAME OUT THE FRONT.
MAYBE NUMBER TEN DUMPS YOU OUT FRONT. LET'S CHECK IT OUT!

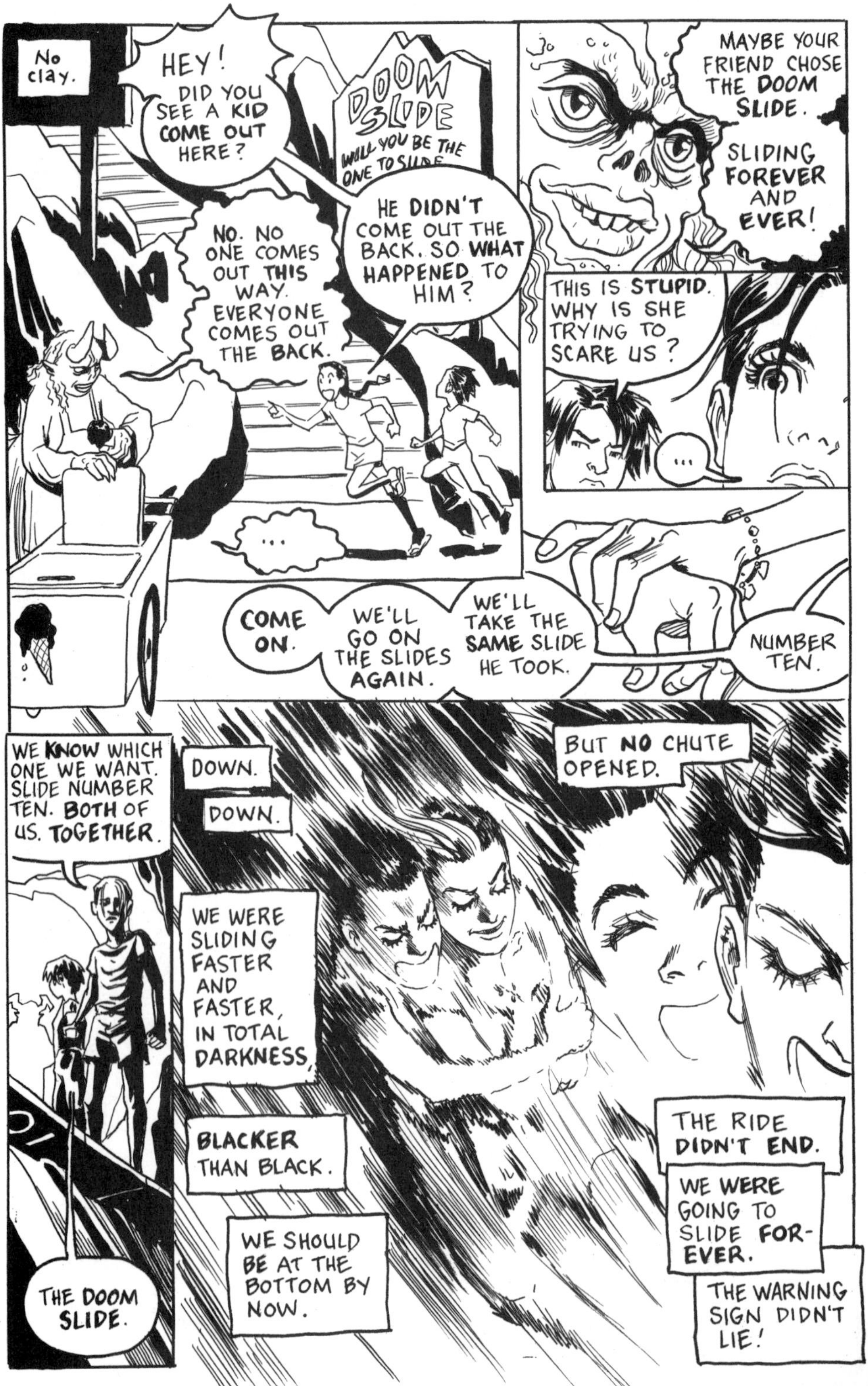
No clay.
HEY! DID YOU SEE A KID COME OUT HERE?
DOOM SLIDE WILL YOU BE THE ONE TO SLIDE
NO. NO ONE COMES OUT THIS WAY. EVERYONE COMES OUT THE BACK.
HE DIDN'T COME OUT THE BACK. SO WHAT HAPPENED TO HIM?
...
MAYBE YOUR FRIEND CHOSE THE DOOM SLIDE.
SLIDING FOREVER AND EVER!
THIS IS STUPID. WHY IS SHE TRYING TO SCARE US?
...
COME ON.
WE'LL GO ON THE SLIDES AGAIN.
WE'LL TAKE THE SAME SLIDE HE TOOK.
NUMBER TEN.
WE KNOW WHICH ONE WE WANT. SLIDE NUMBER TEN. BOTH OF US. TOGETHER.
THE DOOM SLIDE.
DOWN.
DOWN.
WE WERE SLIDING FASTER AND FASTER, IN TOTAL DARKNESS,
BLACKER THAN BLACK.
WE SHOULD BE AT THE BOTTOM BY NOW.
BUT NO CHUTE OPENED.
THE RIDE DIDN'T END.
WE WERE GOING TO SLIDE FOR-EVER.
THE WARNING SIGN DIDN'T LIE!

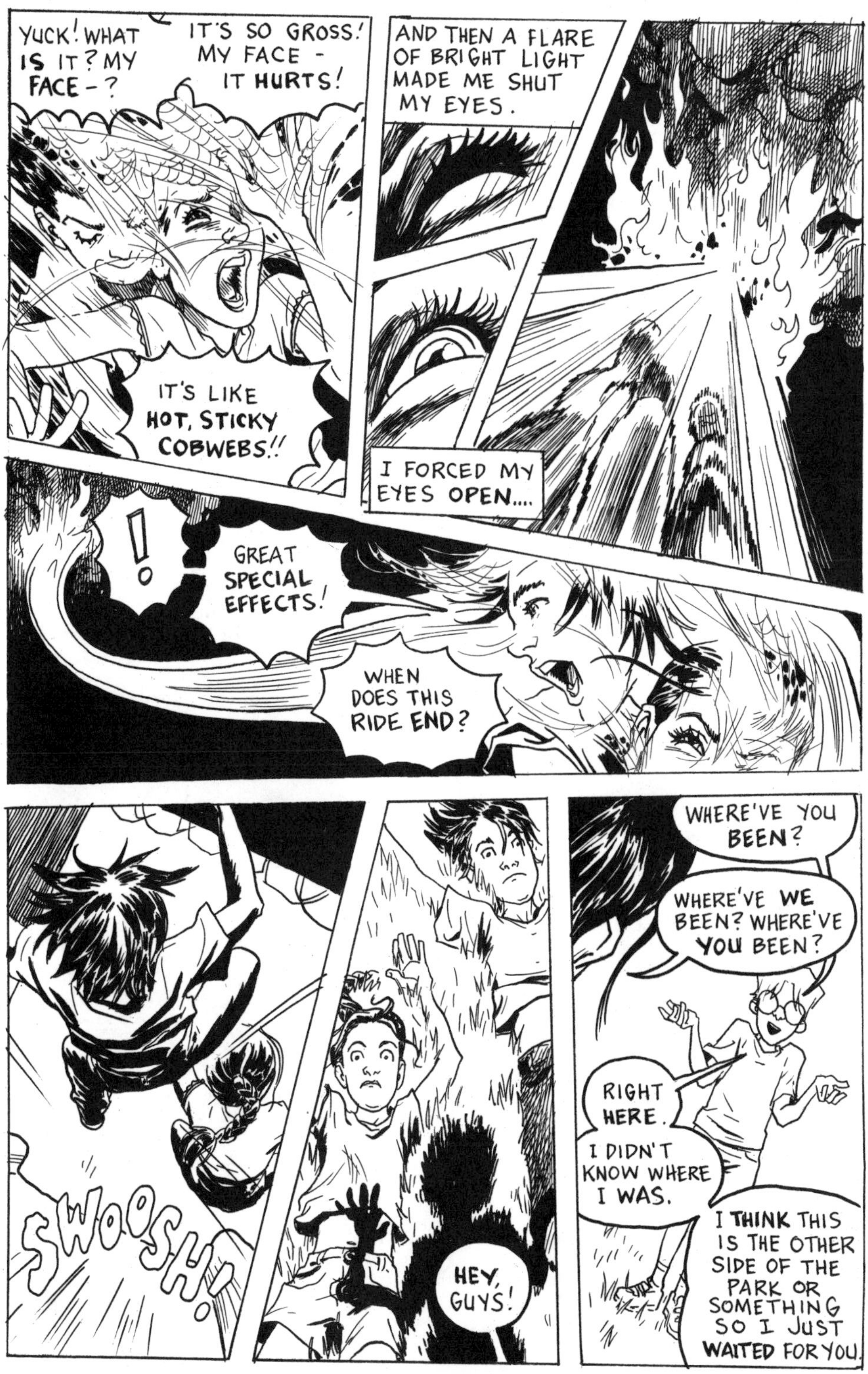
YUCK! WHAT IS IT? MY FACE-?
IT'S SO GROSS! MY FACE - IT HURTS!
IT'S LIKE HOT, STICKY COBWEBS!!
AND THEN A FLARE OF BRIGHT LIGHT MADE ME SHUT MY EYES.
I FORCED MY EYES OPEN....
!
GREAT SPECIAL EFFECTS!
WHEN DOES THIS RIDE END?
SWOOSH!
HEY, GUYS!
WHERE'VE YOU BEEN?
WHERE'VE WE BEEN? WHERE'VE YOU BEEN?
RIGHT HERE.
I DIDN'T KNOW WHERE I WAS.
I THINK THIS IS THE OTHER SIDE OF THE PARK OR SOMETHING SO I JUST WAITED FOR YOU.

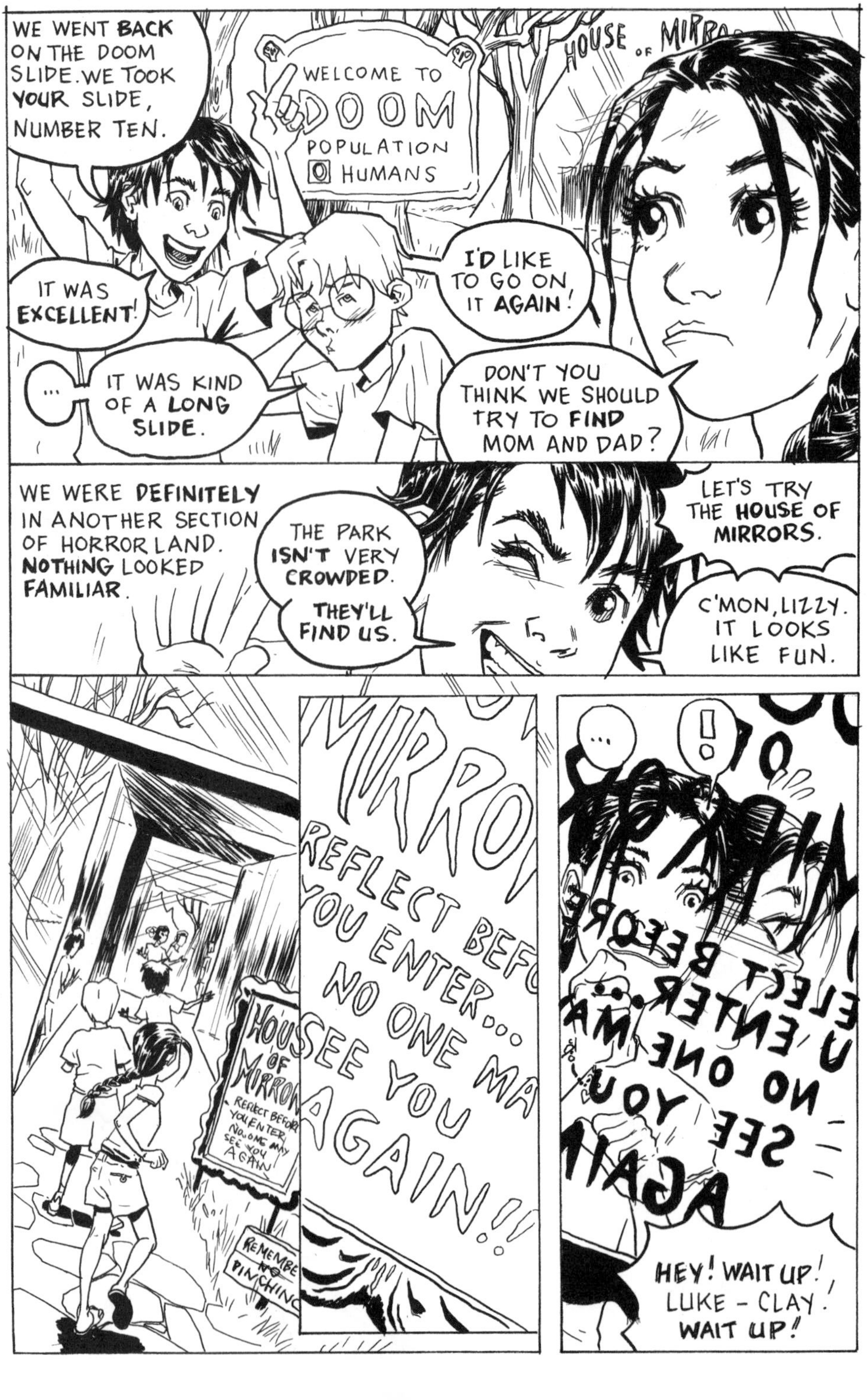
WE WENT BACK ON THE DOOM SLIDE. WE TOOK YOUR SLIDE, NUMBER TEN.
WELCOME TO DOOM POPULATION 0 HUMANS
IT WAS EXCELLENT!
I'D LIKE TO GO ON IT AGAIN!
...
IT WAS KIND OF A LONG SLIDE.
DON'T YOU THINK WE SHOULD TRY TO FIND MOM AND DAD?
WE WERE DEFINITELY IN ANOTHER SECTION OF HORROR LAND. NOTHING LOOKED FAMILIAR.
THE PARK ISN'T VERY CROWDED.
THEY'LL FIND US.
LET'S TRY THE HOUSE OF MIRRORS.
C'MON, LIZZY. IT LOOKS LIKE FUN.
REFLECT BEFORE YOU ENTER. NO ONE MAY SEE YOU AGAIN
...
!
HEY! WAIT UP! LUKE - CLAY! WAIT UP!

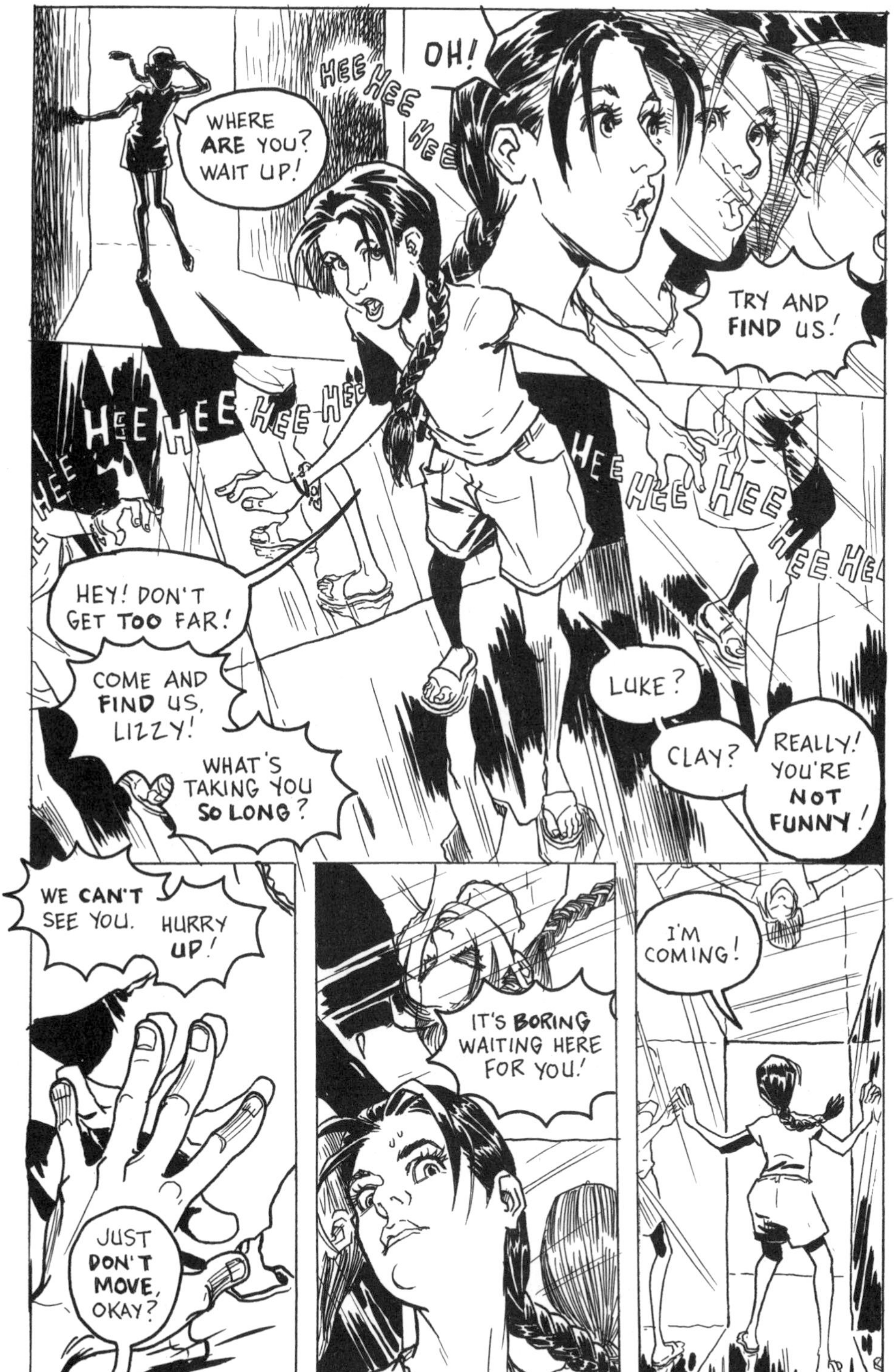
WHERE ARE YOU? WAIT UP!
HEE HEE HEE HEE
OH!
TRY AND FIND US!
HEE HEE HEE HEE HEE
HEE HEE HEE HEE HEE
HEY! DON'T GET TOO FAR!
COME AND FIND US, LIZZY!
WHAT'S TAKING YOU SO LONG?
LUKE?
CLAY?
REALLY! YOU'RE NOT FUNNY!
WE CAN'T SEE YOU. HURRY UP!
JUST DON'T MOVE, OKAY?
IT'S BORING WAITING HERE FOR YOU!
I'M COMING!

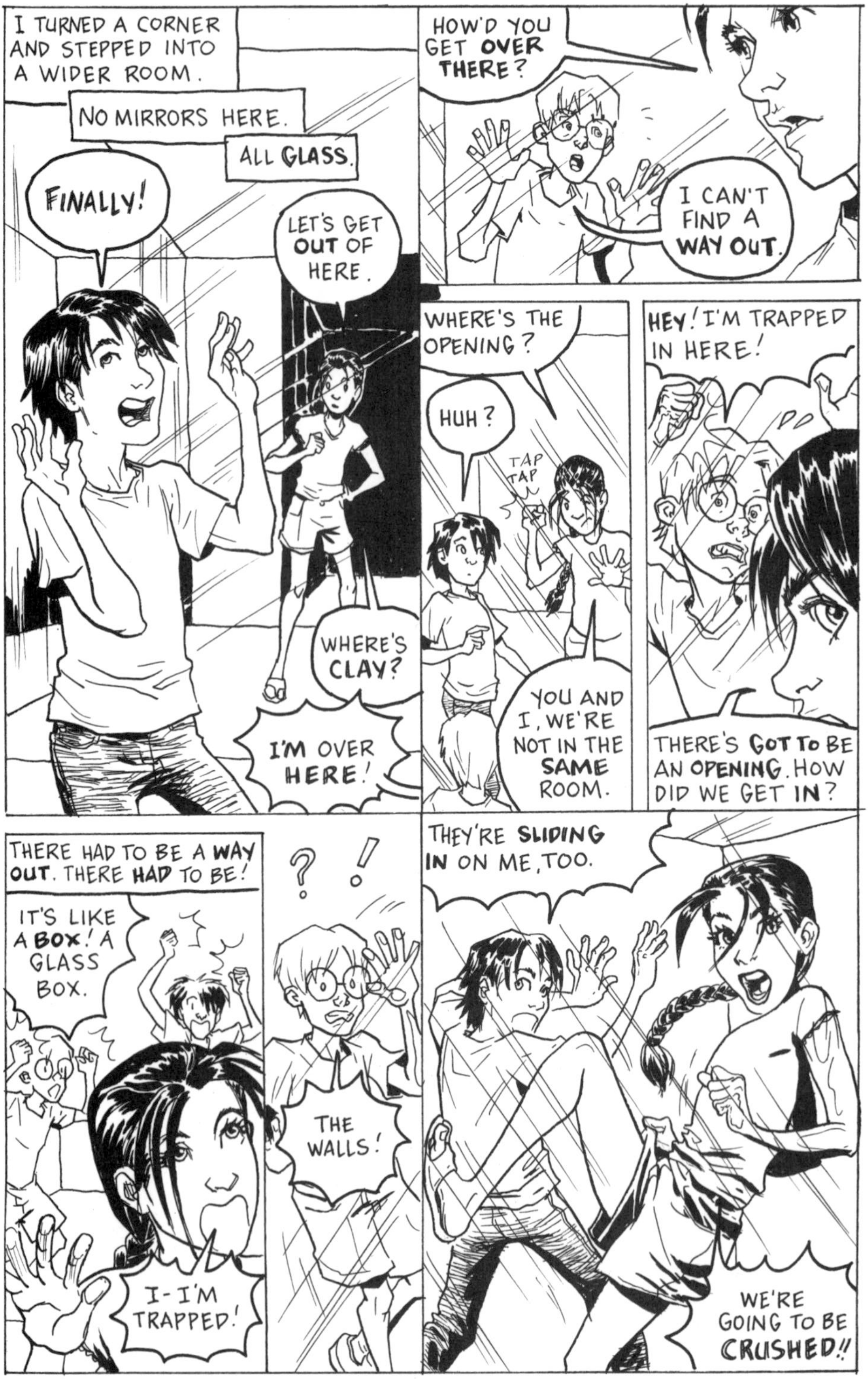
I TURNED A CORNER AND STEPPED INTO A WIDER ROOM.
NO MIRRORS HERE.
ALL GLASS.
FINALLY!
LET'S GET OUT OF HERE.
WHERE'S CLAY?
I'M OVER HERE!
HOW'D YOU GET OVER THERE?
I CAN'T FIND A WAY OUT.
WHERE'S THE OPENING?
HUH?
TAP TAP
YOU AND I, WE'RE NOT IN THE SAME ROOM.
HEY! I'M TRAPPED IN HERE!
THERE'S GOT TO BE AN OPENING. HOW DID WE GET IN?
THERE HAD TO BE A WAY OUT. THERE HAD TO BE!
IT'S LIKE A BOX! A GLASS BOX.
I-I'M TRAPPED!
? !
THE WALLS!
THEY'RE SLIDING IN ON ME, TOO.
WE'RE GOING TO BE CRUSHED!!

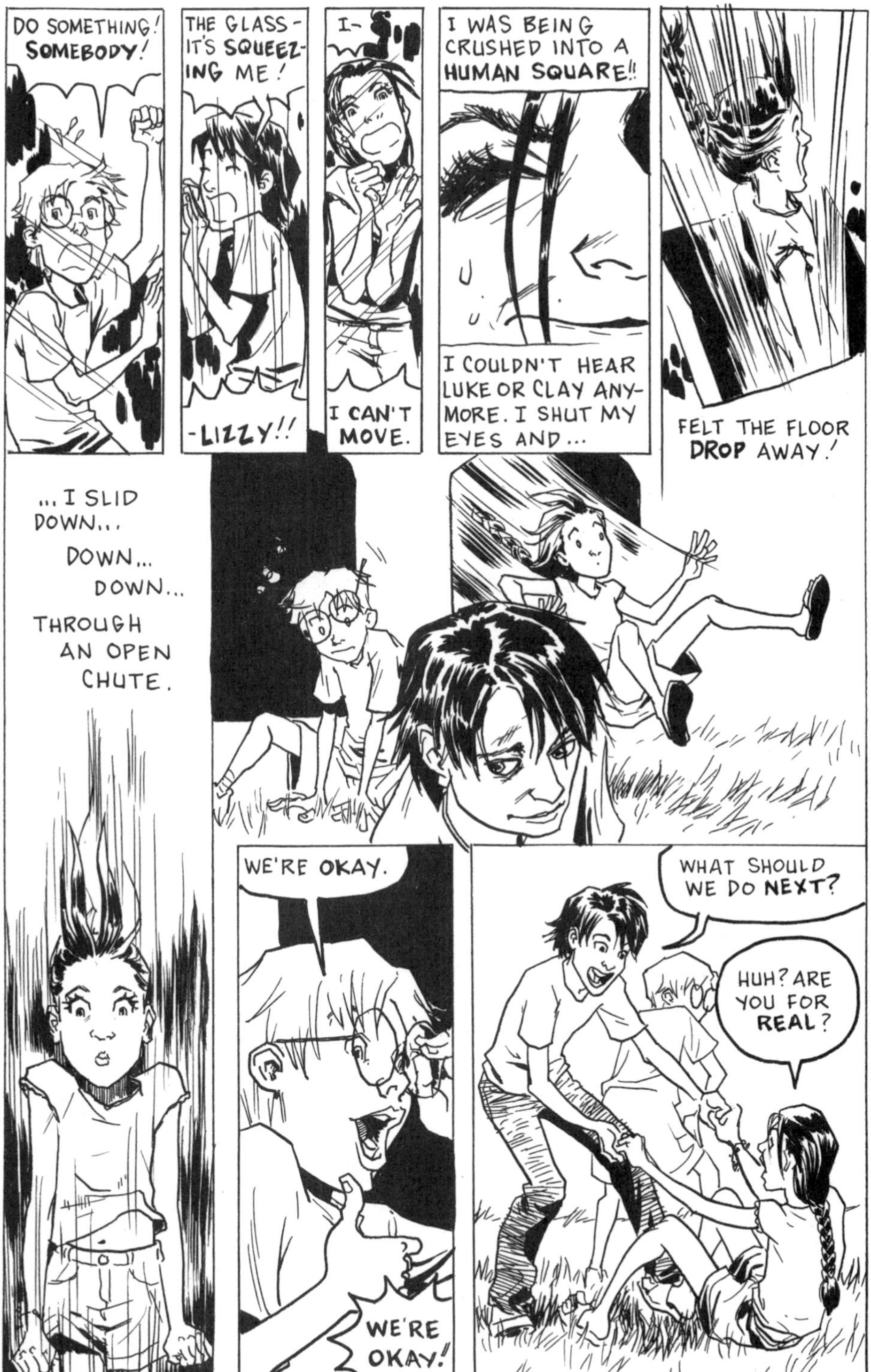
DO SOMETHING! SOMEBODY!
THE GLASS - IT'S SQUEEZ-ING ME!
-LIZZY!!
I-
I CAN'T MOVE.
I WAS BEING CRUSHED INTO A HUMAN SQUARE!!
I COULDN'T HEAR LUKE OR CLAY ANY-MORE. I SHUT MY EYES AND ...
FELT THE FLOOR DROP AWAY!
... I SLID DOWN... DOWN... DOWN... THROUGH AN OPEN CHUTE.
WE'RE OKAY.
WE'RE OKAY!
WHAT SHOULD WE DO NEXT?
HUH? ARE YOU FOR REAL?

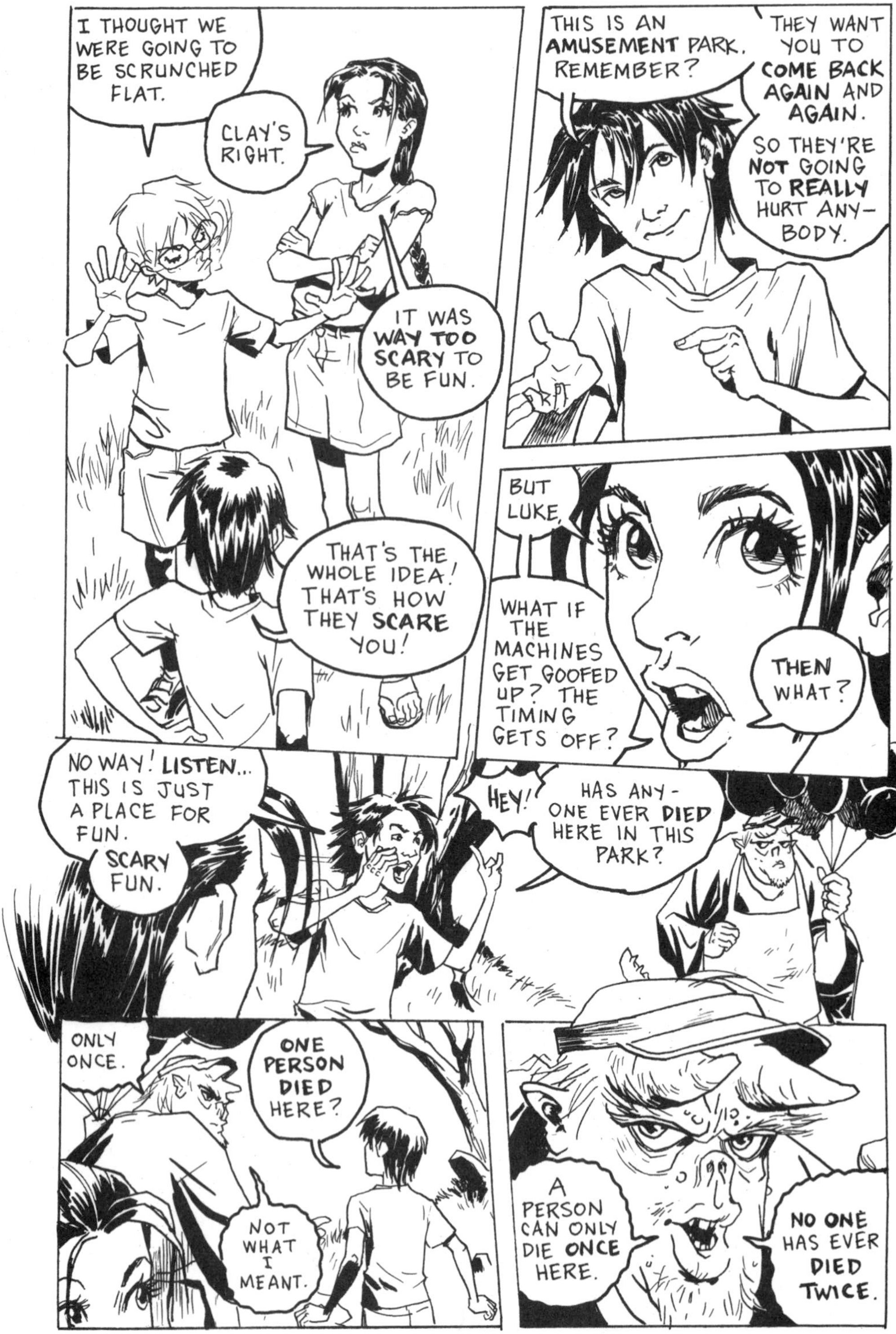
I THOUGHT WE WERE GOING TO BE SCRUNCHED FLAT.
CLAY'S RIGHT.
IT WAS WAY TOO SCARY TO BE FUN.
THAT'S THE WHOLE IDEA! THAT'S HOW THEY SCARE YOU!
THIS IS AN AMUSEMENT PARK. REMEMBER?
THEY WANT YOU TO COME BACK AGAIN AND AGAIN.
SO THEY'RE NOT GOING TO REALLY HURT ANY-BODY.
BUT LUKE,
WHAT IF THE MACHINES GET GOOFED UP? THE TIMING GETS OFF?
THEN WHAT?
NO WAY! LISTEN... THIS IS JUST A PLACE FOR FUN.
SCARY FUN.
HEY!
HAS ANY-ONE EVER DIED HERE IN THIS PARK?
ONLY ONCE.
ONE PERSON DIED HERE?
NOT WHAT I MEANT.
A PERSON CAN ONLY DIE ONCE HERE.
NO ONE HAS EVER DIED TWICE.

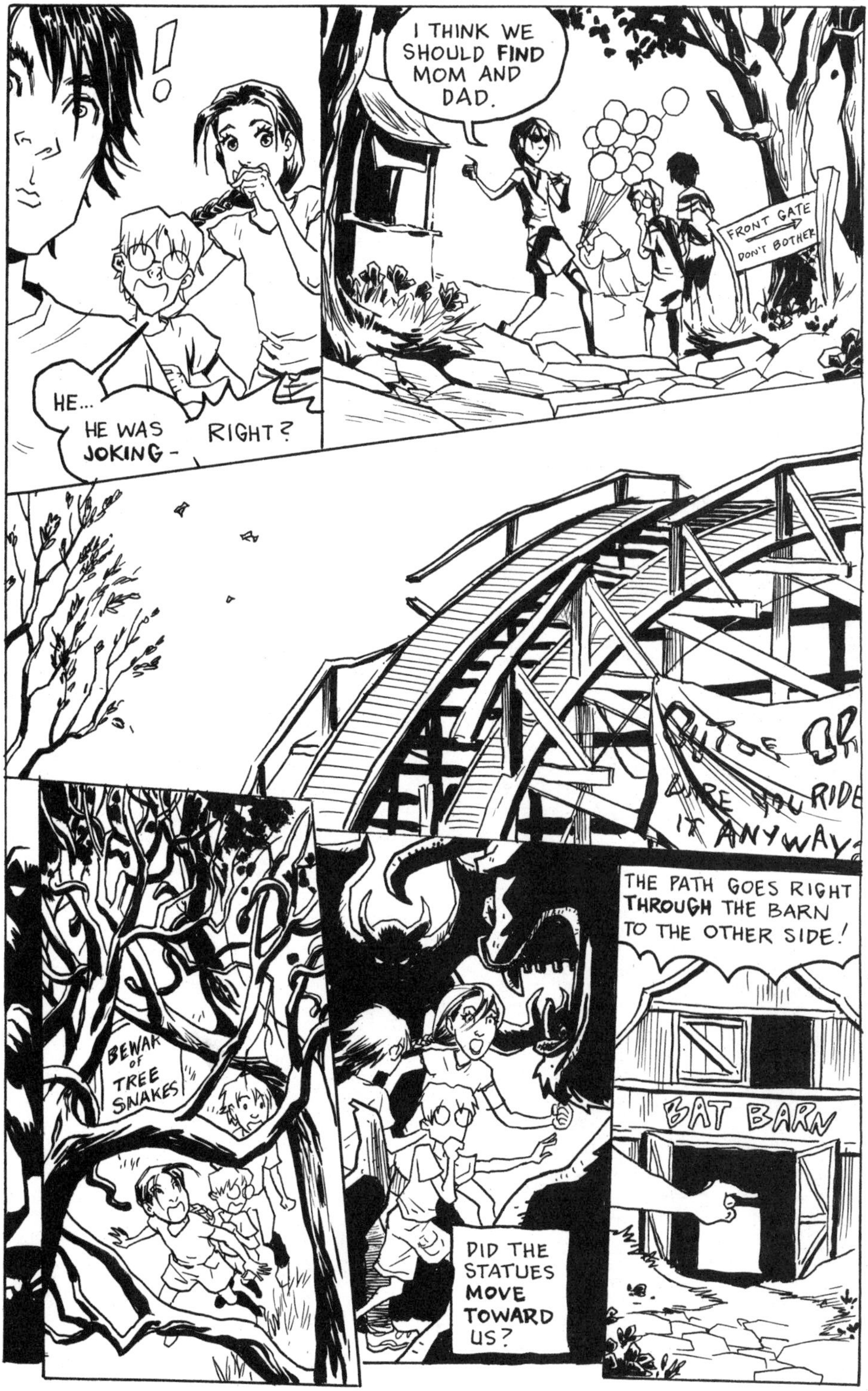
!
HE... HE WAS JOKING- RIGHT?
I THINK WE SHOULD FIND MOM AND DAD.
FRONT GATE
DON'T BOTHER
BEWAR OF TREE SNAKES
DID THE STATUES MOVE TOWARD US?
THE PATH GOES RIGHT THROUGH THE BARN TO THE OTHER SIDE!
BAT BARN

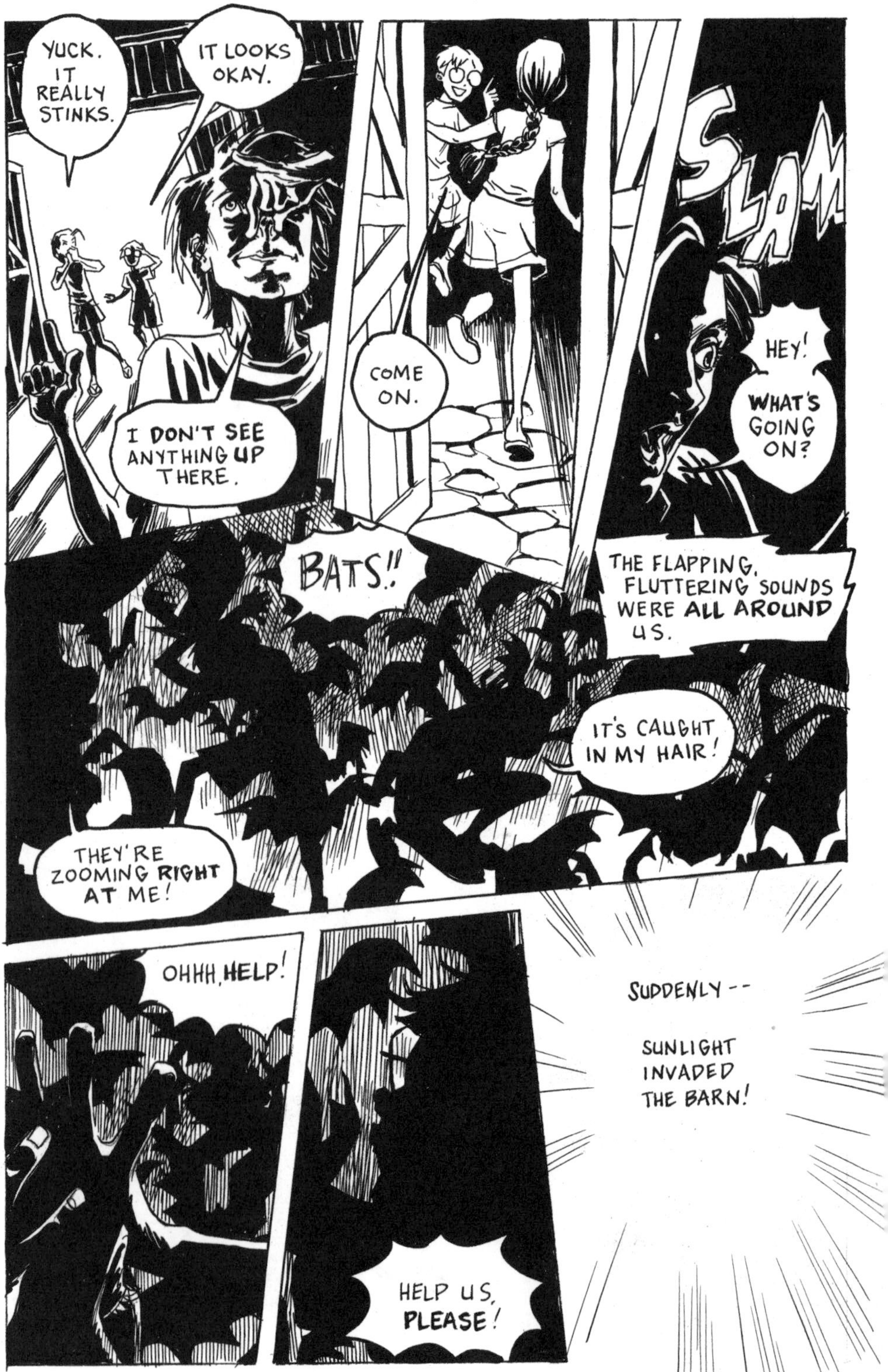
YUCK. IT REALLY STINKS.
IT LOOKS OKAY.
I DON'T SEE ANYTHING UP THERE.
COME ON.
SLAM
HEY! WHAT'S GOING ON?
BATS!!
THE FLAPPING, FLUTTERING SOUNDS WERE ALL AROUND US.
IT'S CAUGHT IN MY HAIR!
THEY'RE ZOOMING RIGHT AT ME!
OHHH, HELP!
HELP US, PLEASE!
SUDDENLY --
SUNLIGHT INVADED THE BARN!

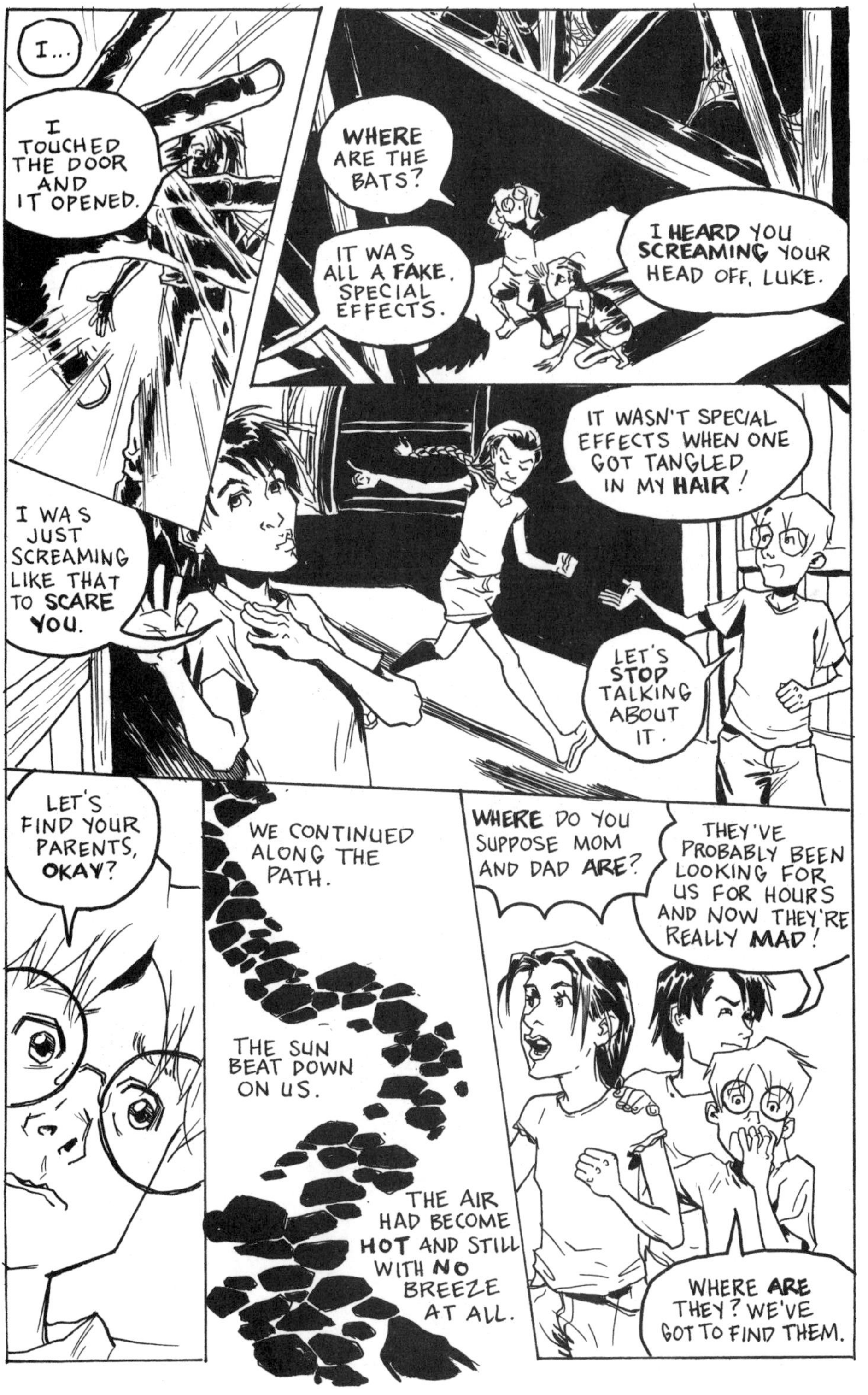
I...
I TOUCHED THE DOOR AND IT OPENED.
WHERE ARE THE BATS?
IT WAS ALL A FAKE. SPECIAL EFFECTS.
I HEARD YOU SCREAMING YOUR HEAD OFF, LUKE.
I WAS JUST SCREAMING LIKE THAT TO SCARE YOU.
IT WASN'T SPECIAL EFFECTS WHEN ONE GOT TANGLED IN MY HAIR!
LET'S STOP TALKING ABOUT IT.
LET'S FIND YOUR PARENTS, OKAY?
WE CONTINUED ALONG THE PATH.
THE SUN BEAT DOWN ON US.
THE AIR HAD BECOME HOT AND STILL WITH NO BREEZE AT ALL.
WHERE DO YOU SUPPOSE MOM AND DAD ARE?
THEY'VE PROBABLY BEEN LOOKING FOR US FOR HOURS AND NOW THEY'RE REALLY MAD!
WHERE ARE THEY? WE'VE GOT TO FIND THEM.

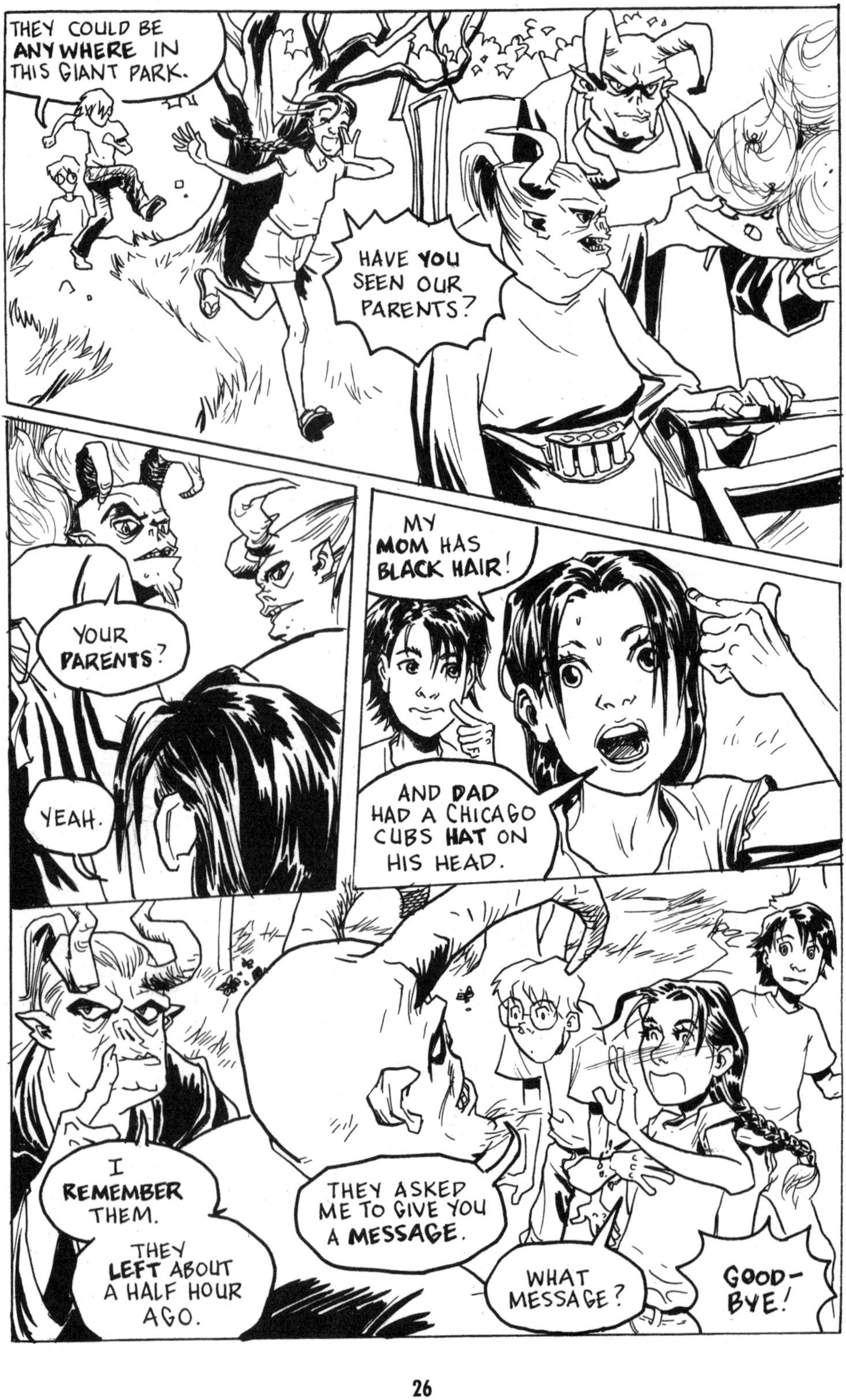
THEY COULD BE **ANYWHERE** IN THIS GIANT PARK.
HAVE **YOU** SEEN OUR PARENTS?
YOUR **PARENTS**?
YEAH.
MY **MOM** HAS **BLACK HAIR**!
AND **DAD** HAD A CHICAGO CUBS **HAT** ON HIS HEAD.
I **REMEMBER** THEM.
THEY **LEFT** ABOUT A HALF HOUR AGO.
THEY ASKED ME TO GIVE YOU A **MESSAGE**.
WHAT MESSAGE?
GOOD-BYE!

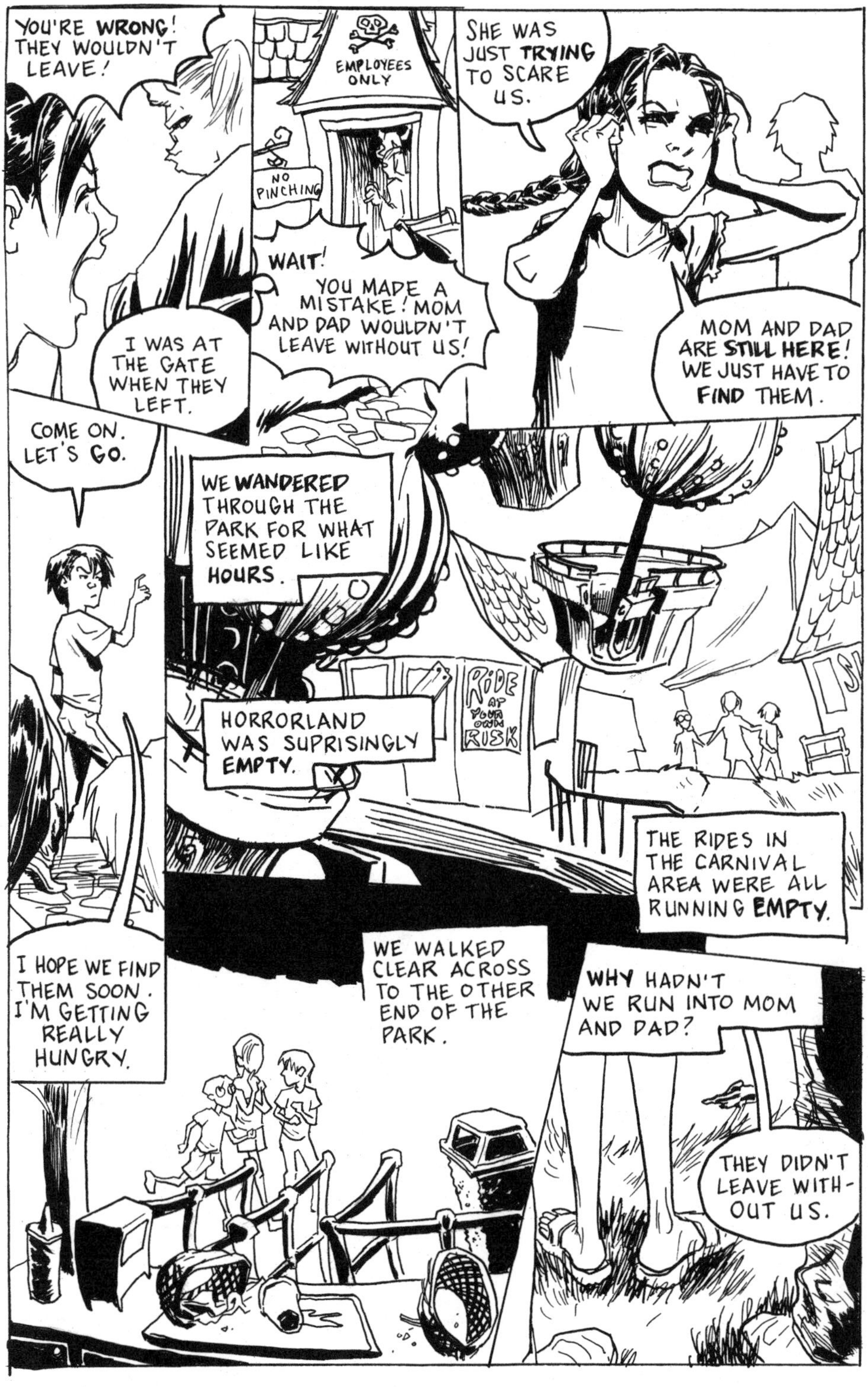
YOU'RE WRONG! THEY WOULDN'T LEAVE!
I WAS AT THE GATE WHEN THEY LEFT.
EMPLOYEES ONLY
NO PINCHING
WAIT! YOU MADE A MISTAKE! MOM AND DAD WOULDN'T LEAVE WITHOUT US!
SHE WAS JUST TRYING TO SCARE US.
MOM AND DAD ARE STILL HERE! WE JUST HAVE TO FIND THEM.
COME ON. LET'S GO.
WE WANDERED THROUGH THE PARK FOR WHAT SEEMED LIKE HOURS.
HORRORLAND WAS SUPRISINGLY EMPTY.
RIDE AT YOUR OWN RISK
THE RIDES IN THE CARNIVAL AREA WERE ALL RUNNING EMPTY.
I HOPE WE FIND THEM SOON. I'M GETTING REALLY HUNGRY.
WE WALKED CLEAR ACROSS TO THE OTHER END OF THE PARK.
WHY HADN'T WE RUN INTO MOM AND DAD?
THEY DIDN'T LEAVE WITH-OUT US.

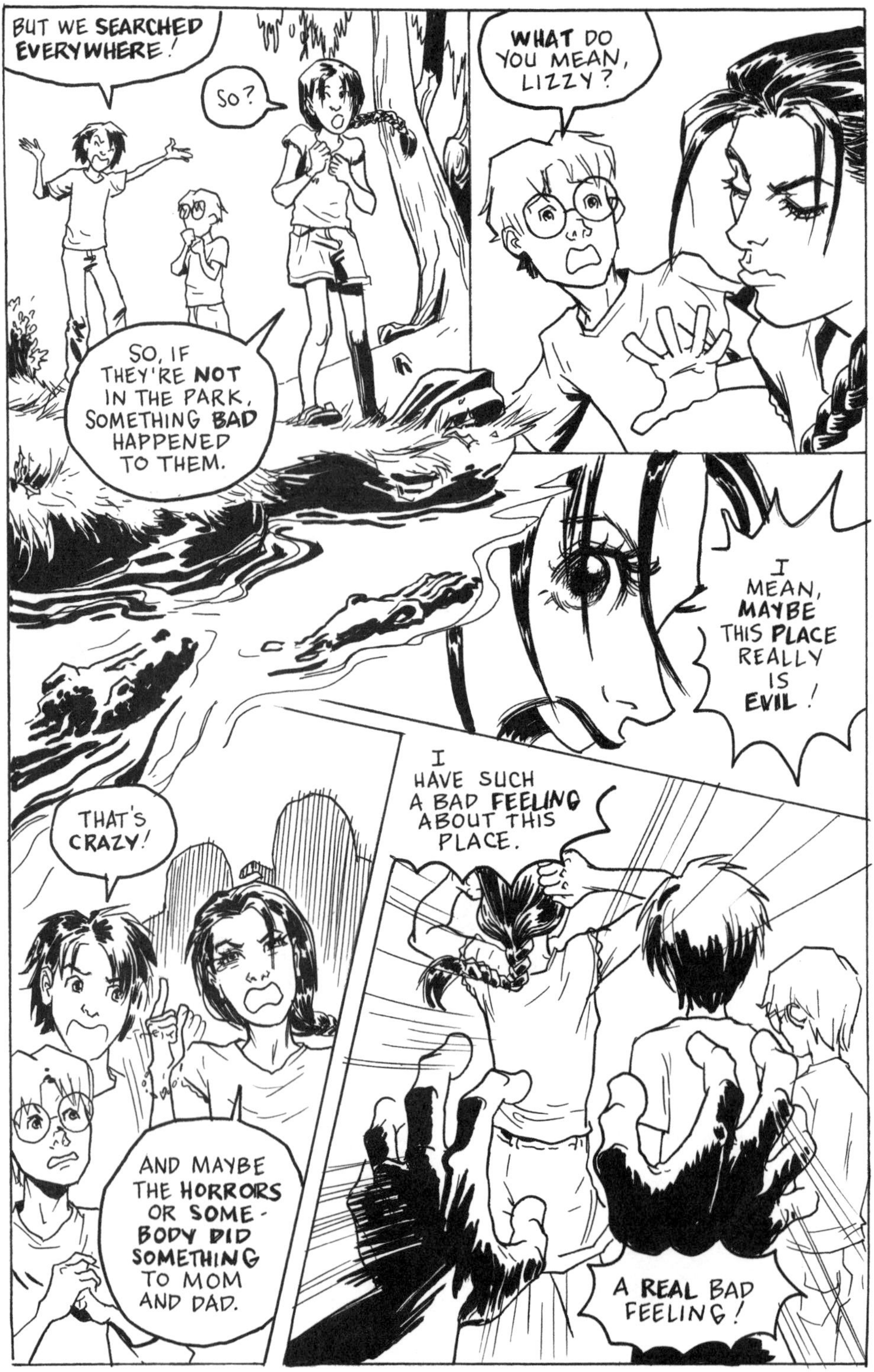
BUT WE SEARCHED EVERYWHERE!
SO?
SO, IF THEY'RE NOT IN THE PARK, SOMETHING BAD HAPPENED TO THEM.
WHAT DO YOU MEAN, LIZZY?
I MEAN, MAYBE THIS PLACE REALLY IS EVIL!
THAT'S CRAZY!
AND MAYBE THE HORRORS OR SOME-BODY DID SOMETHING TO MOM AND DAD.
I HAVE SUCH A BAD FEELING ABOUT THIS PLACE.
A REAL BAD FEELING!

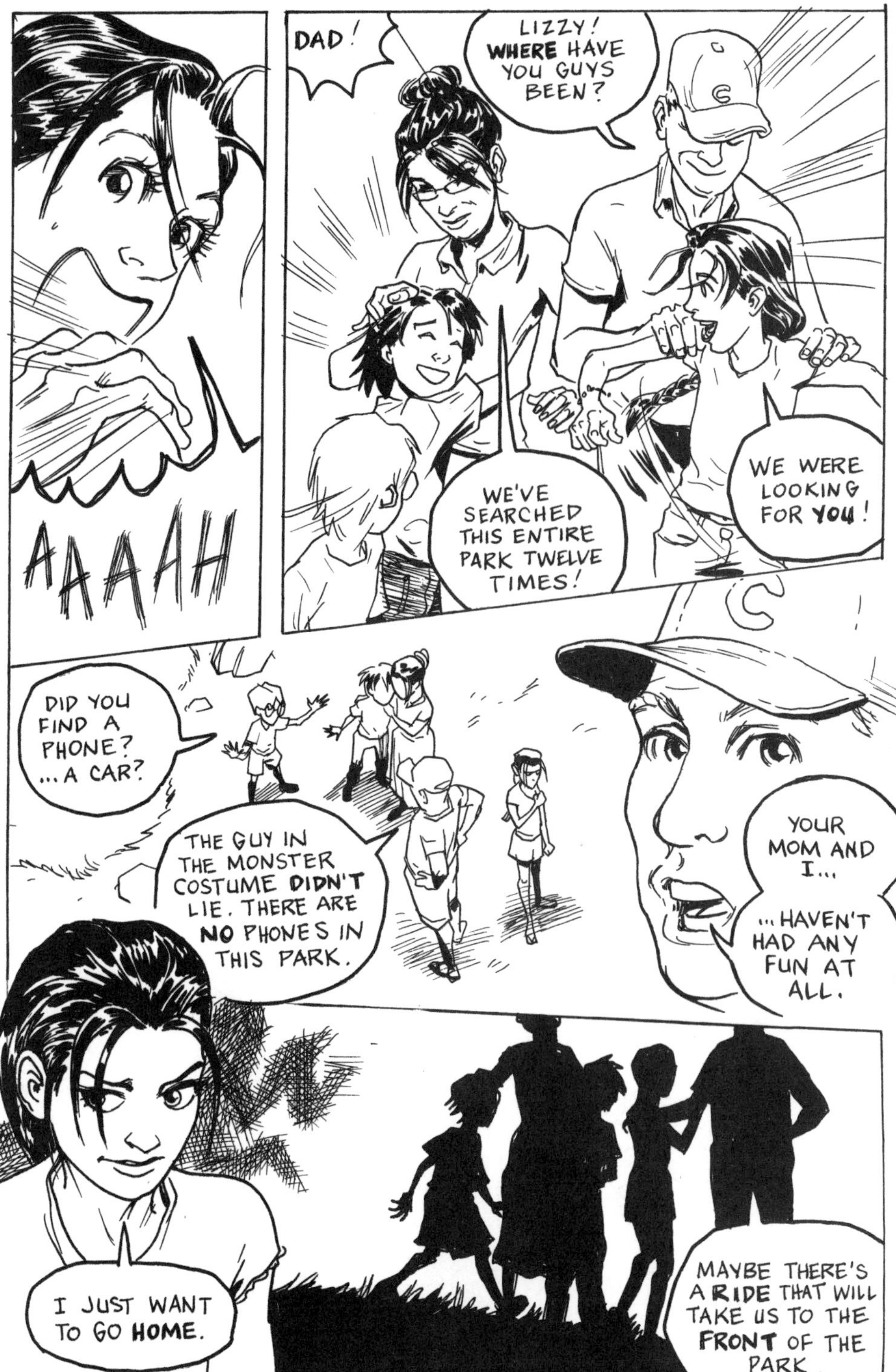
AAAAH
DAD!
LIZZY! WHERE HAVE YOU GUYS BEEN?
WE'VE SEARCHED THIS ENTIRE PARK TWELVE TIMES!
WE WERE LOOKING FOR YOU!
DID YOU FIND A PHONE? ...A CAR?
THE GUY IN THE MONSTER COSTUME DIDN'T LIE. THERE ARE NO PHONES IN THIS PARK.
YOUR MOM AND I...
...HAVEN'T HAD ANY FUN AT ALL.
I JUST WANT TO GO HOME.
MAYBE THERE'S A RIDE THAT WILL TAKE US TO THE FRONT OF THE PARK.

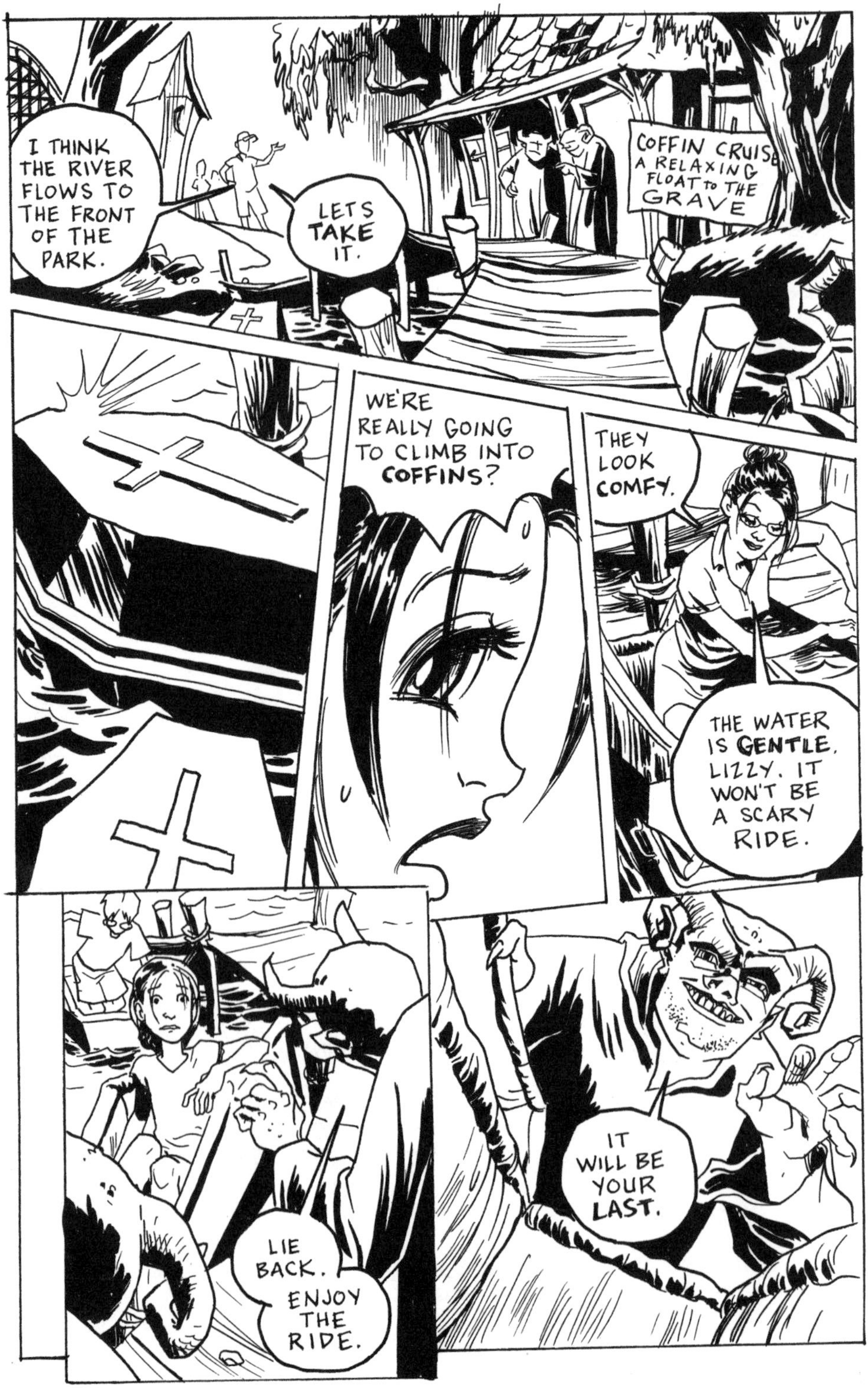
I THINK THE RIVER FLOWS TO THE FRONT OF THE PARK.
LETS TAKE IT.
COFFIN CRUISE A RELAXING FLOAT TO THE GRAVE
WE'RE REALLY GOING TO CLIMB INTO COFFINS?
THEY LOOK COMFY.
THE WATER IS GENTLE, LIZZY. IT WON'T BE A SCARY RIDE.
LIE BACK. ENJOY THE RIDE.
IT WILL BE YOUR LAST.

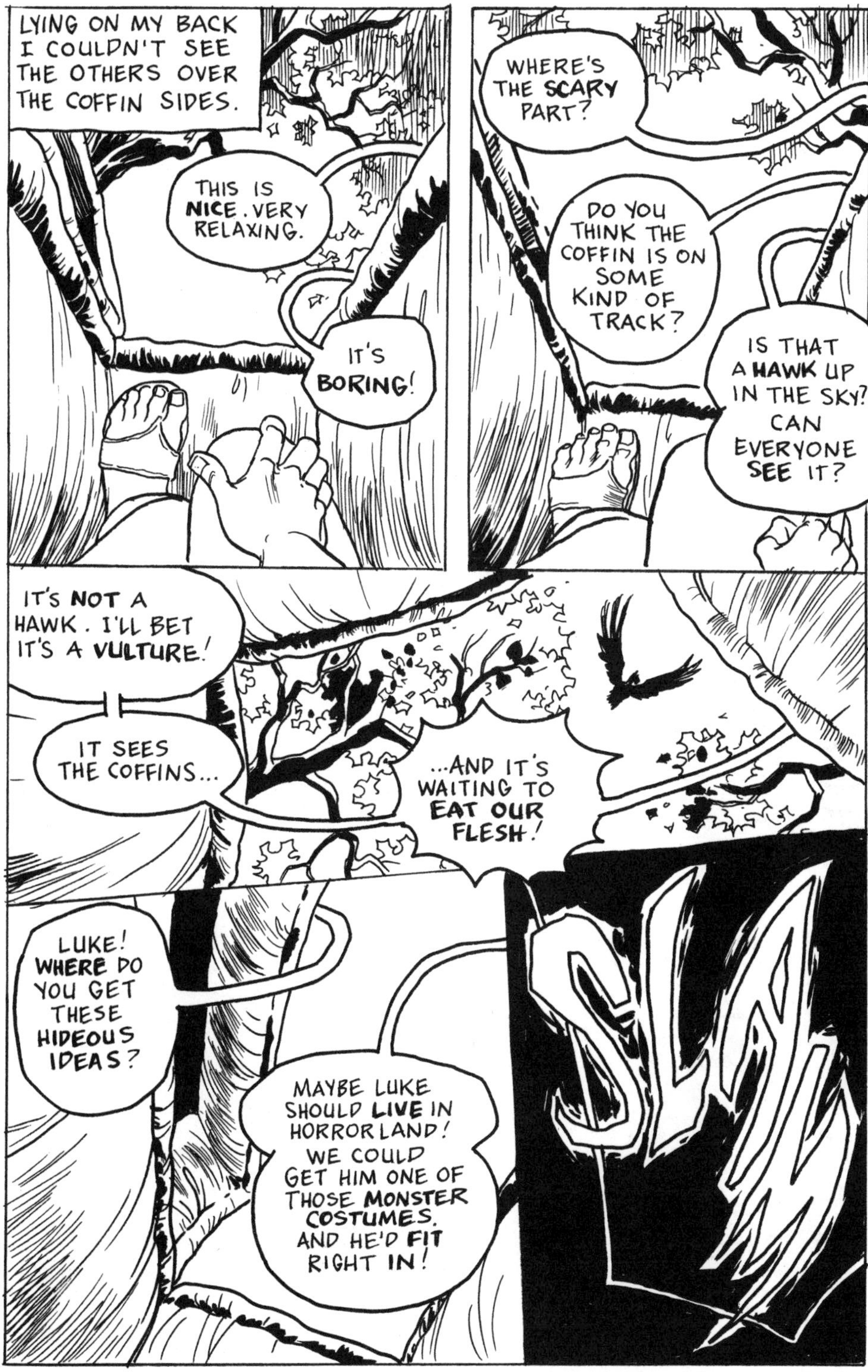
LYING ON MY BACK I COULDN'T SEE THE OTHERS OVER THE COFFIN SIDES.
THIS IS NICE. VERY RELAXING.
IT'S BORING!
WHERE'S THE SCARY PART?
DO YOU THINK THE COFFIN IS ON SOME KIND OF TRACK?
IS THAT A HAWK UP IN THE SKY? CAN EVERYONE SEE IT?
IT'S NOT A HAWK. I'LL BET IT'S A VULTURE!
IT SEES THE COFFINS...
...AND IT'S WAITING TO EAT OUR FLESH!
LUKE! WHERE DO YOU GET THESE HIDEOUS IDEAS?
MAYBE LUKE SHOULD LIVE IN HORRORLAND! WE COULD GET HIM ONE OF THOSE MONSTER COSTUMES. AND HE'D FIT RIGHT IN!
SLAM

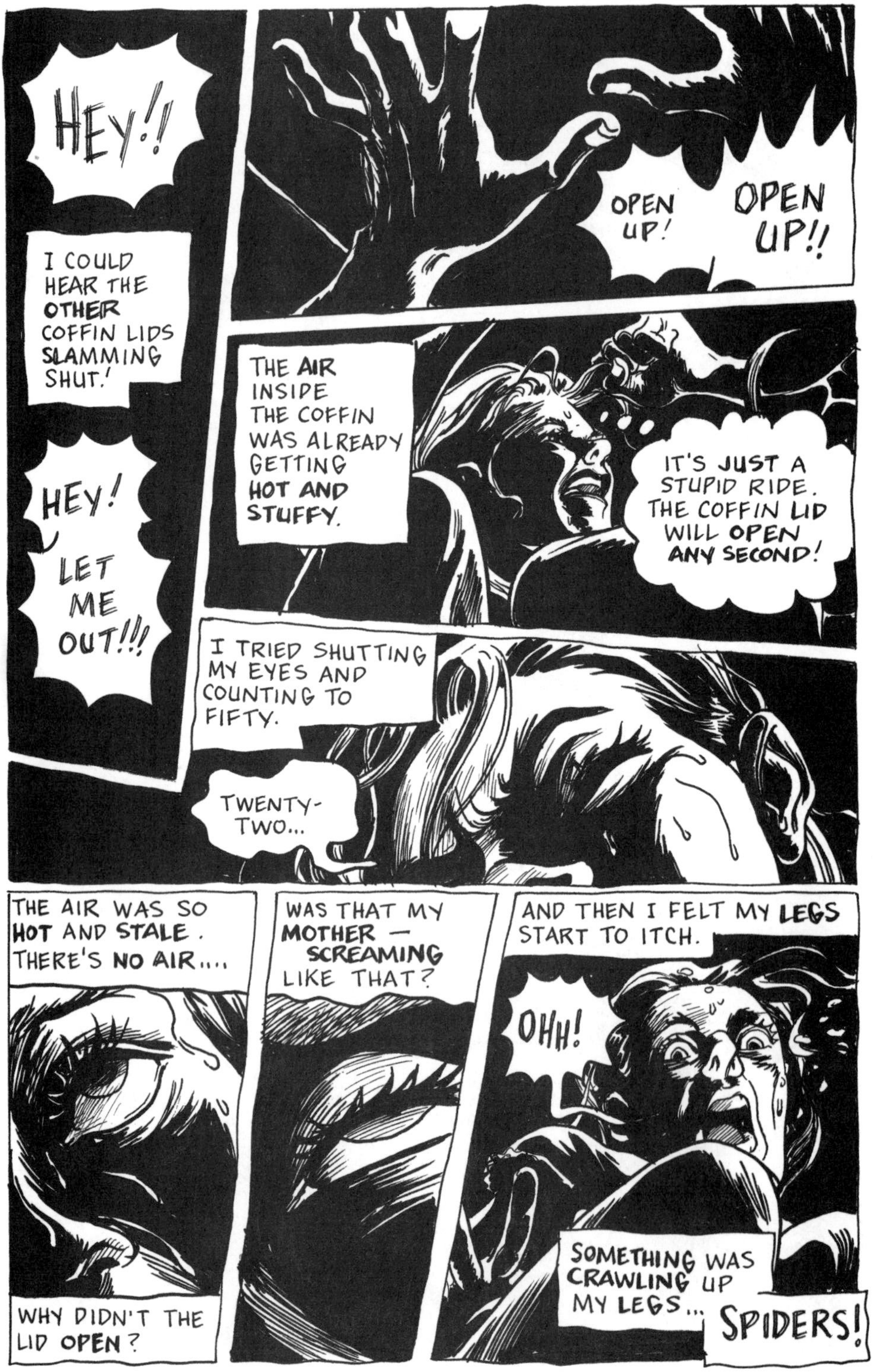
HEY!!
I COULD HEAR THE OTHER COFFIN LIDS SLAMMING SHUT!
HEY! LET ME OUT!!!
OPEN UP!
OPEN UP!!
THE AIR INSIDE THE COFFIN WAS ALREADY GETTING HOT AND STUFFY.
IT'S JUST A STUPID RIDE. THE COFFIN LID WILL OPEN ANY SECOND!
I TRIED SHUTTING MY EYES AND COUNTING TO FIFTY.
TWENTY-TWO...
THE AIR WAS SO HOT AND STALE. THERE'S NO AIR....
WHY DIDN'T THE LID OPEN?
WAS THAT MY MOTHER — SCREAMING LIKE THAT?
AND THEN I FELT MY LEGS START TO ITCH.
OHH!
SOMETHING WAS CRAWLING UP MY LEGS...
SPIDERS!

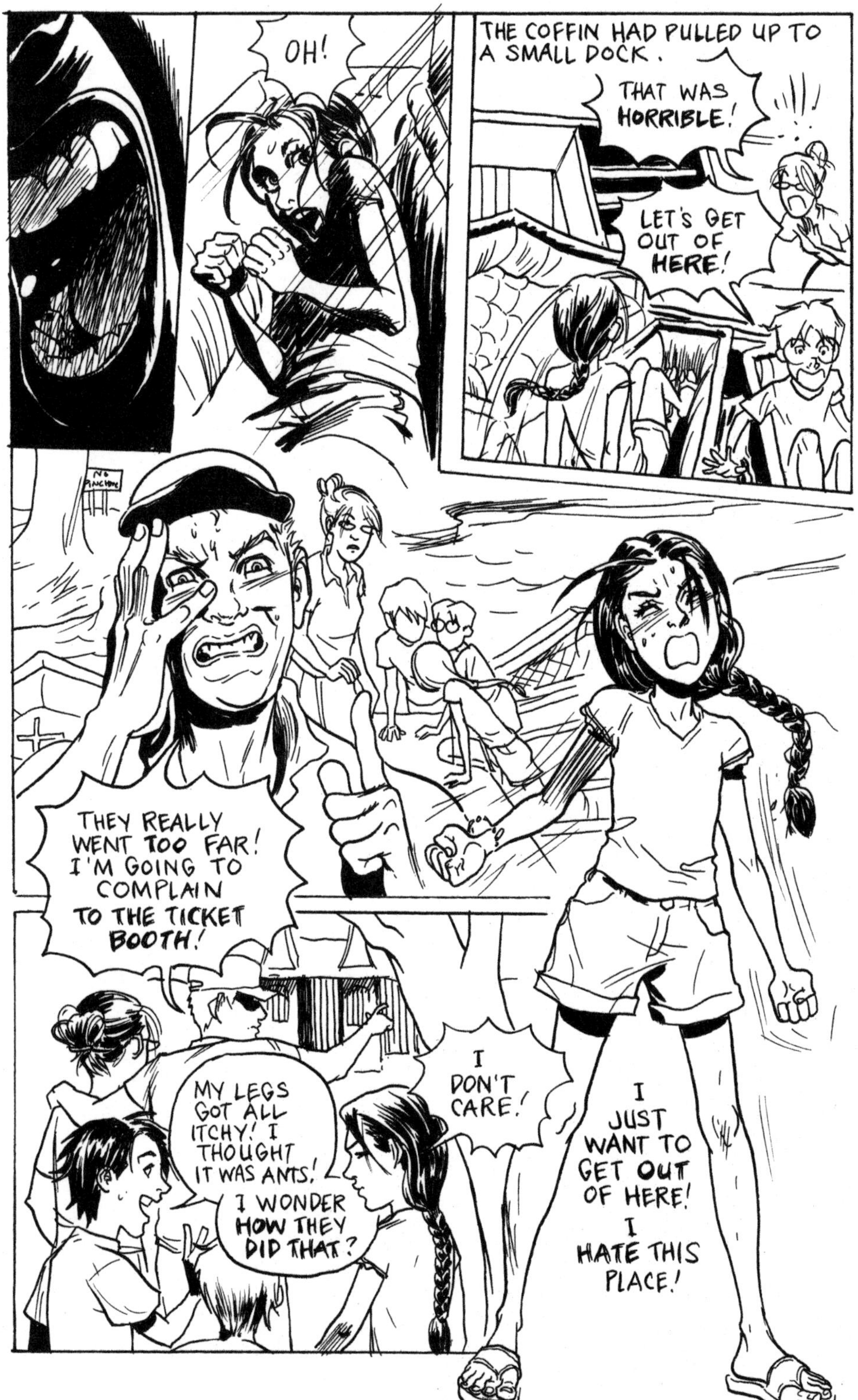
OH!
THE COFFIN HAD PULLED UP TO A SMALL DOCK.
THAT WAS HORRIBLE!
LET'S GET OUT OF HERE!
NO FISHING
THEY REALLY WENT TOO FAR! I'M GOING TO COMPLAIN TO THE TICKET BOOTH!
I JUST WANT TO GET OUT OF HERE! I HATE THIS PLACE!
MY LEGS GOT ALL ITCHY! I THOUGHT IT WAS ANTS!
I WONDER HOW THEY DID THAT?
I DON'T CARE!

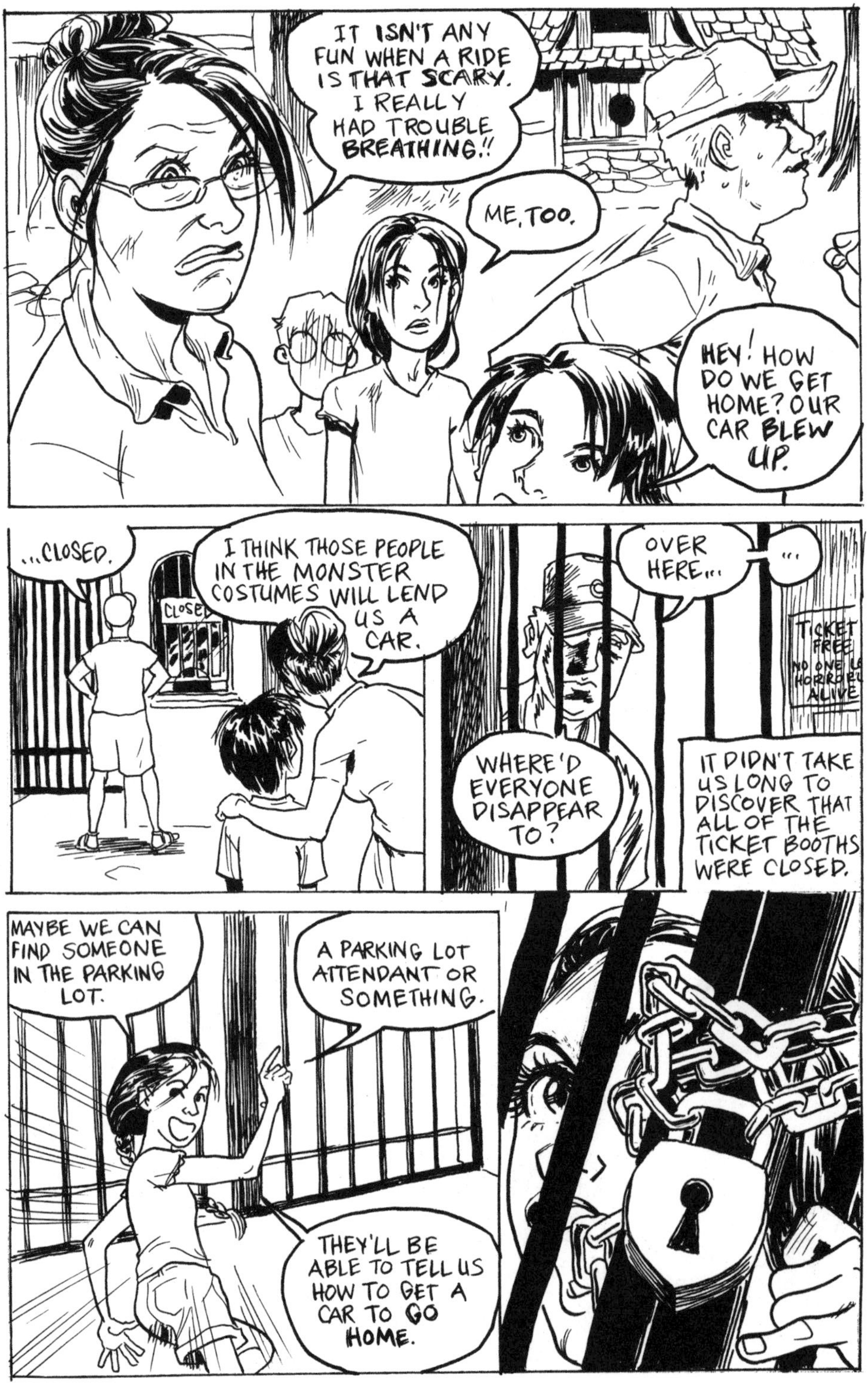
IT ISN'T ANY FUN WHEN A RIDE IS THAT SCARY. I REALLY HAD TROUBLE BREATHING!!
ME, TOO.
HEY! HOW DO WE GET HOME? OUR CAR BLEW UP.
...CLOSED.
I THINK THOSE PEOPLE IN THE MONSTER COSTUMES WILL LEND US A CAR.
OVER HERE...
...
WHERE'D EVERYONE DISAPPEAR TO?
IT DIDN'T TAKE US LONG TO DISCOVER THAT ALL OF THE TICKET BOOTHS WERE CLOSED.
MAYBE WE CAN FIND SOMEONE IN THE PARKING LOT.
A PARKING LOT ATTENDANT OR SOMETHING.
THEY'LL BE ABLE TO TELL US HOW TO GET A CAR TO GO HOME.

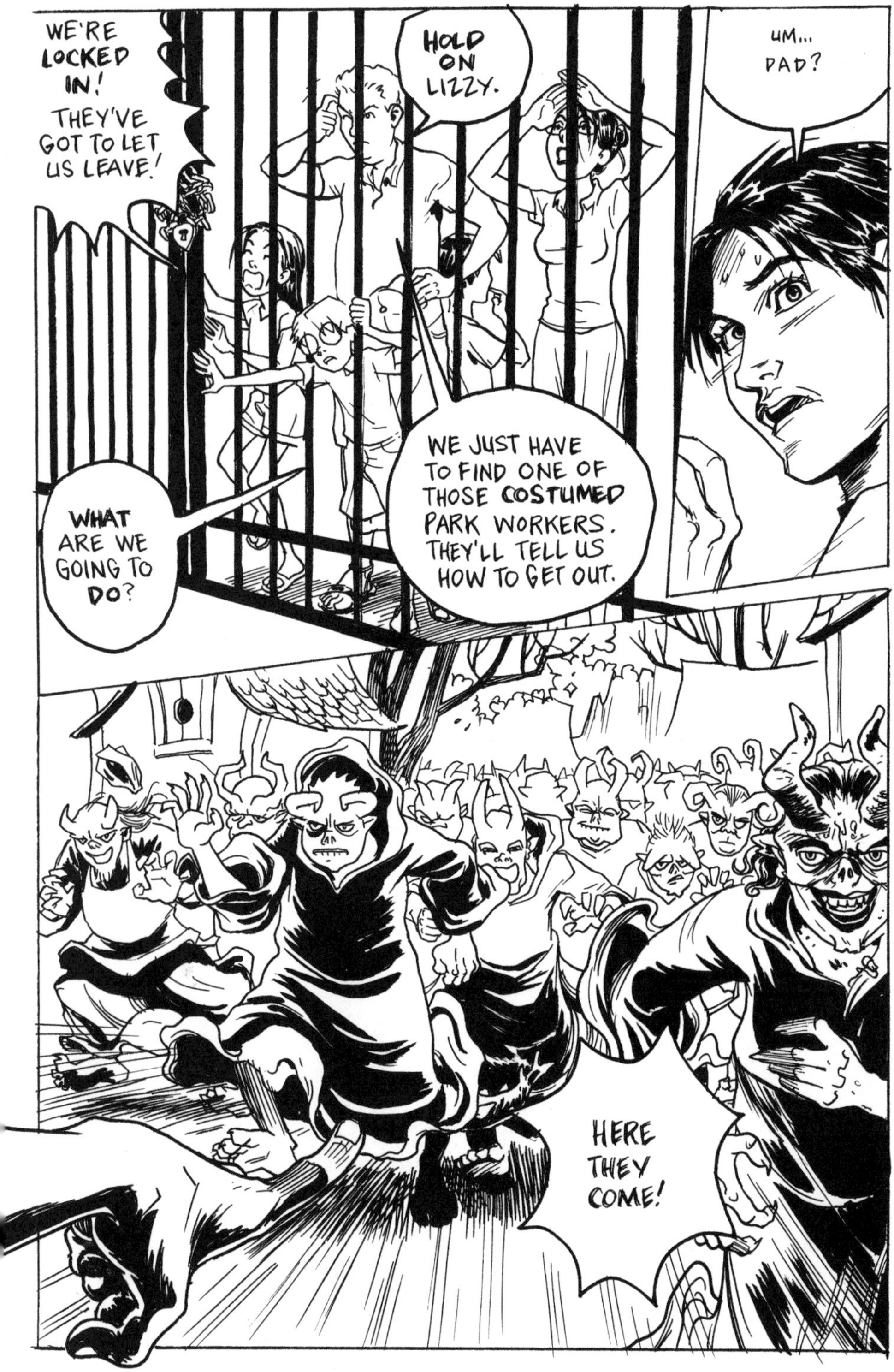
WE'RE LOCKED IN! THEY'VE GOT TO LET US LEAVE!
HOLD ON LIZZY.
WHAT ARE WE GOING TO DO?
WE JUST HAVE TO FIND ONE OF THOSE COSTUMED PARK WORKERS. THEY'LL TELL US HOW TO GET OUT.
UM... DAD?
HERE THEY COME!

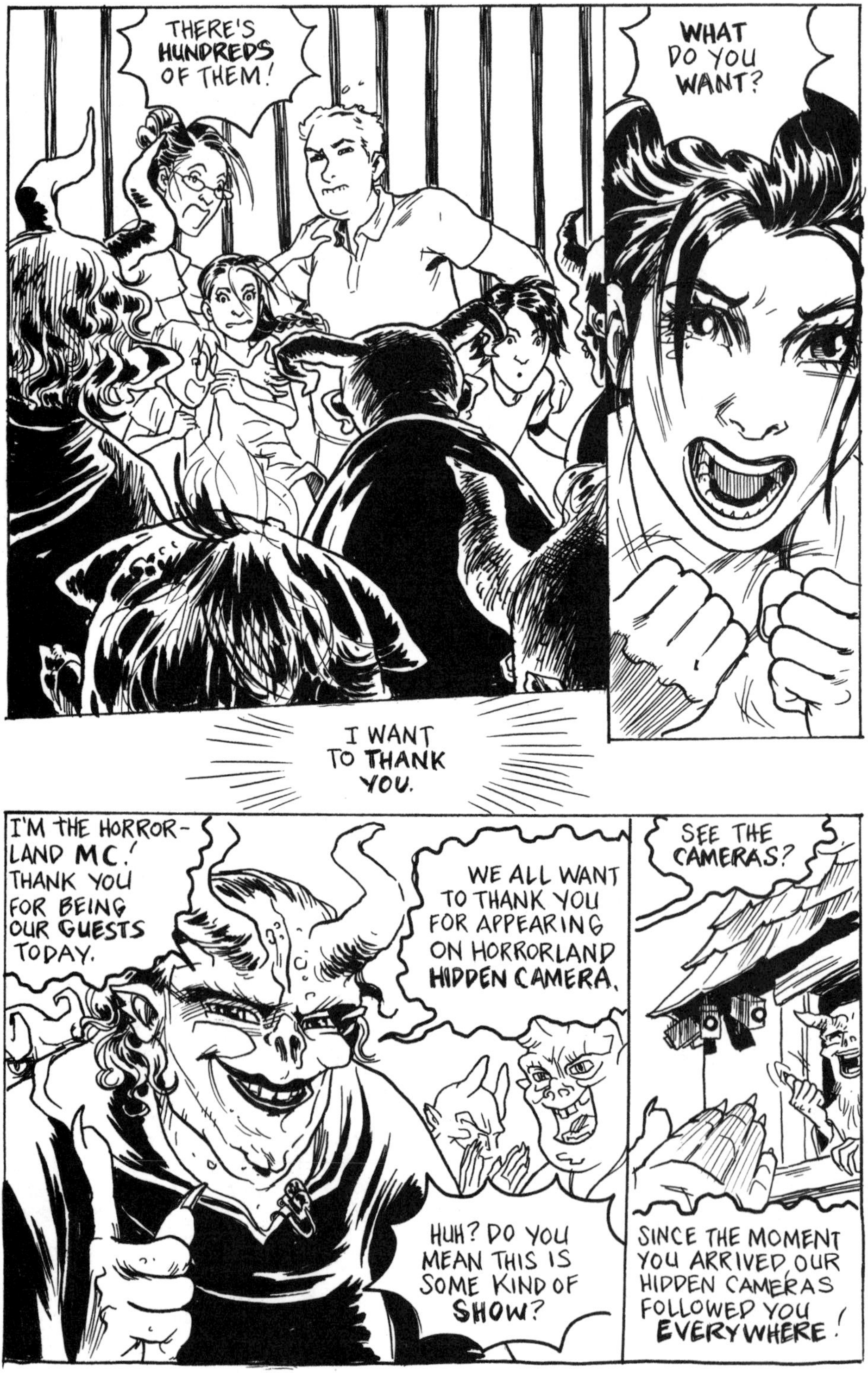
THERE'S HUNDREDS OF THEM!
WHAT DO YOU WANT?
I WANT TO THANK YOU.
I'M THE HORROR-LAND MC! THANK YOU FOR BEING OUR GUESTS TODAY.
WE ALL WANT TO THANK YOU FOR APPEARING ON HORRORLAND HIDDEN CAMERA.
HUH? DO YOU MEAN THIS IS SOME KIND OF SHOW?
SEE THE CAMERAS?
SINCE THE MOMENT YOU ARRIVED OUR HIDDEN CAMERAS FOLLOWED YOU EVERYWHERE!

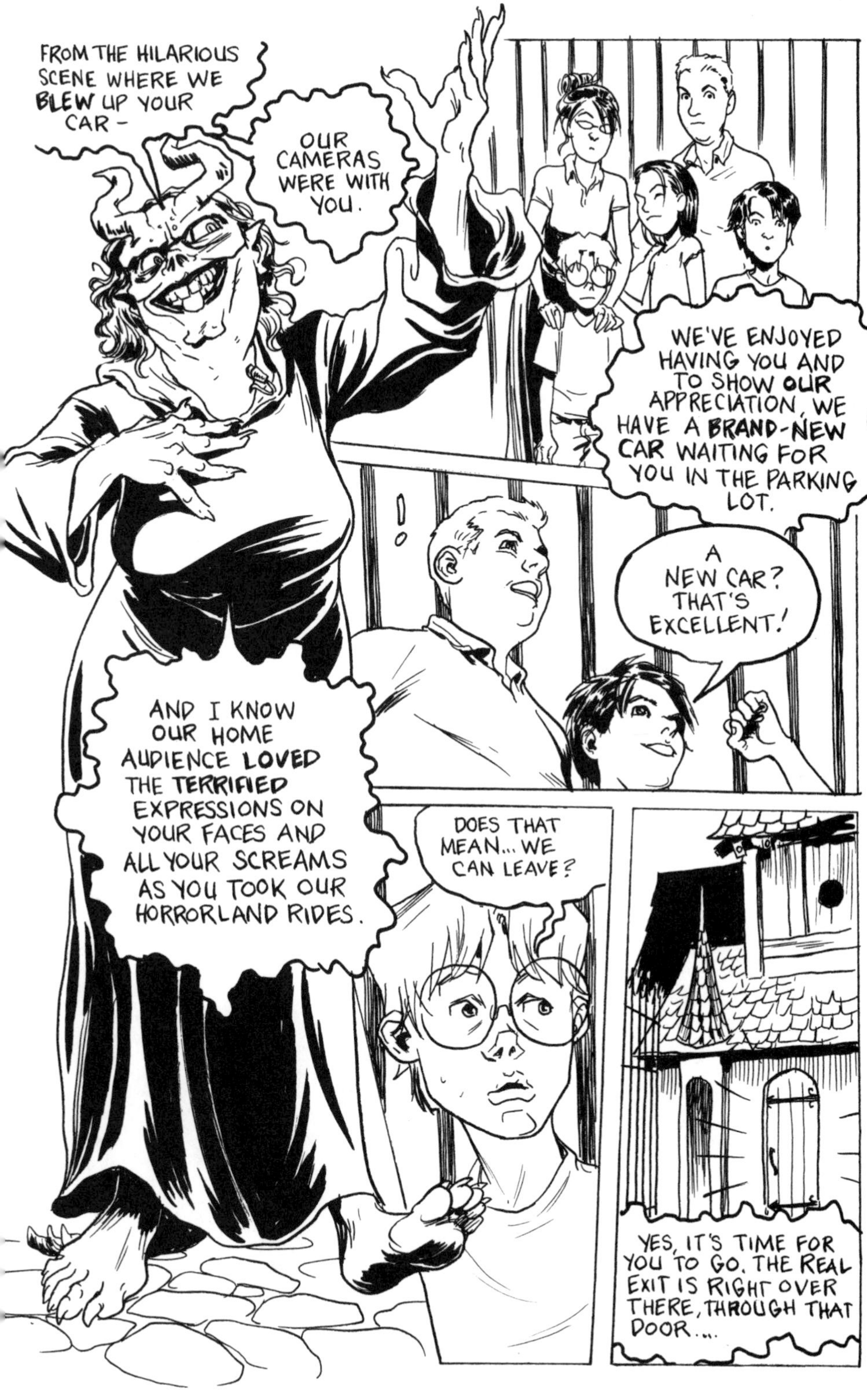
FROM THE HILARIOUS SCENE WHERE WE BLEW UP YOUR CAR -
OUR CAMERAS WERE WITH YOU.
WE'VE ENJOYED HAVING YOU AND TO SHOW OUR APPRECIATION, WE HAVE A BRAND-NEW CAR WAITING FOR YOU IN THE PARKING LOT.
!
A NEW CAR? THAT'S EXCELLENT!
AND I KNOW OUR HOME AUDIENCE LOVED THE TERRIFIED EXPRESSIONS ON YOUR FACES AND ALL YOUR SCREAMS AS YOU TOOK OUR HORRORLAND RIDES.
DOES THAT MEAN... WE CAN LEAVE?
YES, IT'S TIME FOR YOU TO GO. THE REAL EXIT IS RIGHT OVER THERE, THROUGH THAT DOOR....

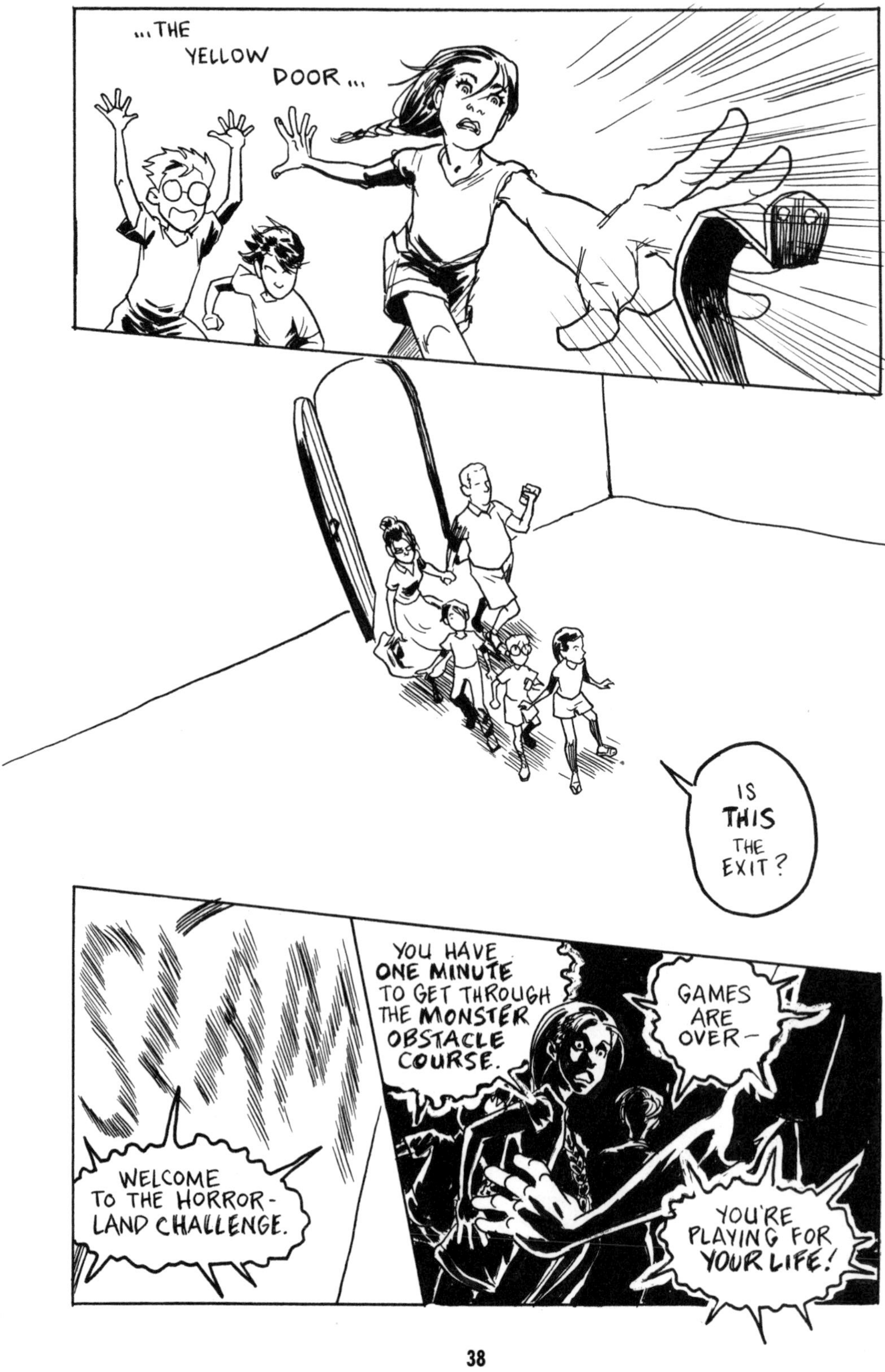
...THE YELLOW DOOR...
IS THIS THE EXIT?
SLAM
WELCOME TO THE HORROR-LAND CHALLENGE.
YOU HAVE ONE MINUTE TO GET THROUGH THE MONSTER OBSTACLE COURSE.
GAMES ARE OVER—
YOU'RE PLAYING FOR YOUR LIFE!

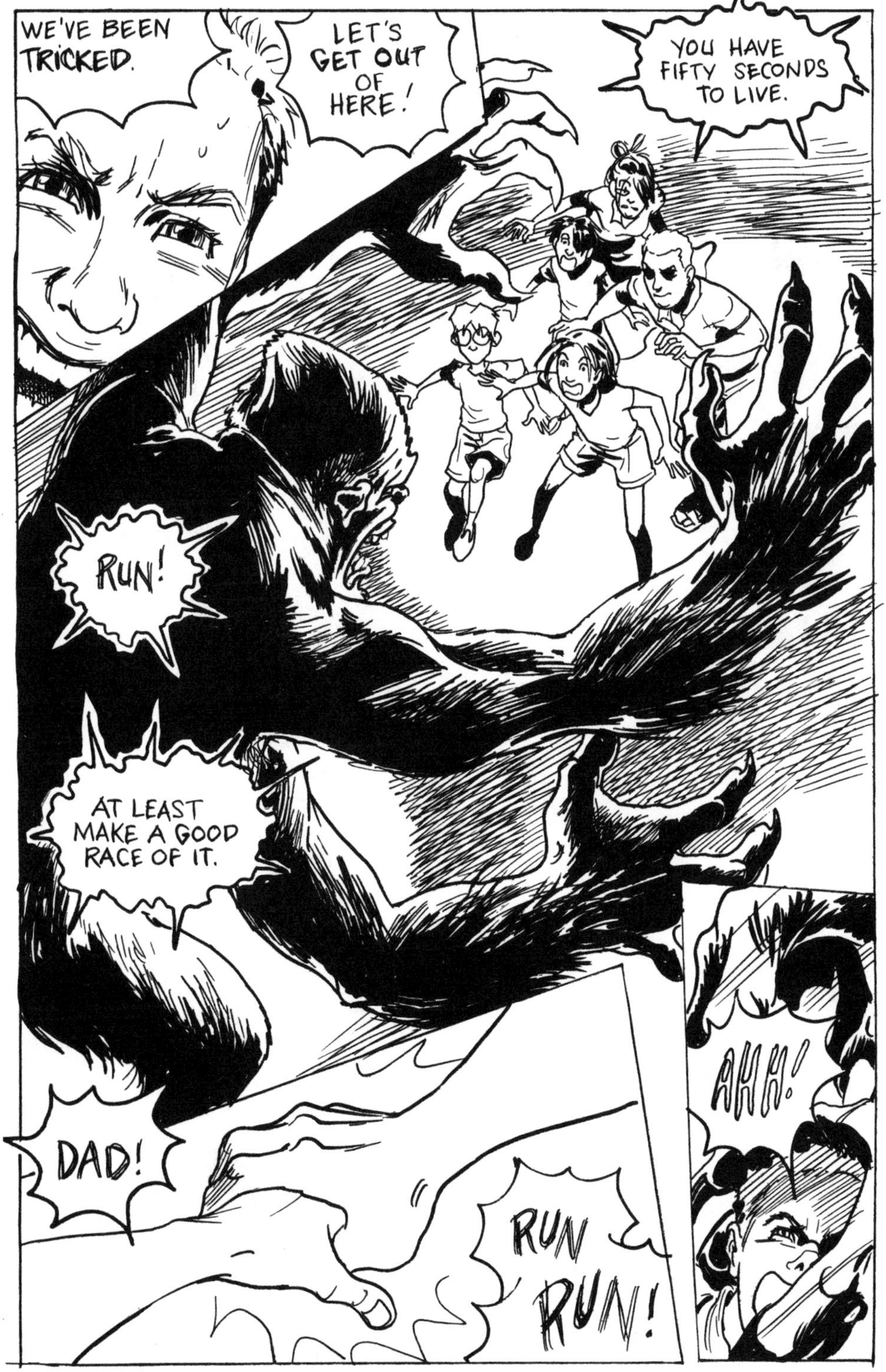
WE'VE BEEN TRICKED.
LET'S GET OUT OF HERE!
YOU HAVE FIFTY SECONDS TO LIVE.
RUN!
AT LEAST MAKE A GOOD RACE OF IT.
DAD!
RUN RUN!
AHH!

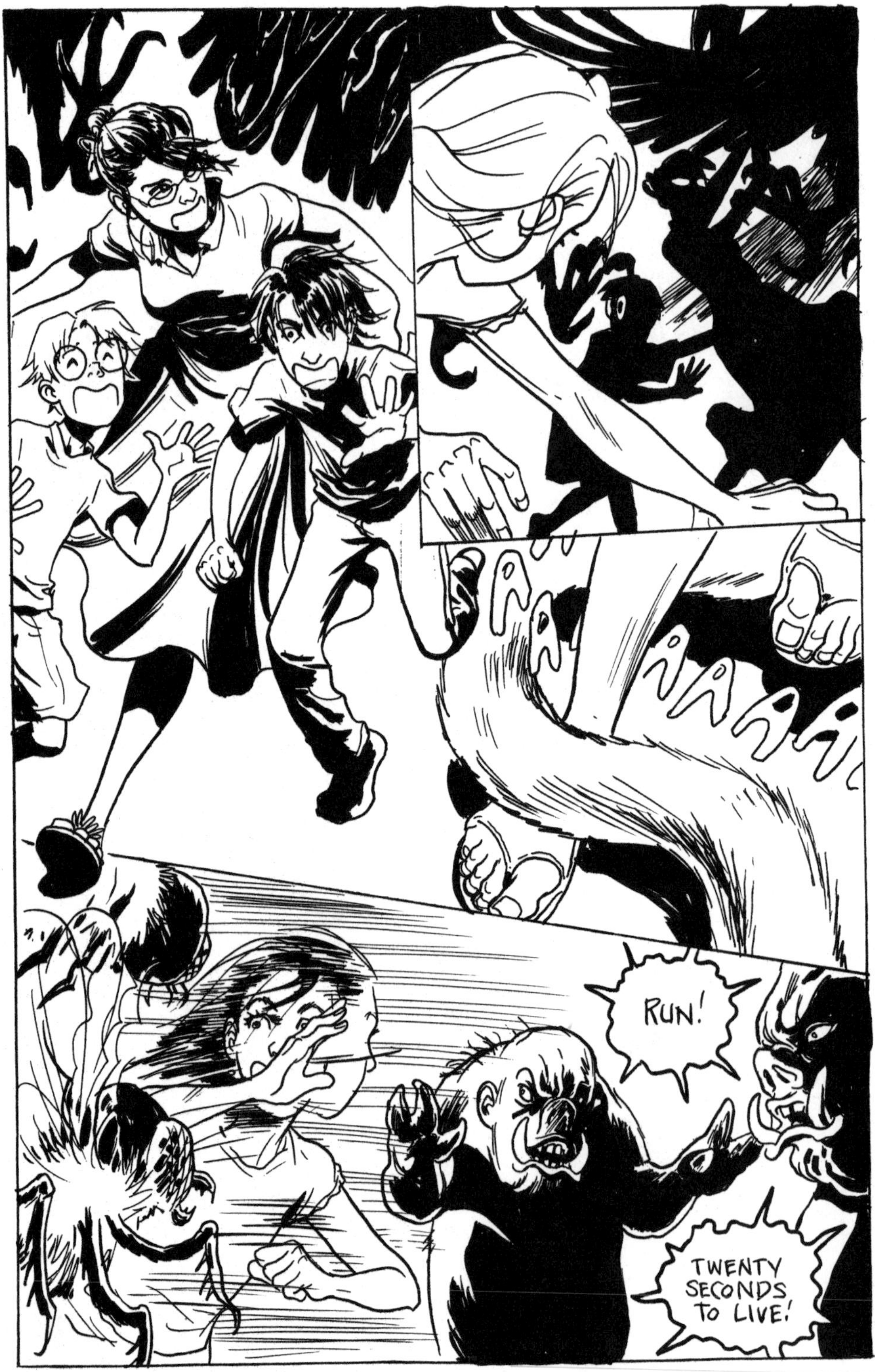
AAAAAAAAAAAAAIII
RUN!
TWENTY SECONDS TO LIVE!

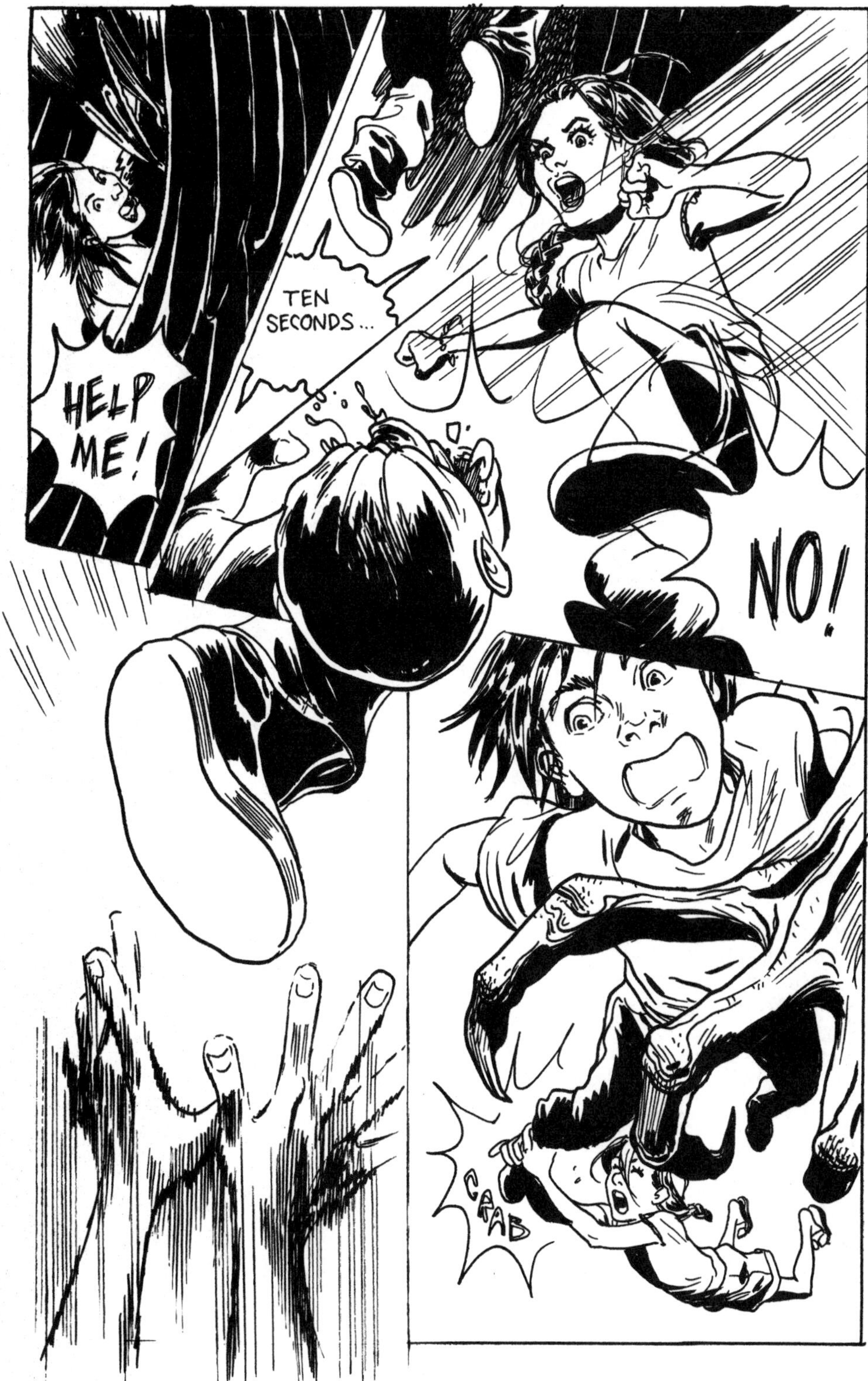
HELP ME!
TEN SECONDS...
NO!
GRAB

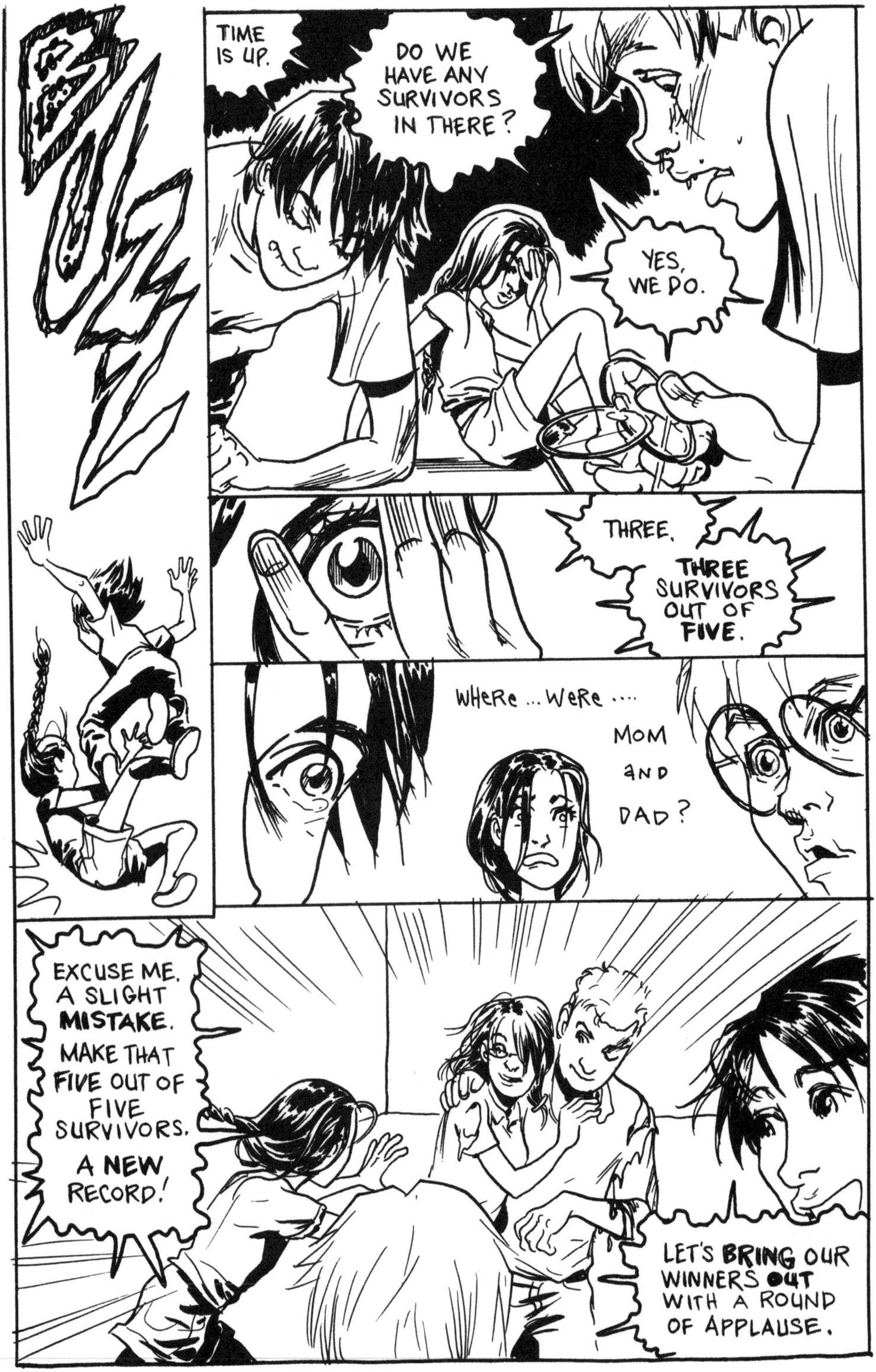
TIME IS UP.
DO WE HAVE ANY SURVIVORS IN THERE?
YES, WE DO.
THREE. **THREE** SURVIVORS OUT OF **FIVE**.
WHERE ... WERE ... MOM AND DAD?
EXCUSE ME. A SLIGHT **MISTAKE**. MAKE THAT **FIVE** OUT OF FIVE SURVIVORS. A **NEW** RECORD!
LET'S **BRING** OUR WINNERS **OUT** WITH A ROUND OF APPLAUSE.

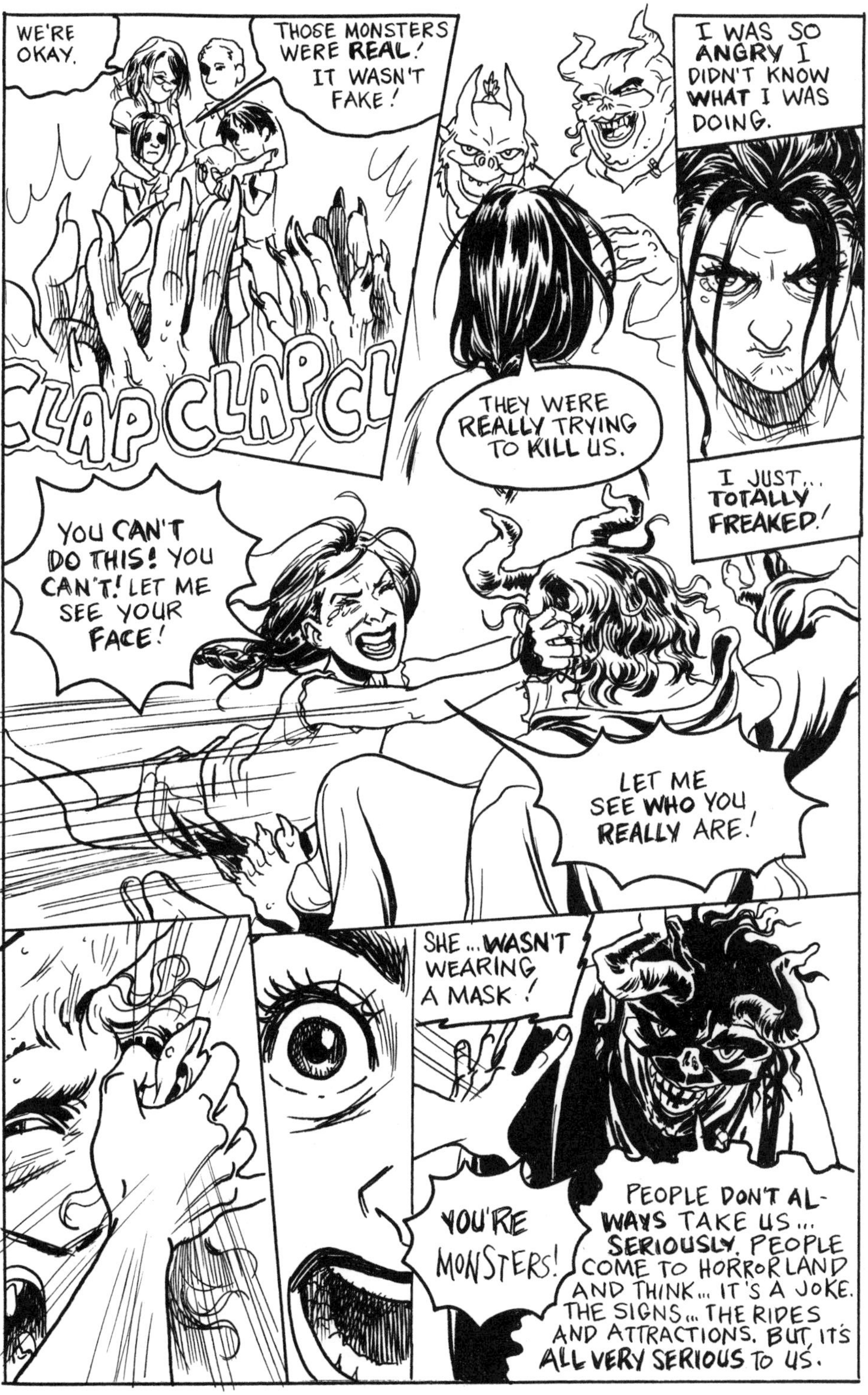
WE'RE OKAY.
THOSE MONSTERS WERE REAL! IT WASN'T FAKE!
CLAP CLAP CL
I WAS SO ANGRY I DIDN'T KNOW WHAT I WAS DOING.
THEY WERE REALLY TRYING TO KILL US.
I JUST... TOTALLY FREAKED!
YOU CAN'T DO THIS! YOU CAN'T! LET ME SEE YOUR FACE!
LET ME SEE WHO YOU REALLY ARE!
SHE... WASN'T WEARING A MASK!
YOU'RE MONSTERS!
PEOPLE DON'T ALWAYS TAKE US... SERIOUSLY. PEOPLE COME TO HORRORLAND AND THINK... IT'S A JOKE. THE SIGNS... THE RIDES AND ATTRACTIONS. BUT IT'S ALL VERY SERIOUS TO US.

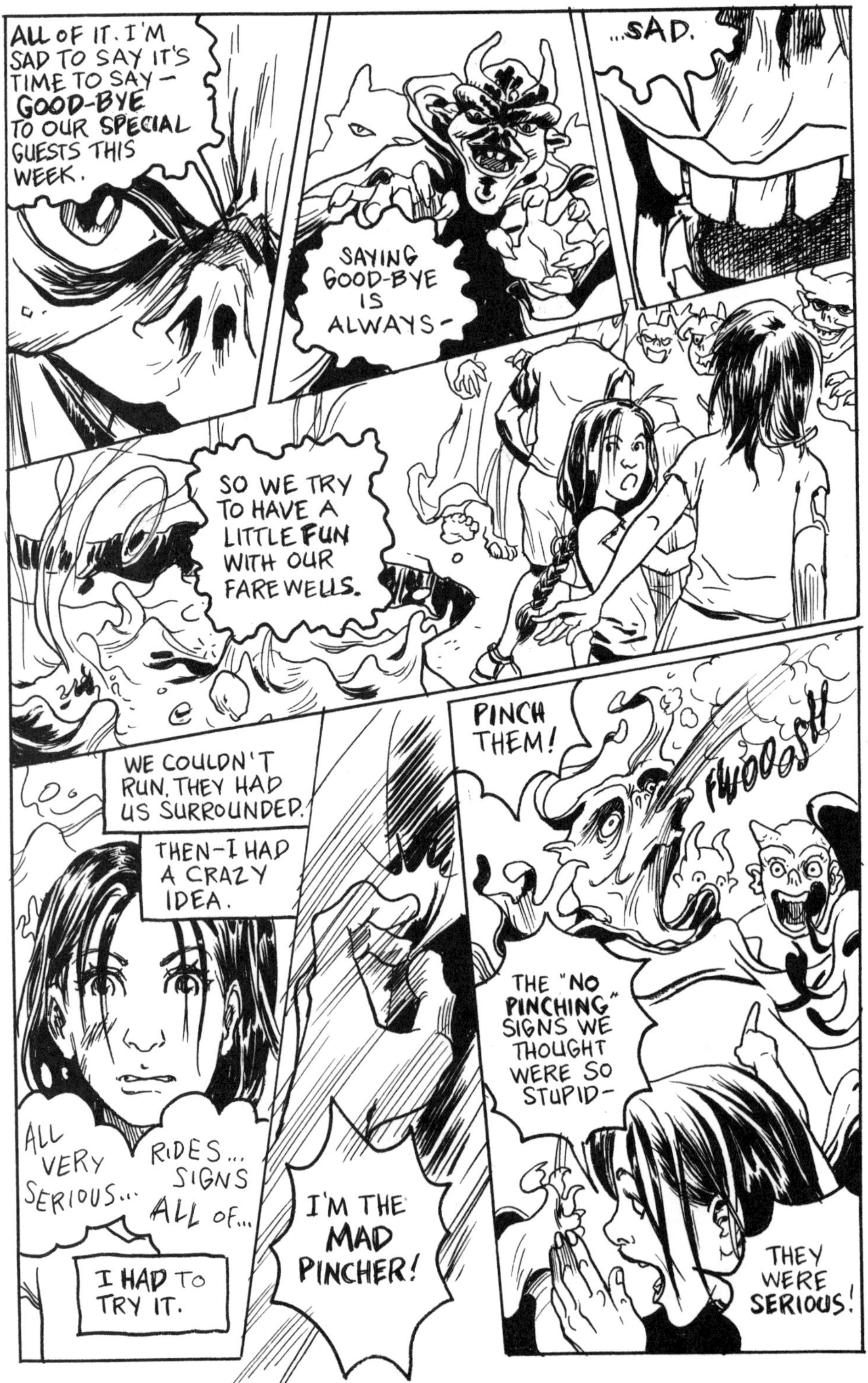
ALL OF IT. I'M SAD TO SAY IT'S TIME TO SAY — GOOD-BYE TO OUR SPECIAL GUESTS THIS WEEK.
SAYING GOOD-BYE IS ALWAYS-
...SAD.
SO WE TRY TO HAVE A LITTLE FUN WITH OUR FAREWELLS.
WE COULDN'T RUN, THEY HAD US SURROUNDED.
THEN-I HAD A CRAZY IDEA.
ALL VERY SERIOUS...
RIDES... SIGNS ALL OF...
I HAD TO TRY IT.
I'M THE MAD PINCHER!
PINCH THEM!
FWOOOSH
THE "NO PINCHING" SIGNS WE THOUGHT WERE SO STUPID-
THEY WERE SERIOUS!

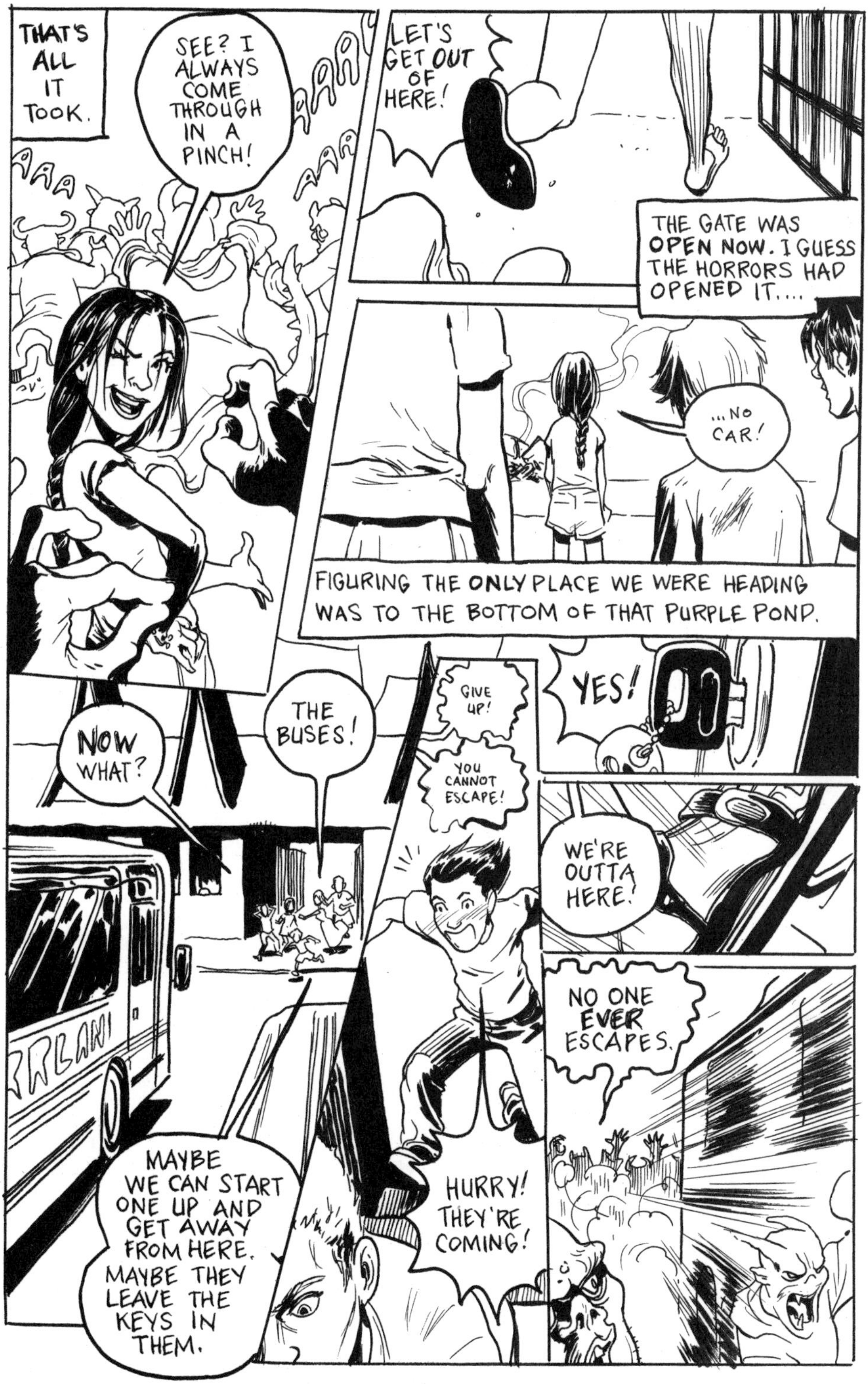
THAT'S ALL IT TOOK.
SEE? I ALWAYS COME THROUGH IN A PINCH!
LET'S GET OUT OF HERE!
THE GATE WAS OPEN NOW. I GUESS THE HORRORS HAD OPENED IT....
...NO CAR!
FIGURING THE ONLY PLACE WE WERE HEADING WAS TO THE BOTTOM OF THAT PURPLE POND.
NOW WHAT?
THE BUSES!
MAYBE WE CAN START ONE UP AND GET AWAY FROM HERE. MAYBE THEY LEAVE THE KEYS IN THEM.
GIVE UP!
YOU CANNOT ESCAPE!
HURRY! THEY'RE COMING!
YES!
WE'RE OUTTA HERE!
NO ONE EVER ESCAPES.

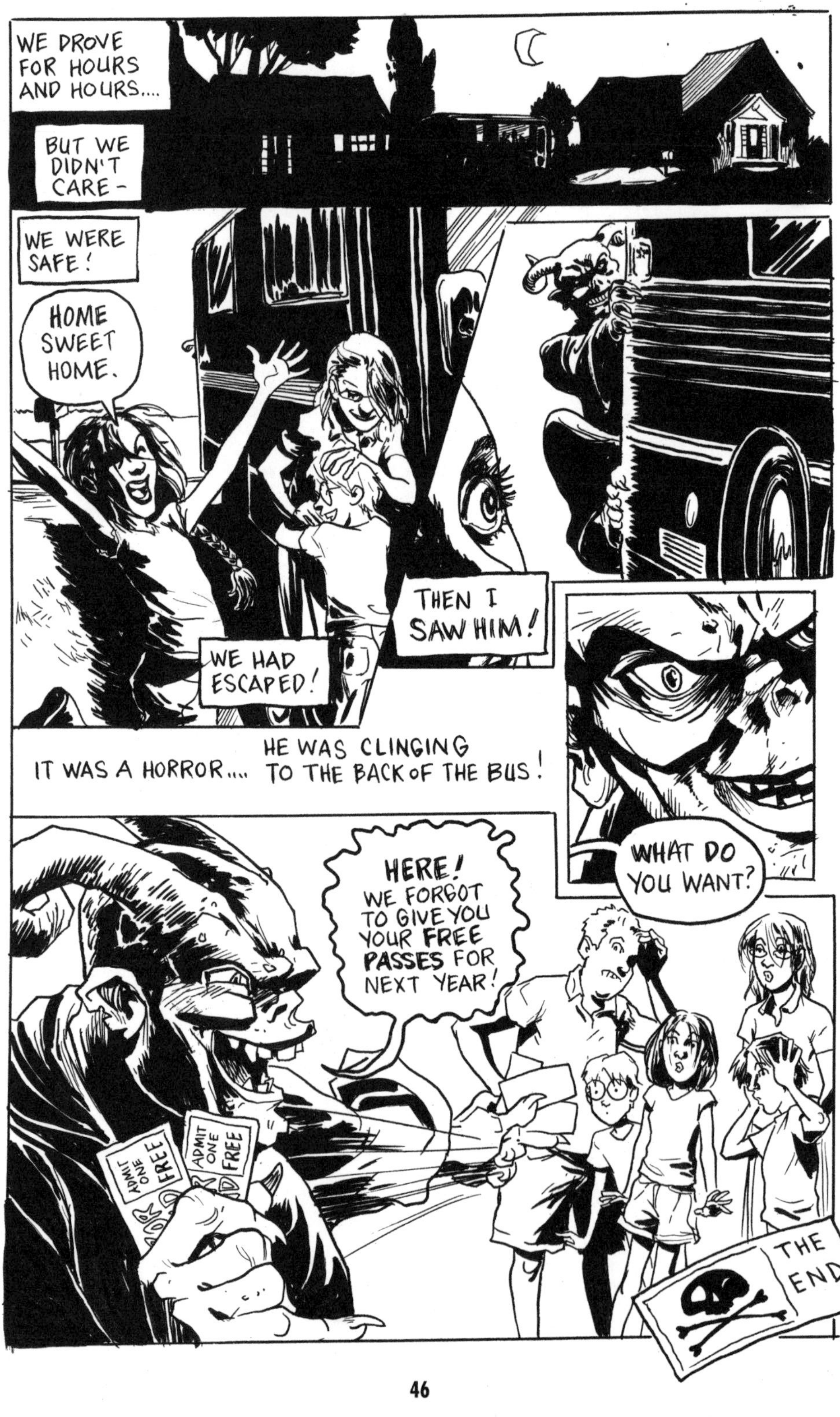
WE DROVE FOR HOURS AND HOURS....
BUT WE DIDN'T CARE -
WE WERE SAFE!
HOME SWEET HOME.
WE HAD ESCAPED!
THEN I SAW HIM!
IT WAS A HORROR....
HE WAS CLINGING TO THE BACK OF THE BUS!
WHAT DO YOU WANT?
HERE! WE FORGOT TO GIVE YOU YOUR FREE PASSES FOR NEXT YEAR!
ADMIT ONE FREE
ADMIT ONE FREE
THE END

A SHOCKER ON SHOCK STREET

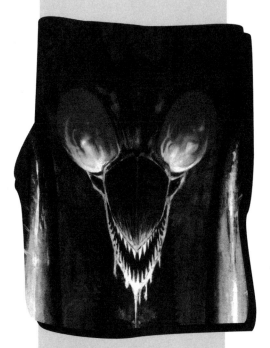

ADAPTED AND ILLUSTRATED BY

Jamie Tolagson

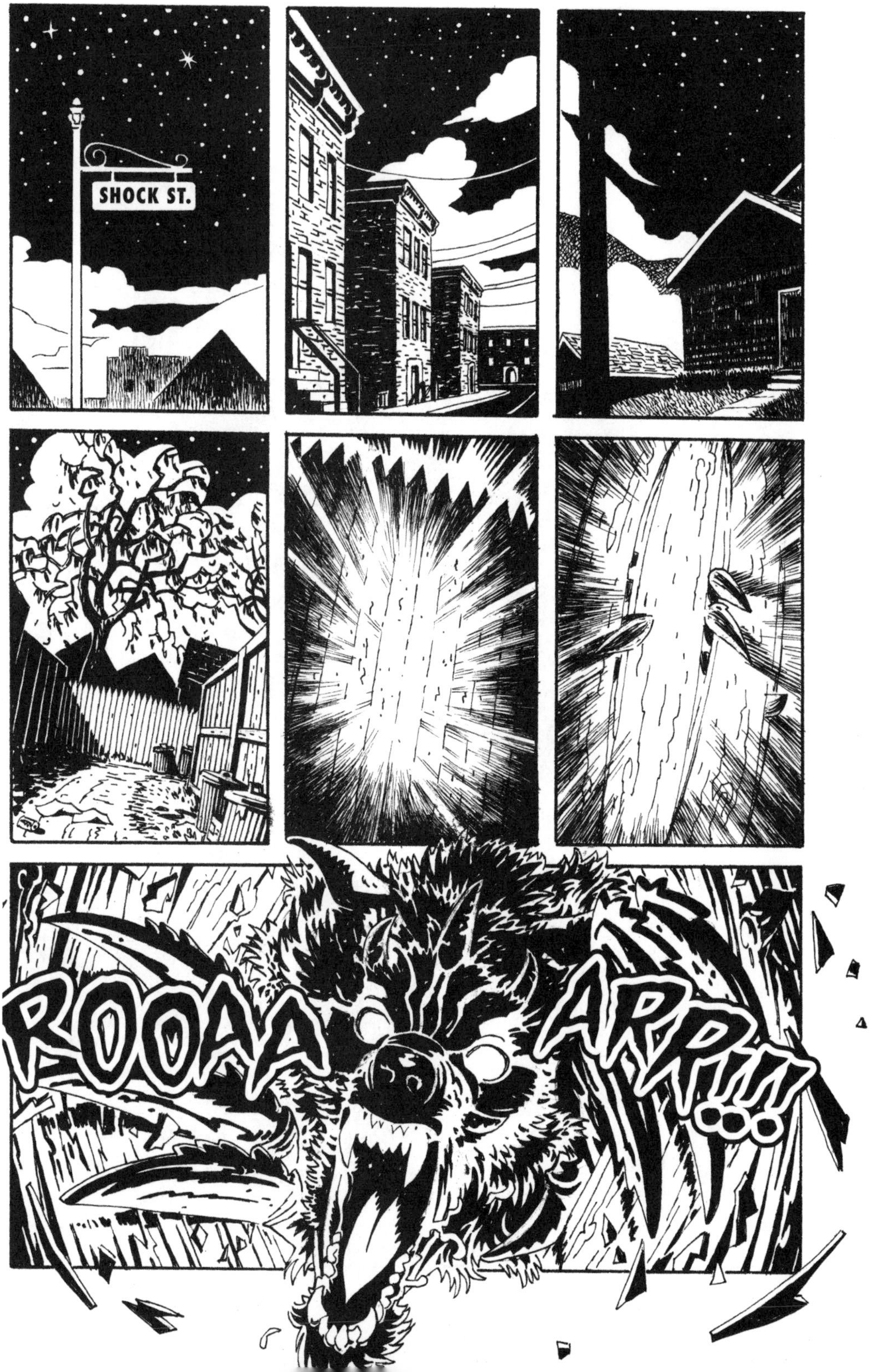
SHOCK ST.
ROOAAARR!!!...

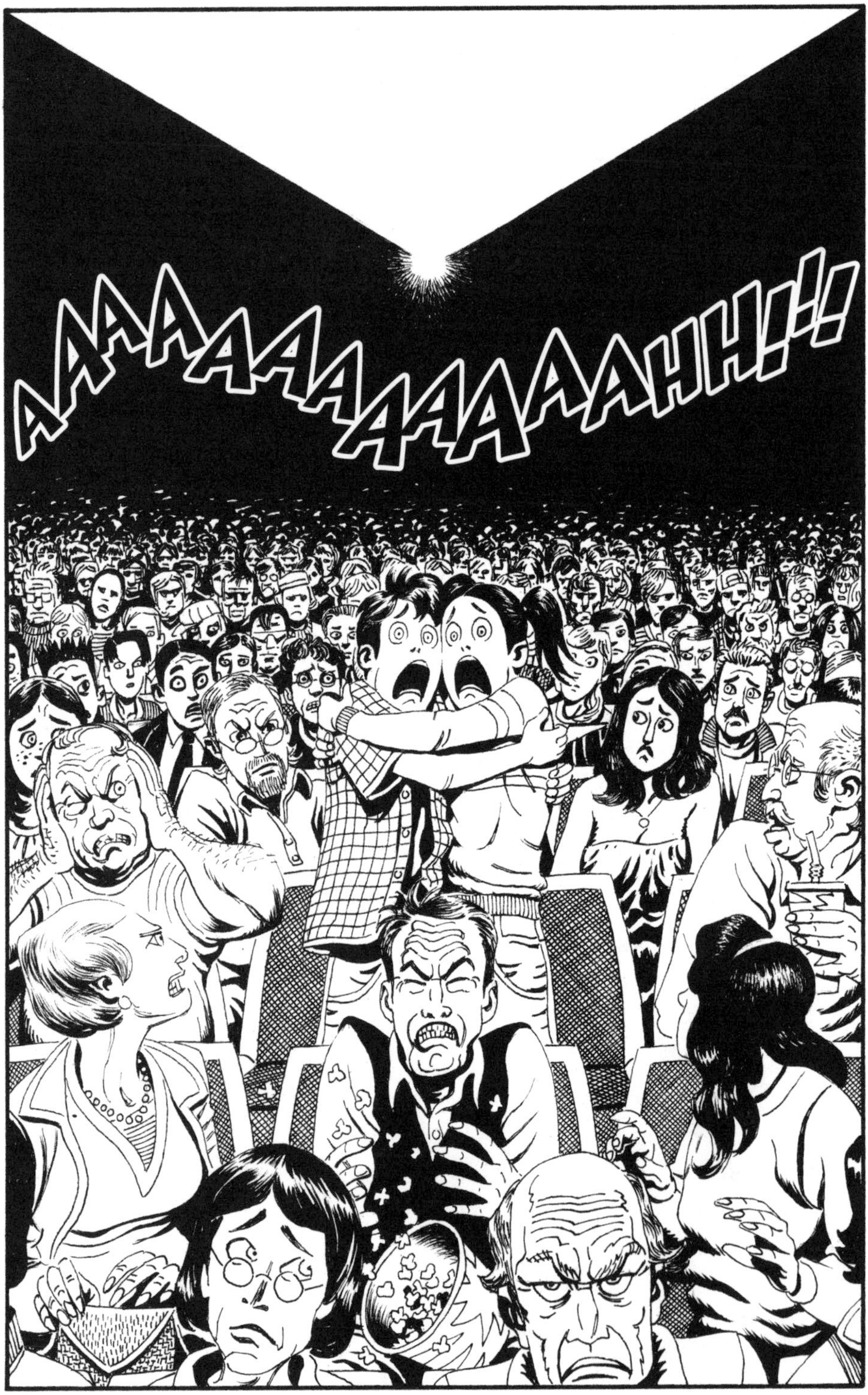
AAAAAAAAAAAAAHH!!!

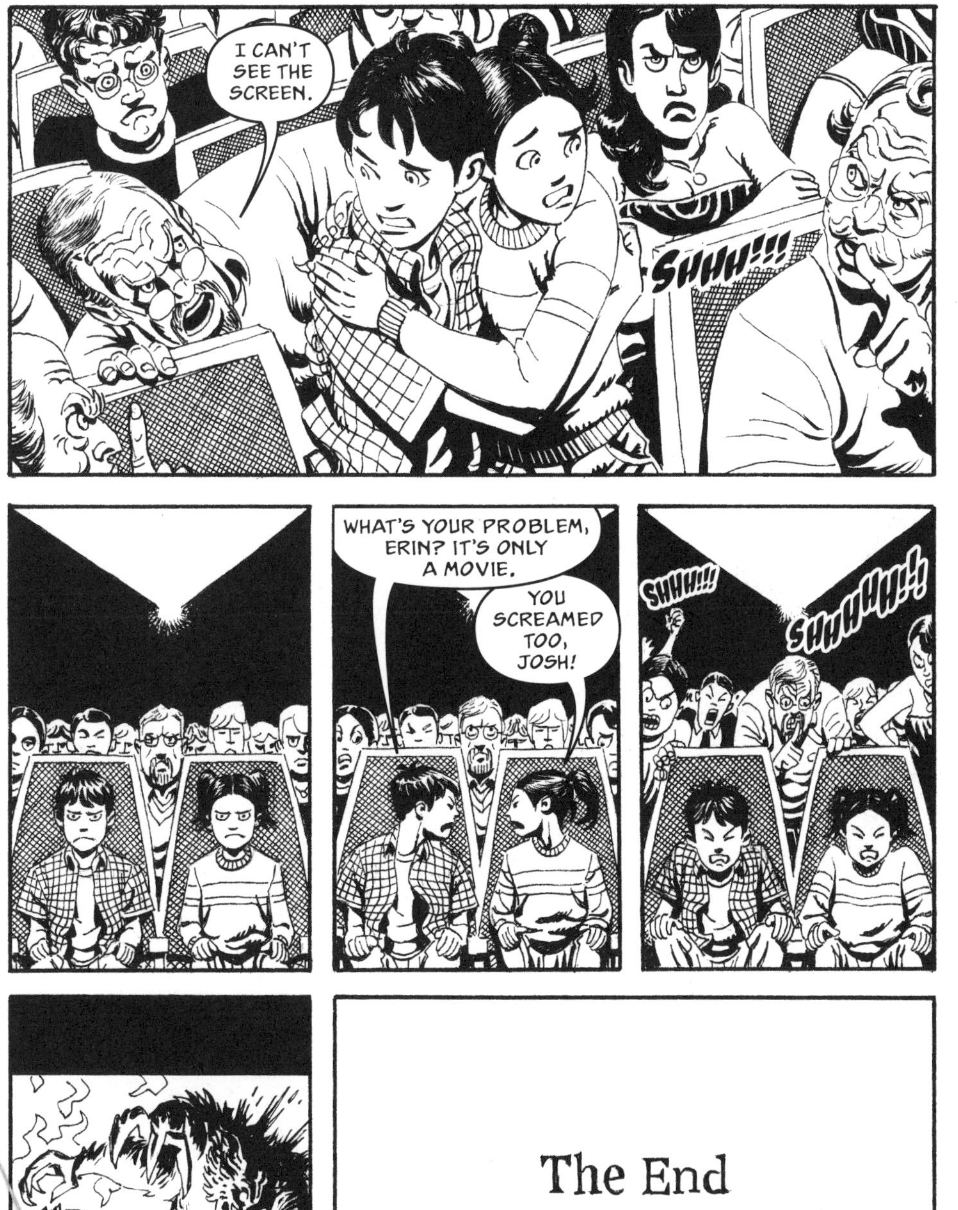
I CAN'T SEE THE SCREEN.
SHHH!!!
WHAT'S YOUR PROBLEM, ERIN? IT'S ONLY A MOVIE.
YOU SCREAMED TOO, JOSH!
SHHH!!!
SHHHHH!!!
BLAM
BLAM
BLAM
BLAM
BLAM
The End
a Shocker Studios Production
CLAP!
CLAP!
CLAP!
CLAP!
CLAP!

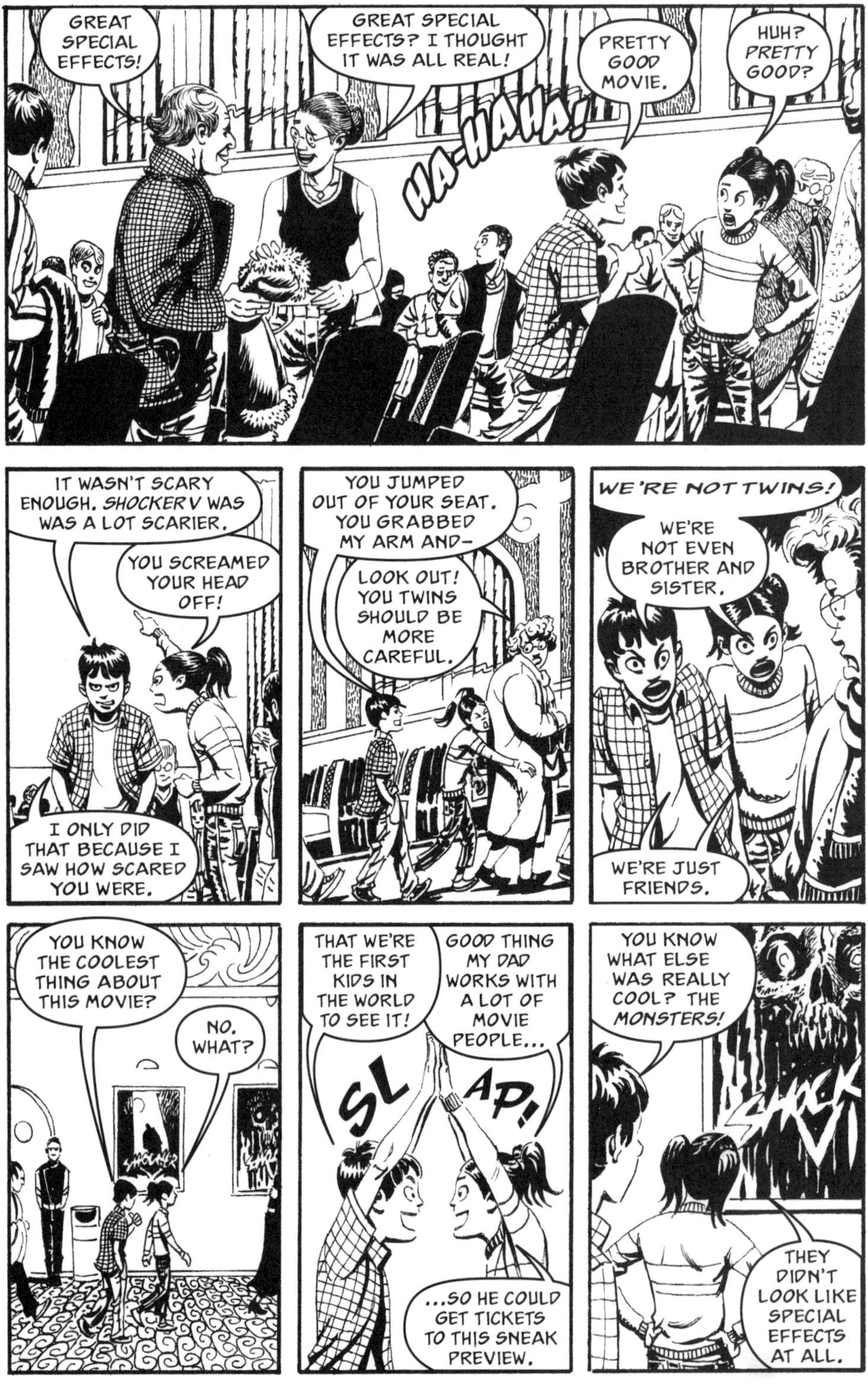
GREAT SPECIAL EFFECTS!
GREAT SPECIAL EFFECTS? I THOUGHT IT WAS ALL REAL!
HA-HAHAHA!
PRETTY GOOD MOVIE.
HUH? PRETTY GOOD?
IT WASN'T SCARY ENOUGH. *SHOCKER V* WAS WAS A LOT SCARIER.
YOU SCREAMED YOUR HEAD OFF!
I ONLY DID THAT BECAUSE I SAW HOW SCARED YOU WERE.
YOU JUMPED OUT OF YOUR SEAT. YOU GRABBED MY ARM AND—
LOOK OUT! YOU TWINS SHOULD BE MORE CAREFUL.
WE'RE NOT TWINS!
WE'RE NOT EVEN BROTHER AND SISTER.
WE'RE JUST FRIENDS.
YOU KNOW THE COOLEST THING ABOUT THIS MOVIE?
NO. WHAT?
THAT WE'RE THE FIRST KIDS IN THE WORLD TO SEE IT!
GOOD THING MY DAD WORKS WITH A LOT OF MOVIE PEOPLE...
SLAP!
...SO HE COULD GET TICKETS TO THIS SNEAK PREVIEW.
YOU KNOW WHAT ELSE WAS REALLY COOL? THE *MONSTERS!*
THEY DIDN'T LOOK LIKE SPECIAL EFFECTS AT ALL.

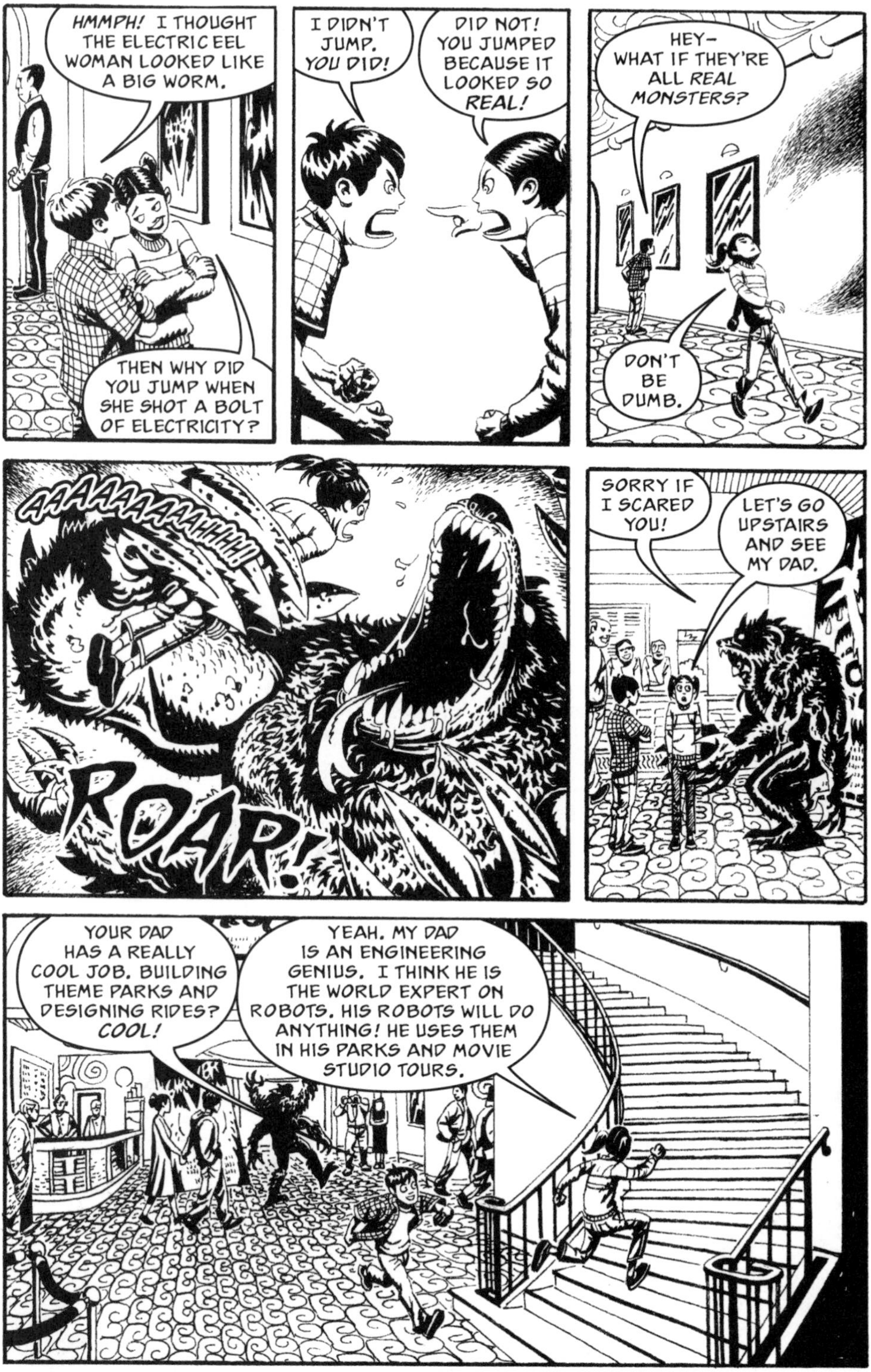
HMMPH! I THOUGHT THE ELECTRIC EEL WOMAN LOOKED LIKE A BIG WORM.
THEN WHY DID YOU JUMP WHEN SHE SHOT A BOLT OF ELECTRICITY?
I DIDN'T JUMP. YOU DID!
DID NOT! YOU JUMPED BECAUSE IT LOOKED SO REAL!
HEY— WHAT IF THEY'RE ALL REAL MONSTERS?
DON'T BE DUMB.
AAAAAAAAAAHHHH!!
ROAR!
SORRY IF I SCARED YOU!
LET'S GO UPSTAIRS AND SEE MY DAD.
YOUR DAD HAS A REALLY COOL JOB. BUILDING THEME PARKS AND DESIGNING RIDES? COOL!
YEAH. MY DAD IS AN ENGINEERING GENIUS. I THINK HE IS THE WORLD EXPERT ON ROBOTS. HIS ROBOTS WILL DO ANYTHING! HE USES THEM IN HIS PARKS AND MOVIE STUDIO TOURS.

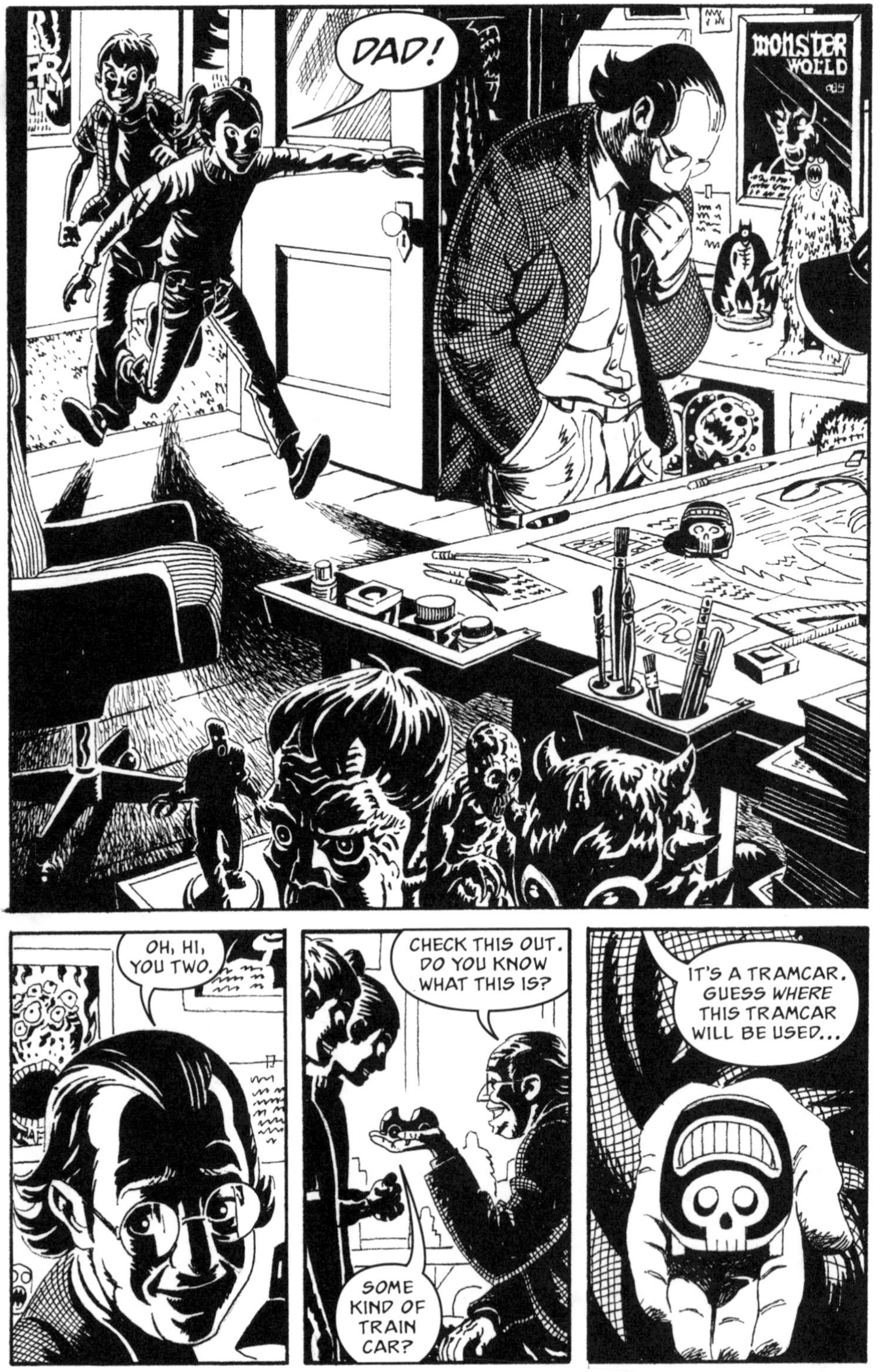
DAD!
MONSTER WORLD
OH, HI, YOU TWO.
CHECK THIS OUT. DO YOU KNOW WHAT THIS IS?
SOME KIND OF TRAIN CAR?
IT'S A TRAMCAR. GUESS *WHERE* THIS TRAMCAR WILL BE USED...

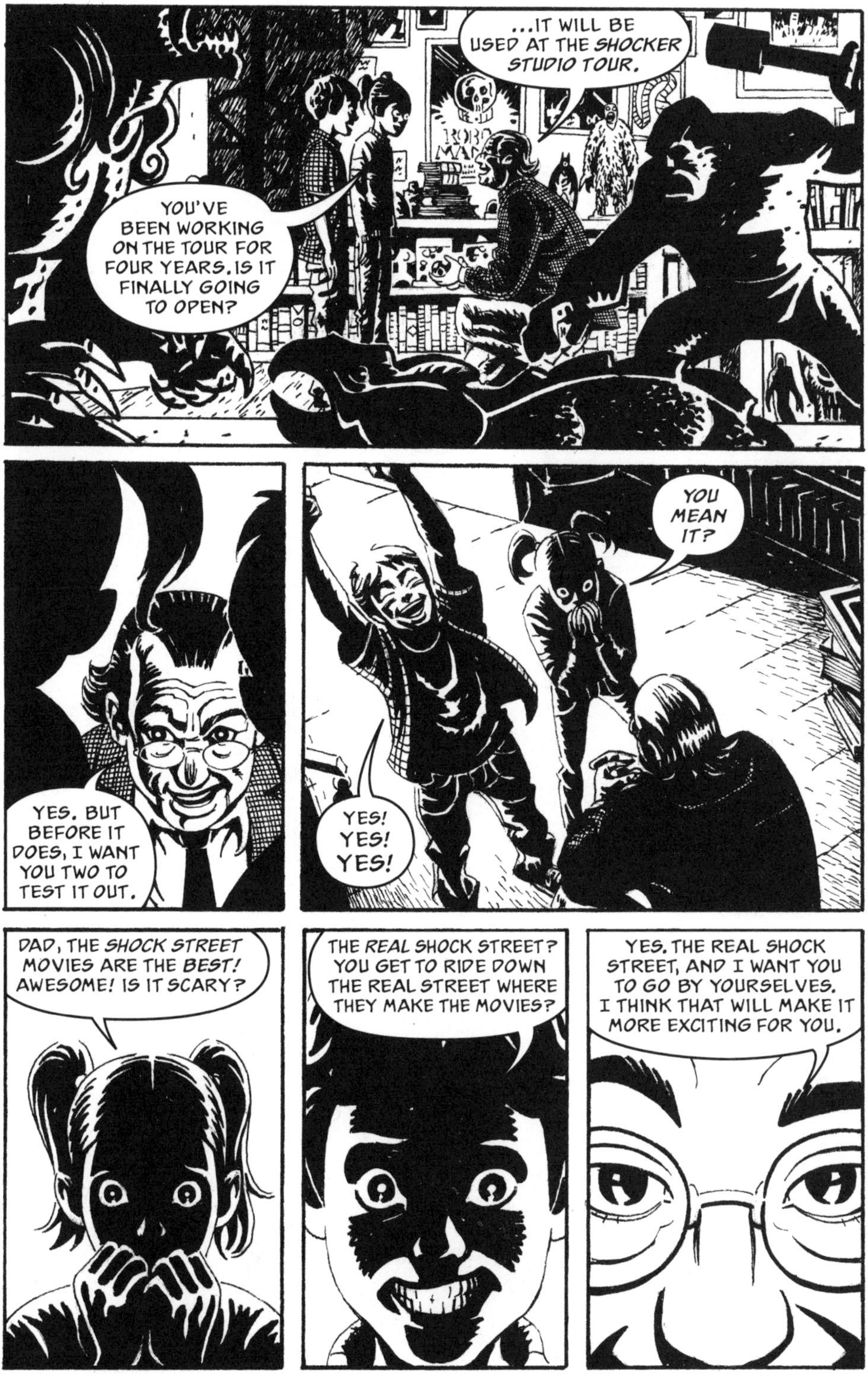
...IT WILL BE USED AT THE *SHOCKER STUDIO TOUR.*
YOU'VE BEEN WORKING ON THE TOUR FOR FOUR YEARS. IS IT FINALLY GOING TO OPEN?
YES. BUT BEFORE IT DOES, I WANT YOU TWO TO TEST IT OUT.
YOU MEAN IT?
YES! YES! YES!
DAD, THE *SHOCK STREET* MOVIES ARE THE *BEST!* AWESOME! IS IT SCARY?
THE *REAL* SHOCK STREET? YOU GET TO RIDE DOWN THE REAL STREET WHERE THEY MAKE THE MOVIES?
YES. THE REAL SHOCK STREET, AND I WANT YOU TO GO BY YOURSELVES. I THINK THAT WILL MAKE IT MORE EXCITING FOR YOU.

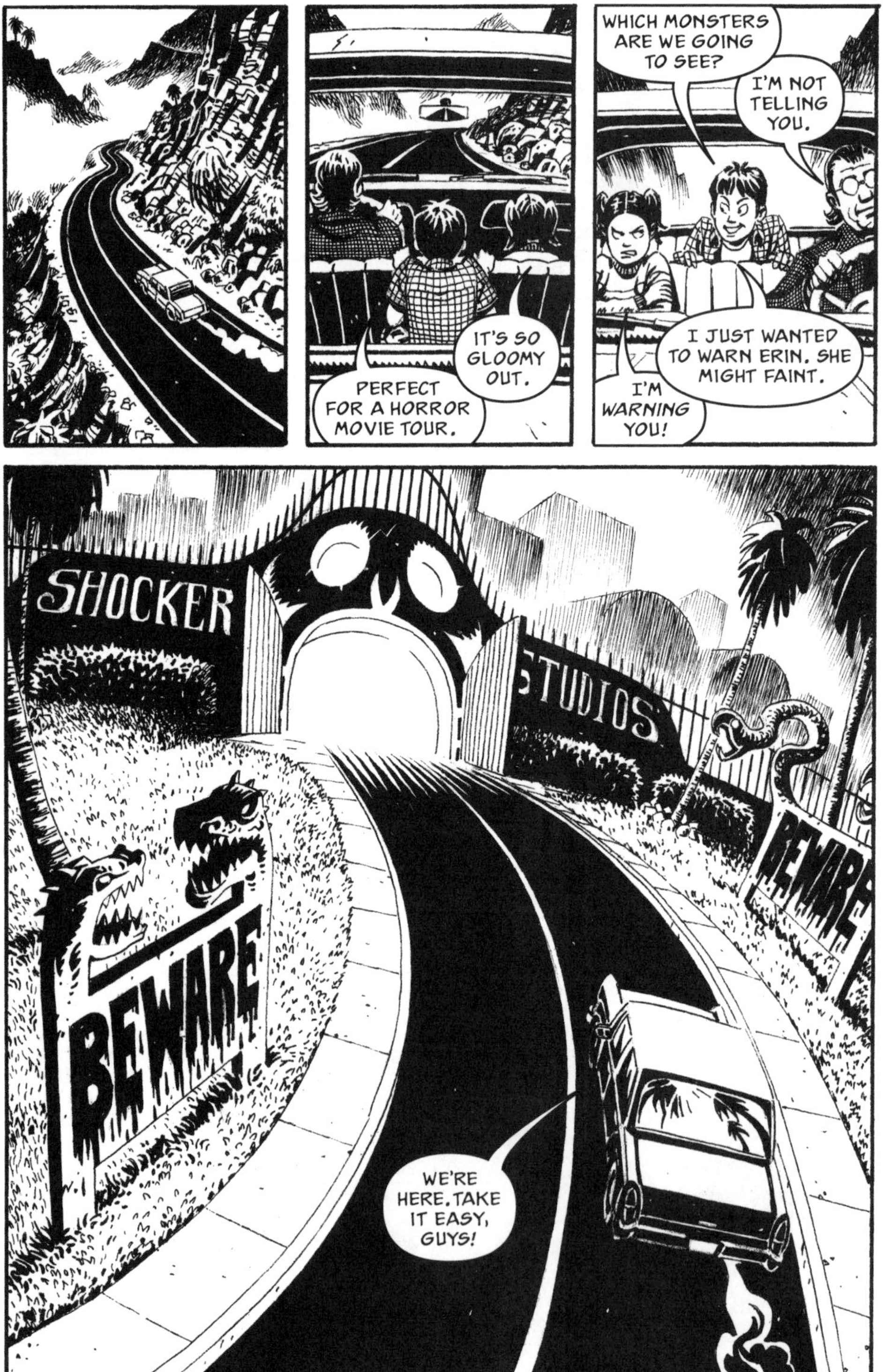
IT'S SO GLOOMY OUT.
PERFECT FOR A HORROR MOVIE TOUR.
WHICH MONSTERS ARE WE GOING TO SEE?
I'M NOT TELLING YOU.
I JUST WANTED TO WARN ERIN. SHE MIGHT FAINT.
I'M WARNING YOU!
SHOCKER
STUDIOS
BEWARE
BEWARE
WE'RE HERE. TAKE IT EASY, GUYS!

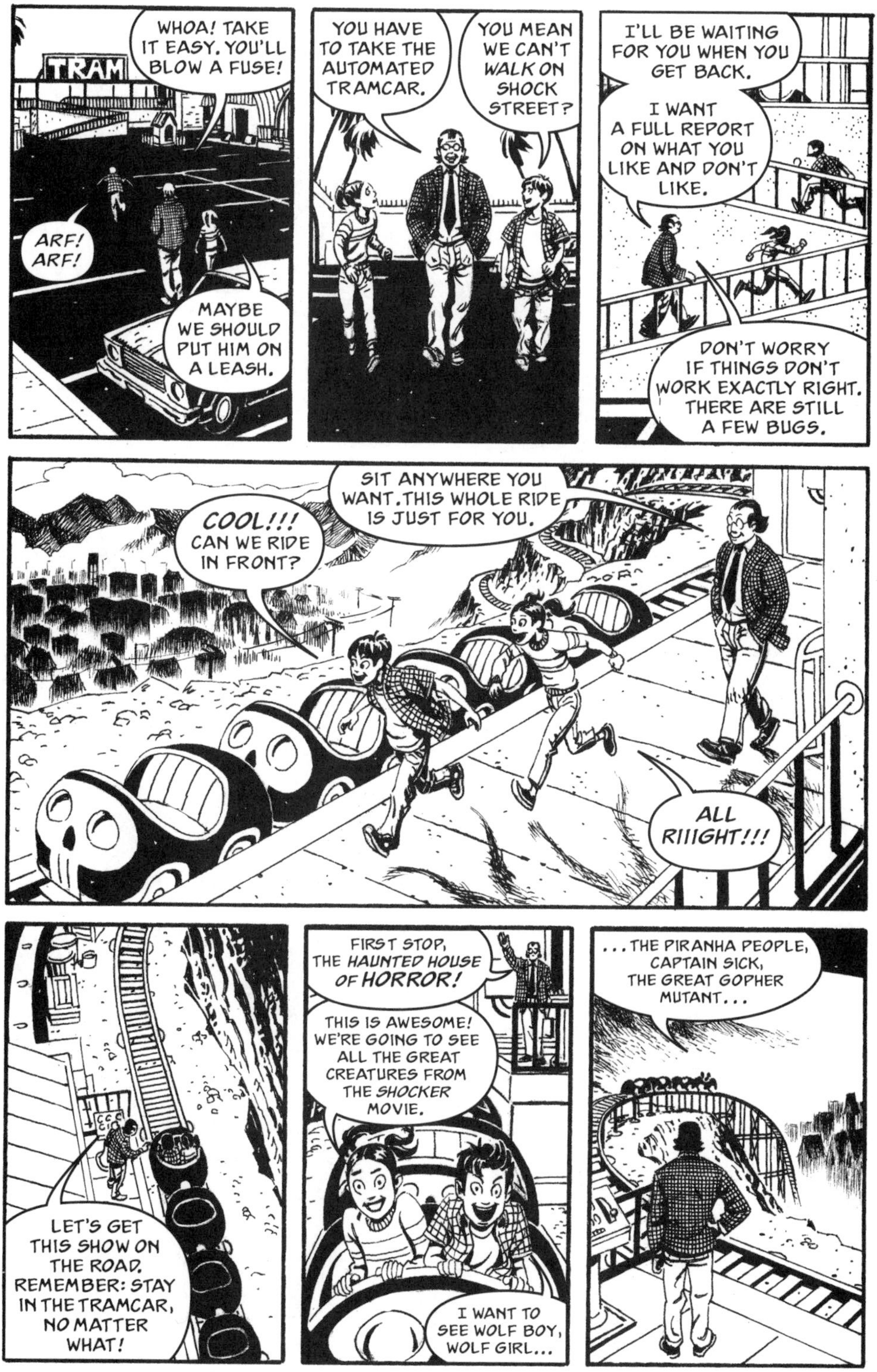
WHOA! TAKE IT EASY. YOU'LL BLOW A FUSE!
TRAM
ARF! ARF!
MAYBE WE SHOULD PUT HIM ON A LEASH.
YOU HAVE TO TAKE THE AUTOMATED TRAMCAR.
YOU MEAN WE CAN'T WALK ON SHOCK STREET?
I'LL BE WAITING FOR YOU WHEN YOU GET BACK.
I WANT A FULL REPORT ON WHAT YOU LIKE AND DON'T LIKE.
DON'T WORRY IF THINGS DON'T WORK EXACTLY RIGHT. THERE ARE STILL A FEW BUGS.
COOL!!! CAN WE RIDE IN FRONT?
SIT ANYWHERE YOU WANT. THIS WHOLE RIDE IS JUST FOR YOU.
ALL RIIIGHT!!!
LET'S GET THIS SHOW ON THE ROAD. REMEMBER: STAY IN THE TRAMCAR, NO MATTER WHAT!
FIRST STOP, THE HAUNTED HOUSE OF HORROR!
THIS IS AWESOME! WE'RE GOING TO SEE ALL THE GREAT CREATURES FROM THE SHOCKER MOVIE.
I WANT TO SEE WOLF BOY, WOLF GIRL...
...THE PIRANHA PEOPLE, CAPTAIN SICK, THE GREAT GOPHER MUTANT...

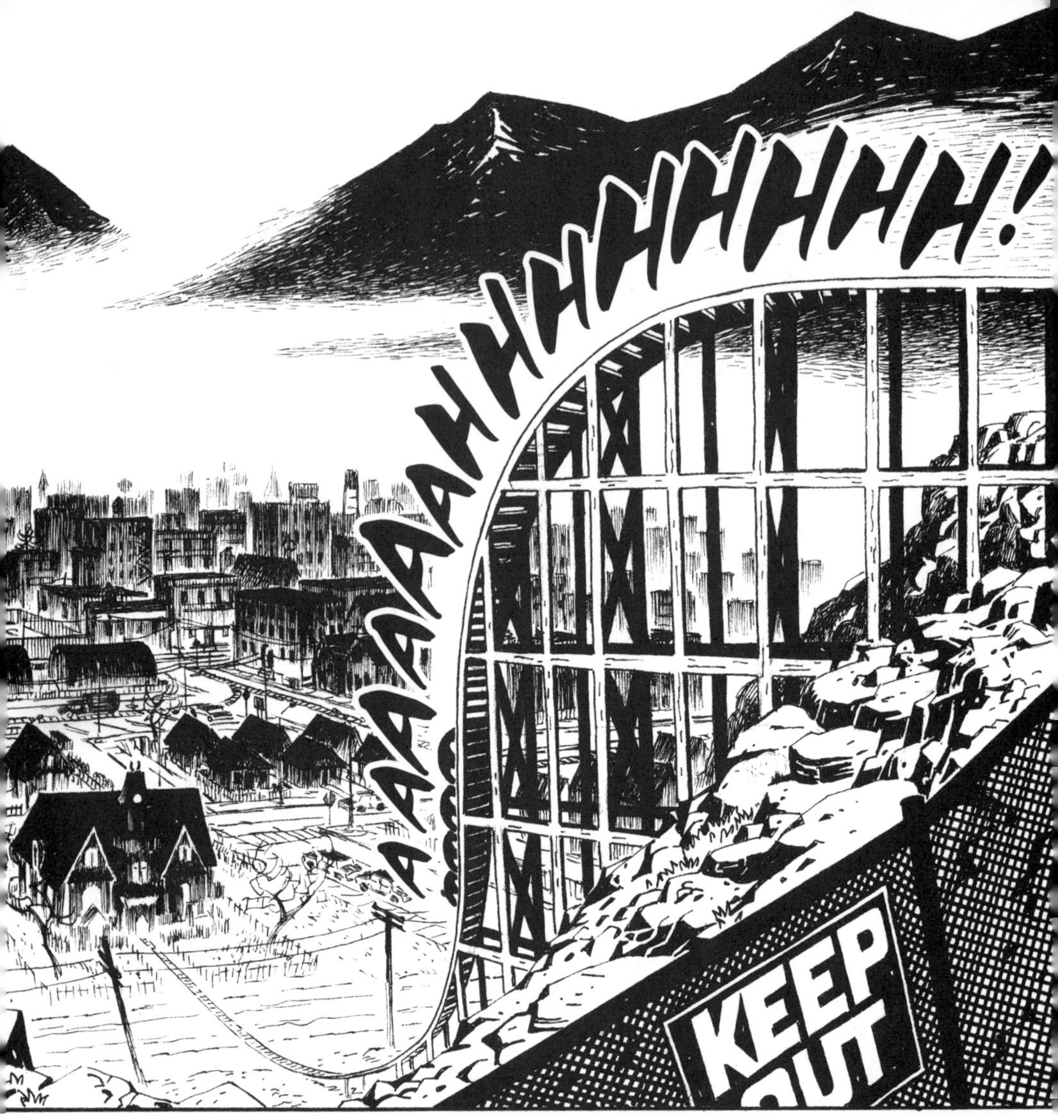
AAAAAAAHHHHHHHHHHHHH!
KEEP OUT

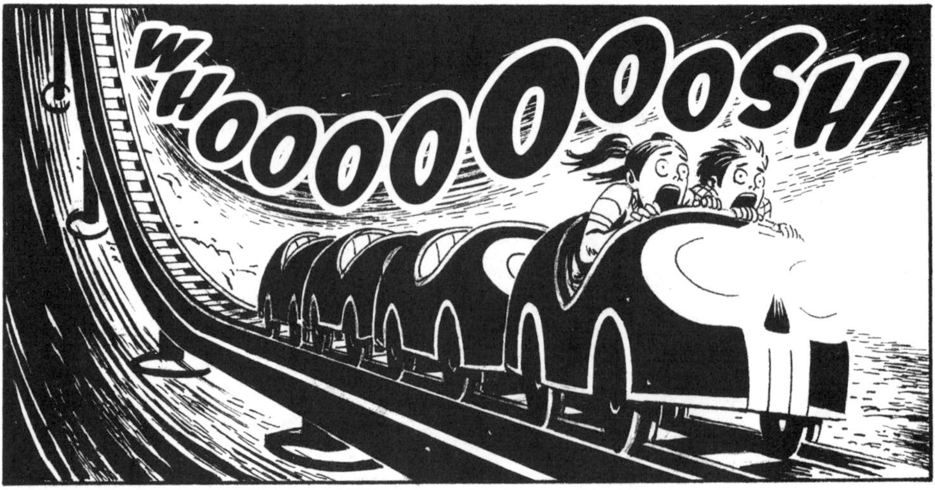
WHOOOOOOOOSH

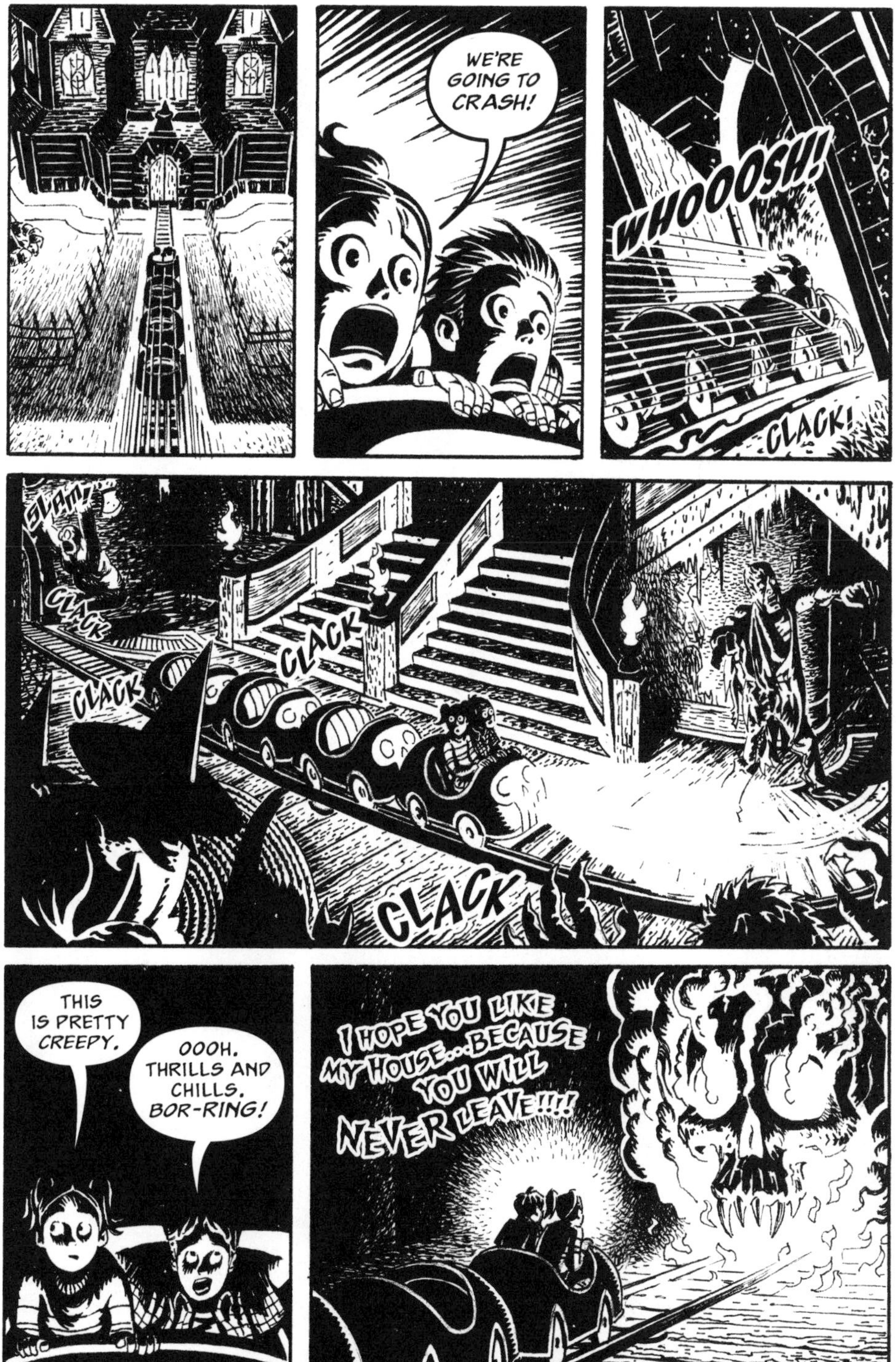
WE'RE GOING TO CRASH!
WHOOOSH!
CLACK!
SLAM!
CLACK
CLACK
CLACK
CLACK
THIS IS PRETTY CREEPY.
OOOH. THRILLS AND CHILLS. BOR-RING!
I HOPE YOU LIKE MY HOUSE...BECAUSE YOU WILL NEVER LEAVE!!!!

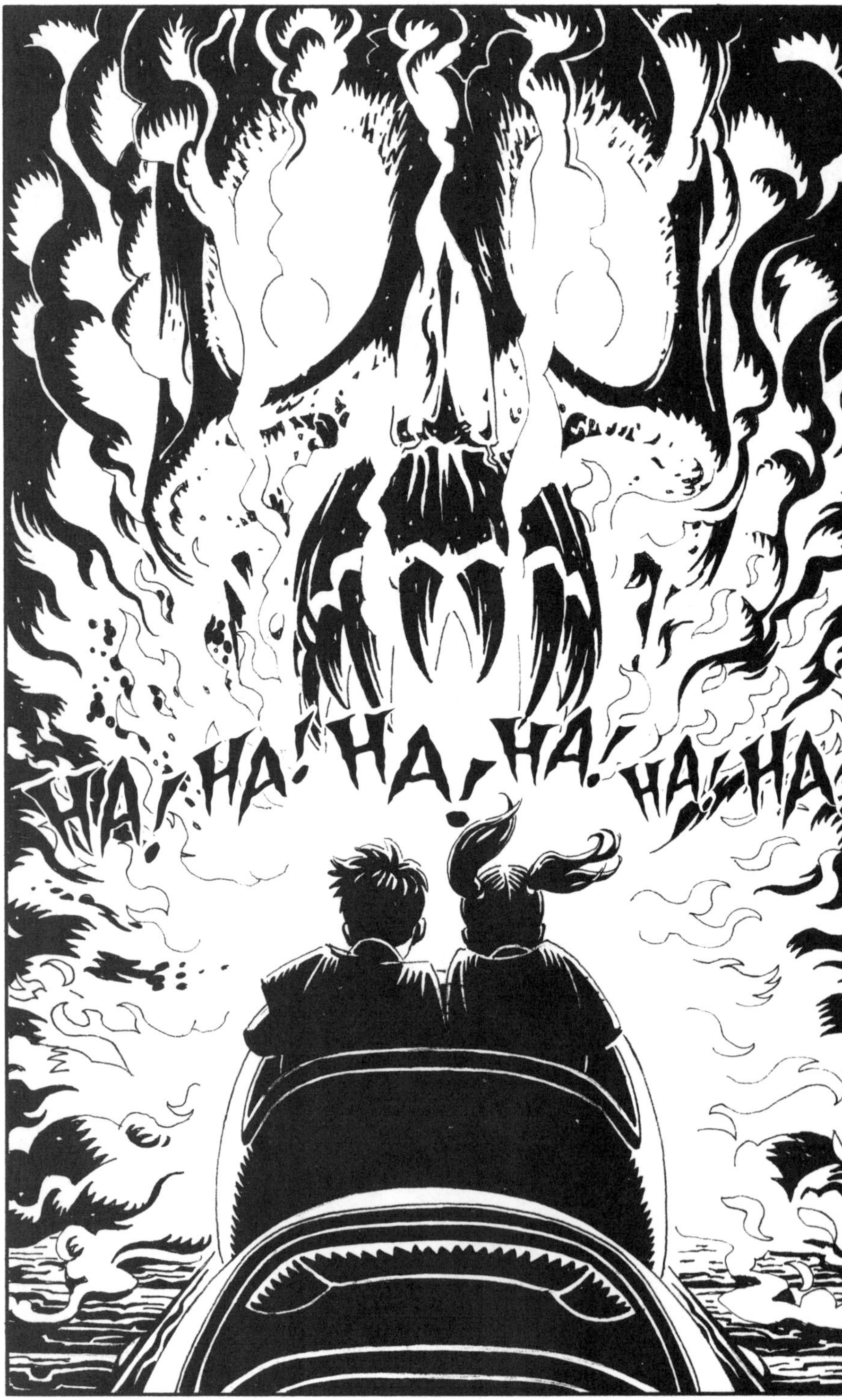
HA! HA! HA! HA! HA! HA!

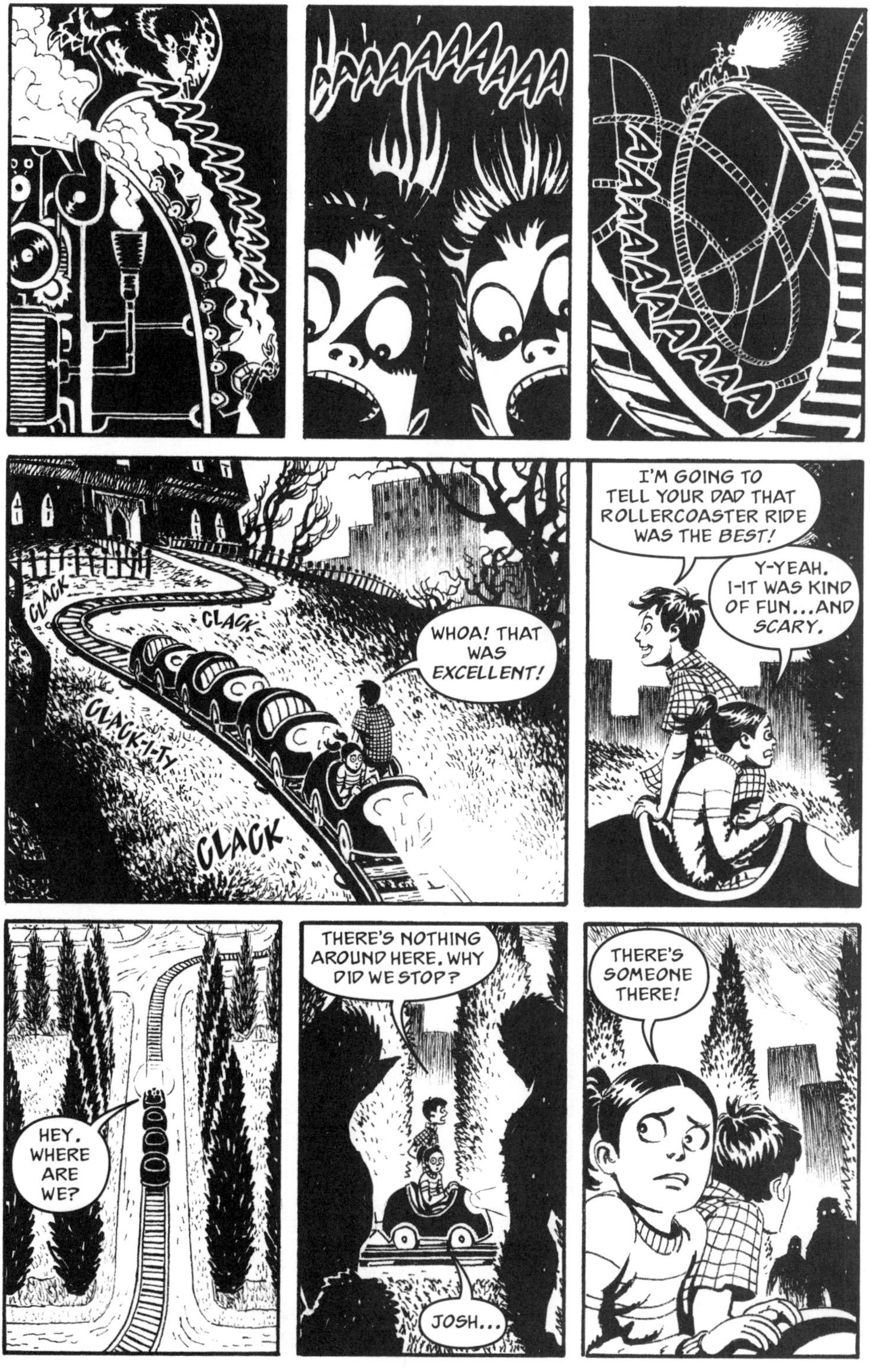
AAAAAAAAAAAA
AAAAAAAAAAA
AAAAAAAAAAAAAA
CLACK
CLACK
CLACK-I-TY
CLACK
WHOA! THAT WAS *EXCELLENT!*
I'M GOING TO TELL YOUR DAD THAT ROLLERCOASTER RIDE WAS THE *BEST!*
Y-YEAH. I-IT WAS KIND OF FUN...AND *SCARY.*
HEY. WHERE ARE WE?
THERE'S NOTHING AROUND HERE. WHY DID WE STOP?
JOSH...
THERE'S SOMEONE THERE!

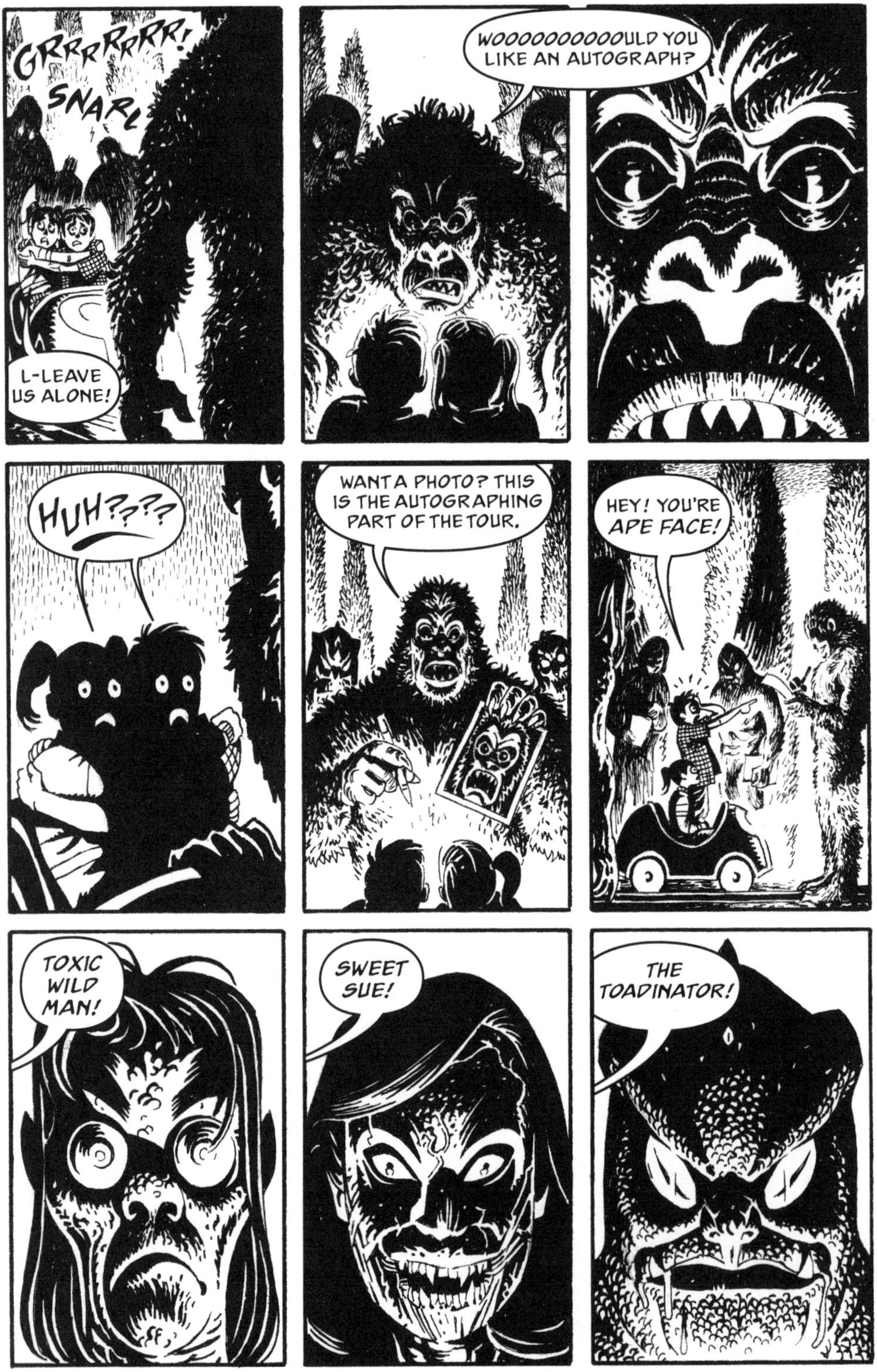
GRRRRRRR!
SNARL
L-LEAVE US ALONE!
WOOOOOOOOOOULD YOU LIKE AN AUTOGRAPH?
HUH????
WANT A PHOTO? THIS IS THE AUTOGRAPHING PART OF THE TOUR.
HEY! YOU'RE APE FACE!
TOXIC WILD MAN!
SWEET SUE!
THE TOADINATOR!

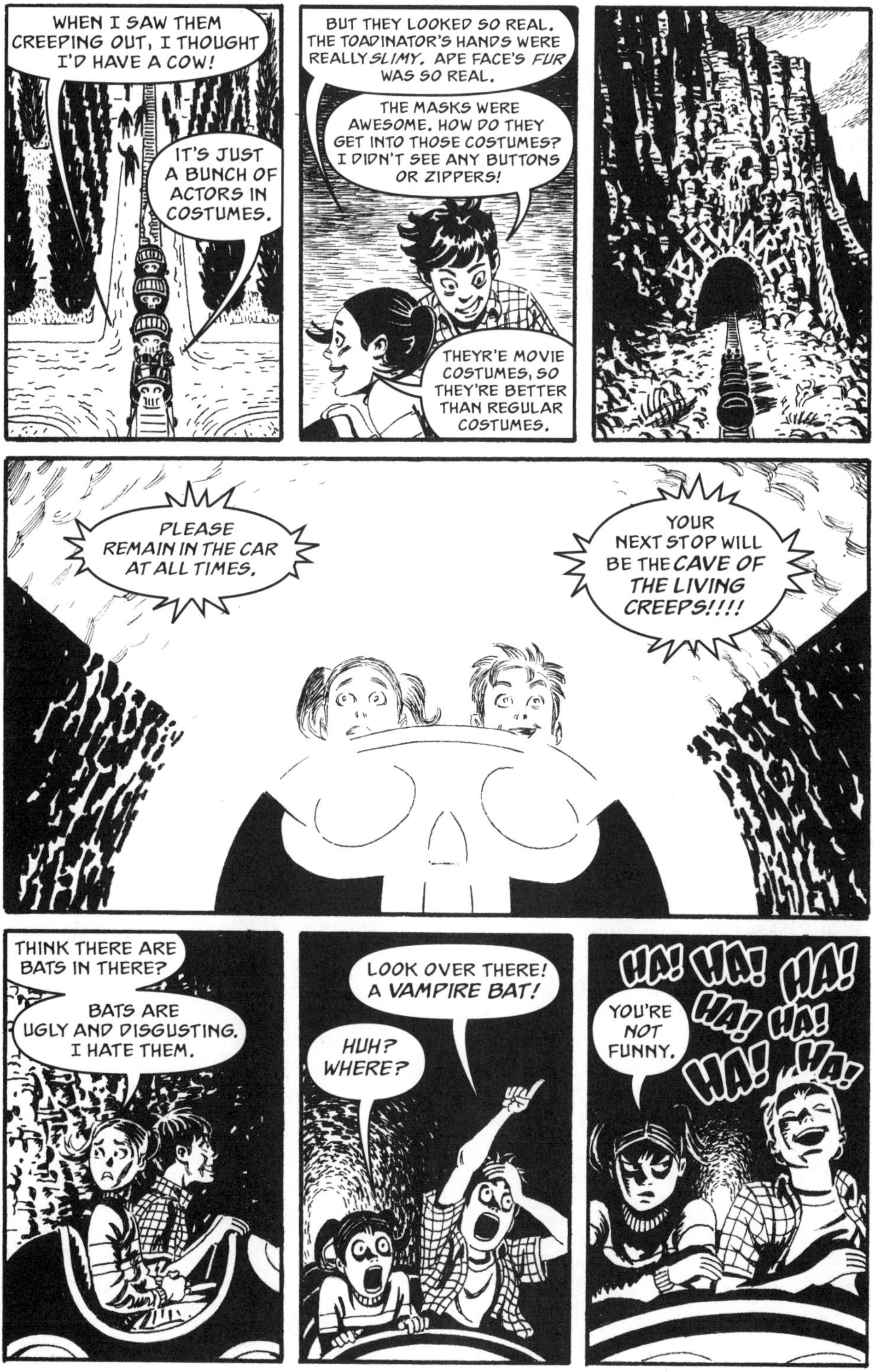
WHEN I SAW THEM CREEPING OUT, I THOUGHT I'D HAVE A COW!
IT'S JUST A BUNCH OF ACTORS IN COSTUMES.
BUT THEY LOOKED SO REAL. THE TOADINATOR'S HANDS WERE REALLY *SLIMY*. APE FACE'S *FUR* WAS SO REAL.
THE MASKS WERE AWESOME. HOW DO THEY GET INTO THOSE COSTUMES? I DIDN'T SEE ANY BUTTONS OR ZIPPERS!
THEYR'E MOVIE COSTUMES, SO THEY'RE BETTER THAN REGULAR COSTUMES.
BEWARE
PLEASE REMAIN IN THE CAR AT ALL TIMES.
YOUR NEXT STOP WILL BE THE *CAVE OF THE LIVING CREEPS!!!!*
THINK THERE ARE BATS IN THERE?
BATS ARE UGLY AND DISGUSTING. I HATE THEM.
LOOK OVER THERE! A *VAMPIRE BAT!*
HUH? WHERE?
HA! HA! HA! HA! HA! HA! HA!
YOU'RE *NOT* FUNNY.

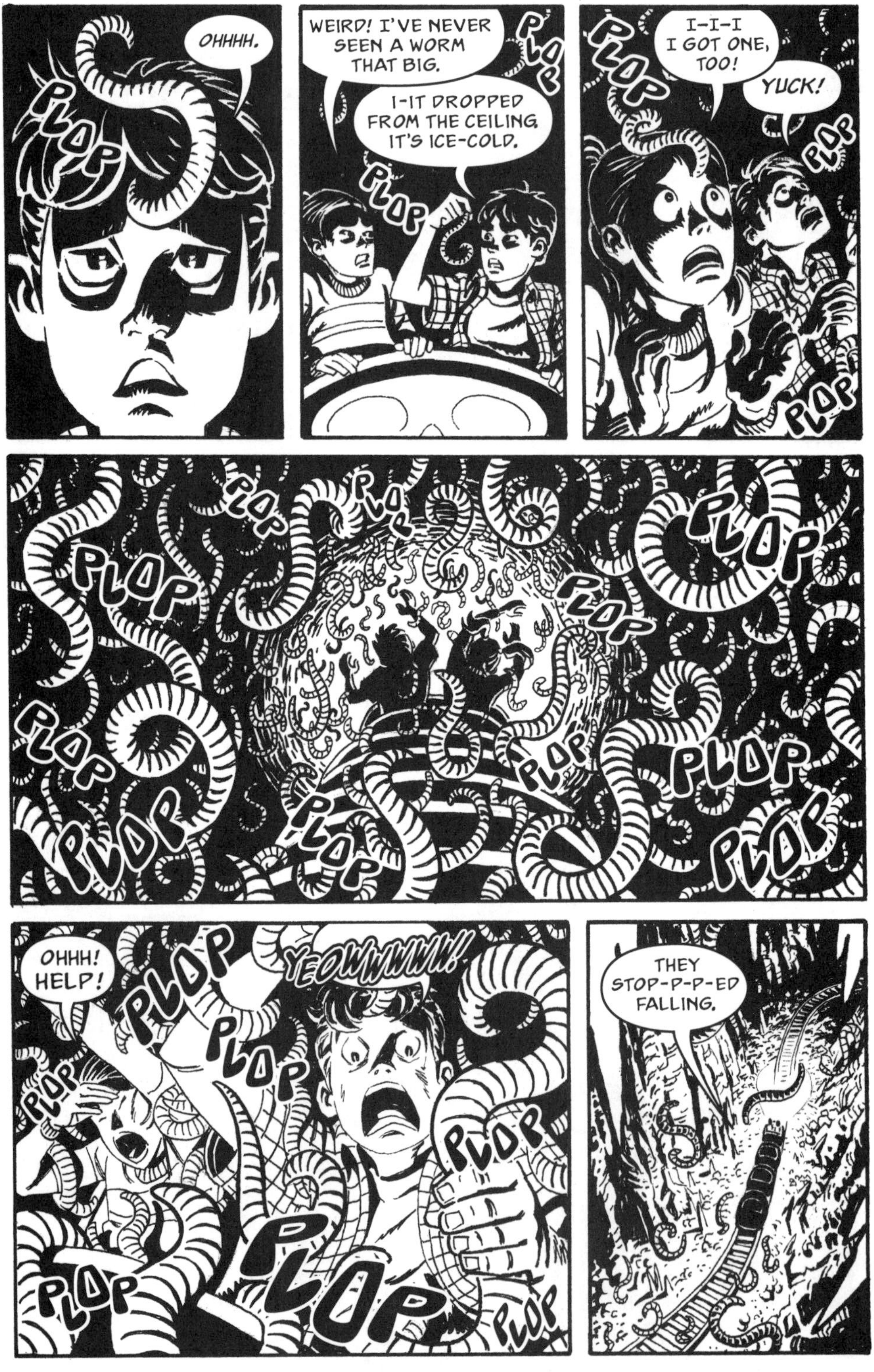
OHHHH.
PLOP
WEIRD! I'VE NEVER SEEN A WORM THAT BIG.
PLOP
I-IT DROPPED FROM THE CEILING. IT'S ICE-COLD.
PLOP
PLOP
I-I-I I GOT ONE, TOO!
YUCK!
PLOP
PLOP
PLOP
PLOP
PLOP
PLOP
PLOP
PLOP
PLOP
PLOP
PLOP
PLOP
PLOP
PLOP
PLOP
OHHH! HELP!
PLOP
PLOP
YEOWWWWW!
PLOP
PLOP
PLOP
PLOP
PLOP
PLOP
THEY STOP-P-P-ED FALLING.

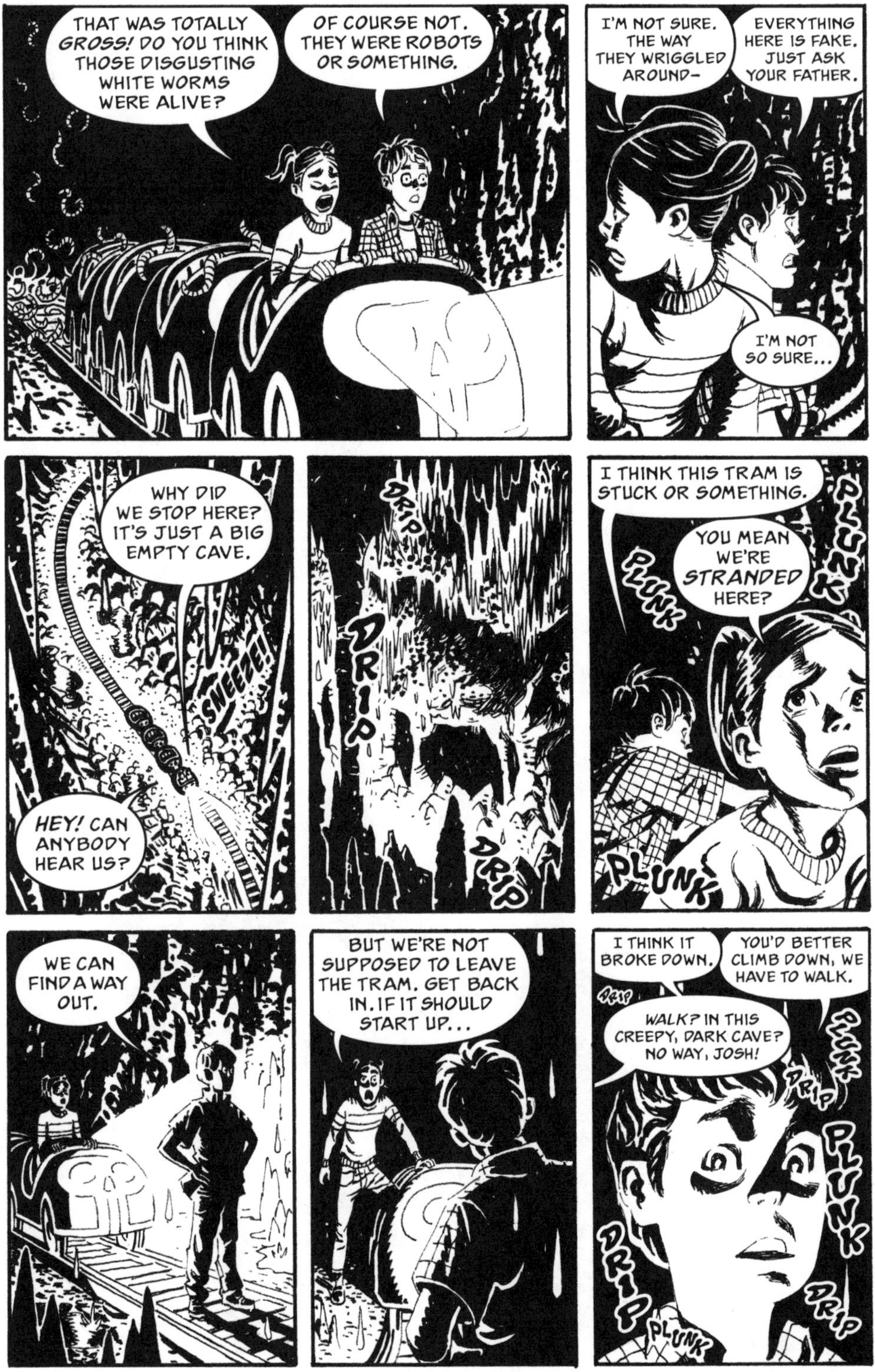
THAT WAS TOTALLY *GROSS!* DO YOU THINK THOSE DISGUSTING WHITE WORMS WERE ALIVE?
OF COURSE NOT. THEY WERE ROBOTS OR SOMETHING.
I'M NOT SURE. THE WAY THEY WRIGGLED AROUND–
EVERYTHING HERE IS FAKE. JUST ASK YOUR FATHER.
I'M NOT SO SURE...
WHY DID WE STOP HERE? IT'S JUST A BIG EMPTY CAVE.
SNEEZE!!
HEY! CAN ANYBODY HEAR US?
DRIP
DRIP
DRIP
I THINK THIS TRAM IS STUCK OR SOMETHING.
PLUNK
YOU MEAN WE'RE *STRANDED* HERE?
PLUNK
PLUNK
WE CAN FIND A WAY OUT.
BUT WE'RE NOT SUPPOSED TO LEAVE THE TRAM. GET BACK IN. IF IT SHOULD START UP...
I THINK IT BROKE DOWN.
YOU'D BETTER CLIMB DOWN, WE HAVE TO WALK.
DRIP
PLUNK
WALK? IN THIS CREEPY, DARK CAVE? NO WAY, JOSH!
DRIP
PLUNK
DRIP
DRIP
PLUNK

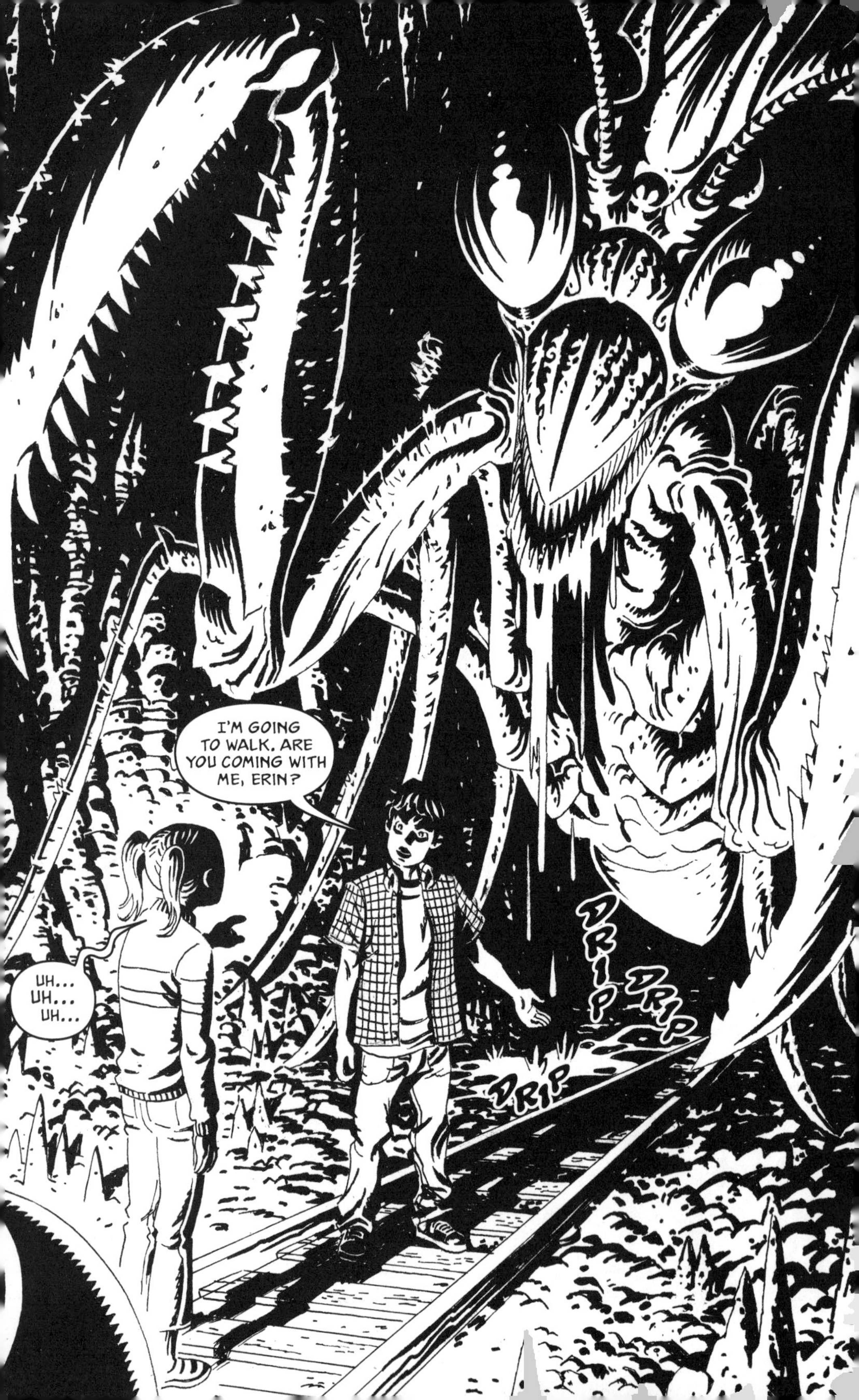
I'M GOING TO WALK. ARE YOU COMING WITH ME, ERIN?
UH... UH... UH...
DRIP
DRIP
DRIP

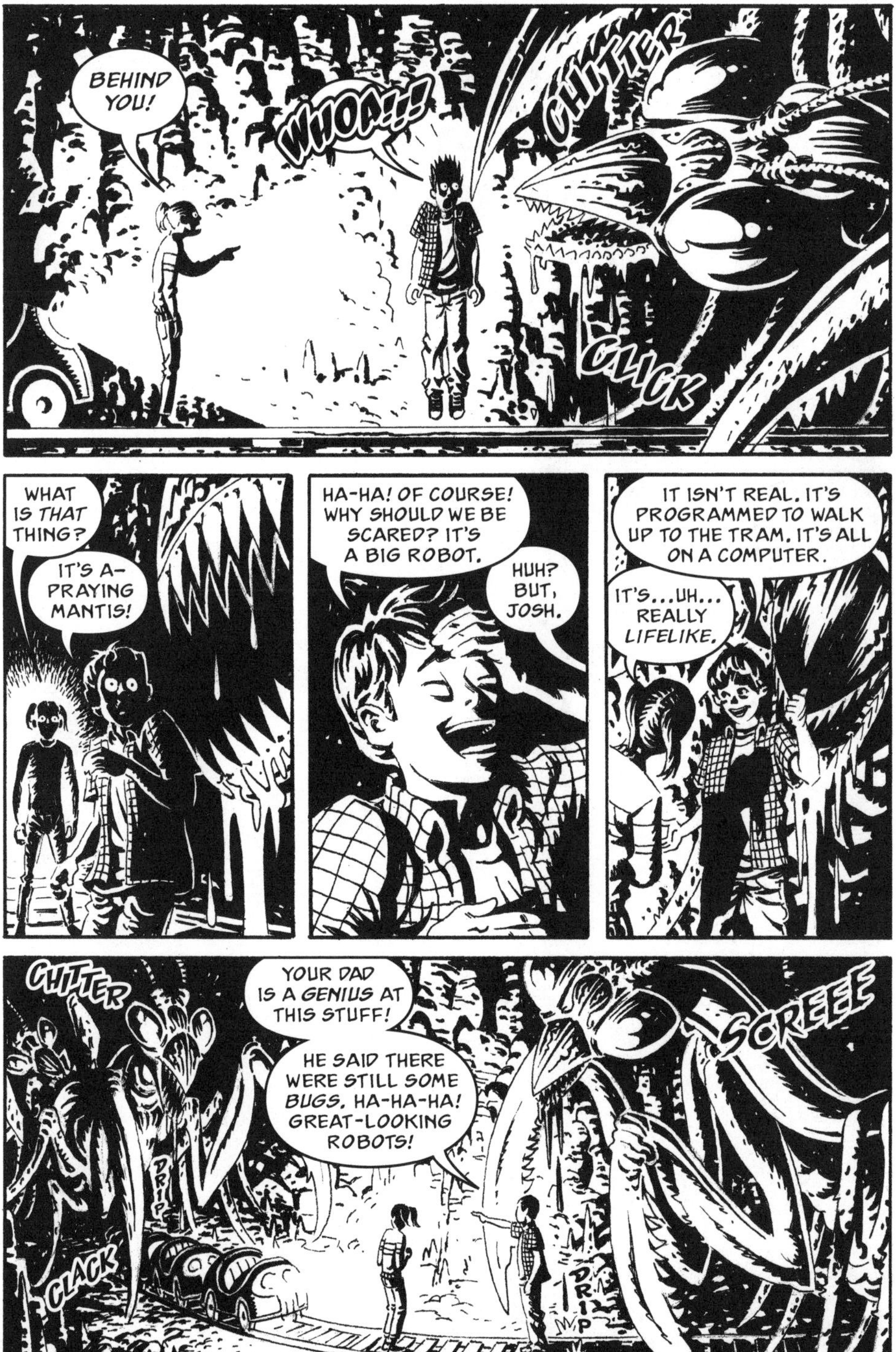
BEHIND YOU!
WHOA!!!
CHITTER
CLICK
WHAT IS THAT THING?
IT'S A- PRAYING MANTIS!
HA-HA! OF COURSE! WHY SHOULD WE BE SCARED? IT'S A BIG ROBOT.
HUH? BUT, JOSH.
IT ISN'T REAL. IT'S PROGRAMMED TO WALK UP TO THE TRAM. IT'S ALL ON A COMPUTER.
IT'S...UH... REALLY LIFELIKE.
CHITTER
YOUR DAD IS A GENIUS AT THIS STUFF!
HE SAID THERE WERE STILL SOME BUGS. HA-HA-HA! GREAT-LOOKING ROBOTS!
SCREEEE
DRIP
CLACK
DRIP
DRIP

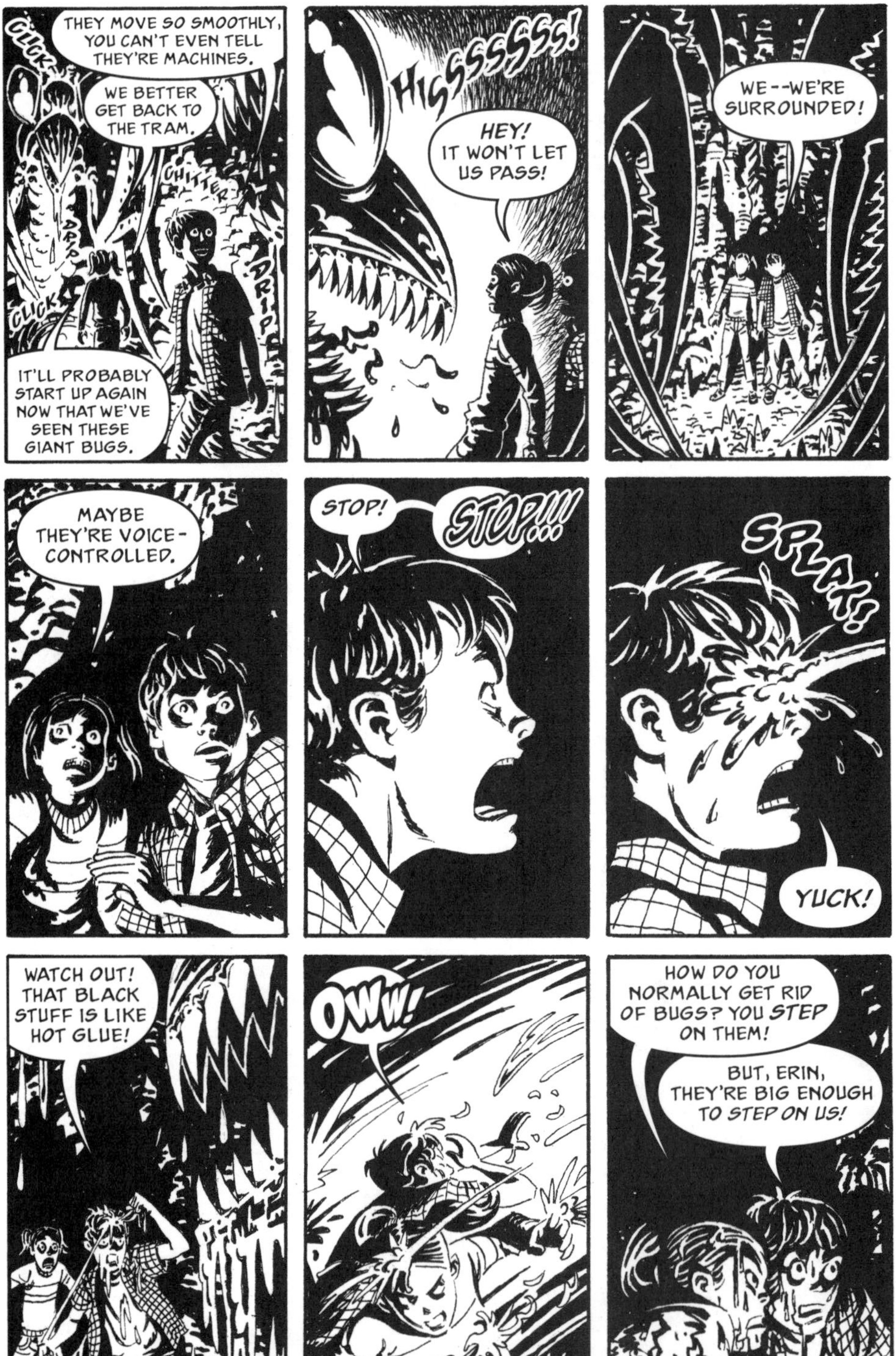
CLICK
THEY MOVE SO SMOOTHLY, YOU CAN'T EVEN TELL THEY'RE MACHINES.
WE BETTER GET BACK TO THE TRAM.
CHITTER
DRIP
CLICK
DRIP
IT'LL PROBABLY START UP AGAIN NOW THAT WE'VE SEEN THESE GIANT BUGS.
HISSSSSSS!
HEY! IT WON'T LET US PASS!
WE--WE'RE SURROUNDED!
MAYBE THEY'RE VOICE-CONTROLLED.
STOP!
STOP!!!
SPLAK!
YUCK!
WATCH OUT! THAT BLACK STUFF IS LIKE HOT GLUE!
OWW!
HOW DO YOU NORMALLY GET RID OF BUGS? YOU STEP ON THEM!
BUT, ERIN, THEY'RE BIG ENOUGH TO STEP ON US!

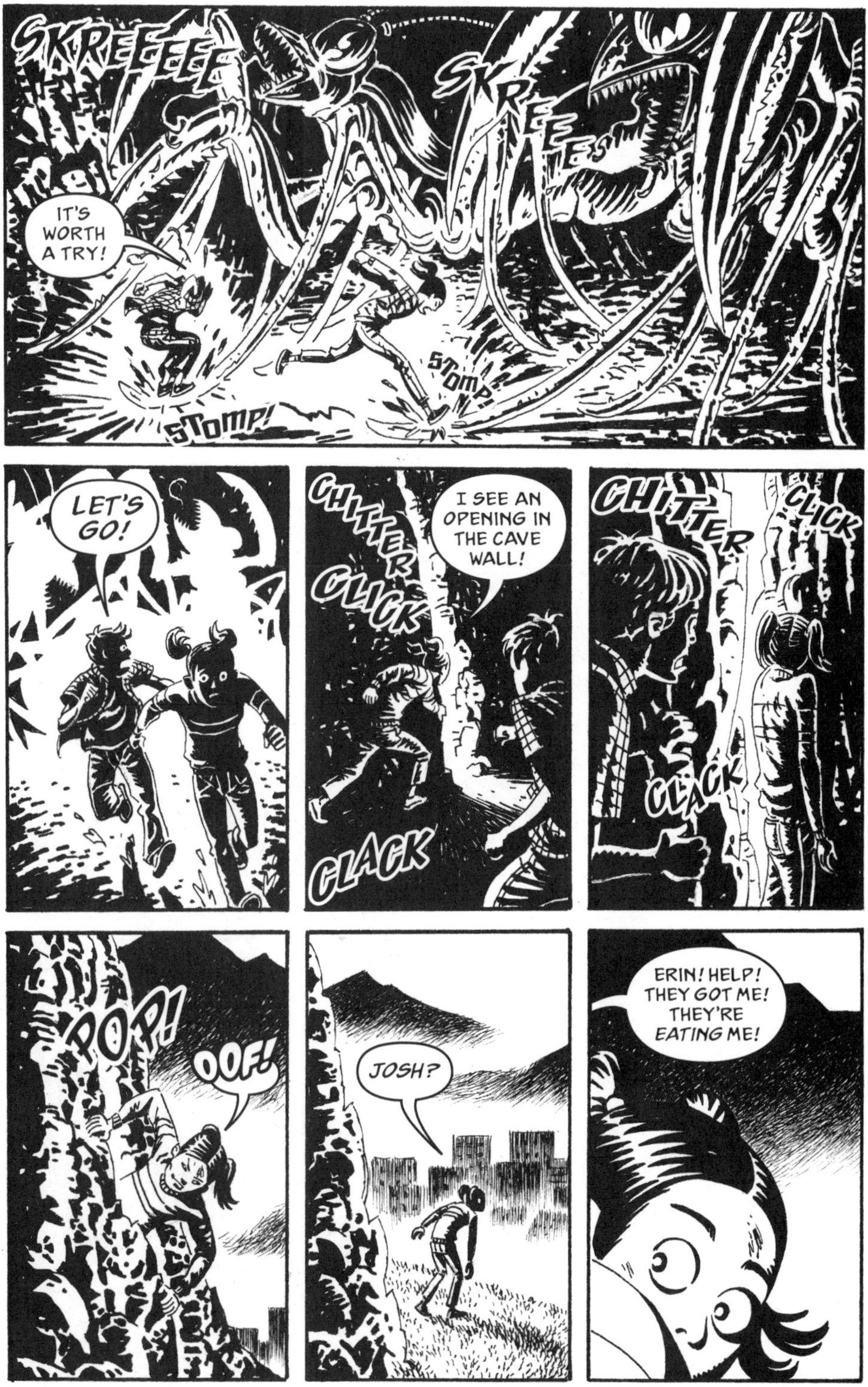
SKREEEEE
SKREEES
IT'S WORTH A TRY!
STOMP!
STOMP!
LET'S GO!
CHITTER
CLICK
I SEE AN OPENING IN THE CAVE WALL!
CLACK
CHITTER
CLICK
CLACK
POP!
OOF!
JOSH?
ERIN! HELP! THEY GOT ME! THEY'RE EATING ME!

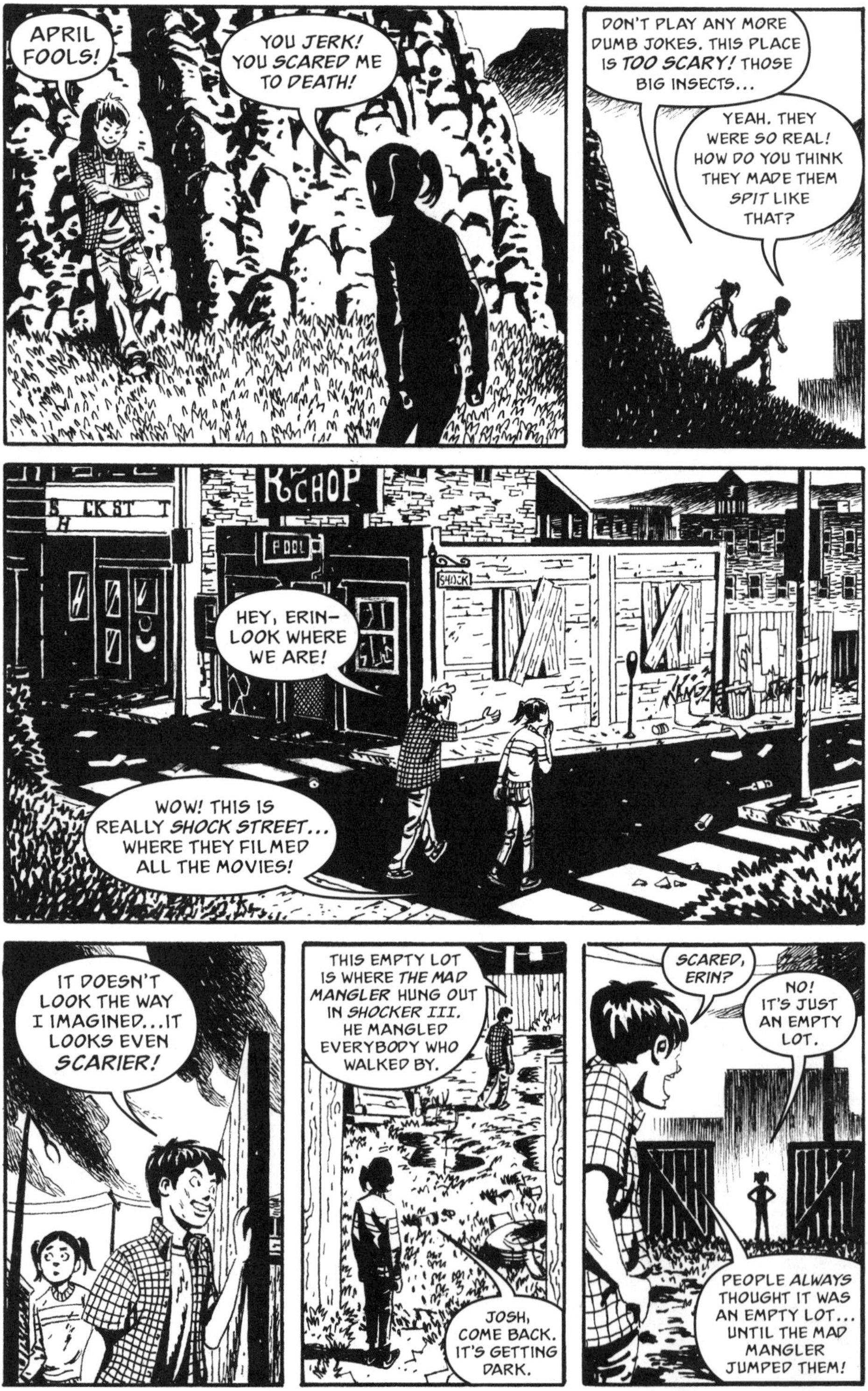
APRIL FOOLS!
YOU JERK! YOU SCARED ME TO DEATH!
DON'T PLAY ANY MORE DUMB JOKES. THIS PLACE IS TOO SCARY! THOSE BIG INSECTS...
YEAH. THEY WERE SO REAL! HOW DO YOU THINK THEY MADE THEM SPIT LIKE THAT?
POOL
HEY, ERIN- LOOK WHERE WE ARE!
WOW! THIS IS REALLY SHOCK STREET... WHERE THEY FILMED ALL THE MOVIES!
IT DOESN'T LOOK THE WAY I IMAGINED...IT LOOKS EVEN SCARIER!
THIS EMPTY LOT IS WHERE THE MAD MANGLER HUNG OUT IN SHOCKER III. HE MANGLED EVERYBODY WHO WALKED BY.
JOSH, COME BACK. IT'S GETTING DARK.
SCARED, ERIN?
NO! IT'S JUST AN EMPTY LOT.
PEOPLE ALWAYS THOUGHT IT WAS AN EMPTY LOT... UNTIL THE MAD MANGLER JUMPED THEM!

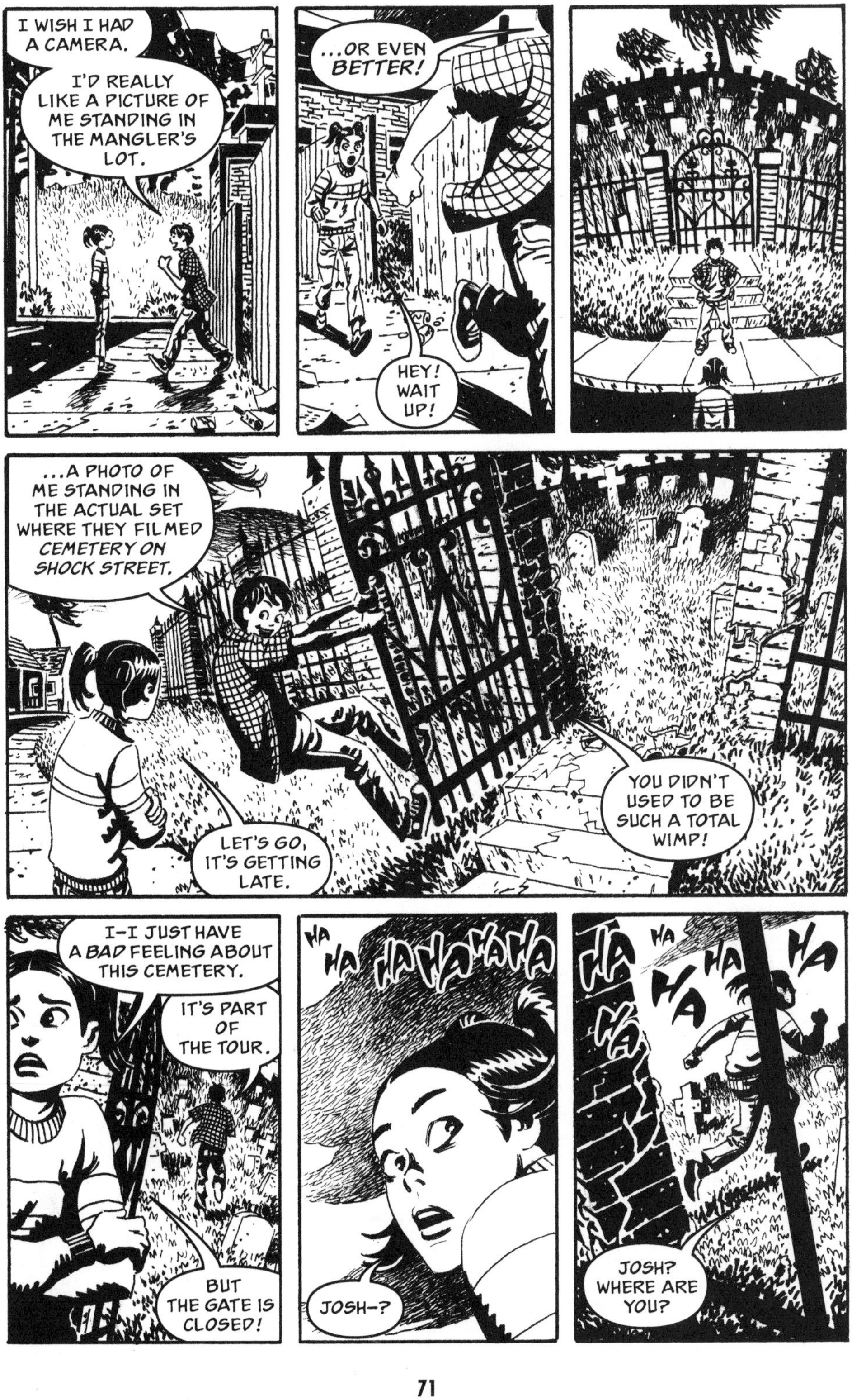
I WISH I HAD A CAMERA.
I'D REALLY LIKE A PICTURE OF ME STANDING IN THE MANGLER'S LOT.
...OR EVEN BETTER!
HEY! WAIT UP!
...A PHOTO OF ME STANDING IN THE ACTUAL SET WHERE THEY FILMED CEMETERY ON SHOCK STREET.
LET'S GO, IT'S GETTING LATE.
YOU DIDN'T USED TO BE SUCH A TOTAL WIMP!
I-I JUST HAVE A BAD FEELING ABOUT THIS CEMETERY.
IT'S PART OF THE TOUR.
BUT THE GATE IS CLOSED!
HA HA HA HA HA HA HA
JOSH-?
HA HA HA HA HA HA HA HA
JOSH? WHERE ARE YOU?

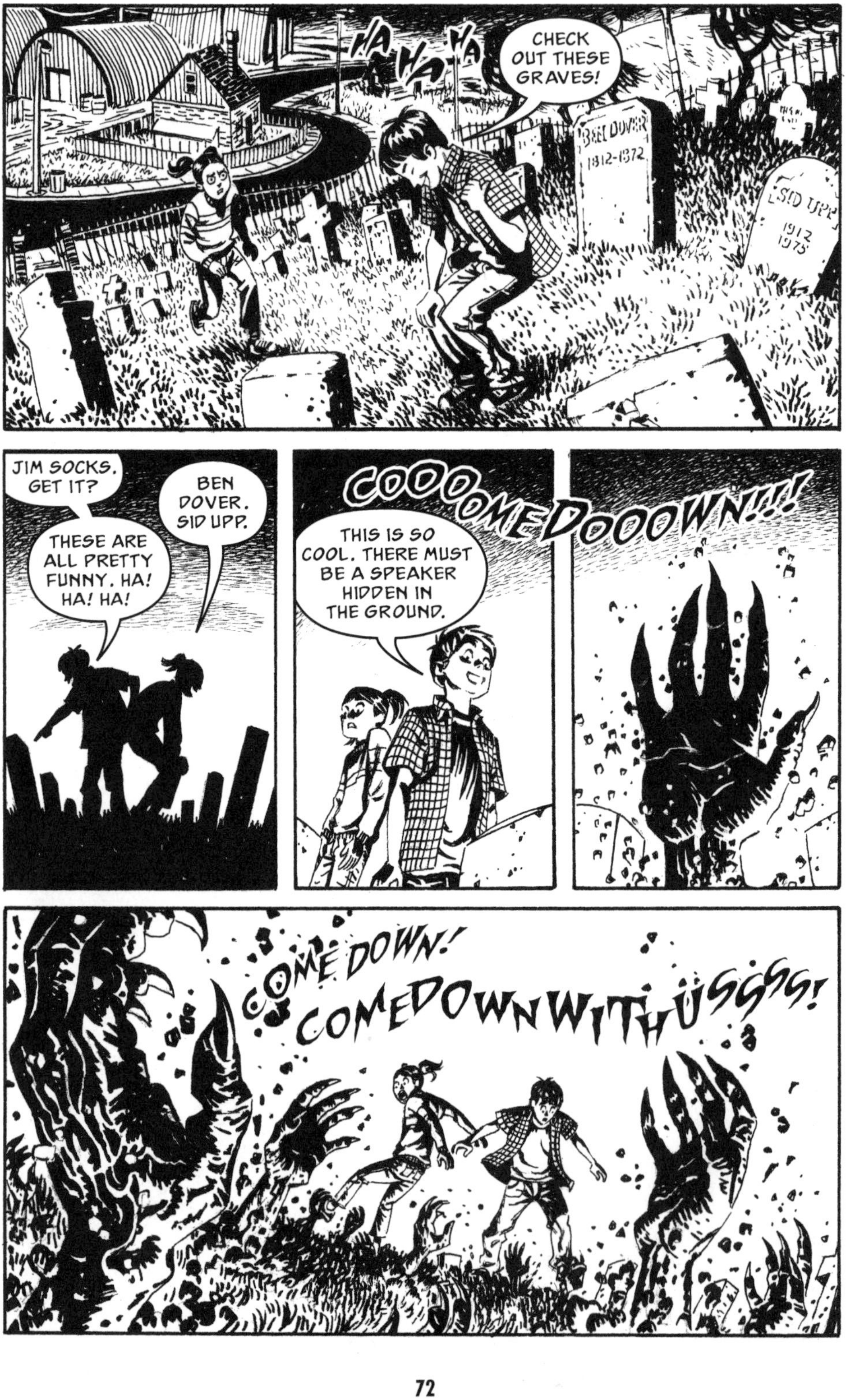
HA HA HA
CHECK OUT THESE GRAVES!
BEN DOVER 1812-1872
SID UPP 1912 1975
JIM SOCKS. GET IT?
BEN DOVER. SID UPP.
THESE ARE ALL PRETTY FUNNY. HA! HA! HA!
COOOOME DOOOOWN!!!
THIS IS SO COOL. THERE MUST BE A SPEAKER HIDDEN IN THE GROUND.
COME DOWN!
COMEDOWNWITHUSSSS!

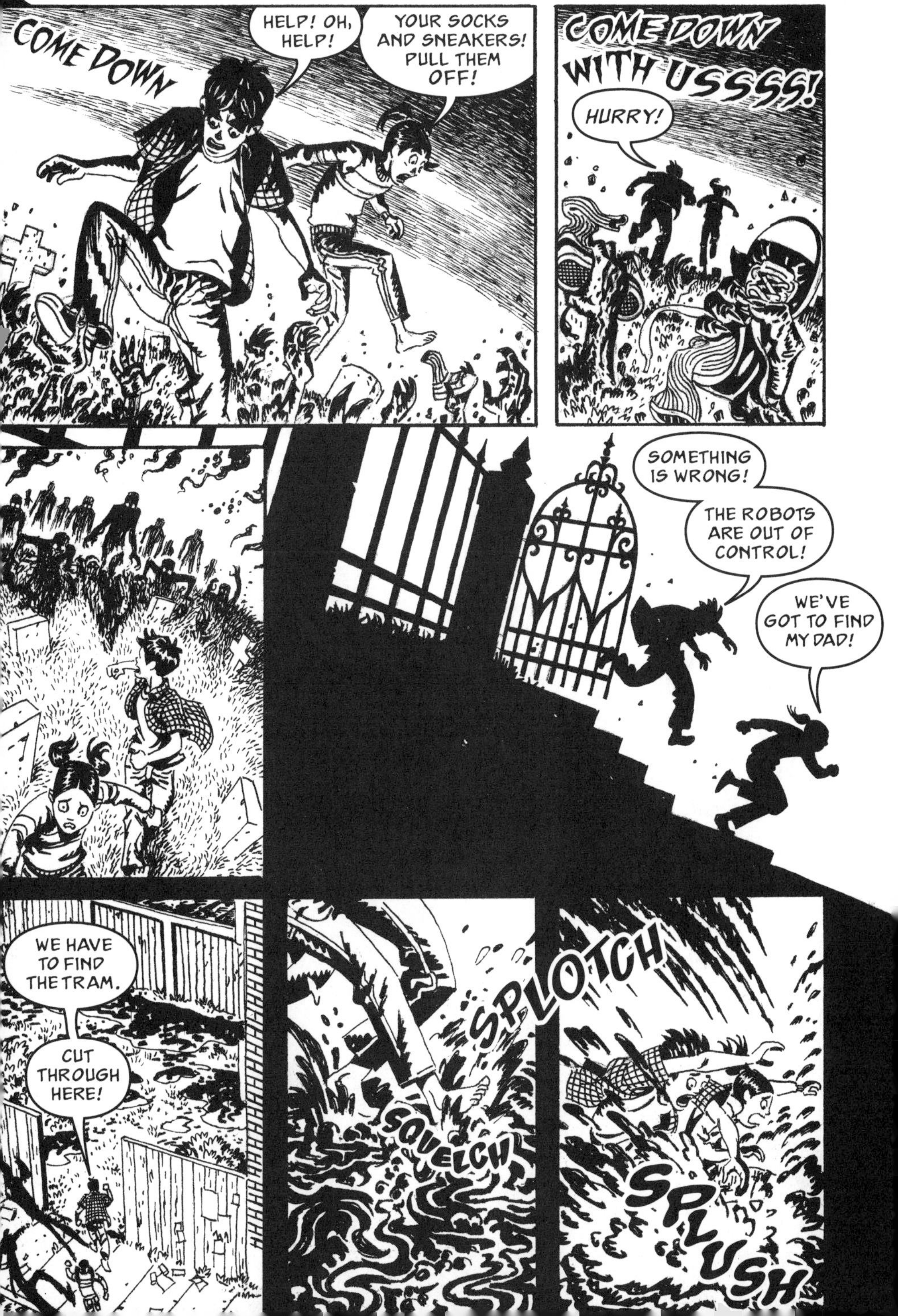
COME DOWN
HELP! OH, HELP!
YOUR SOCKS AND SNEAKERS! PULL THEM OFF!
COME DOWN WITH USSSSS!
HURRY!
SOMETHING IS WRONG!
THE ROBOTS ARE OUT OF CONTROL!
WE'VE GOT TO FIND MY DAD!
WE HAVE TO FIND THE TRAM.
CUT THROUGH HERE!
SPLOTCH
SQUELCH
SPLUSH

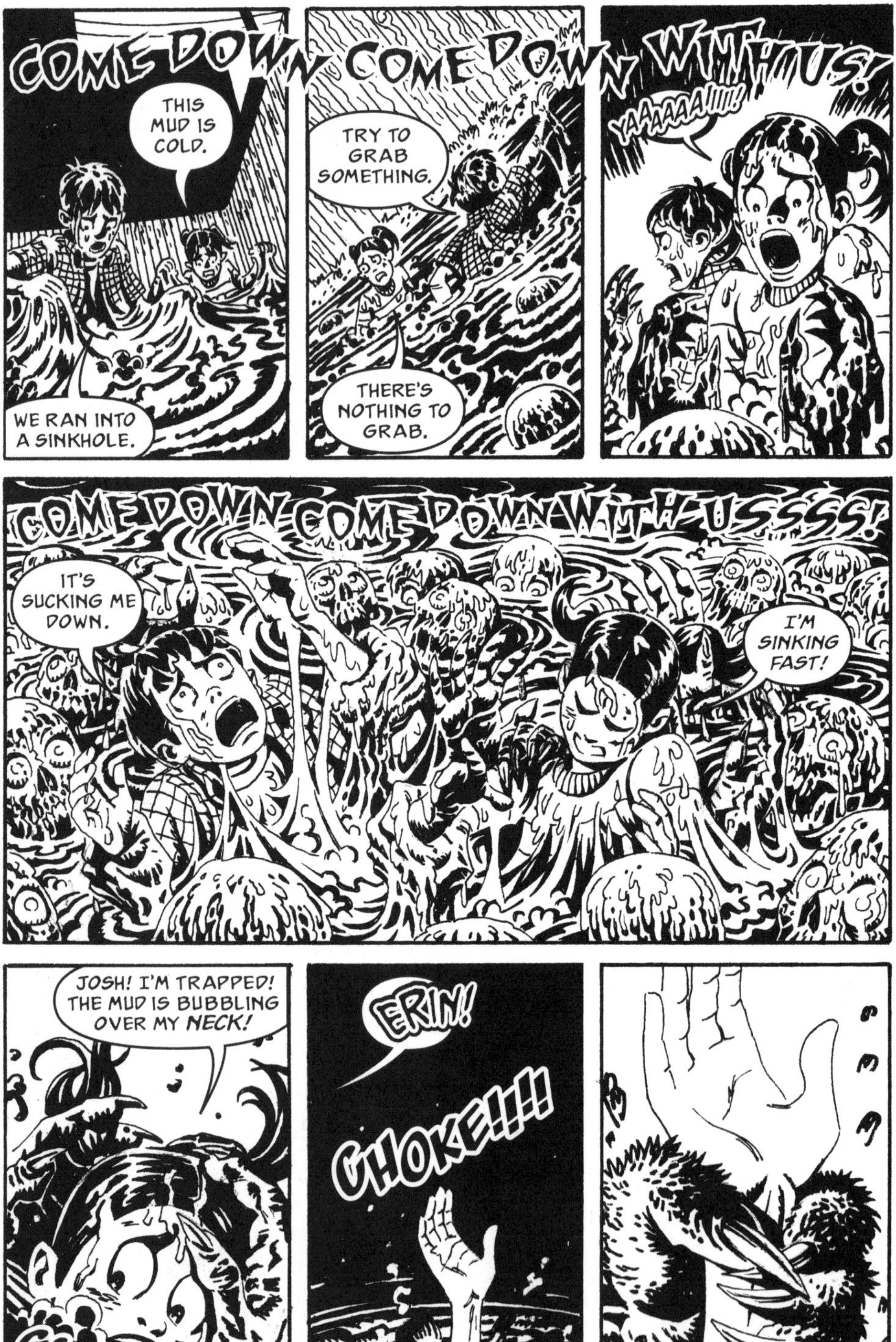
COME DOWN COME DOWN WITH US!
THIS MUD IS COLD.
WE RAN INTO A SINKHOLE.
TRY TO GRAB SOMETHING.
THERE'S NOTHING TO GRAB.
YAAAAAA!!!!!
COME DOWN COME DOWN WITH USSSS!
IT'S SUCKING ME DOWN.
I'M SINKING FAST!
JOSH! I'M TRAPPED! THE MUD IS BUBBLING OVER MY NECK!
GLUB
ERIN!
CHOKE!!!!

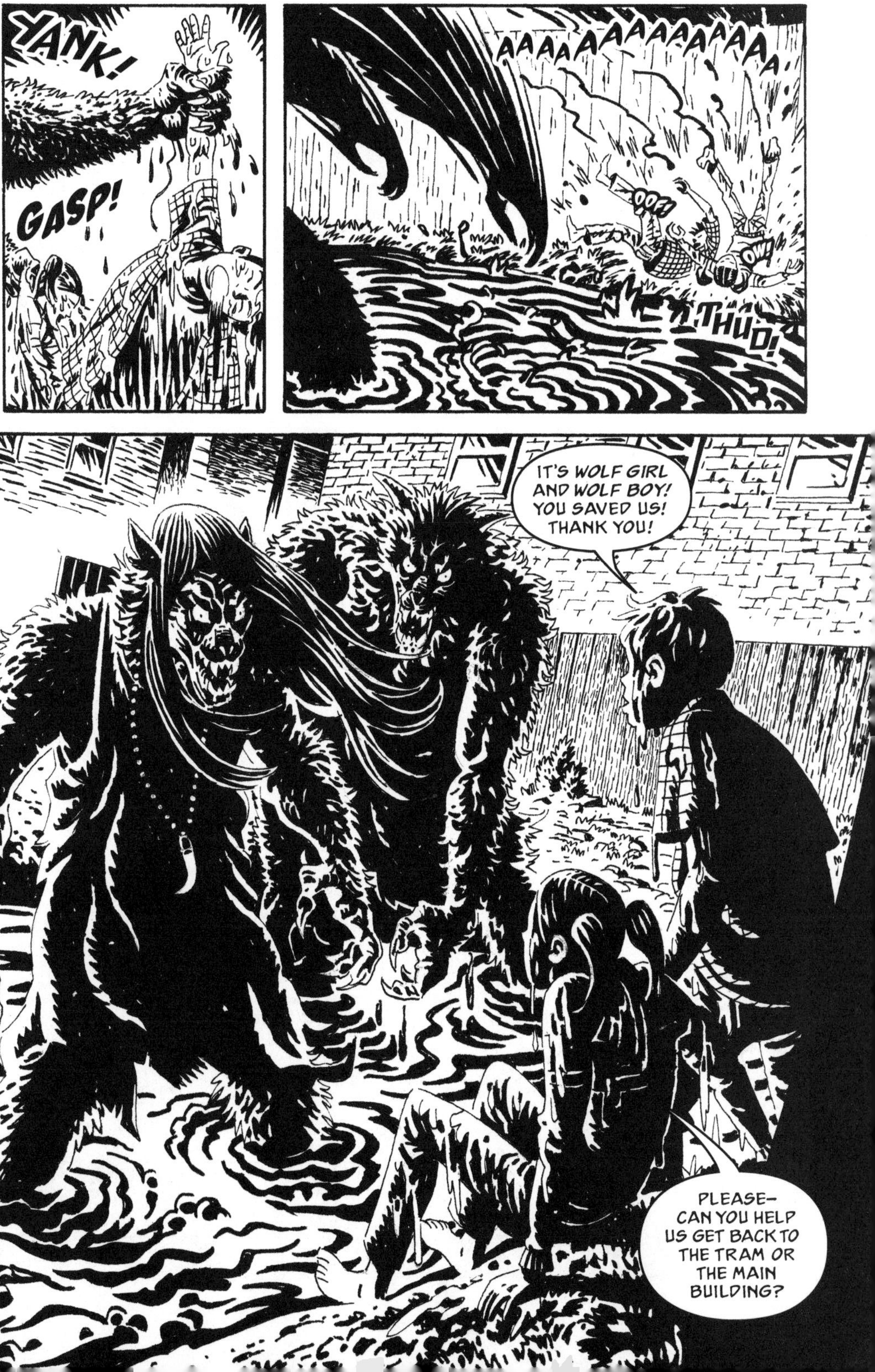
YANK!
GASP!
AAAAAAAAAAAAAA
OOF!
OW!
THUD!
IT'S WOLF GIRL AND WOLF BOY! YOU SAVED US! THANK YOU!
PLEASE— CAN YOU HELP US GET BACK TO THE TRAM OR THE MAIN BUILDING?

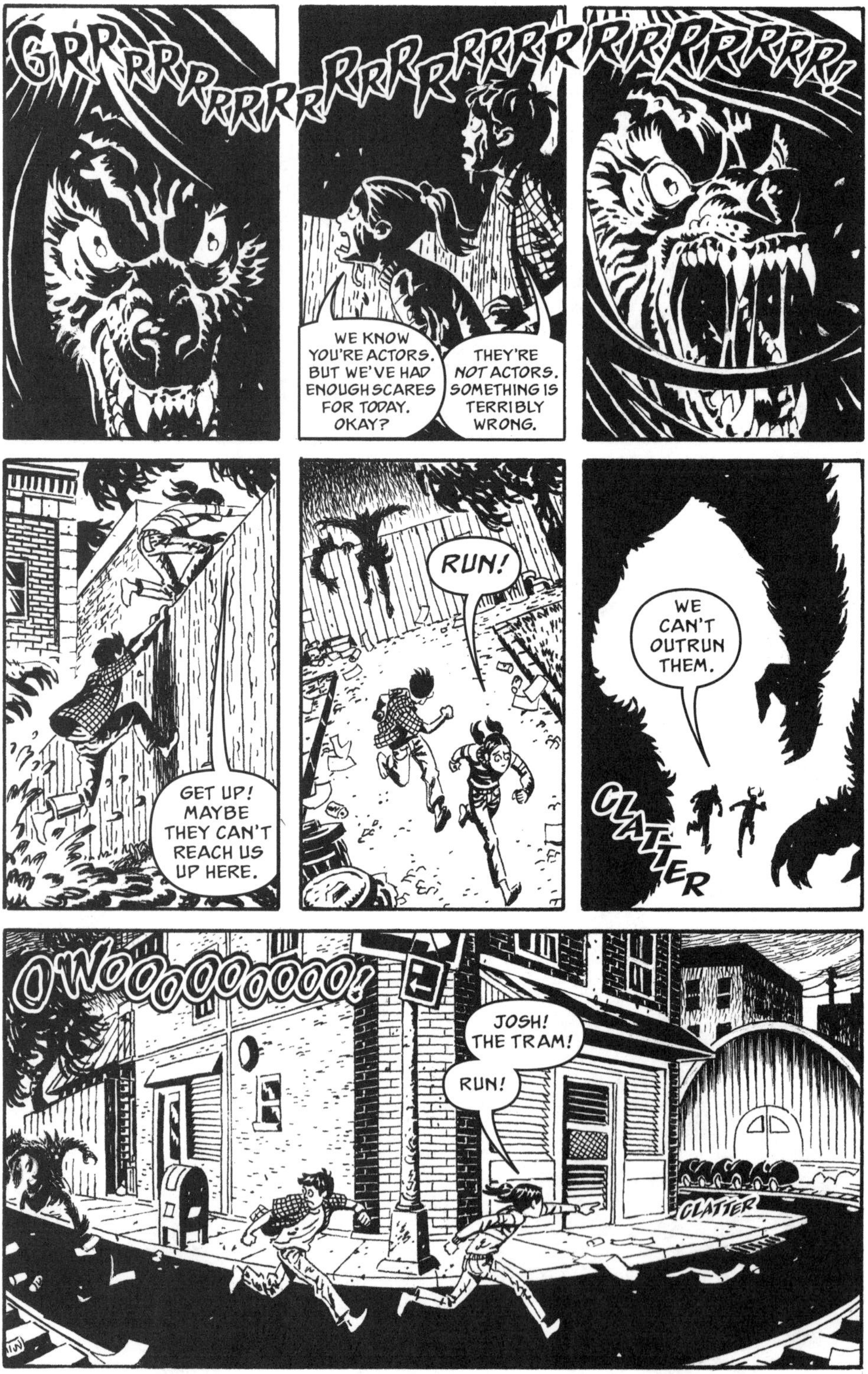
GRRRRRRRRRRRRRRRRRRRRRRRRRRRR!
WE KNOW YOU'RE ACTORS. BUT WE'VE HAD ENOUGH SCARES FOR TODAY. OKAY?
THEY'RE NOT ACTORS. SOMETHING IS TERRIBLY WRONG.
GET UP! MAYBE THEY CAN'T REACH US UP HERE.
RUN!
WE CAN'T OUTRUN THEM.
CLATTER
OWOOOOOOOOOO!
JOSH! THE TRAM!
RUN!
CLATTER

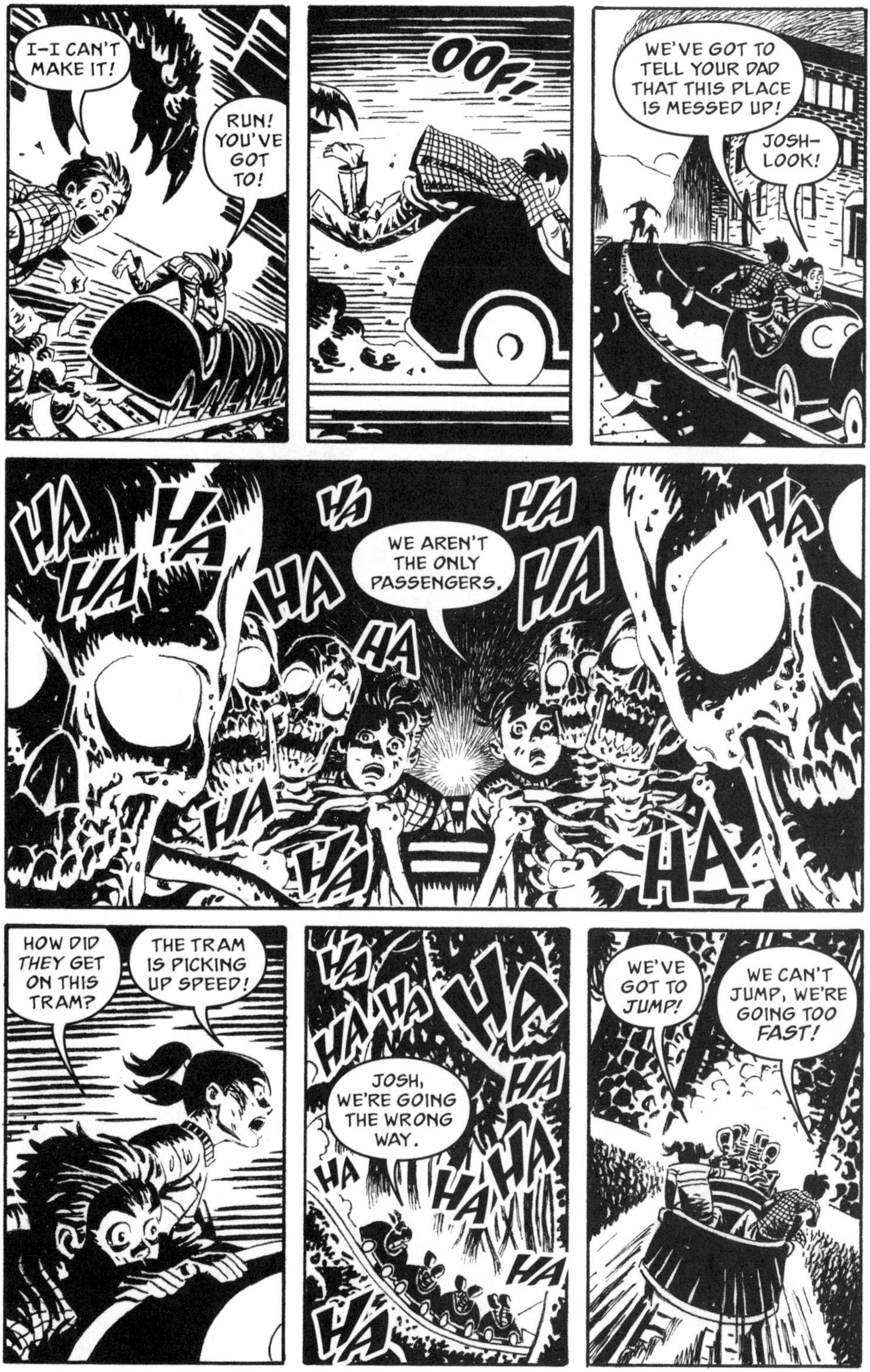
I–I CAN'T MAKE IT!
RUN! YOU'VE GOT TO!
OOF!
WE'VE GOT TO TELL YOUR DAD THAT THIS PLACE IS MESSED UP!
JOSH— LOOK!
HA HA HA HA HA HA HA HA HA
WE AREN'T THE ONLY PASSENGERS.
HA HA HA HA HA
HOW DID THEY GET ON THIS TRAM?
THE TRAM IS PICKING UP SPEED!
HA HA HA HA HA HA
JOSH, WE'RE GOING THE WRONG WAY.
HA HA HA HA HA HA HA
WE'VE GOT TO JUMP!
WE CAN'T JUMP, WE'RE GOING TOO FAST!

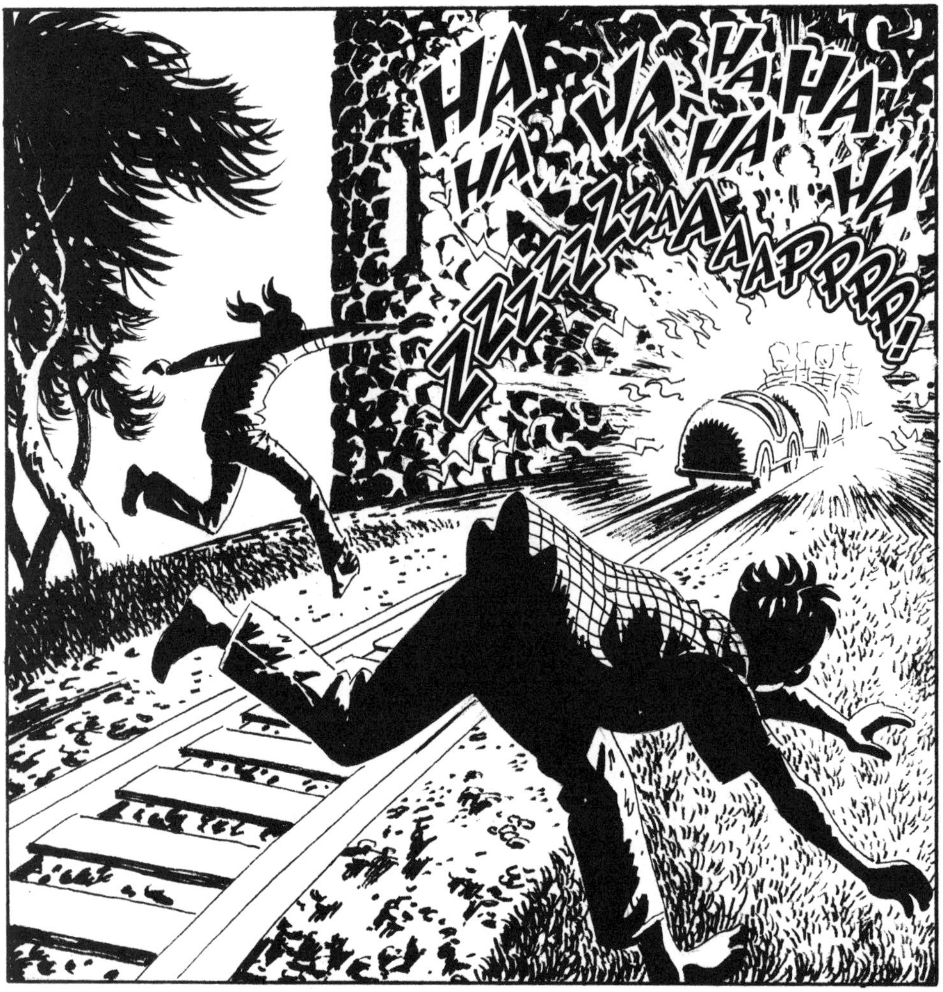
HA HA HA HA HA HA HA
ZZZZZZZAAAAAPPPP!

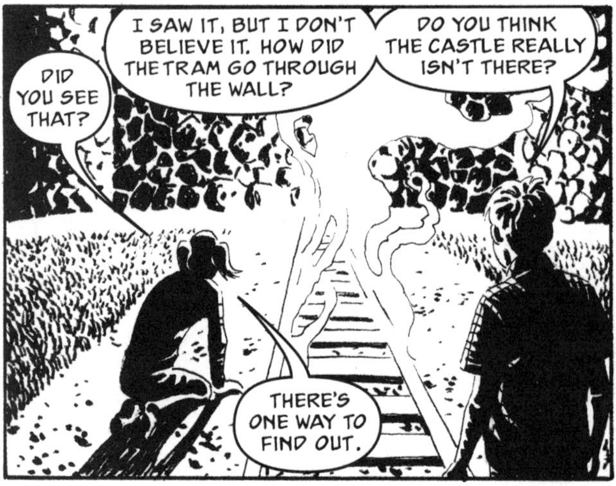
DID YOU SEE THAT?
I SAW IT, BUT I DON'T BELIEVE IT. HOW DID THE TRAM GO THROUGH THE WALL?
DO YOU THINK THE CASTLE REALLY ISN'T THERE?
THERE'S ONE WAY TO FIND OUT.

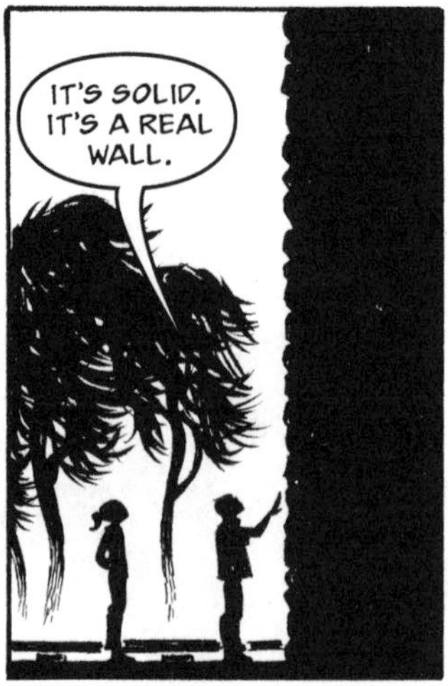
IT'S SOLID. IT'S A REAL WALL.

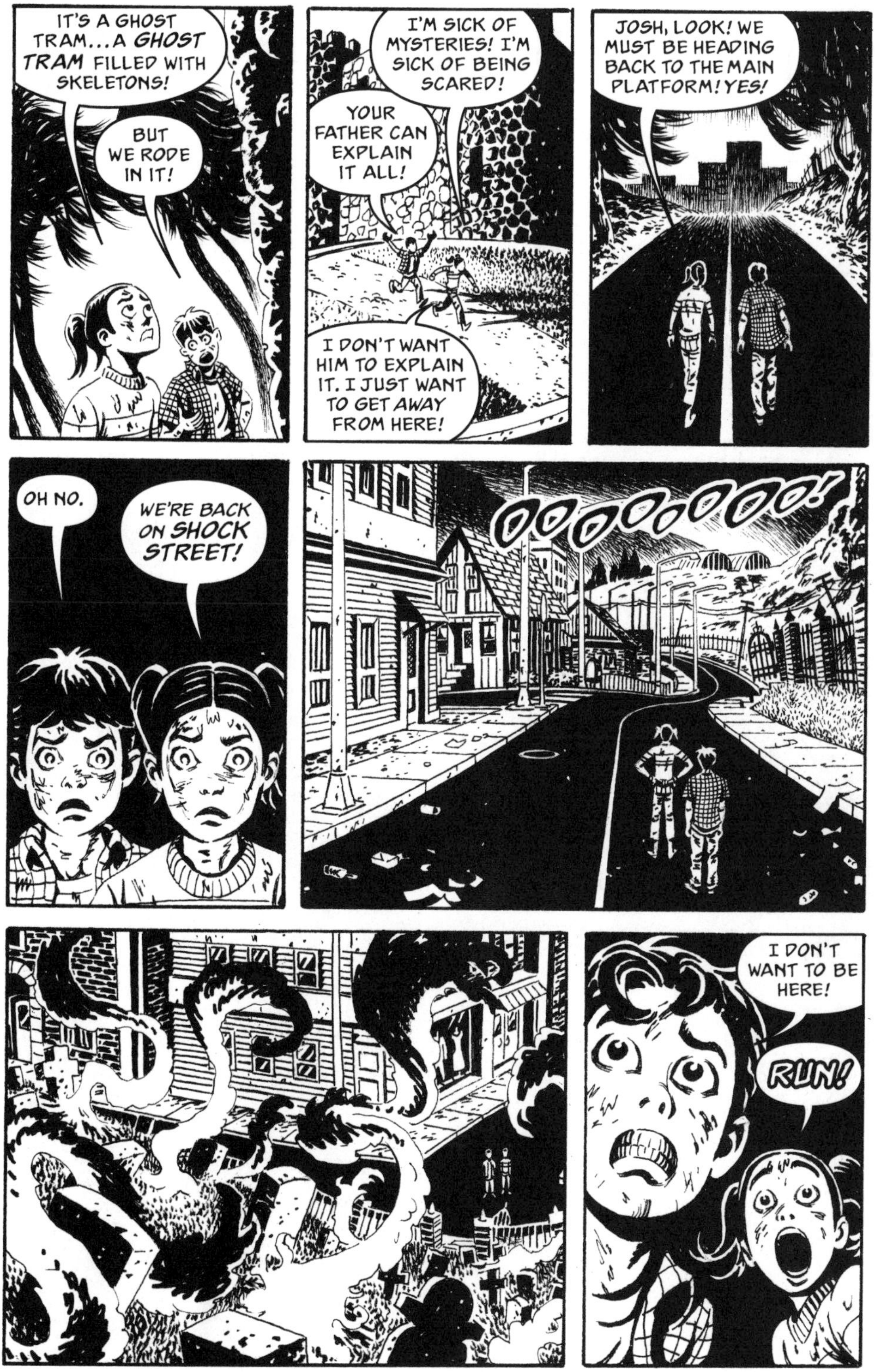
IT'S A GHOST TRAM... A GHOST TRAM FILLED WITH SKELETONS!
BUT WE RODE IN IT!
I'M SICK OF MYSTERIES! I'M SICK OF BEING SCARED!
YOUR FATHER CAN EXPLAIN IT ALL!
I DON'T WANT HIM TO EXPLAIN IT. I JUST WANT TO GET AWAY FROM HERE!
JOSH, LOOK! WE MUST BE HEADING BACK TO THE MAIN PLATFORM! YES!
OH NO.
WE'RE BACK ON SHOCK STREET!
OOOOOOOO!
I DON'T WANT TO BE HERE!
RUN!

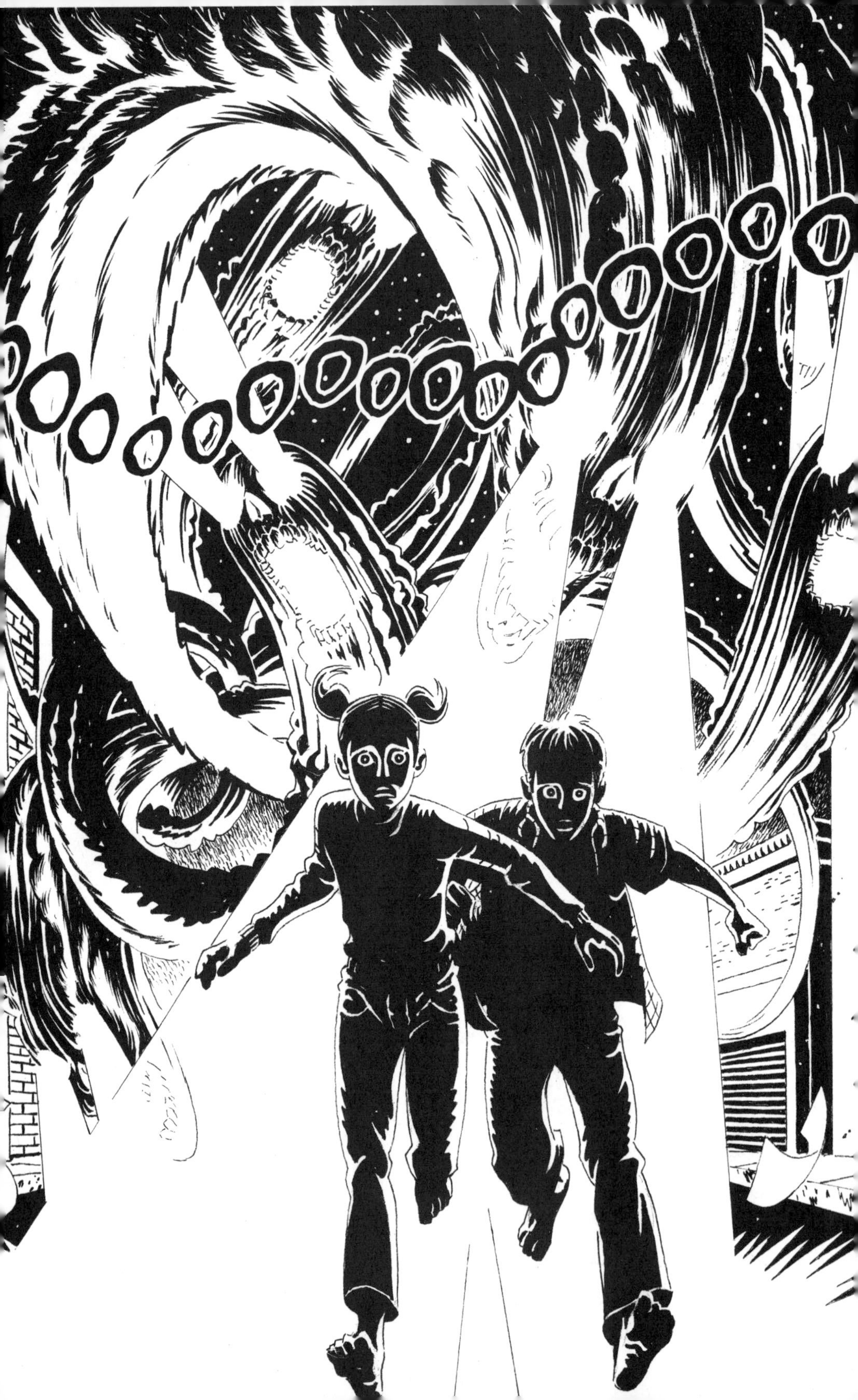

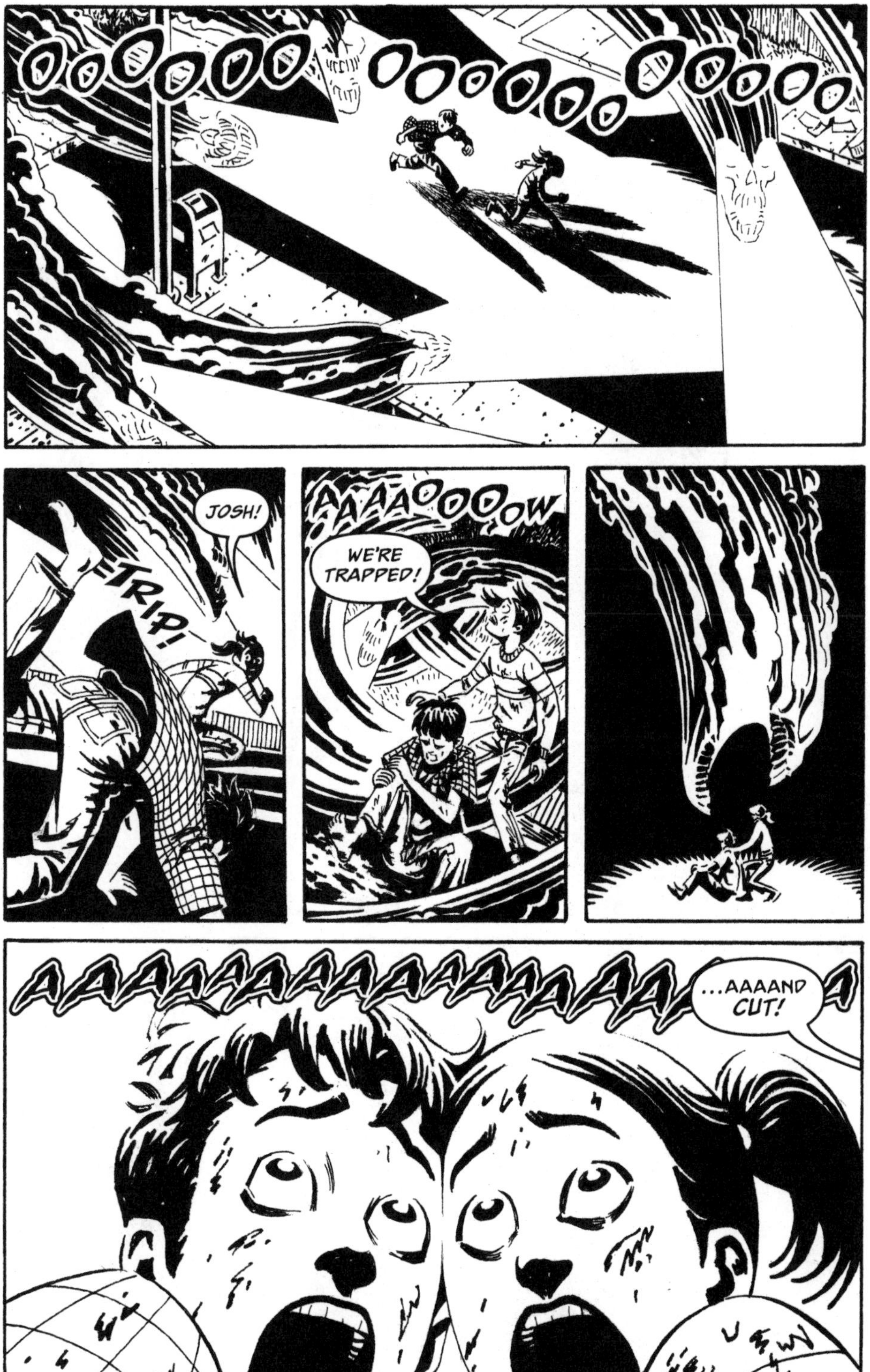
OOOOOOOOOOOOOOOOOOO
JOSH!
TRIP!
AAAAOOOOOW
WE'RE TRAPPED!
AAAAAAAAAAAAAAAAAAAAA
...AAAAND CUT!

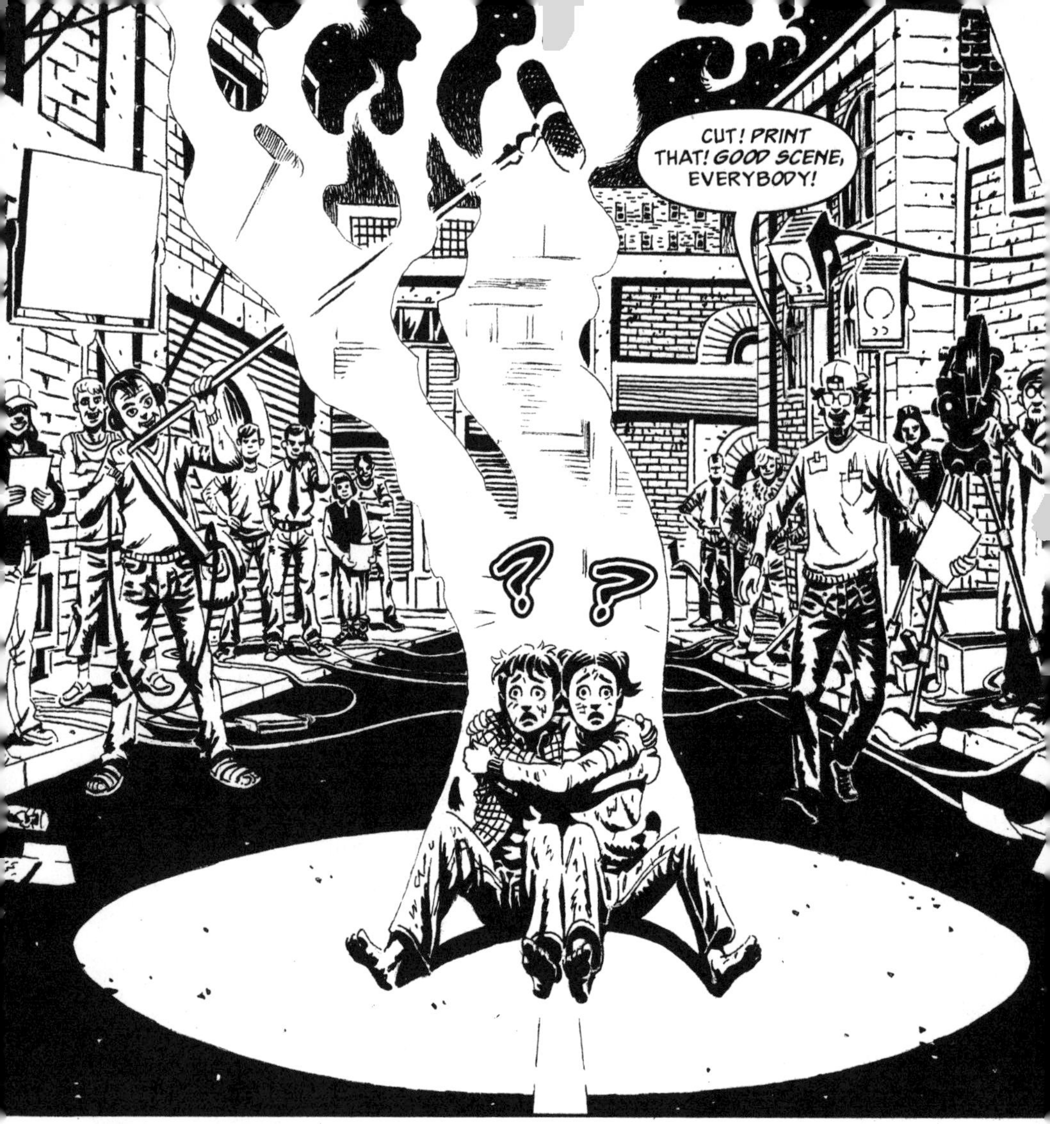
CUT! PRINT THAT! GOOD SCENE, EVERYBODY!
?
?

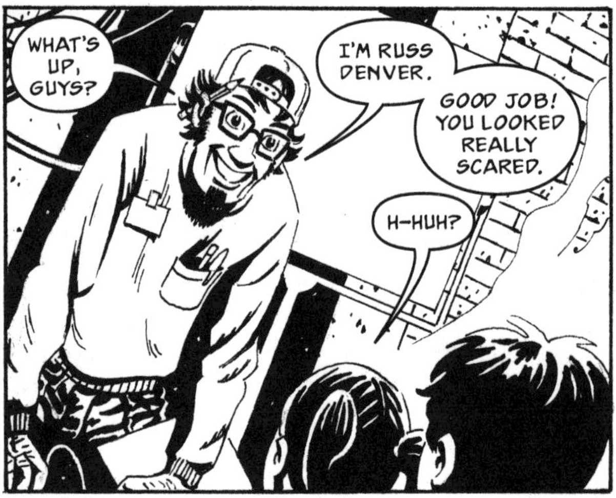
WHAT'S UP, GUYS?
I'M RUSS DENVER.
GOOD JOB! YOU LOOKED REALLY SCARED.
H-HUH?

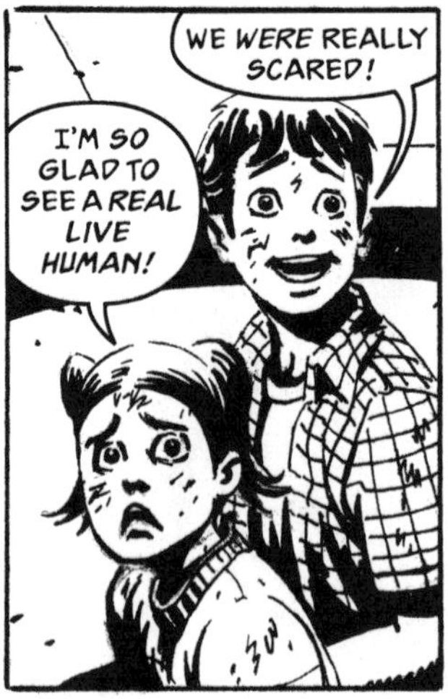
WE WERE REALLY SCARED!
I'M SO GLAD TO SEE A REAL LIVE HUMAN!

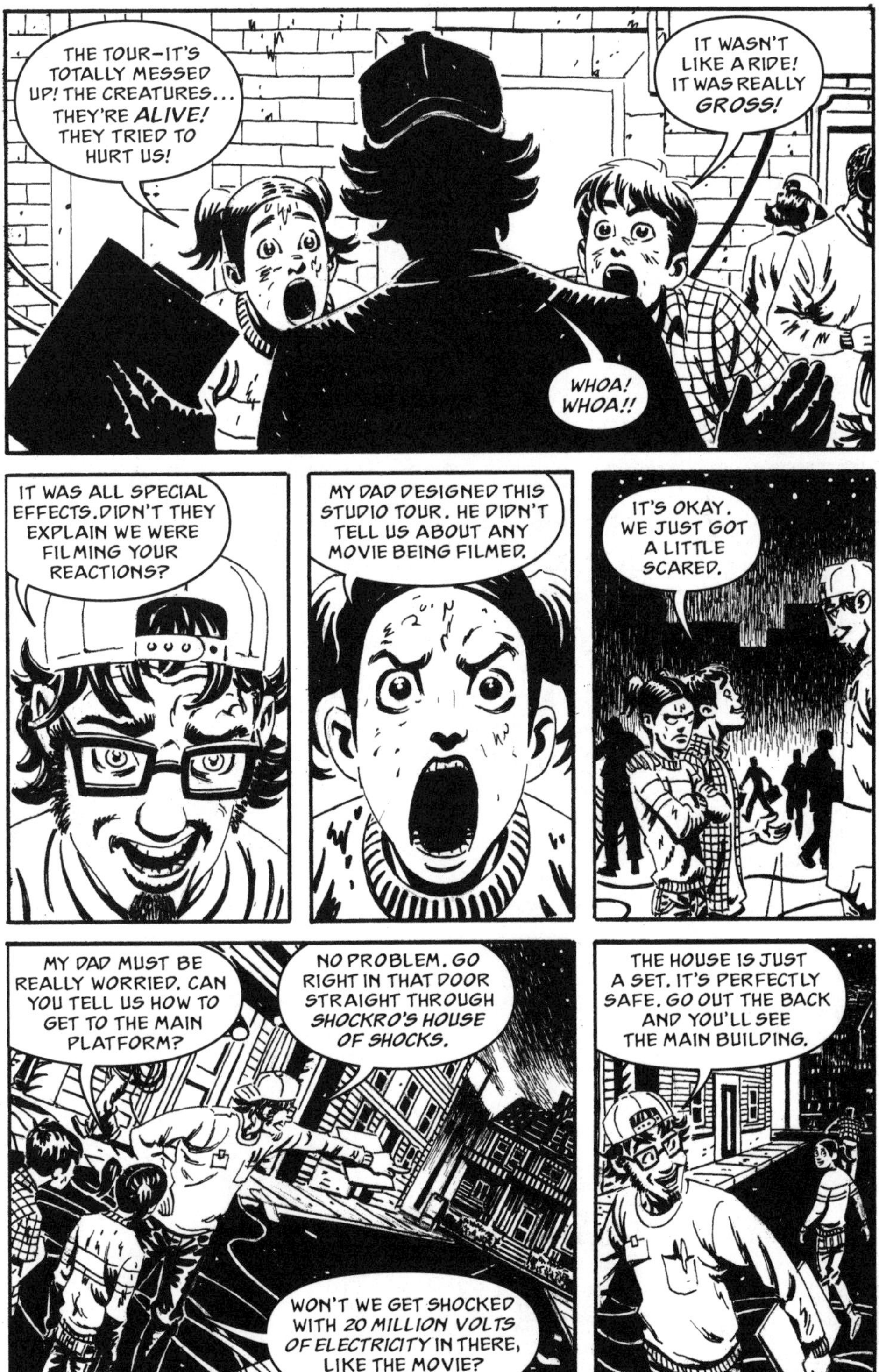
THE TOUR—IT'S TOTALLY MESSED UP! THE CREATURES... THEY'RE *ALIVE!* THEY TRIED TO HURT US!
IT WASN'T LIKE A RIDE! IT WAS REALLY *GROSS!*
WHOA! WHOA!!
IT WAS ALL SPECIAL EFFECTS. DIDN'T THEY EXPLAIN WE WERE FILMING YOUR REACTIONS?
MY DAD DESIGNED THIS STUDIO TOUR. HE DIDN'T TELL US ABOUT ANY MOVIE BEING FILMED.
IT'S OKAY. WE JUST GOT A LITTLE SCARED.
MY DAD MUST BE REALLY WORRIED. CAN YOU TELL US HOW TO GET TO THE MAIN PLATFORM?
NO PROBLEM. GO RIGHT IN THAT DOOR STRAIGHT THROUGH *SHOCKRO'S HOUSE OF SHOCKS.*
WON'T WE GET SHOCKED WITH *20 MILLION VOLTS OF ELECTRICITY* IN THERE, LIKE THE MOVIE?
THE HOUSE IS JUST A SET. IT'S PERFECTLY SAFE. GO OUT THE BACK AND YOU'LL SEE THE MAIN BUILDING.

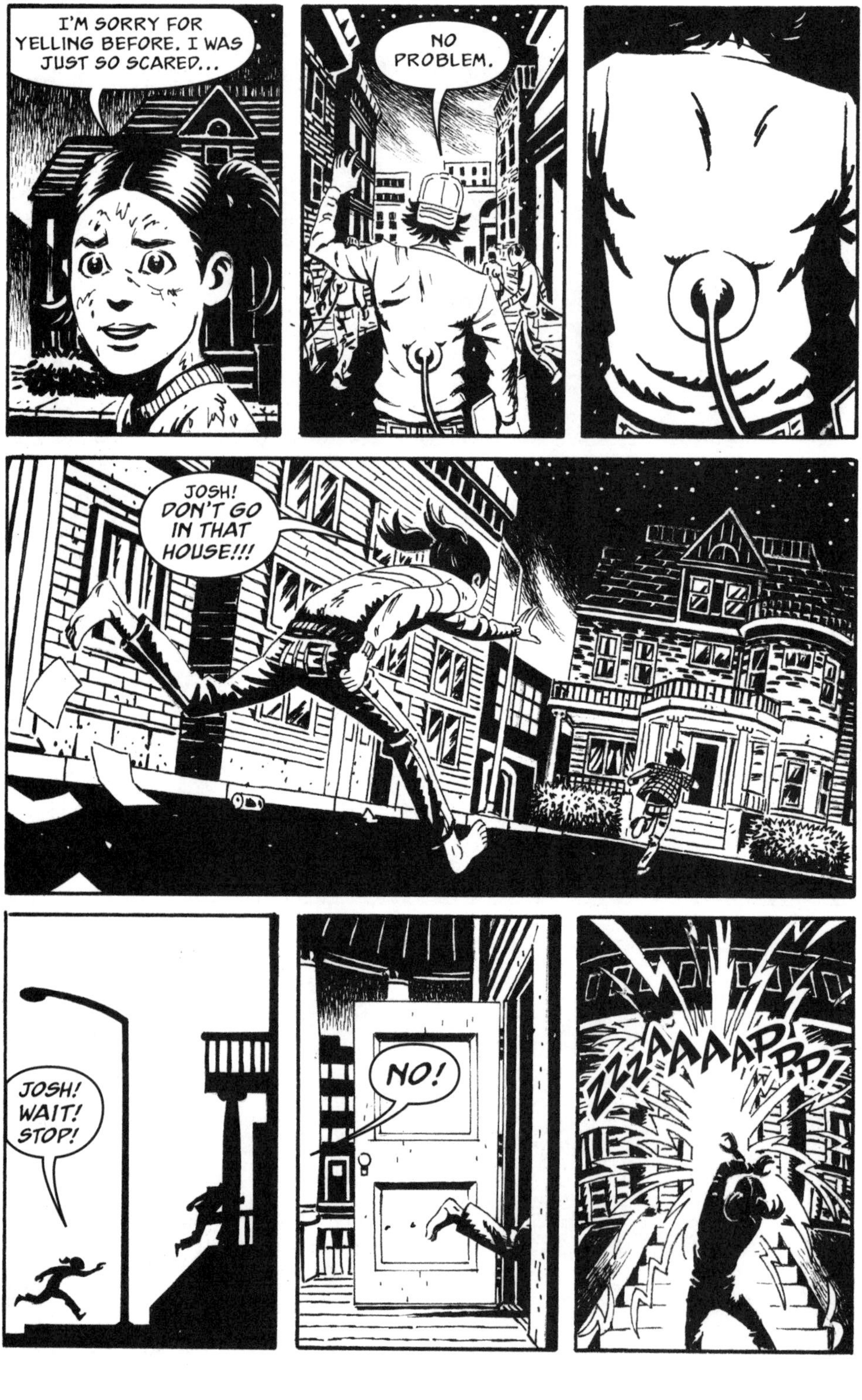
I'M SORRY FOR YELLING BEFORE. I WAS JUST SO SCARED...
NO PROBLEM.
JOSH! DON'T GO IN THAT HOUSE!!!
JOSH! WAIT! STOP!
NO!
ZZZAAAAAPPP!

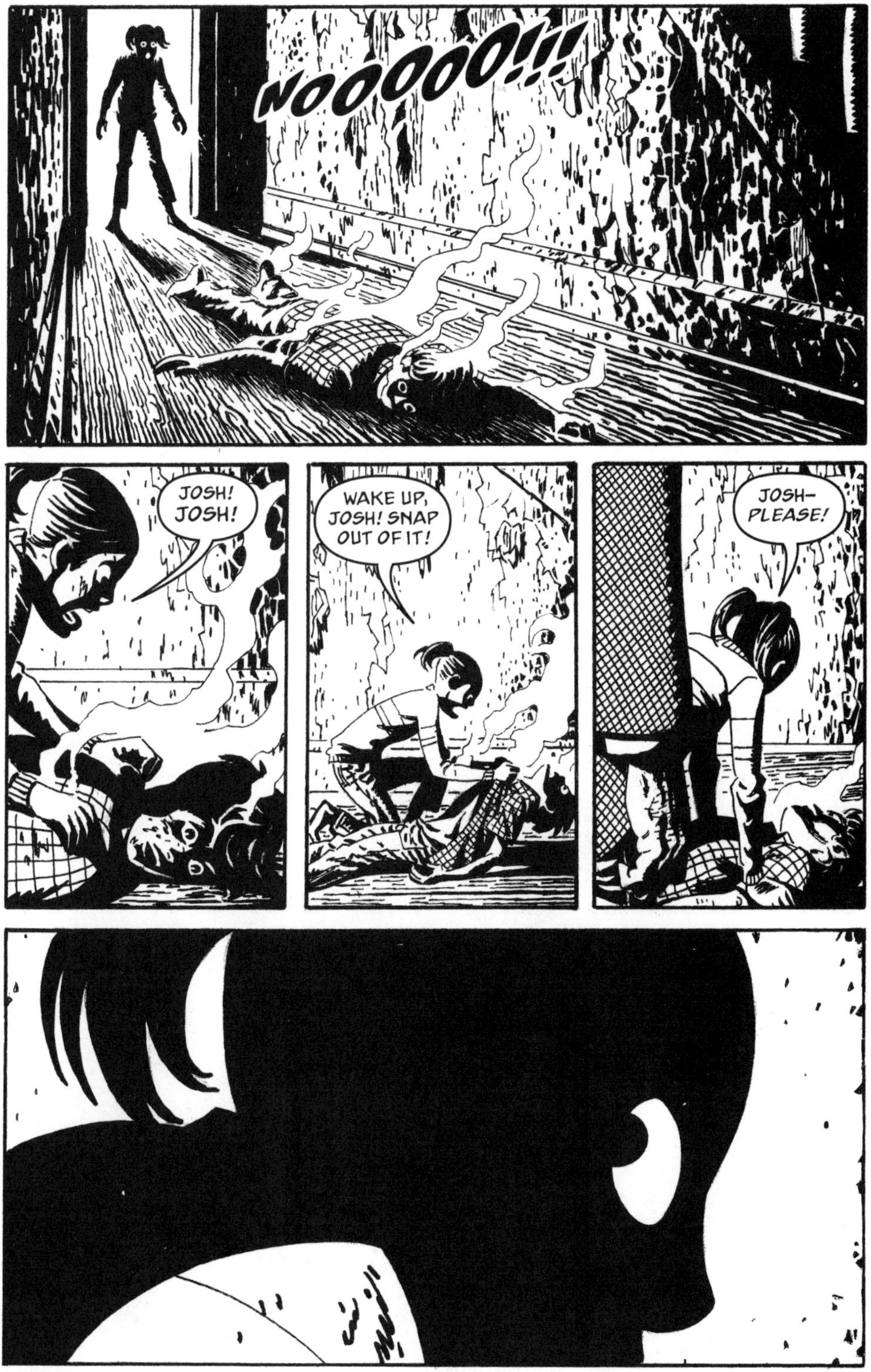
WOOOOO!!!
JOSH! JOSH!
WAKE UP, JOSH! SNAP OUT OF IT!
JOSH- PLEASE!

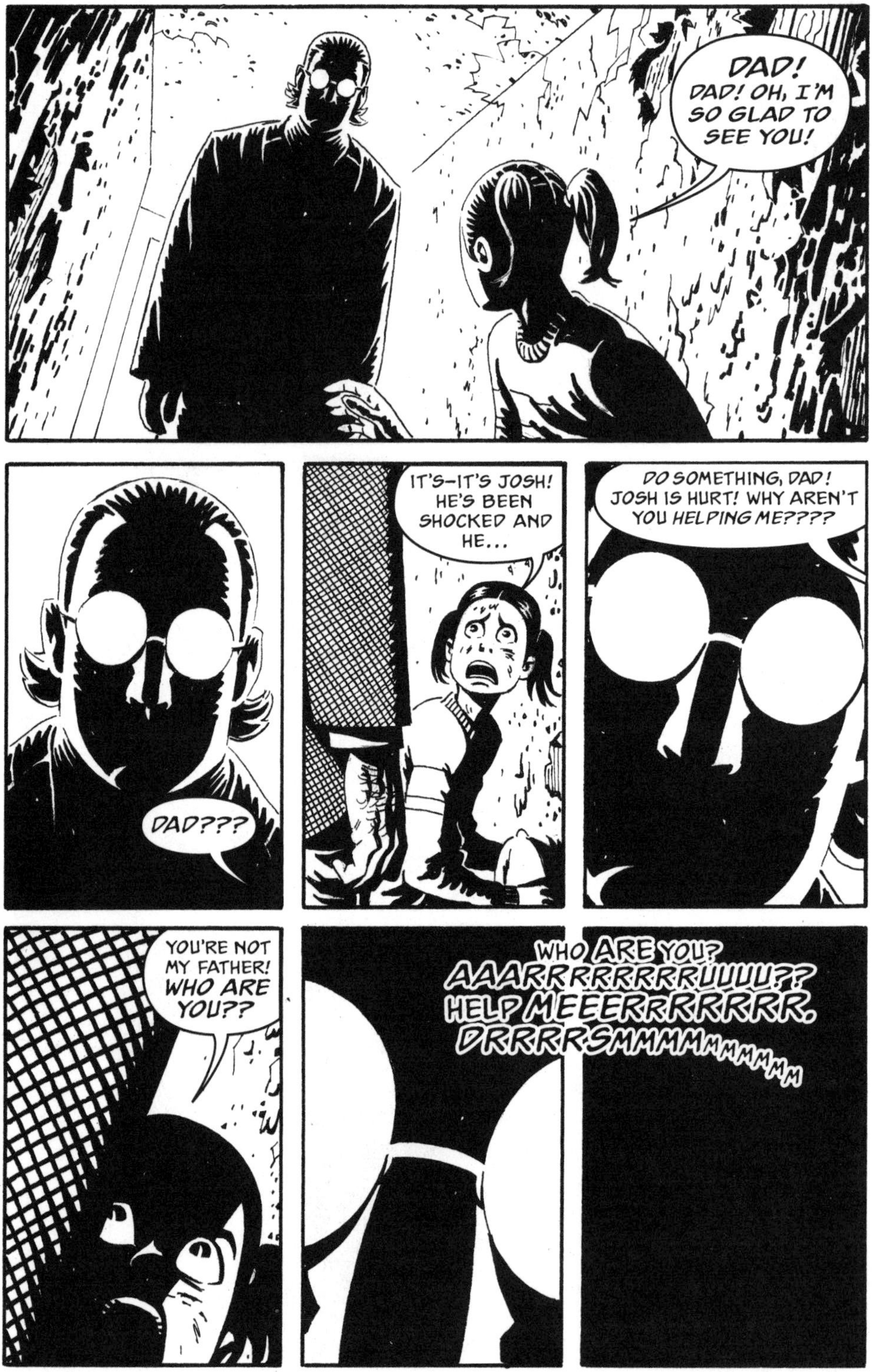
DAD! DAD! OH, I'M SO GLAD TO SEE YOU!
DAD???
IT'S–IT'S JOSH! HE'S BEEN SHOCKED AND HE...
DO SOMETHING, DAD! JOSH IS HURT! WHY AREN'T YOU HELPING ME????
YOU'RE NOT MY FATHER! WHO ARE YOU??
WHO ARE YOU? AAARRRRRRRUUUU?? HELP MEEERRRRRRR. DRRRRSMMMMMMMMM

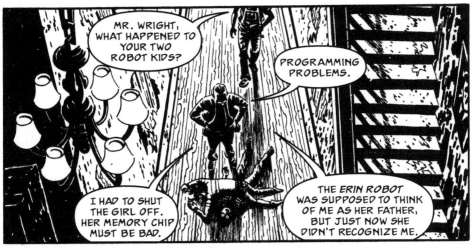

MR. WRIGHT, WHAT HAPPENED TO YOUR TWO ROBOT KIDS?

PROGRAMMING PROBLEMS.

I HAD TO SHUT THE GIRL OFF. HER MEMORY CHIP MUST BE BAD.

THE *ERIN ROBOT* WAS SUPPOSED TO THINK OF ME AS HER FATHER, BUT JUST NOW SHE DIDN'T RECOGNIZE ME.

WHAT ABOUT THE *JOSH ROBOT*?

I THINK THE ELECTRICAL SYSTEM SHORTED.

WHAT A SHAME, BUT IT WAS A GREAT IDEA TO MAKE ROBOT KIDS TO TEST THE PARK.

WE'LL REPROGRAM THESE TWO AND TRY THEM OUT ON THE *SHOCKER STUDIO* TOUR AGAIN...

...BEFORE WE OPEN THE PARK TO *REAL KIDS.*

DEEP TROUBLE

ADAPTED AND ILLUSTRATED BY

Amy Kim Ganter

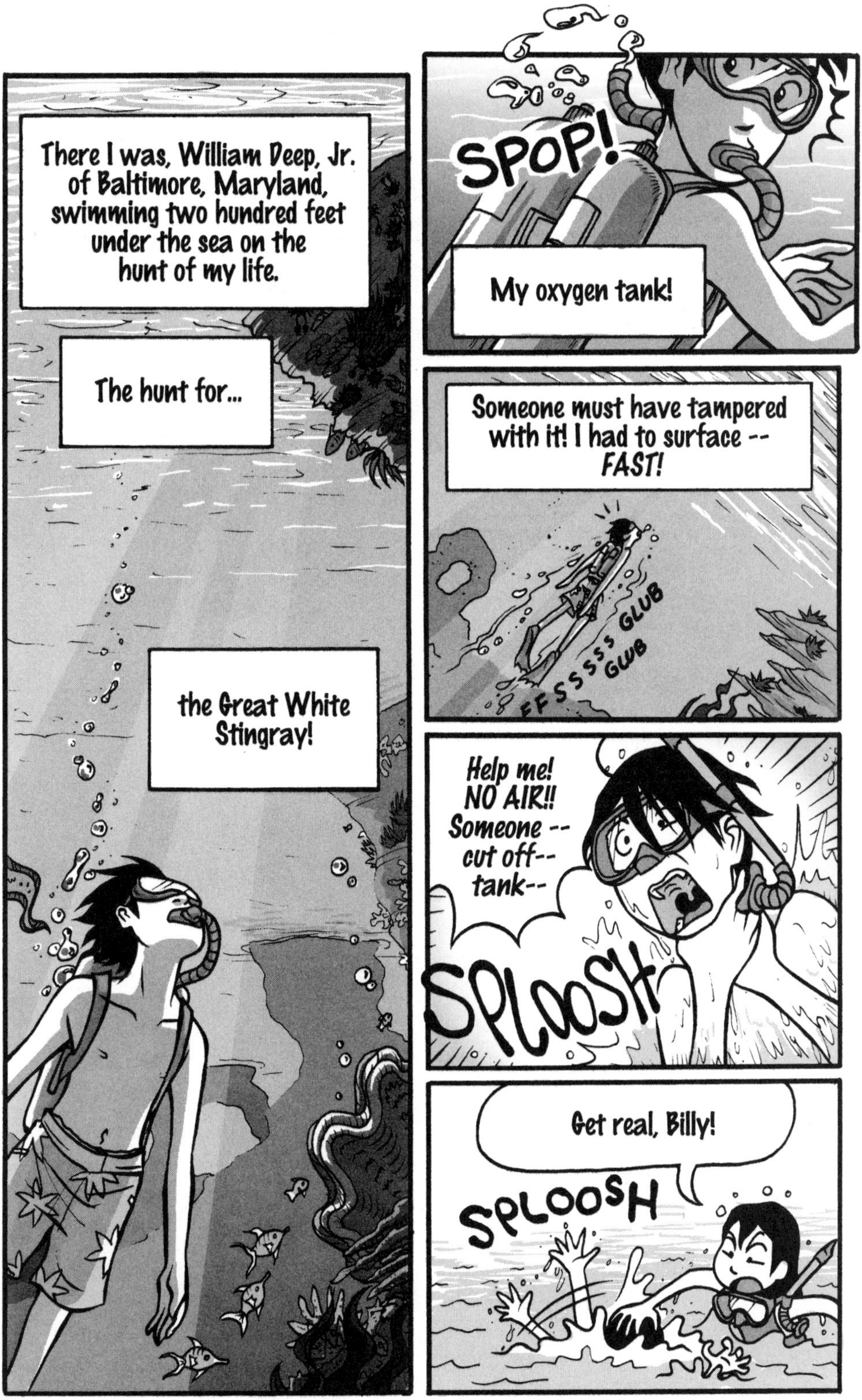
There I was, William Deep, Jr. of Baltimore, Maryland, swimming two hundred feet under the sea on the hunt of my life.
The hunt for...
the Great White Stingray!
SPOP!
My oxygen tank!
Someone must have tampered with it! I had to surface -- *FAST!*
FFSSSSSS GLUB GLUB
Help me! NO AIR!! Someone -- cut off-- tank--
SPLOOSH
Get real, Billy!
SPLOOSH

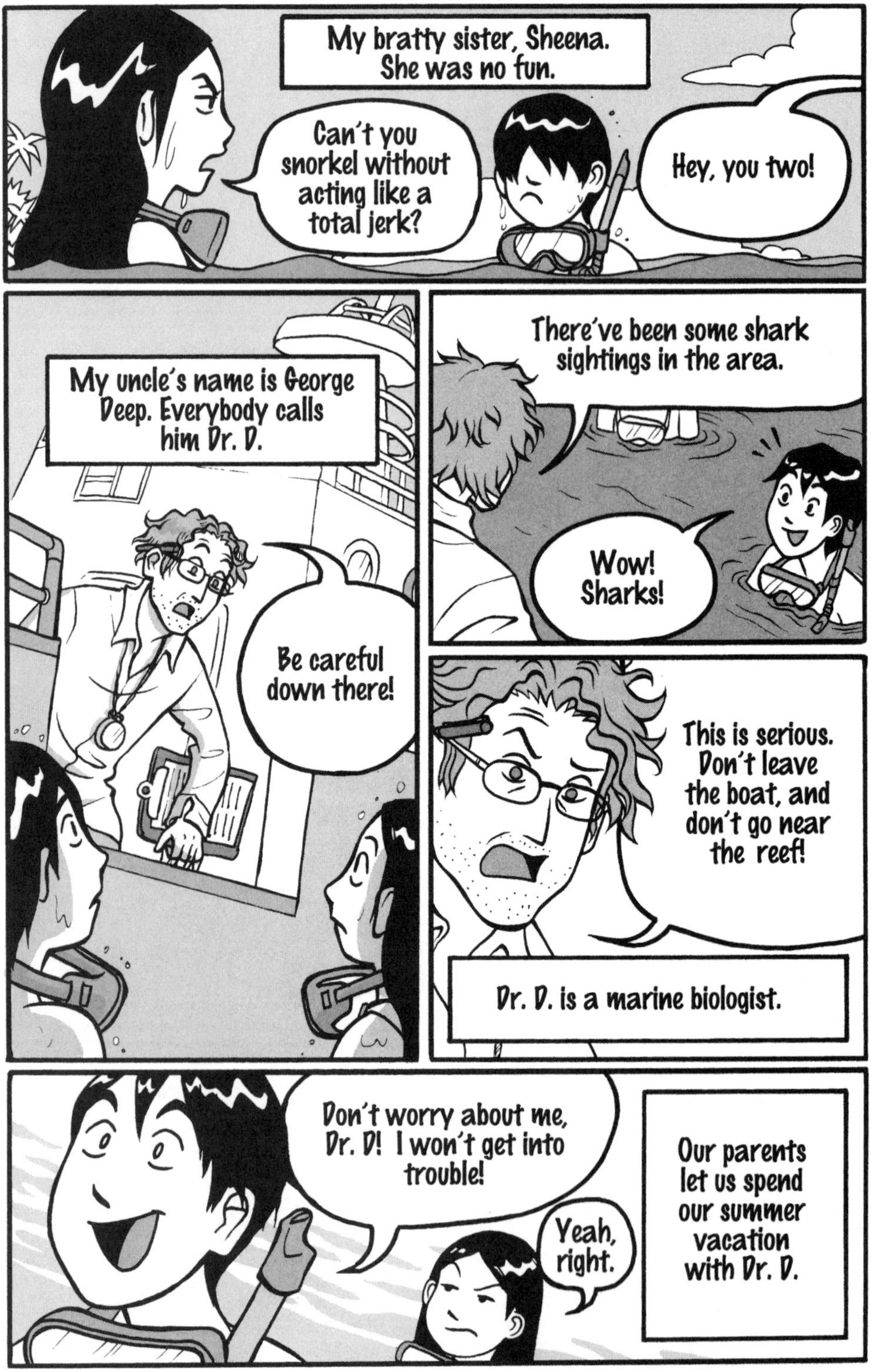
My bratty sister, Sheena. She was no fun.
Can't you snorkel without acting like a total jerk?
Hey, you two!
My uncle's name is George Deep. Everybody calls him Dr. D.
Be careful down there!
There've been some shark sightings in the area.
Wow! Sharks!
This is serious. Don't leave the boat, and don't go near the reef!
Dr. D. is a marine biologist.
Don't worry about me, Dr. D! I won't get into trouble!
Yeah, right.
Our parents let us spend our summer vacation with Dr. D.

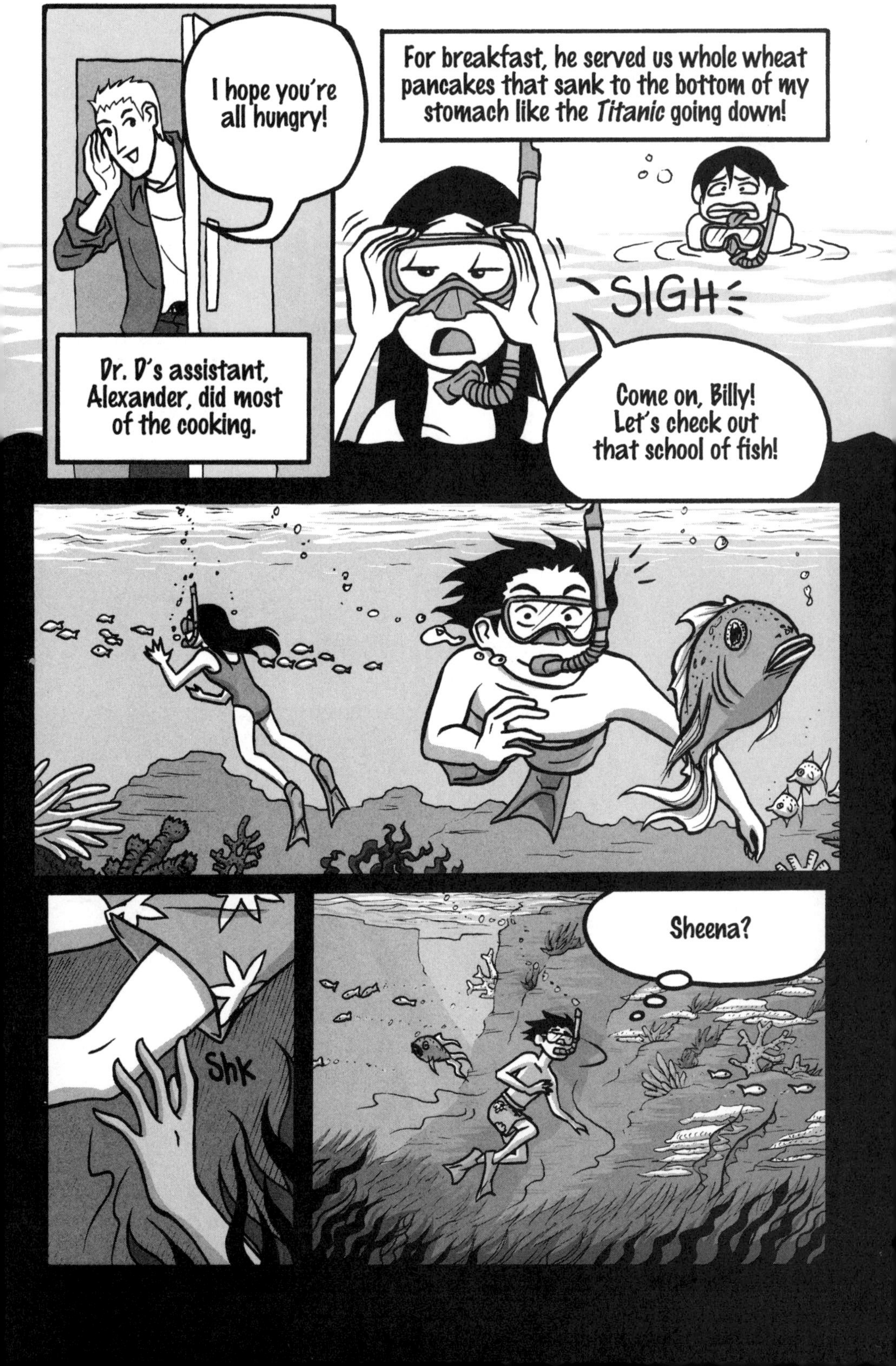
I hope you're all hungry!
Dr. D's assistant, Alexander, did most of the cooking.
For breakfast, he served us whole wheat pancakes that sank to the bottom of my stomach like the *Titanic* going down!
SIGH
Come on, Billy! Let's check out that school of fish!
Shk
Sheena?

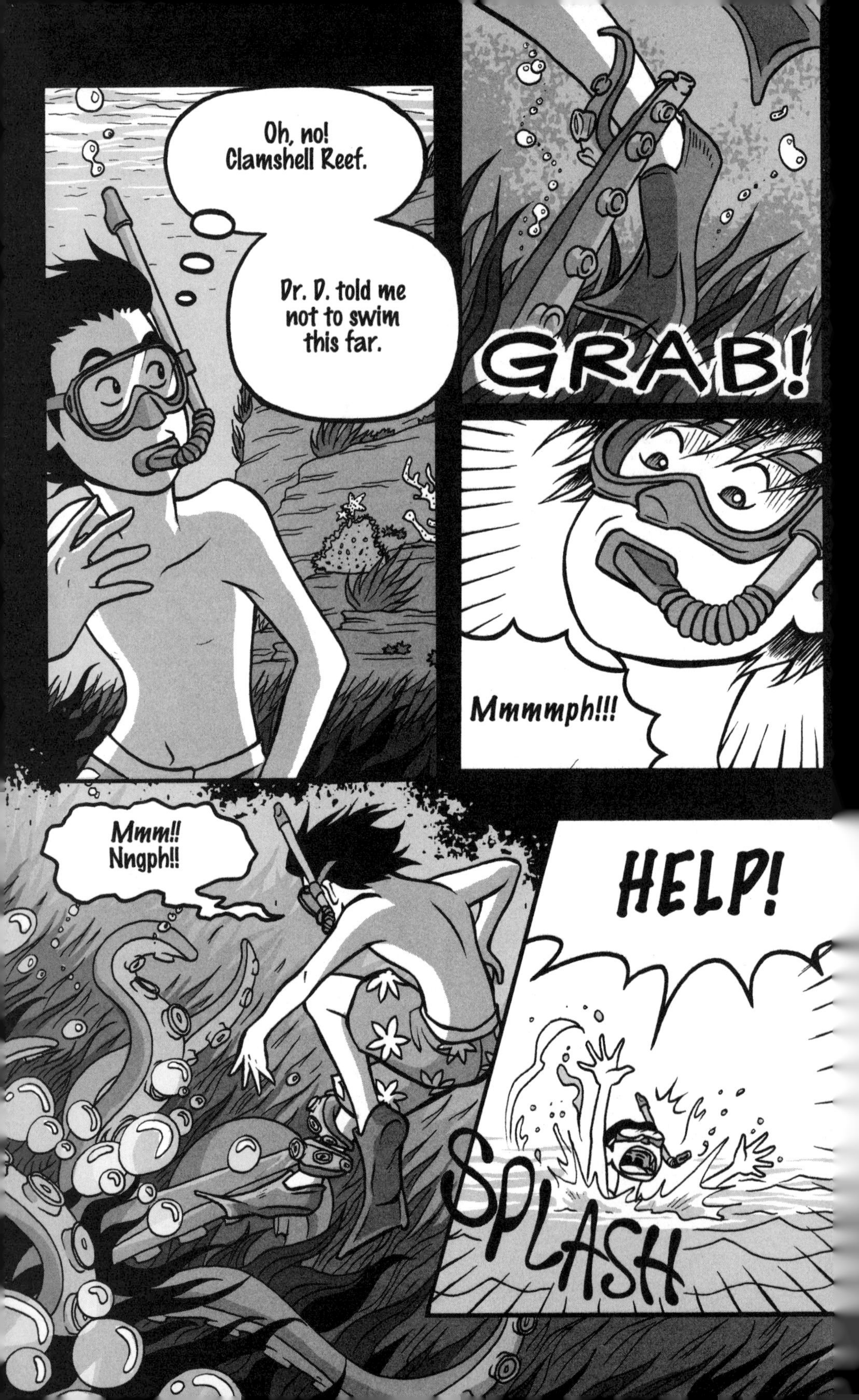
Oh, no! Clamshell Reef.
Dr. D. told me not to swim this far.
GRAB!
Mmmmph!!!
Mmm!! Nngph!!
HELP!
SPLASH

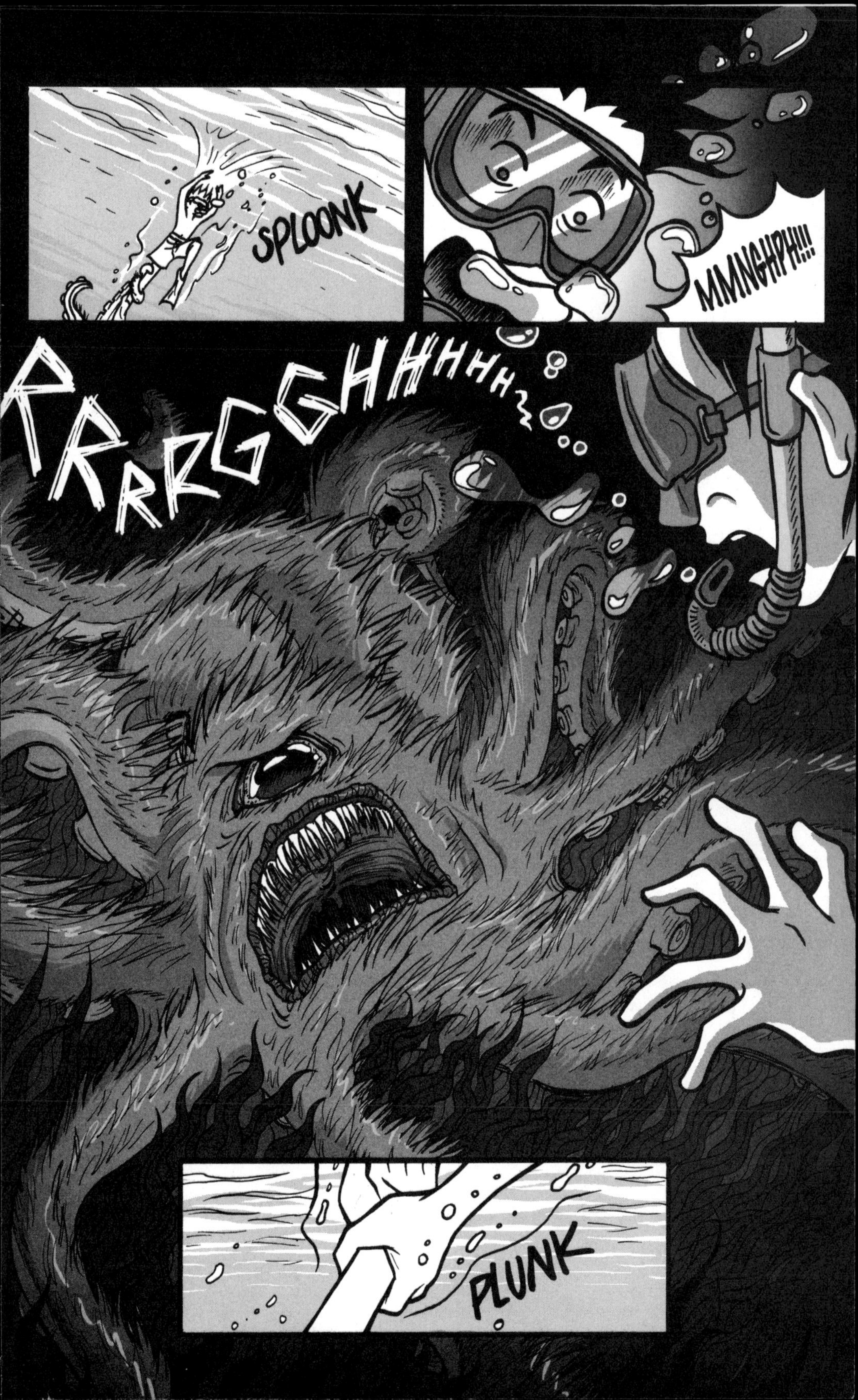
SPLOONK
MMNGHPH!!!
RRRRGGHHHHH
PLUNK

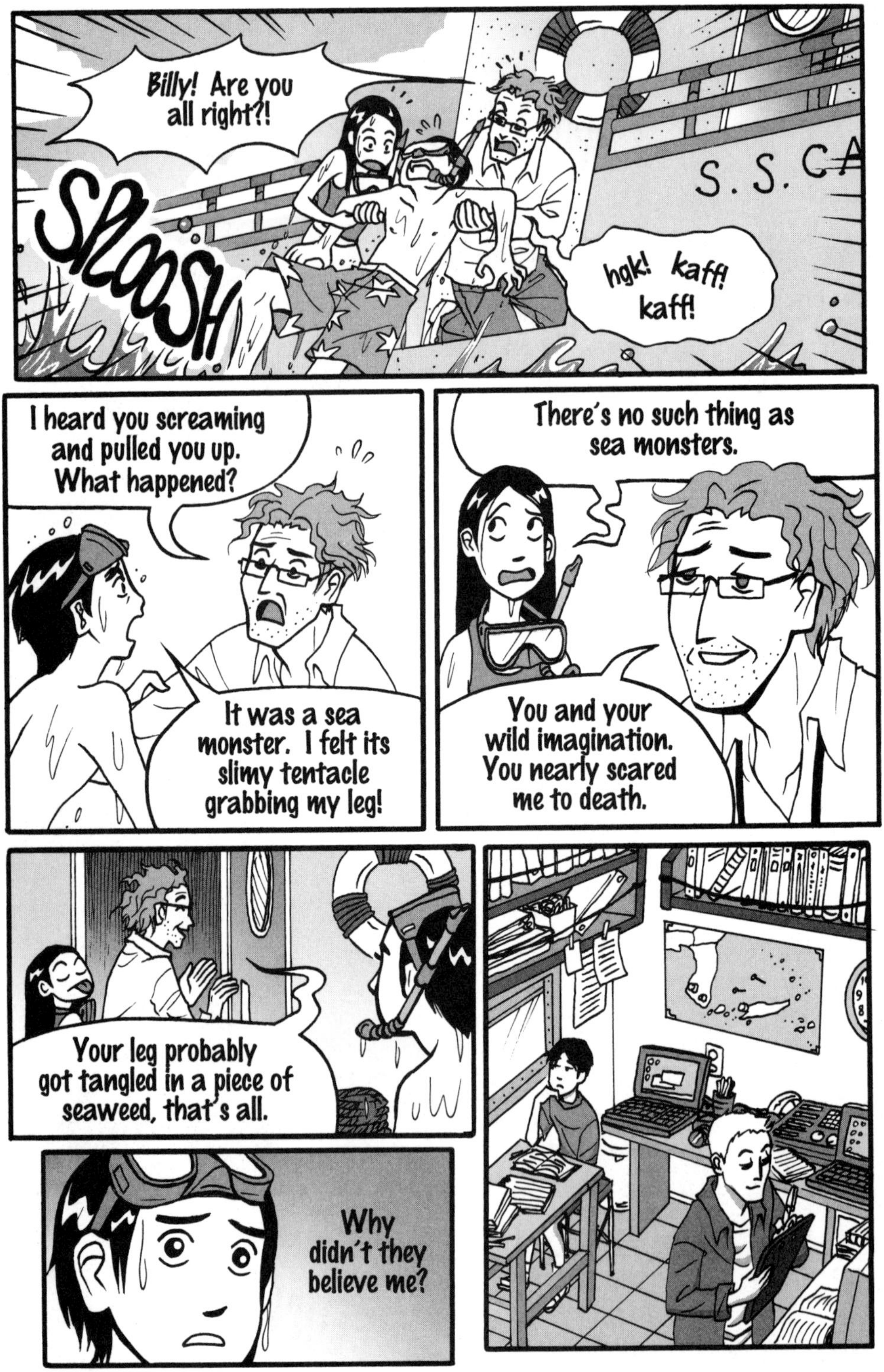
Billy! Are you all right?!
SPLOOSH
S.S. CA
hgk! kaff! kaff!
I heard you screaming and pulled you up. What happened?
It was a sea monster. I felt its slimy tentacle grabbing my leg!
There's no such thing as sea monsters.
You and your wild imagination. You nearly scared me to death.
Your leg probably got tangled in a piece of seaweed, that's all.
Why didn't they believe me?

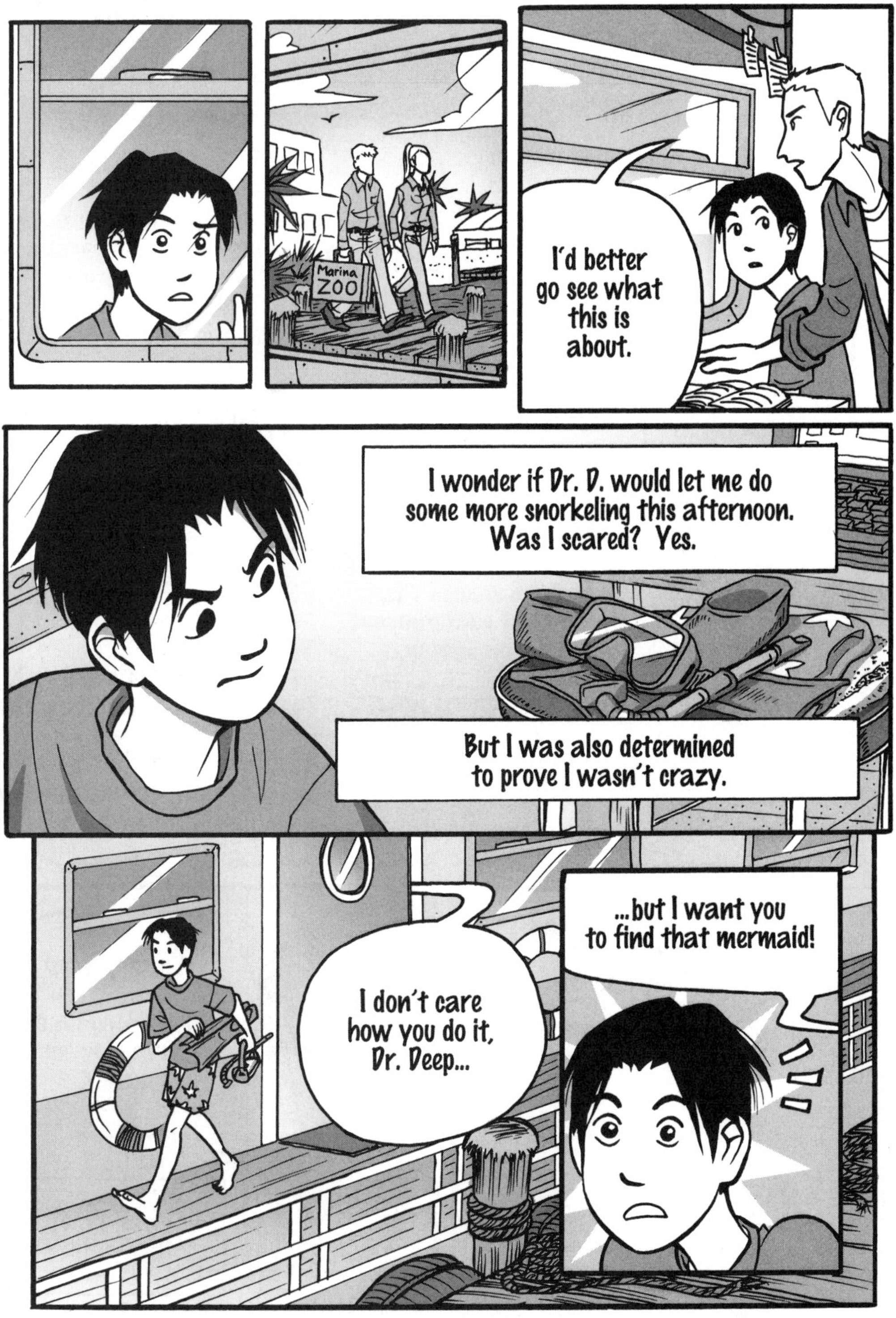
Marina ZOO
I'd better go see what this is about.
I wonder if Dr. D. would let me do some more snorkeling this afternoon. Was I scared? Yes.
But I was also determined to prove I wasn't crazy.
I don't care how you do it, Dr. Deep...
...but I want you to find that mermaid!

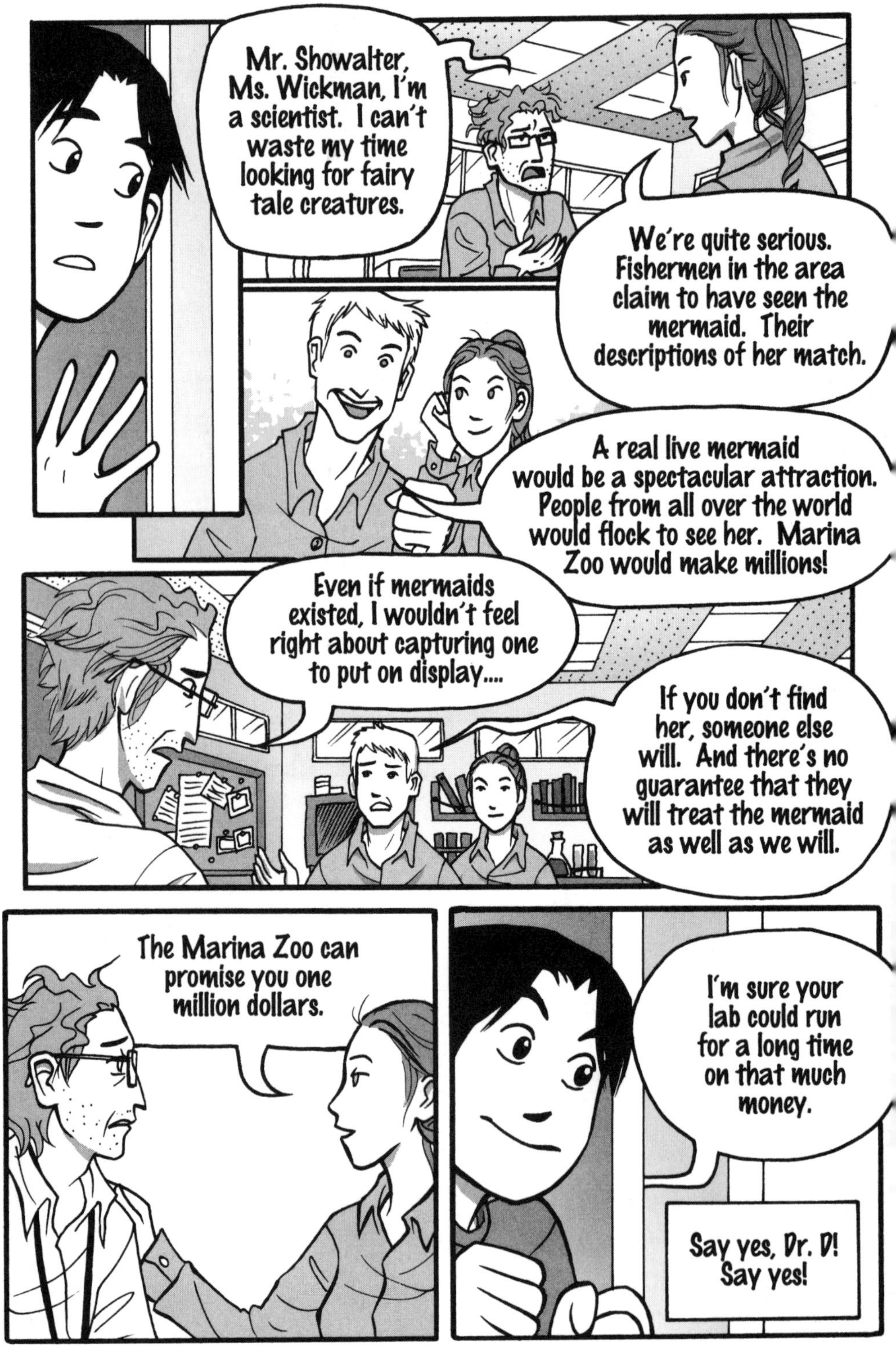
Mr. Showalter, Ms. Wickman, I'm a scientist. I can't waste my time looking for fairy tale creatures.
We're quite serious. Fishermen in the area claim to have seen the mermaid. Their descriptions of her match.
A real live mermaid would be a spectacular attraction. People from all over the world would flock to see her. Marina Zoo would make millions!
Even if mermaids existed, I wouldn't feel right about capturing one to put on display....
If you don't find her, someone else will. And there's no guarantee that they will treat the mermaid as well as we will.
The Marina Zoo can promise you one million dollars.
I'm sure your lab could run for a long time on that much money.
Say yes, Dr. D! Say yes!

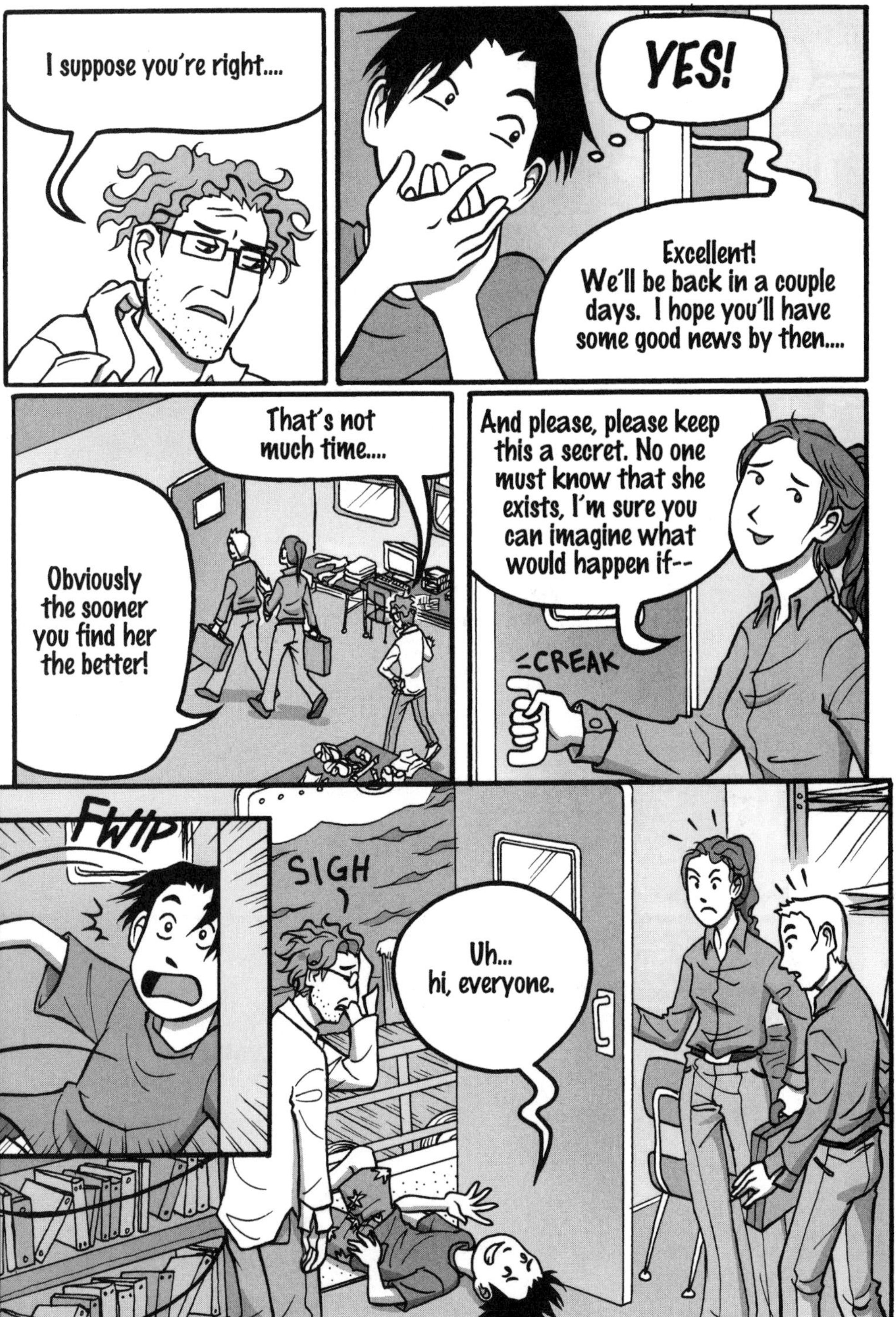
I suppose you're right....
YES!
Excellent! We'll be back in a couple days. I hope you'll have some good news by then....
That's not much time....
Obviously the sooner you find her the better!
And please, please keep this a secret. No one must know that she exists, I'm sure you can imagine what would happen if--
CREAK
FWIP
SIGH
Uh... hi, everyone.

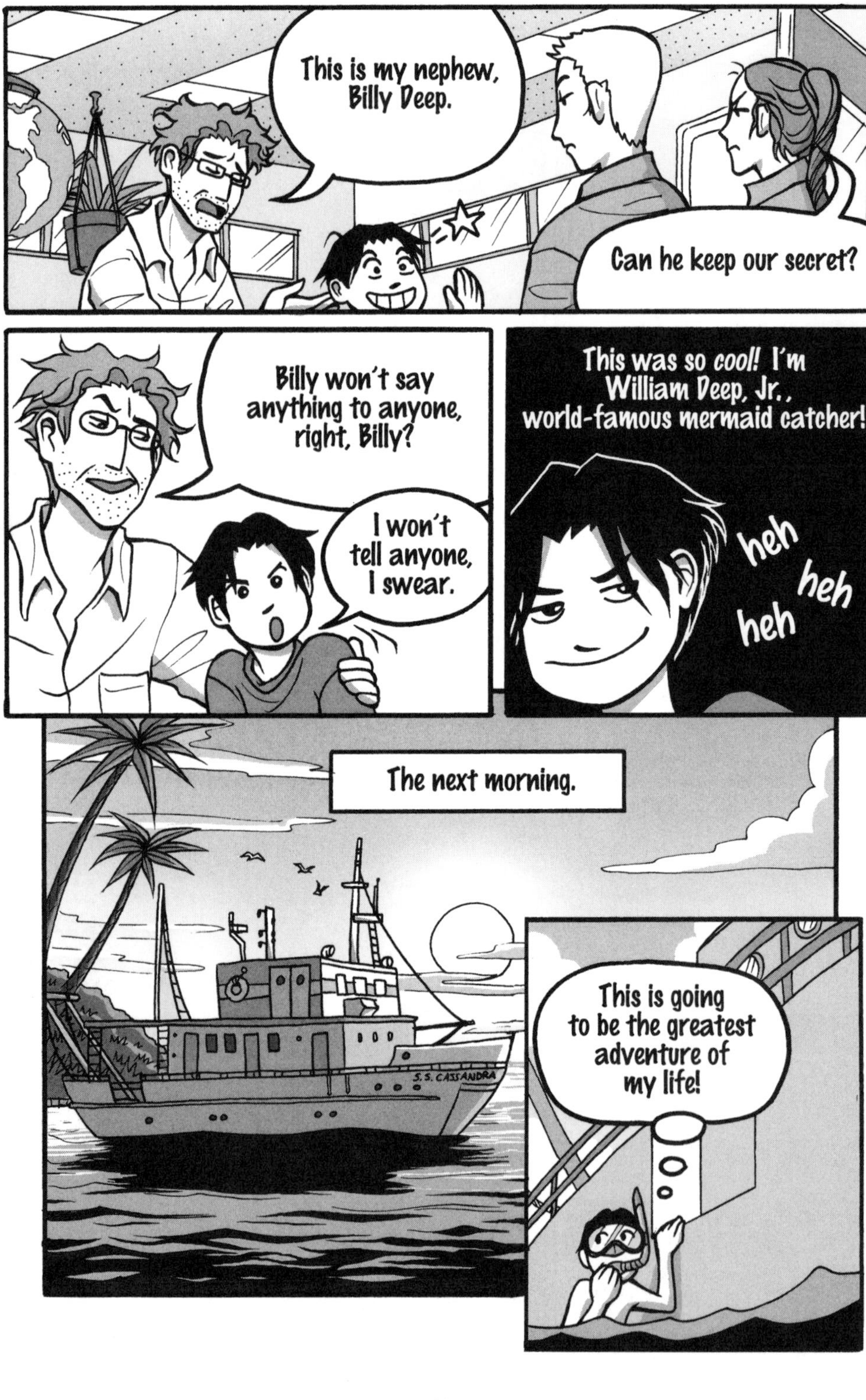
This is my nephew, Billy Deep.
Can he keep our secret?
Billy won't say anything to anyone, right, Billy?
I won't tell anyone, I swear.
This was so *cool!* I'm William Deep, Jr., world-famous mermaid catcher!
heh heh heh
The next morning.
S.S. CASSANDRA
This is going to be the greatest adventure of my life!

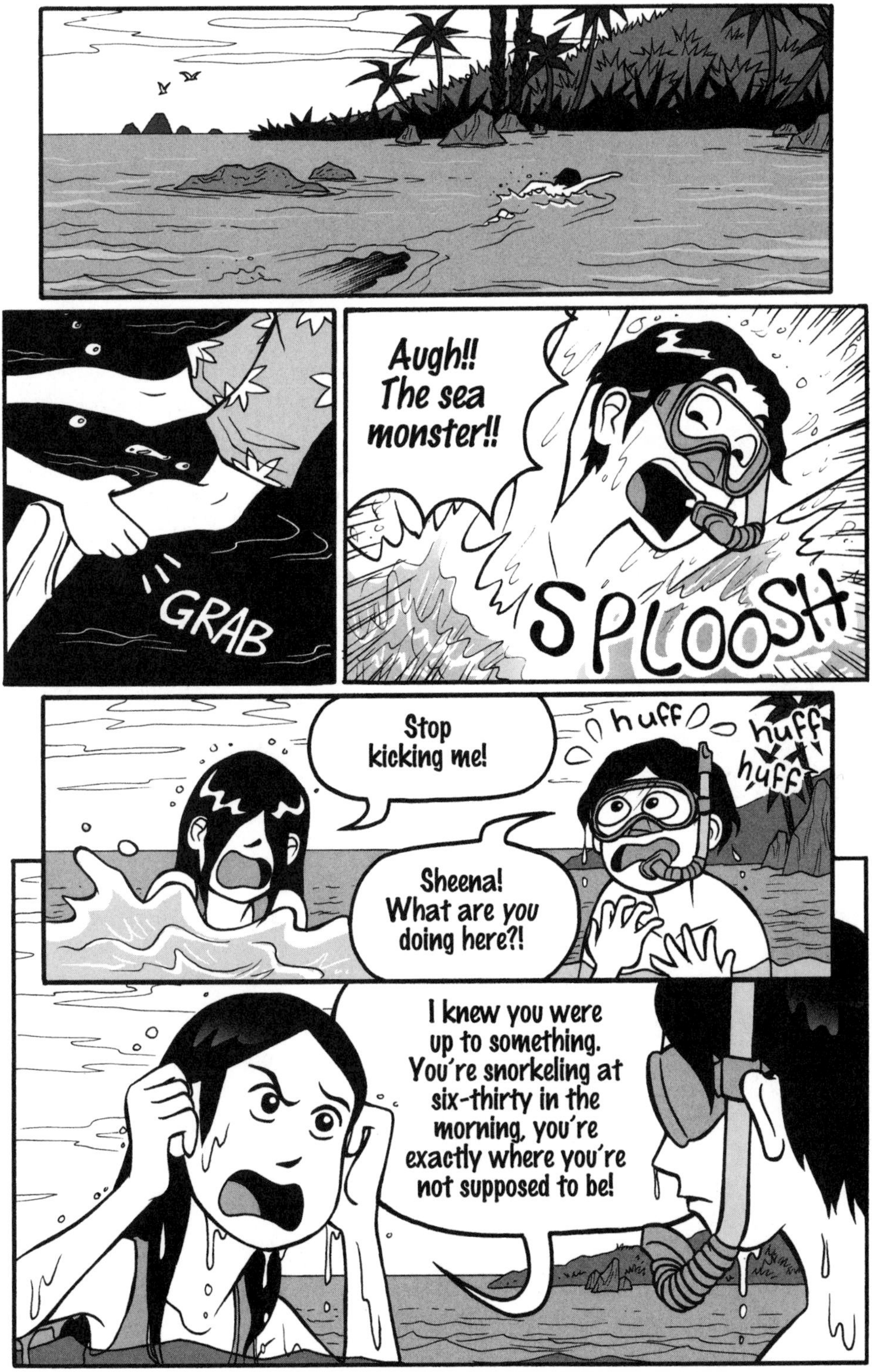
GRAB
Augh!! The sea monster!!
SPLOOSH
Stop kicking me!
huff
huff
huff
Sheena! What are you doing here?!
I knew you were up to something. You're snorkeling at six-thirty in the morning, you're exactly where you're not supposed to be!

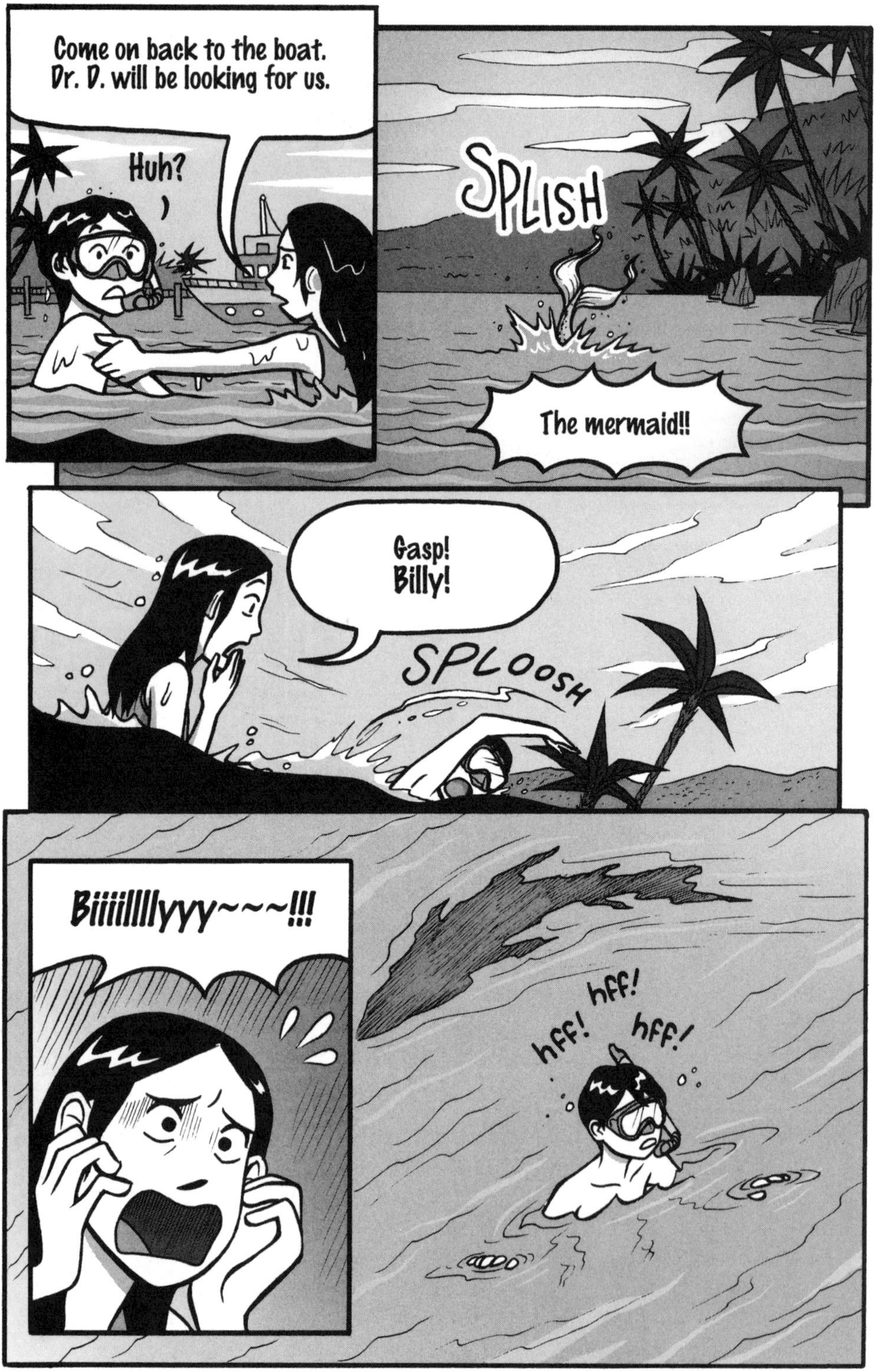
Come on back to the boat. Dr. D. will be looking for us.
Huh?
SPLISH
The mermaid!!
Gasp! Billy!
SPLOOSH
Biiiilllllyyy~~~!!!
hff!
hff!
hff!

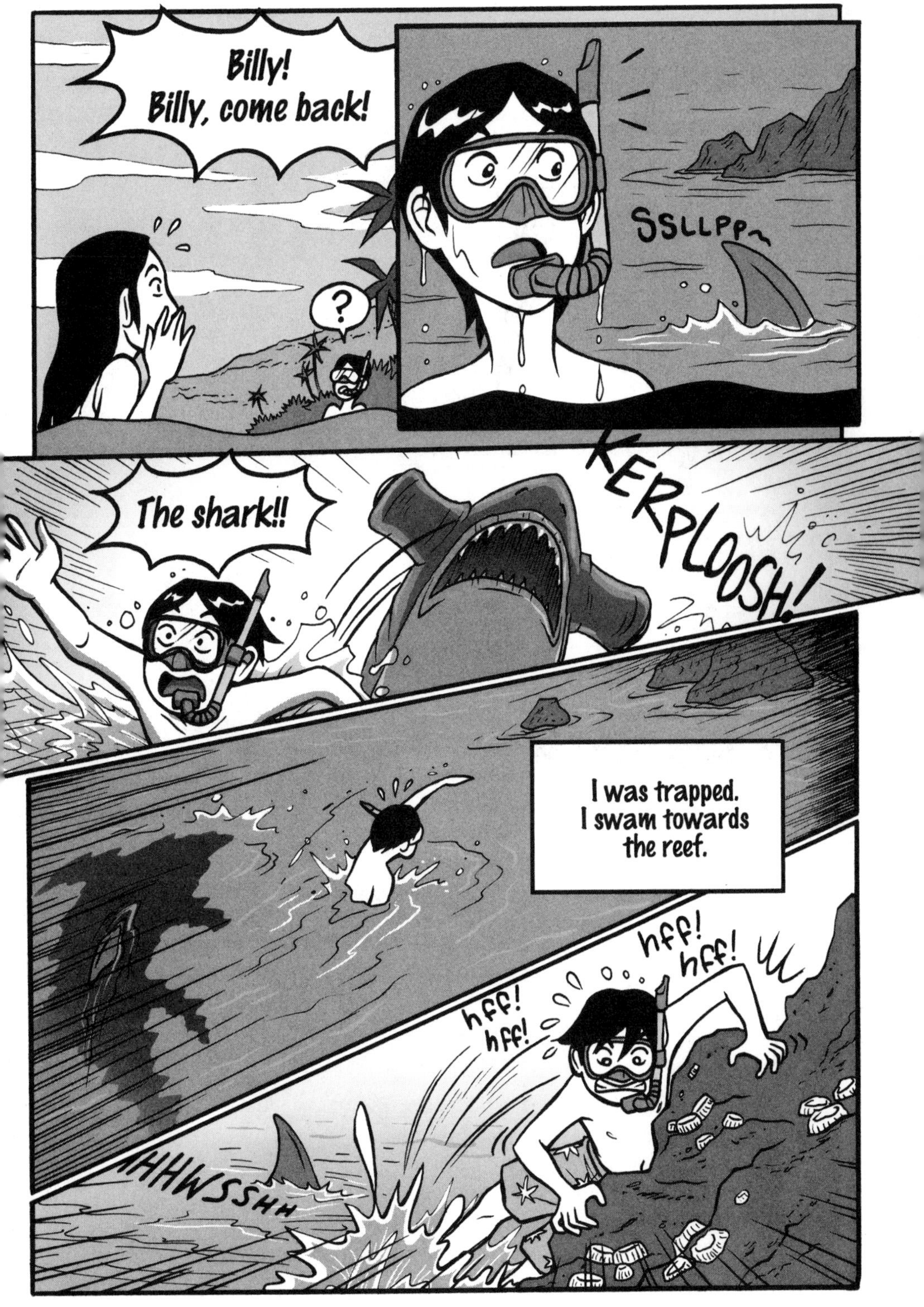
Billy!
Billy, come back!
?
SSLLPP
The shark!!
KERPLOOSH!
I was trapped. I swam towards the reef.
hff! hff!
hff! hff!
HHWSSHH

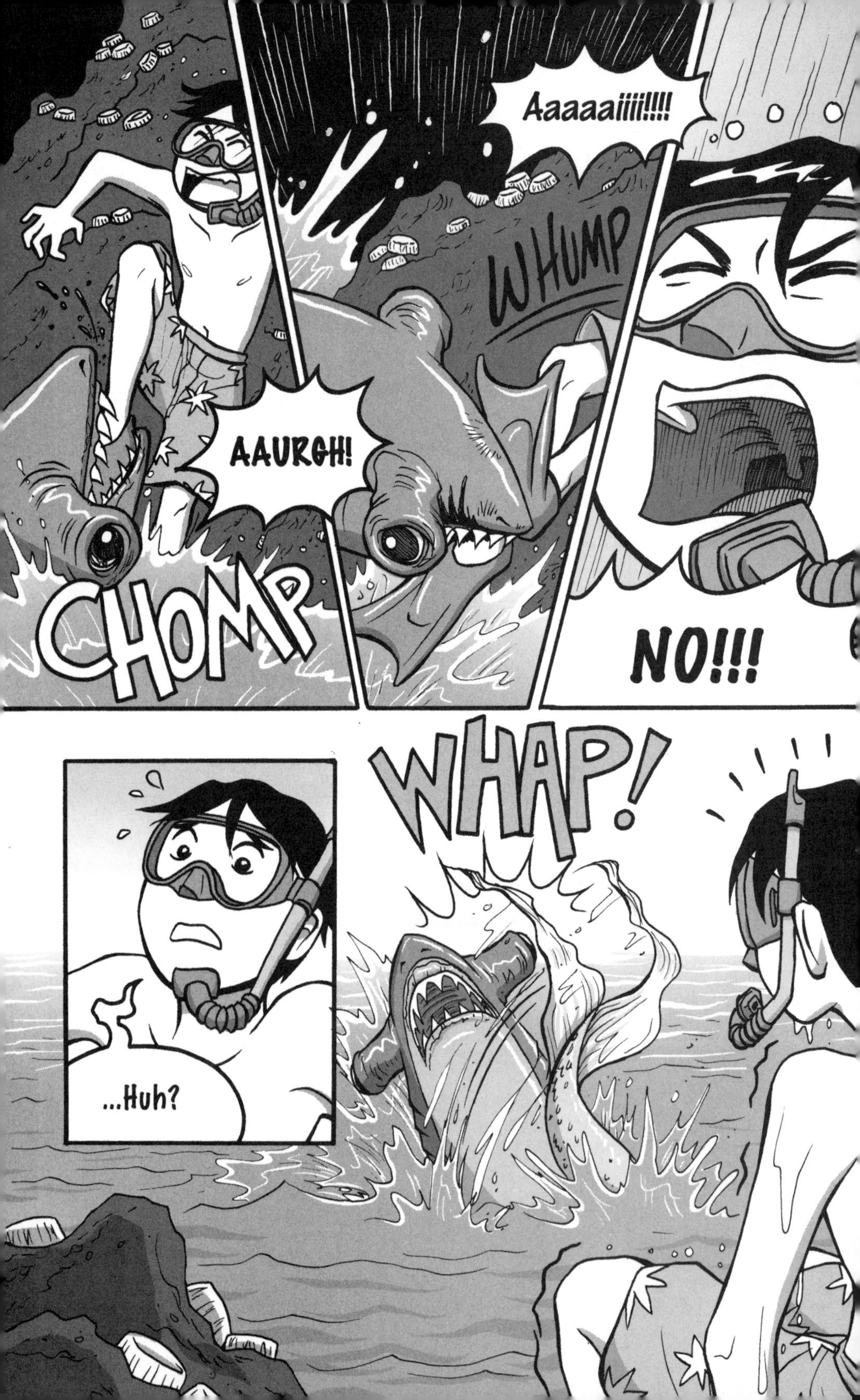
AAURGH!
CHOMP
Aaaaaiiiii!!!!
WHUMP
NO!!!
...Huh?
WHAP!

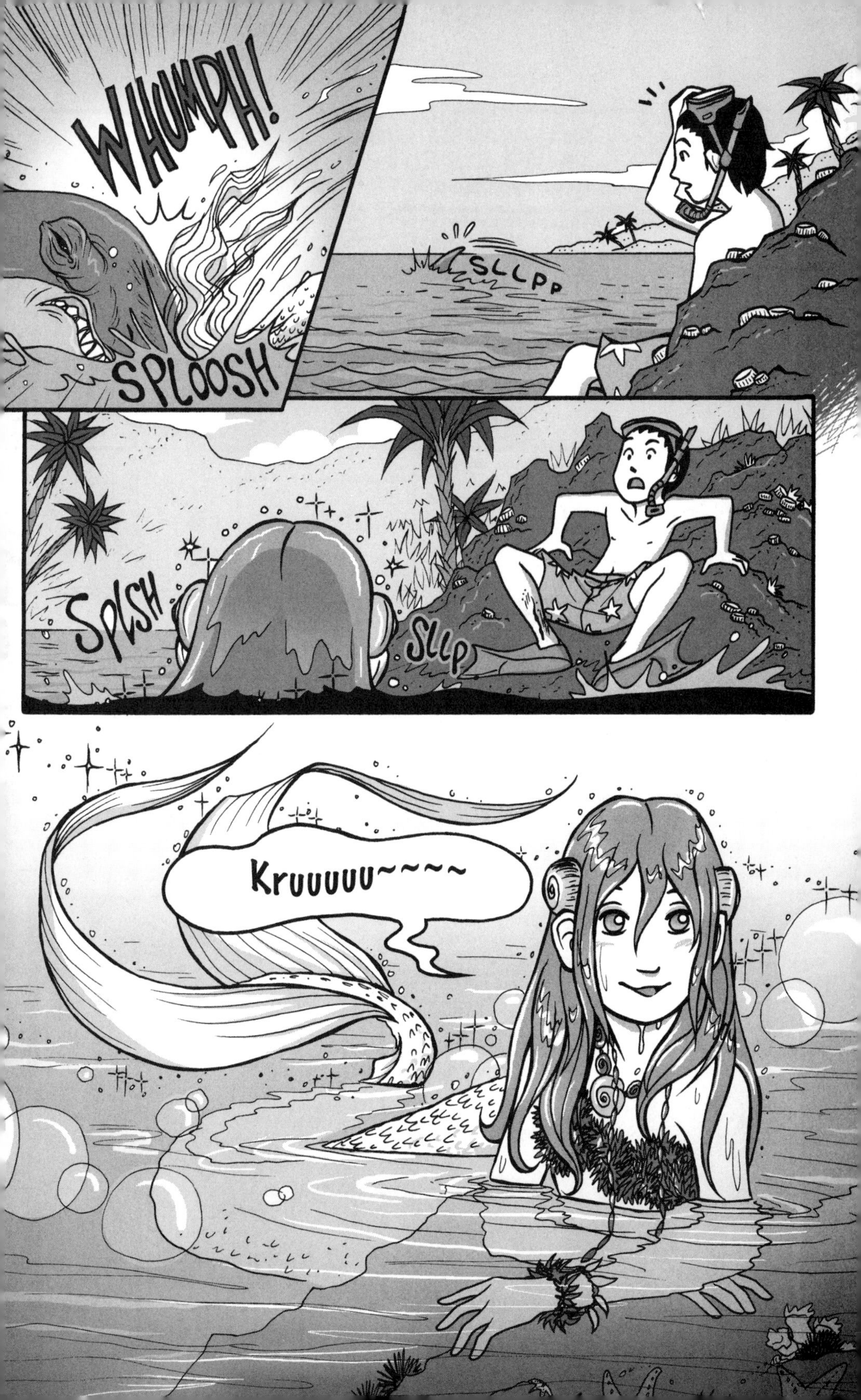
WHUMPH!
SPLOOSH
SLLPP
SPLSH
SLLP
Kruuuuu~~~~

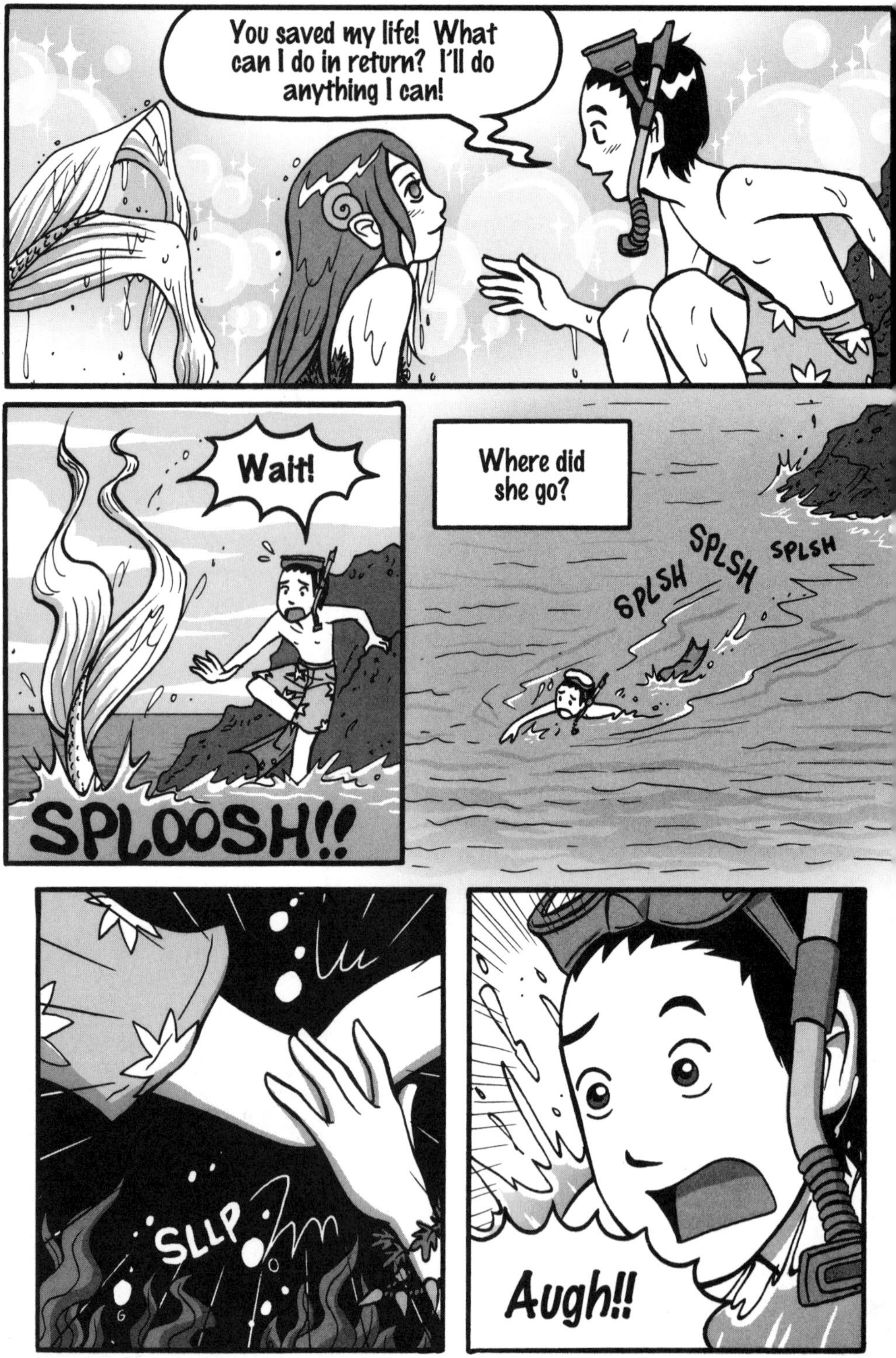
You saved my life! What can I do in return? I'll do anything I can!
Wait!
SPLOOSH!!
Where did she go?
SPLSH
SPLSH
SPLSH
SLLP
Augh!!

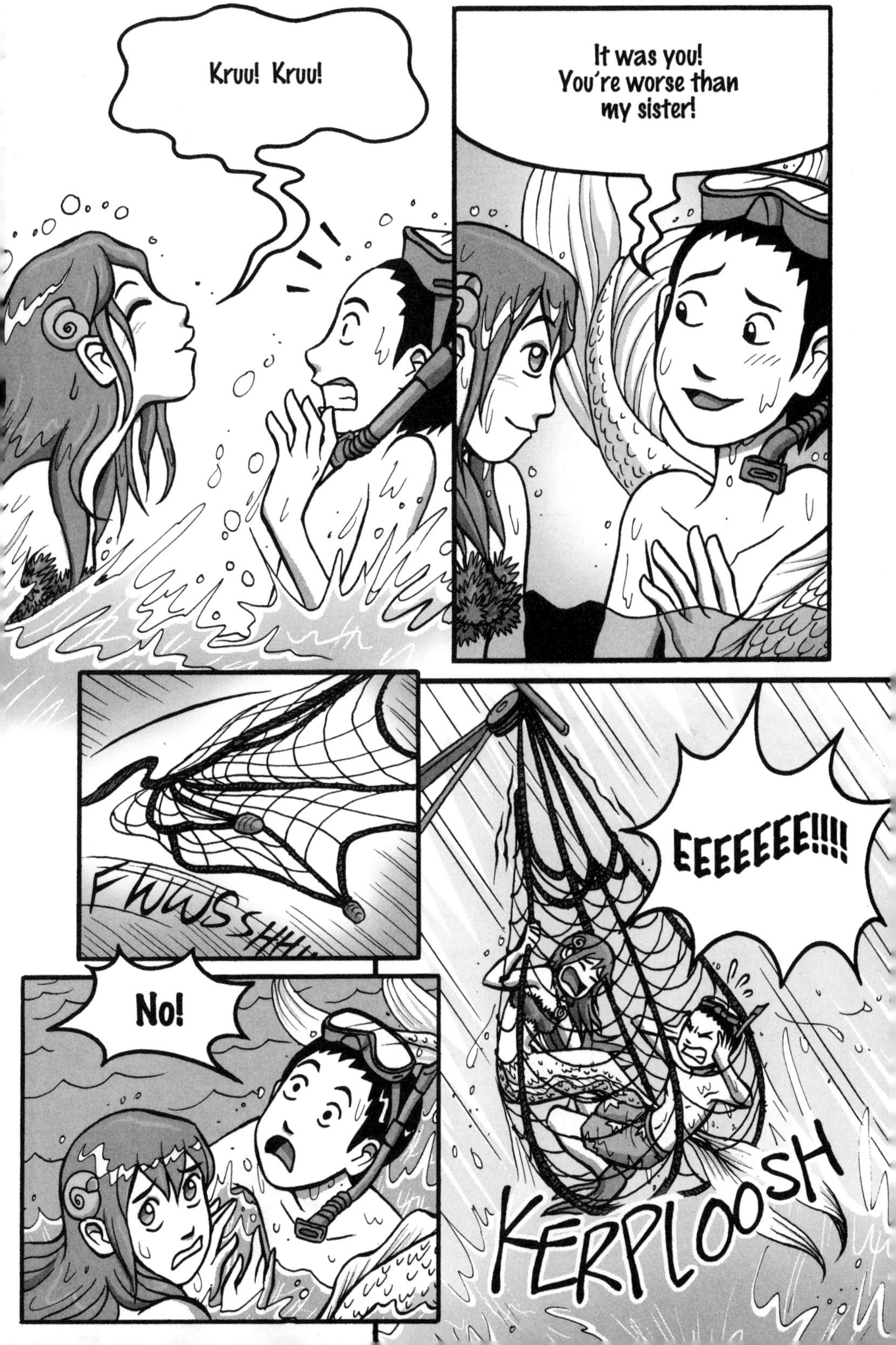
Kruu! Kruu!
It was you! You're worse than my sister!
FWWSSHH
EEEEEEE!!!!
No!
KERPLOOSH

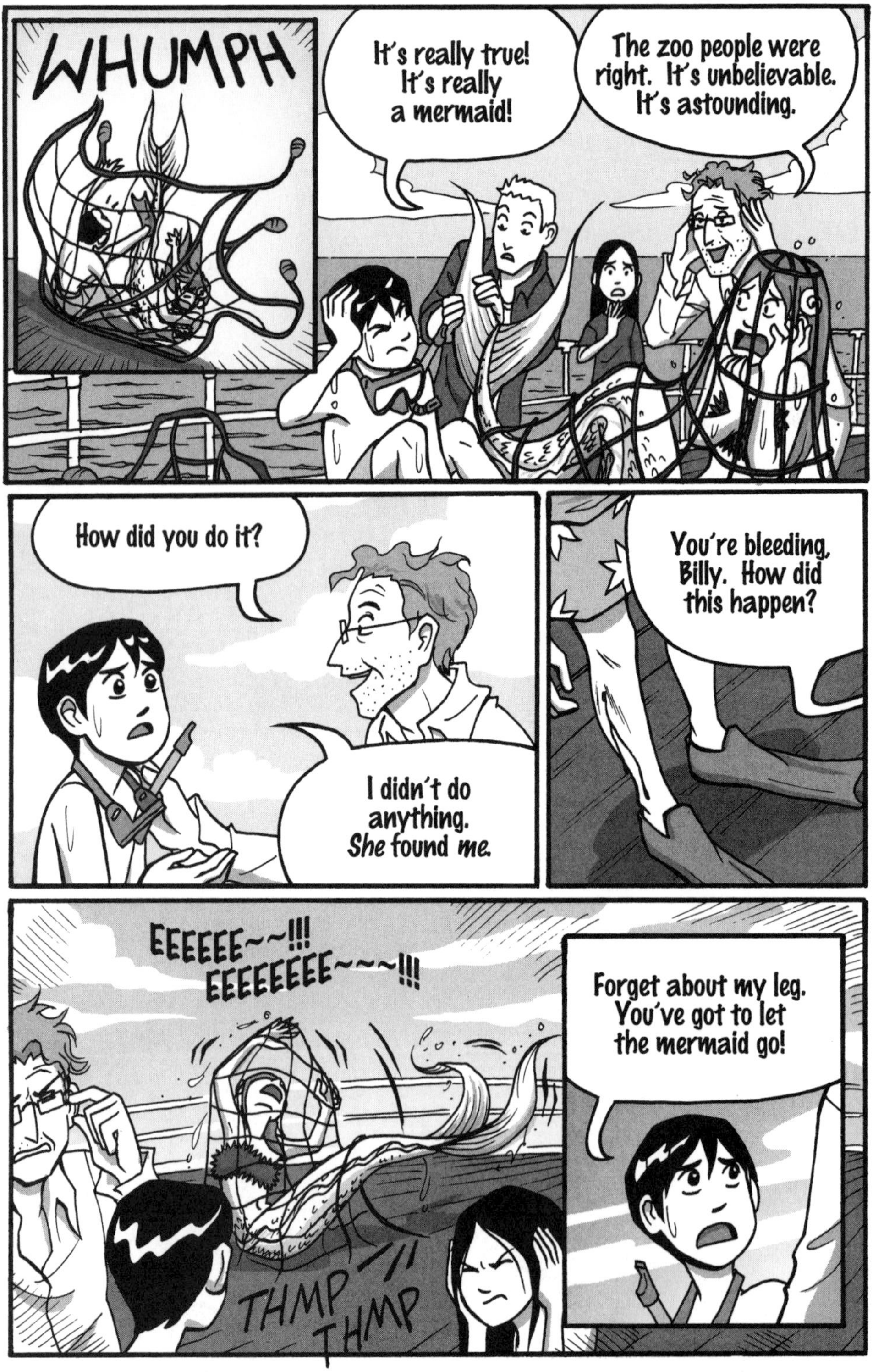
WHUMPH
It's really true! It's really a mermaid!
The zoo people were right. It's unbelievable. It's astounding.
How did you do it?
I didn't do anything. *She* found *me*.
You're bleeding, Billy. How did this happen?
EEEEEE~~!!! EEEEEEEE~~~!!!
Forget about my leg. You've got to let the mermaid go!
THMP THMP

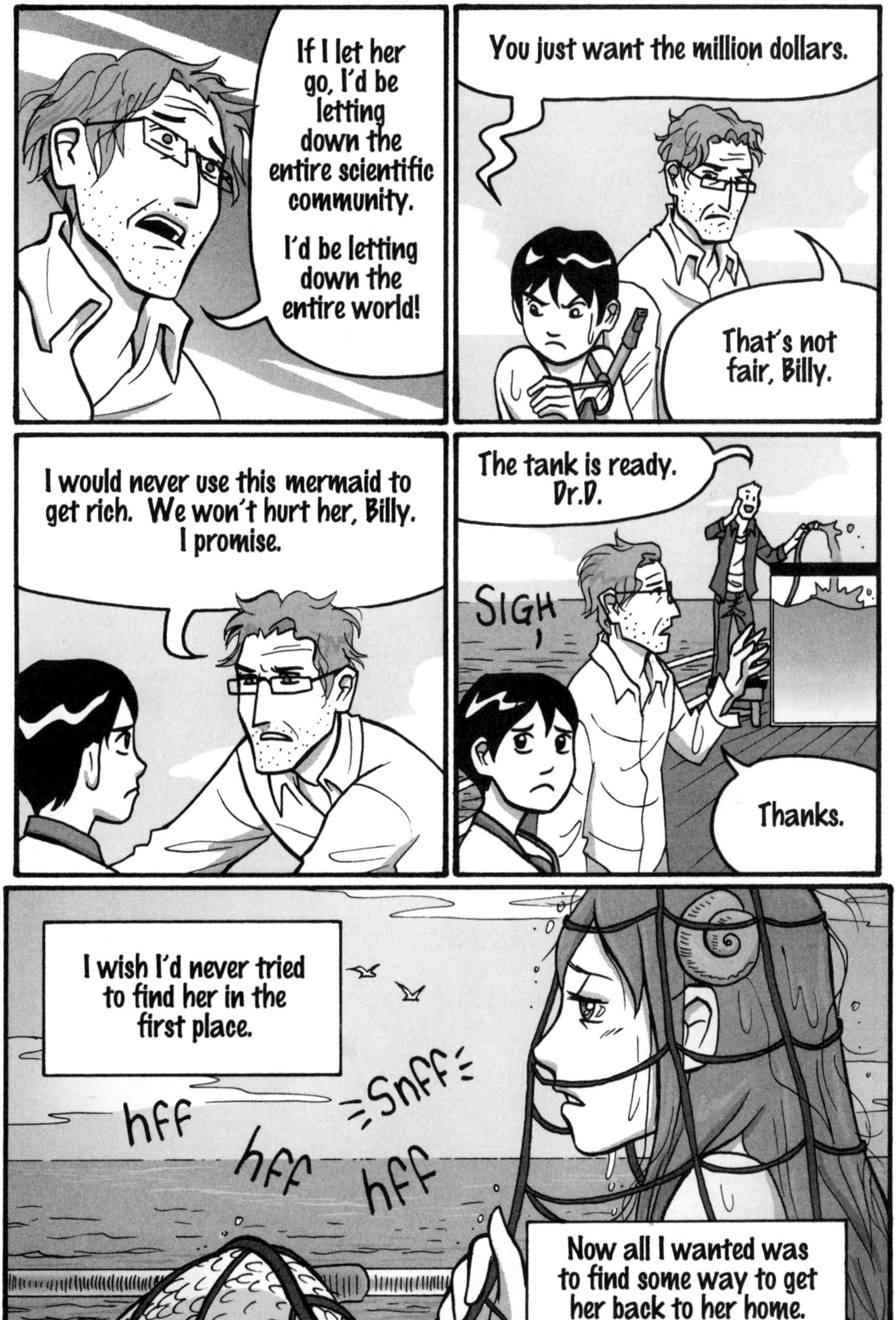
If I let her go, I'd be letting down the entire scientific community.
I'd be letting down the entire world!
You just want the million dollars.
That's not fair, Billy.
I would never use this mermaid to get rich. We won't hurt her, Billy. I promise.
The tank is ready. Dr.D.
SIGH
Thanks.
I wish I'd never tried to find her in the first place.
hff
Snff
hff
hff
Now all I wanted was to find some way to get her back to her home.

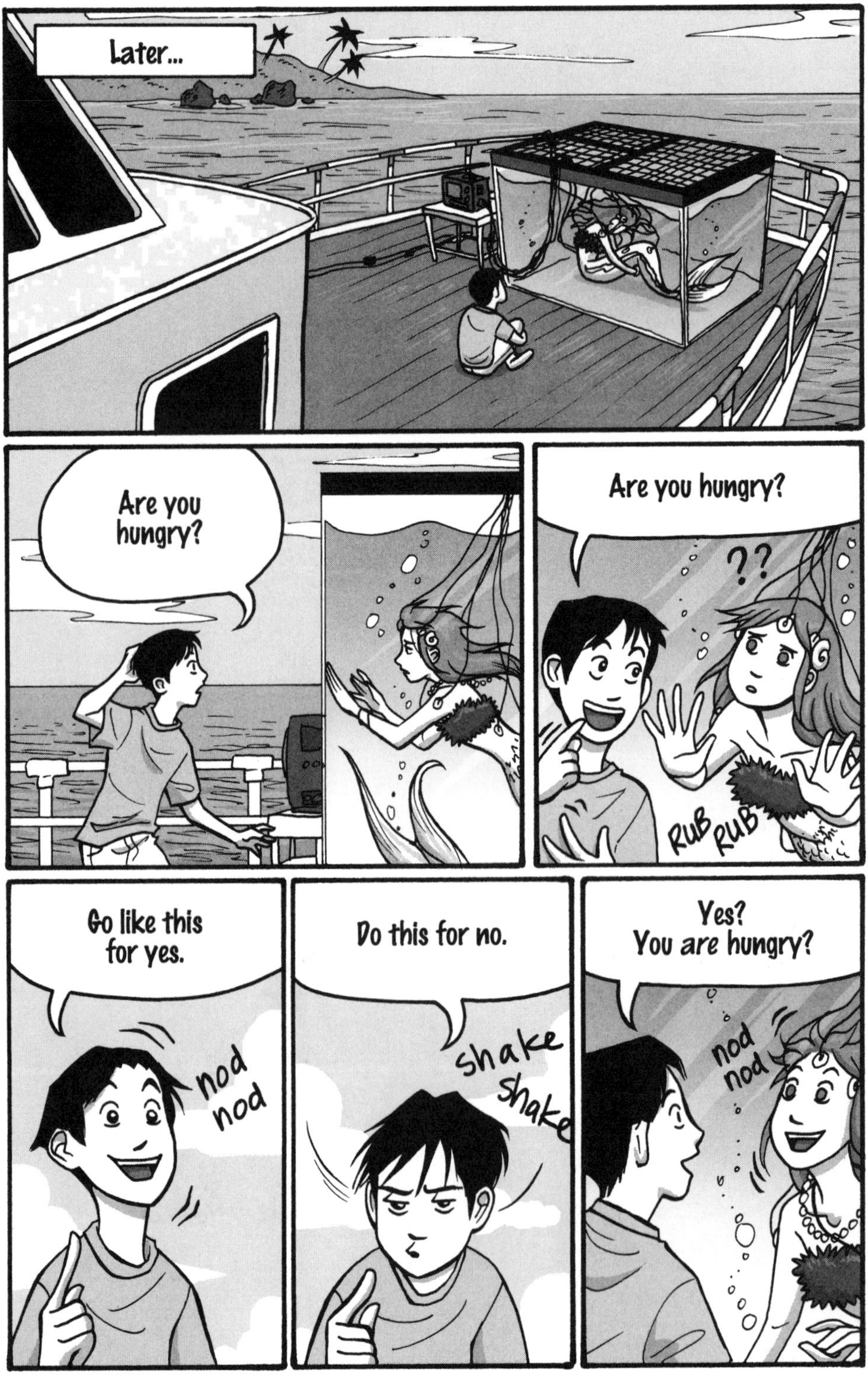
Later...
Are you hungry?
Are you hungry?
??
RUB RUB
Go like this for yes.
nod nod
Do this for no.
shake shake
Yes? You are hungry?
nod nod

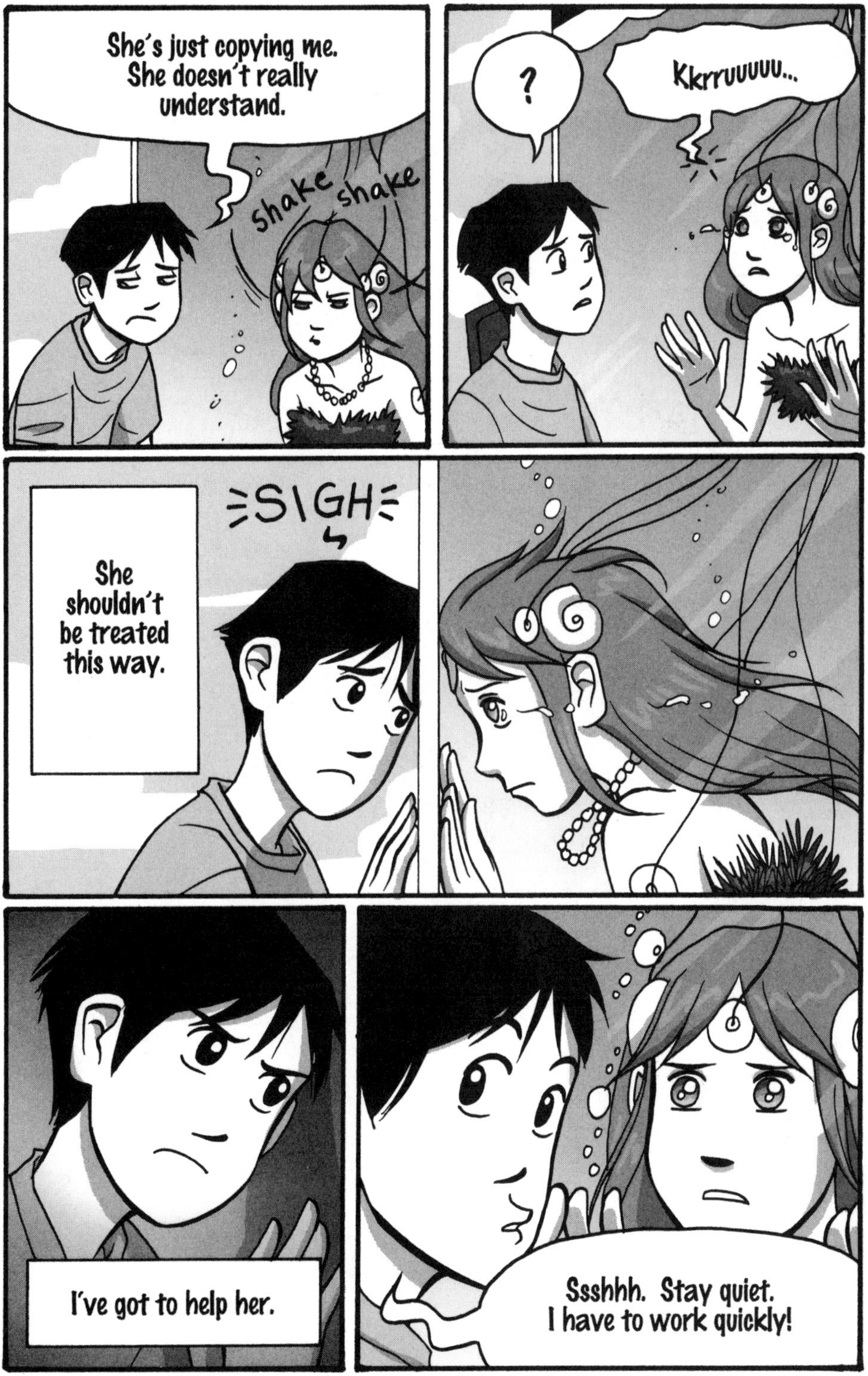
She's just copying me.
She doesn't really understand.
shake shake
?
Kkrruuuuu...
=SIGH=
She shouldn't be treated this way.
I've got to help her.
Ssshhh. Stay quiet.
I have to work quickly!

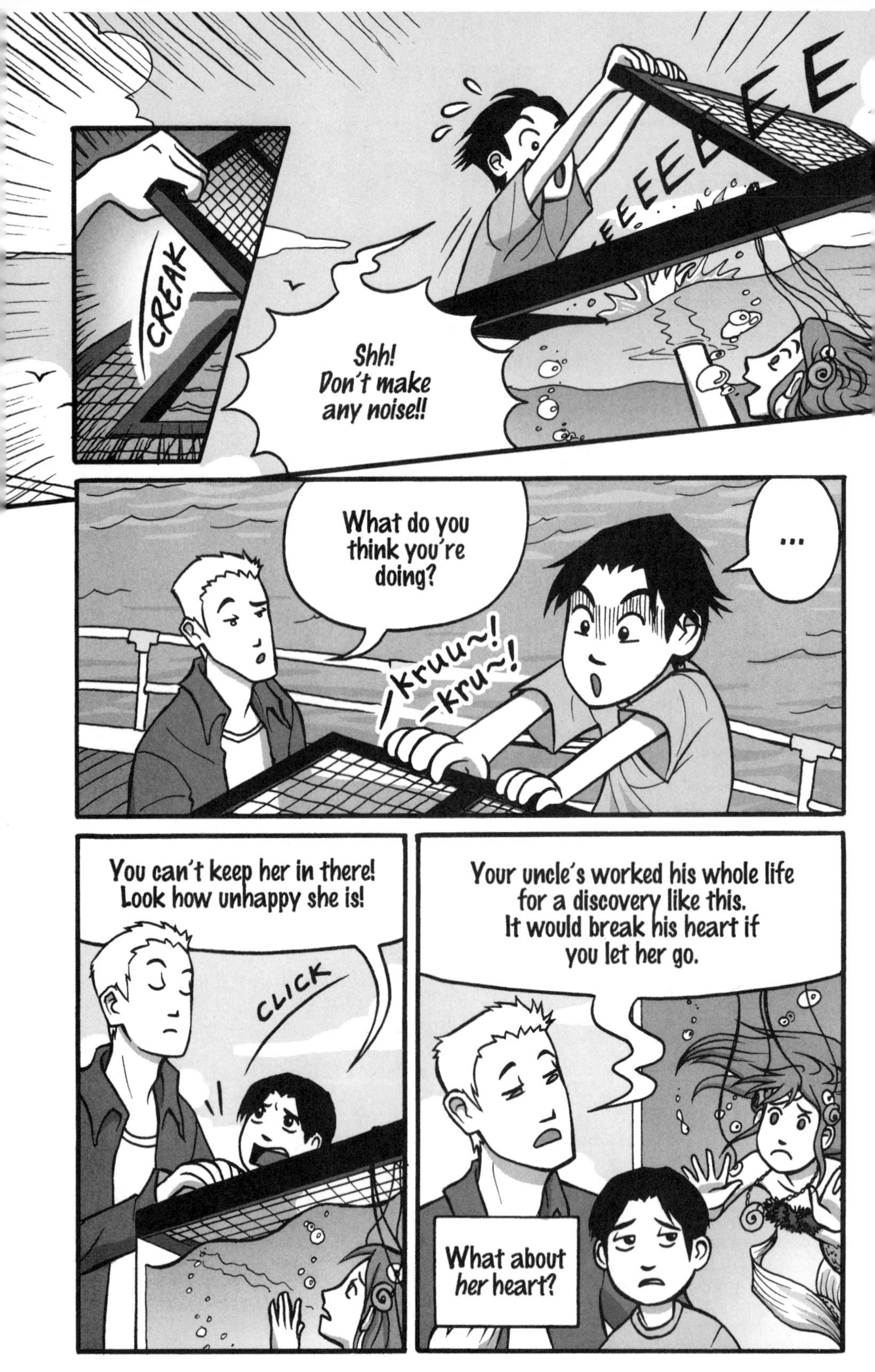
CREAK
EEEEEEEEE
Shh! Don't make any noise!!
What do you think you're doing?
...
kruu~! kru~!
You can't keep her in there! Look how unhappy she is!
CLICK
Your uncle's worked his whole life for a discovery like this. It would break his heart if you let her go.
What about her heart?

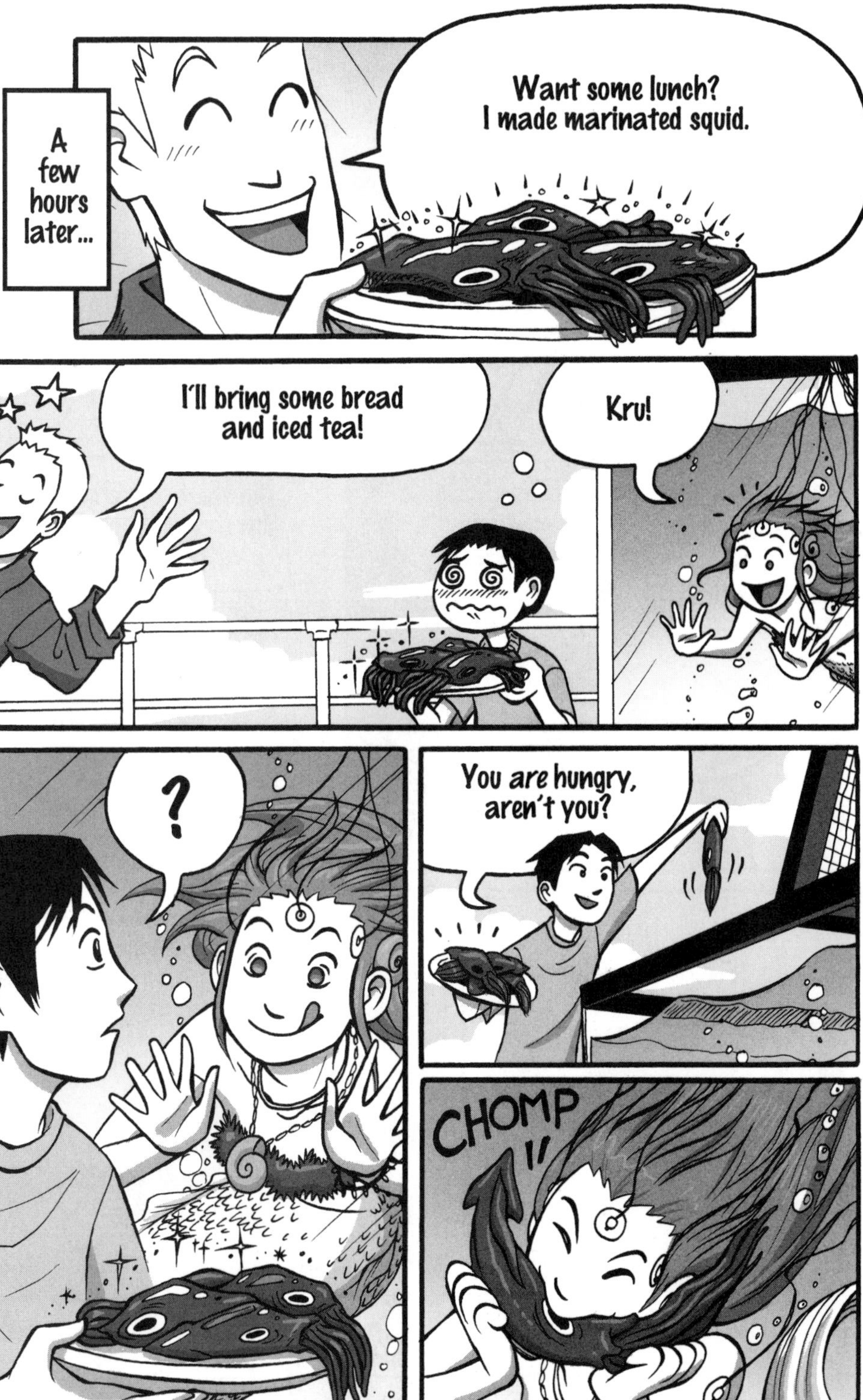
A few hours later...
Want some lunch? I made marinated squid.
I'll bring some bread and iced tea!
Kru!
?
You are hungry, aren't you?
CHOMP

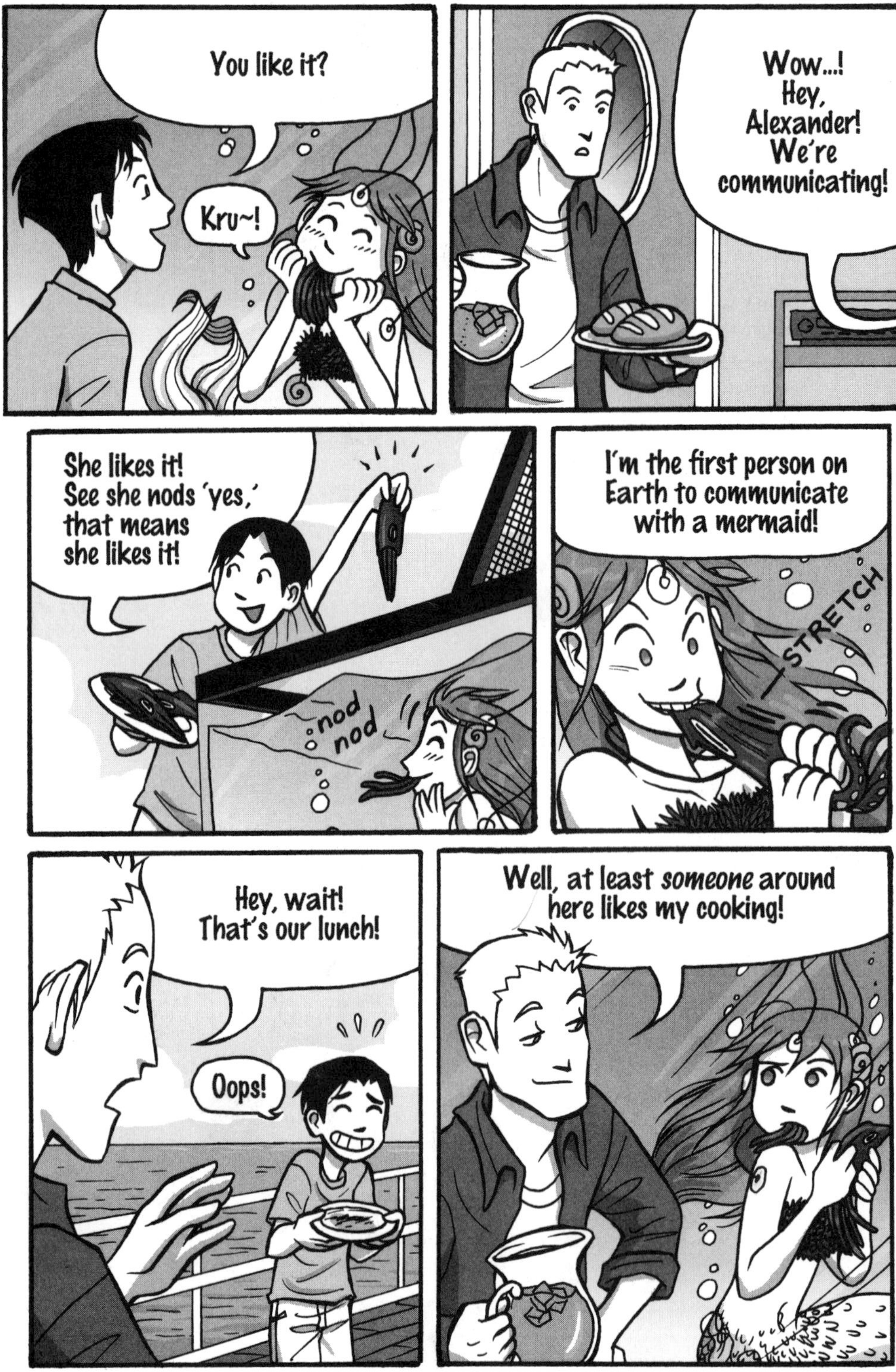
You like it?
Kru~!
Wow...! Hey, Alexander! We're communicating!
She likes it! See she nods 'yes,' that means she likes it!
nod nod
I'm the first person on Earth to communicate with a mermaid!
STRETCH
Hey, wait! That's our lunch!
Oops!
Well, at least *someone* around here likes my cooking!

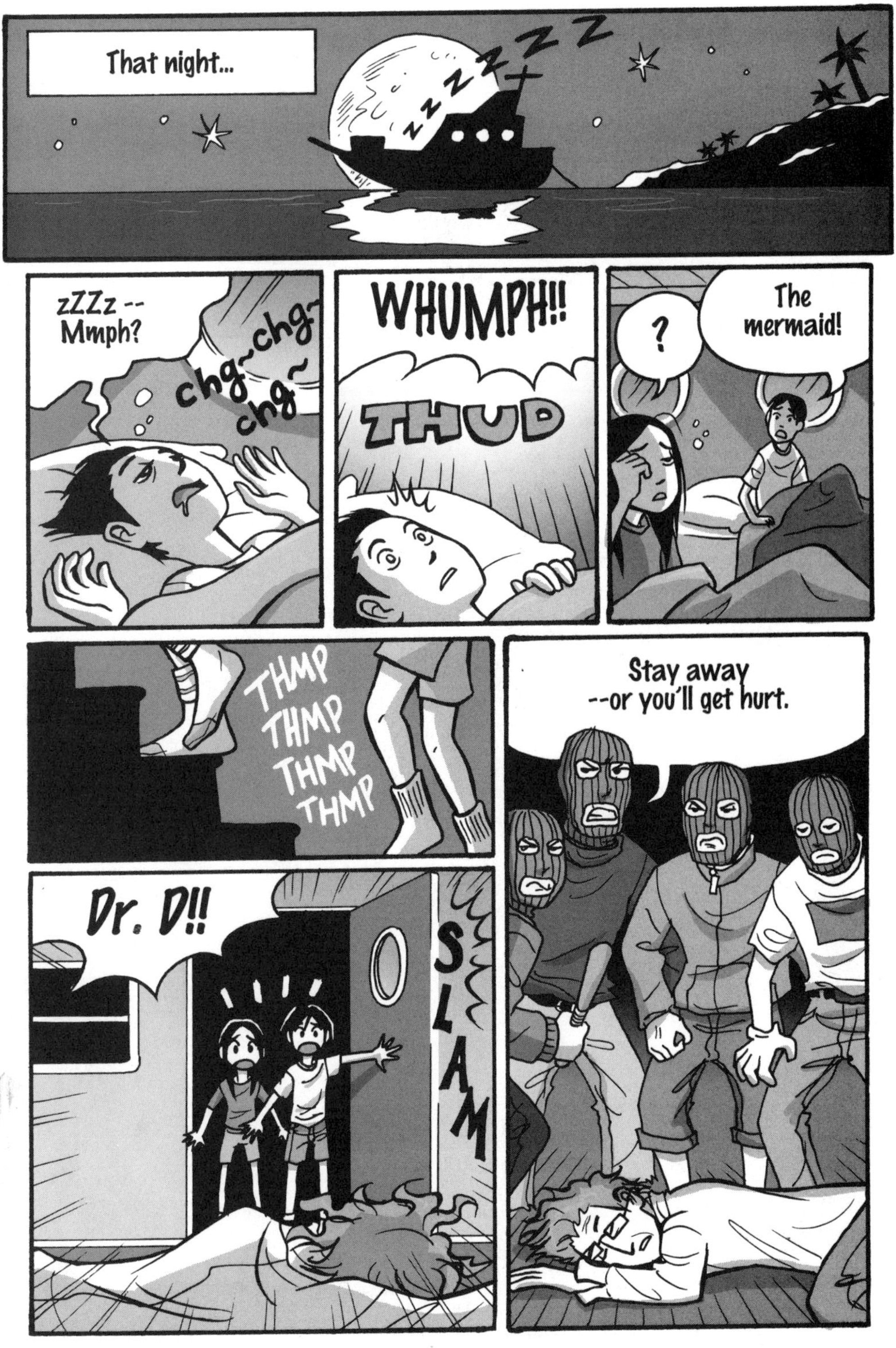
That night...
ZZZZZZZ
zZZz --
Mmph?
chg~chg~
chg~
WHUMPH!!
THUD
?
The mermaid!
THMP
THMP
THMP
THMP
Stay away
--or you'll get hurt.
Dr. D!!
SLAM

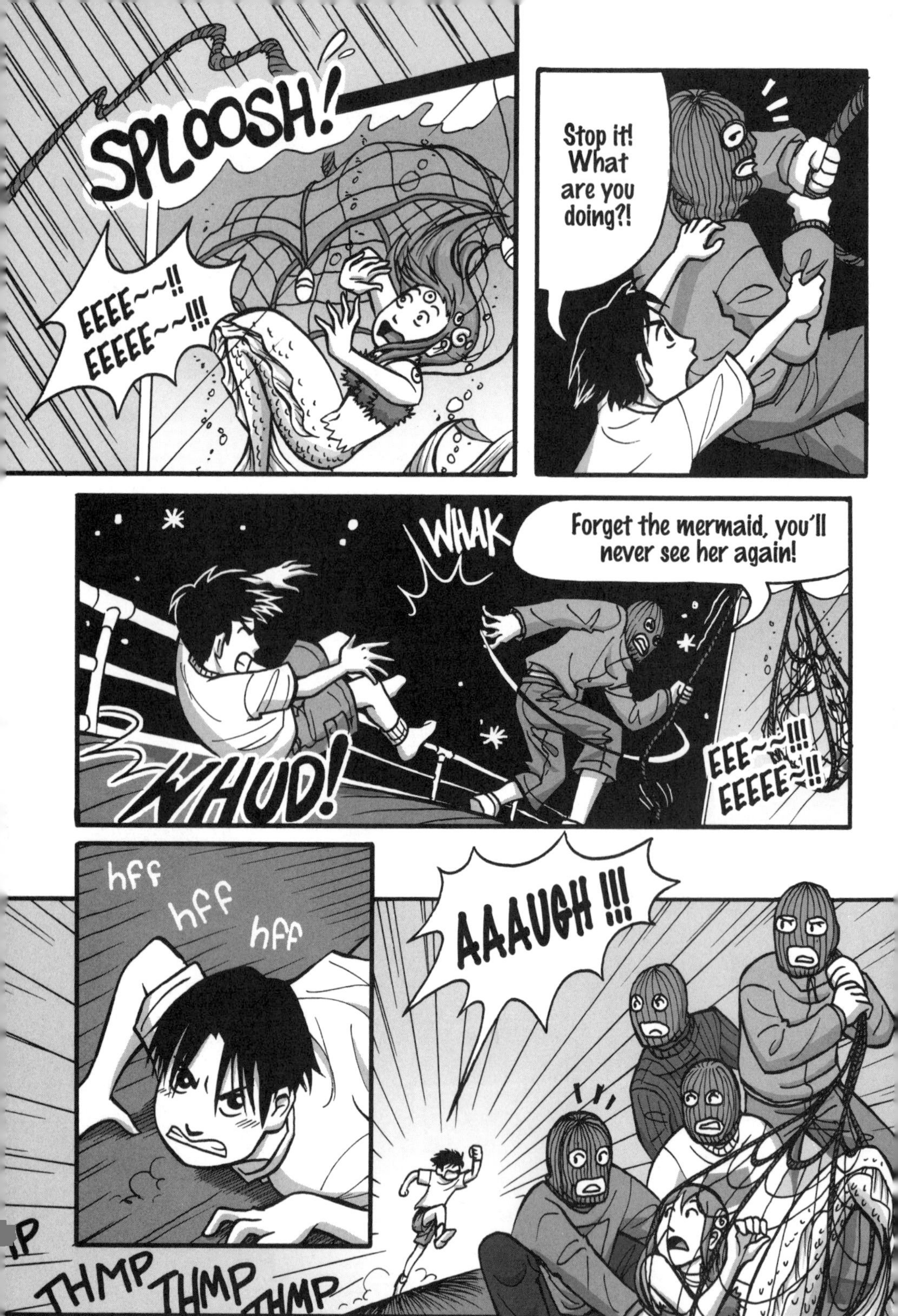
SPLOOSH!
EEEE~~!!
EEEEE~~!!!
Stop it! What are you doing?!
WHAK
Forget the mermaid, you'll never see her again!
WHUD!
EEE~~!!!
EEEEE~!!
hff
hff
hff
THMP
THMP
THMP
AAAUGH !!!

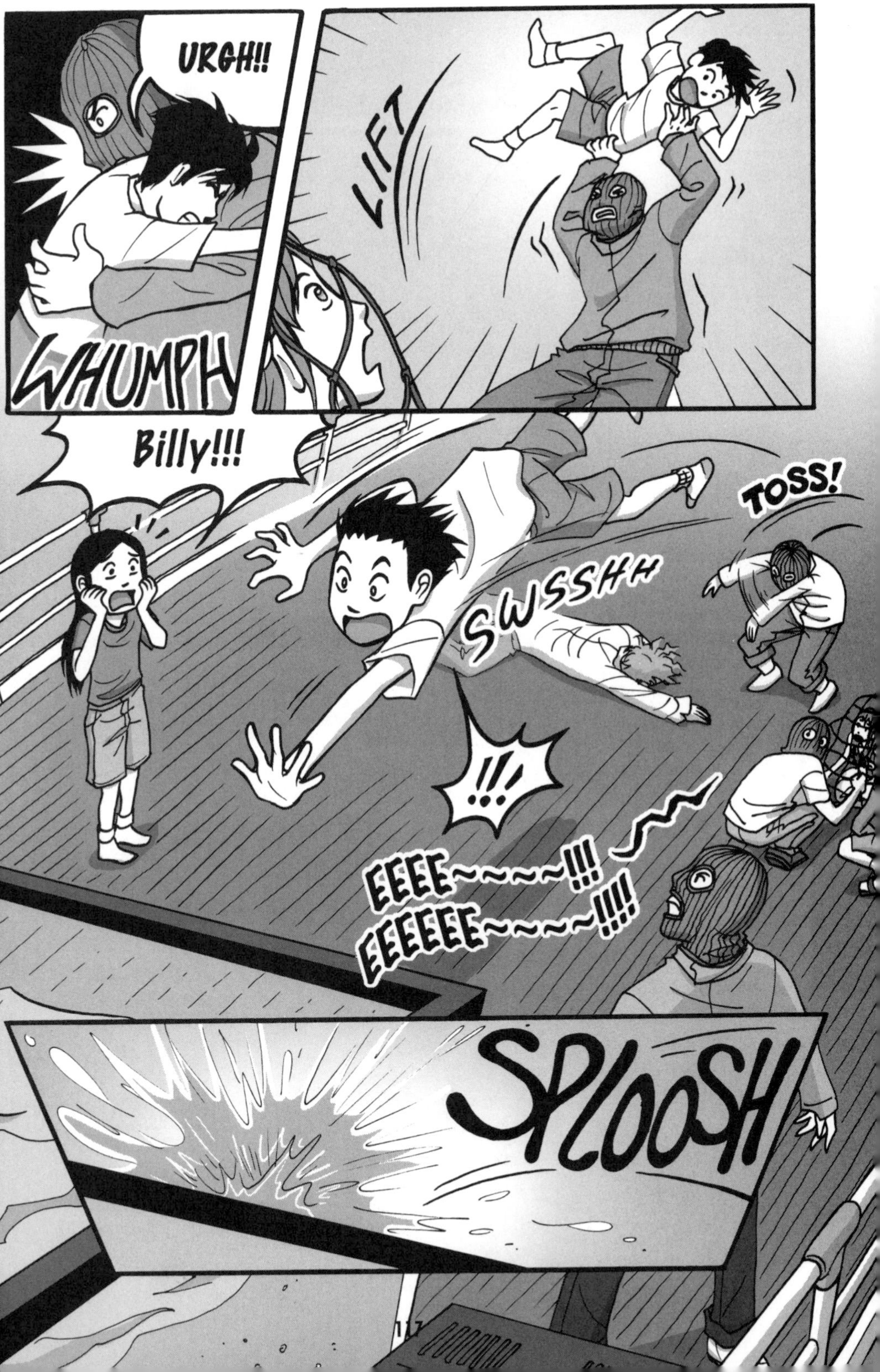
URGH!!
WHUMPH
LIFT
Billy!!!!
TOSS!
SWSSHH
!!!
EEEE~~~~!!!
EEEEEE~~~~!!!!
SPLOOSH

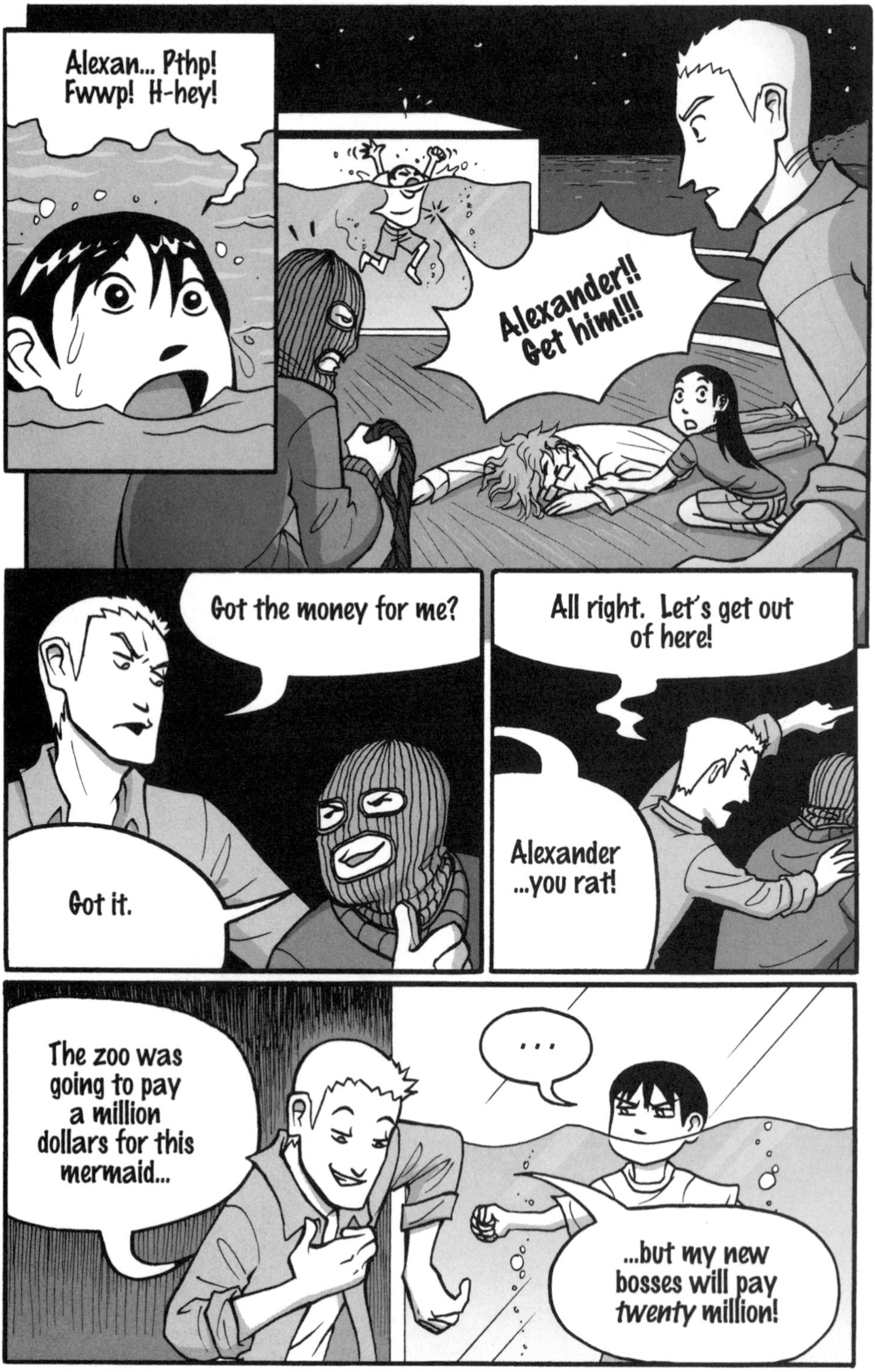
Alexan... Pthp! Fwwp! H-hey!
Alexander!! Get him!!!
Got the money for me?
Got it.
All right. Let's get out of here!
Alexander ...you rat!
The zoo was going to pay a million dollars for this mermaid...
...
...but my new bosses will pay *twenty* million!

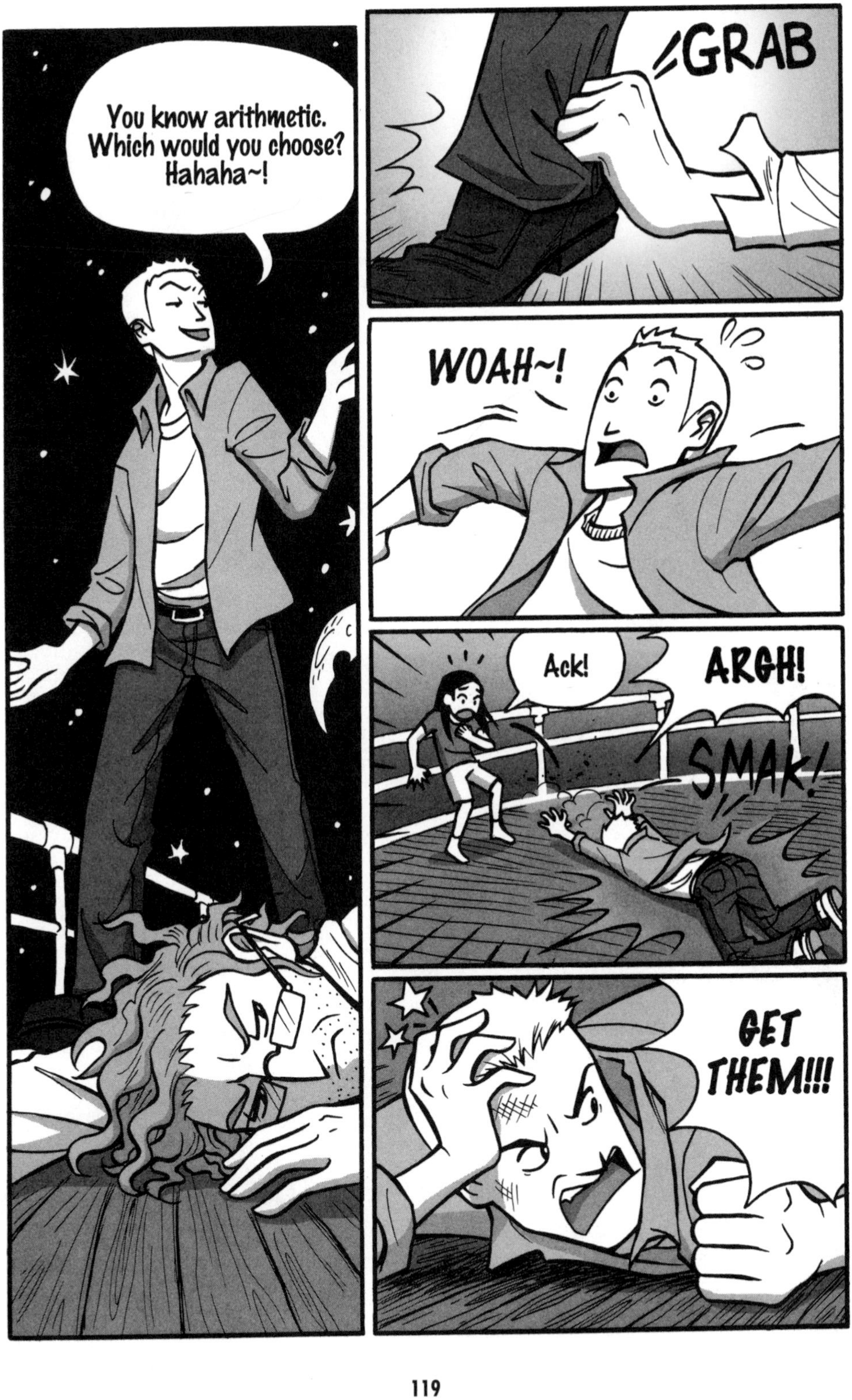
You know arithmetic. Which would you choose? Hahaha~!
GRAB
WOAH~!
Ack!
ARGH!
SMAK!
GET THEM!!!

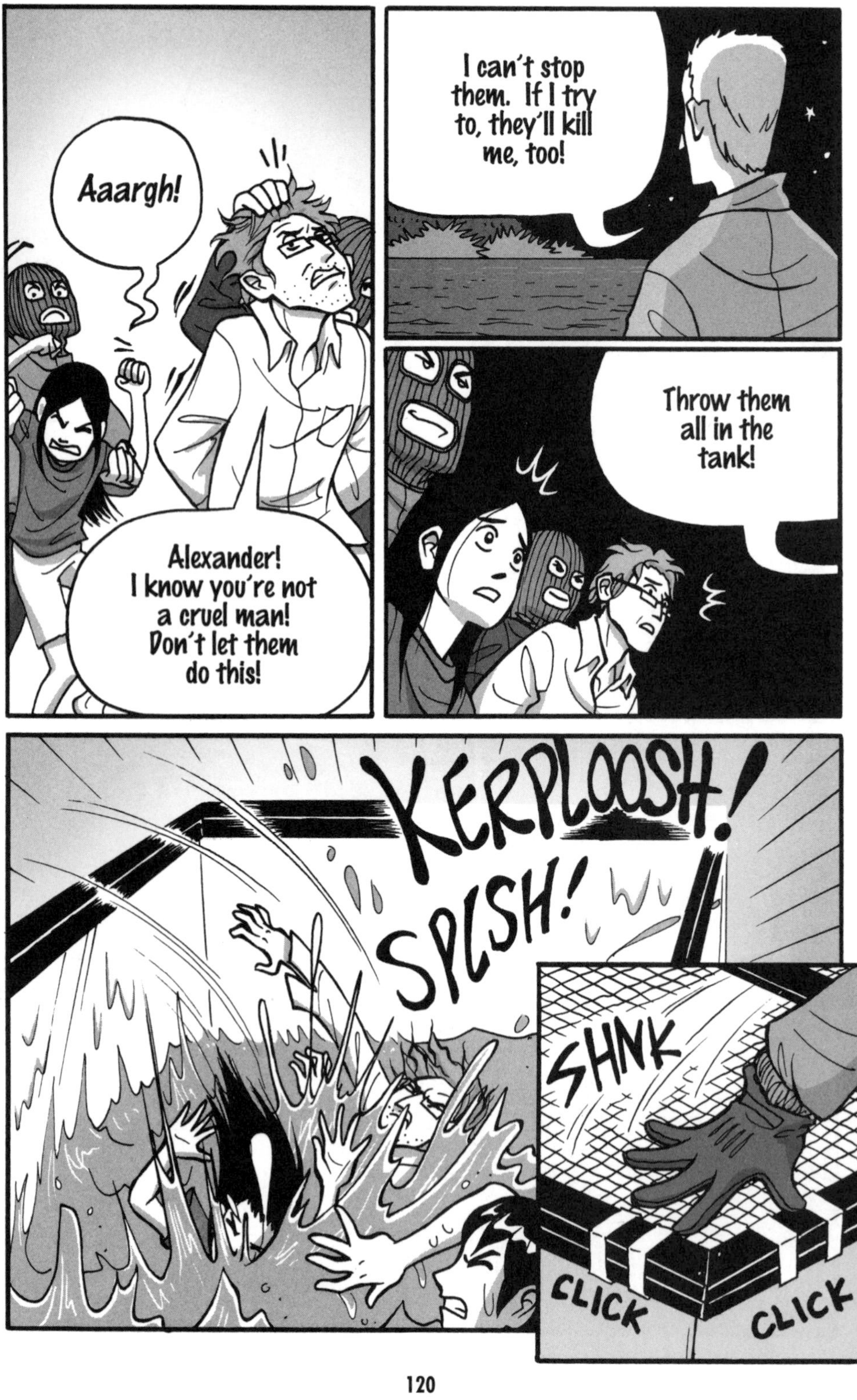
Aaargh!
Alexander! I know you're not a cruel man! Don't let them do this!
I can't stop them. If I try to, they'll kill me, too!
Throw them all in the tank!
KERPLOOSH!
SPLSH!
SHNK
CLICK
CLICK

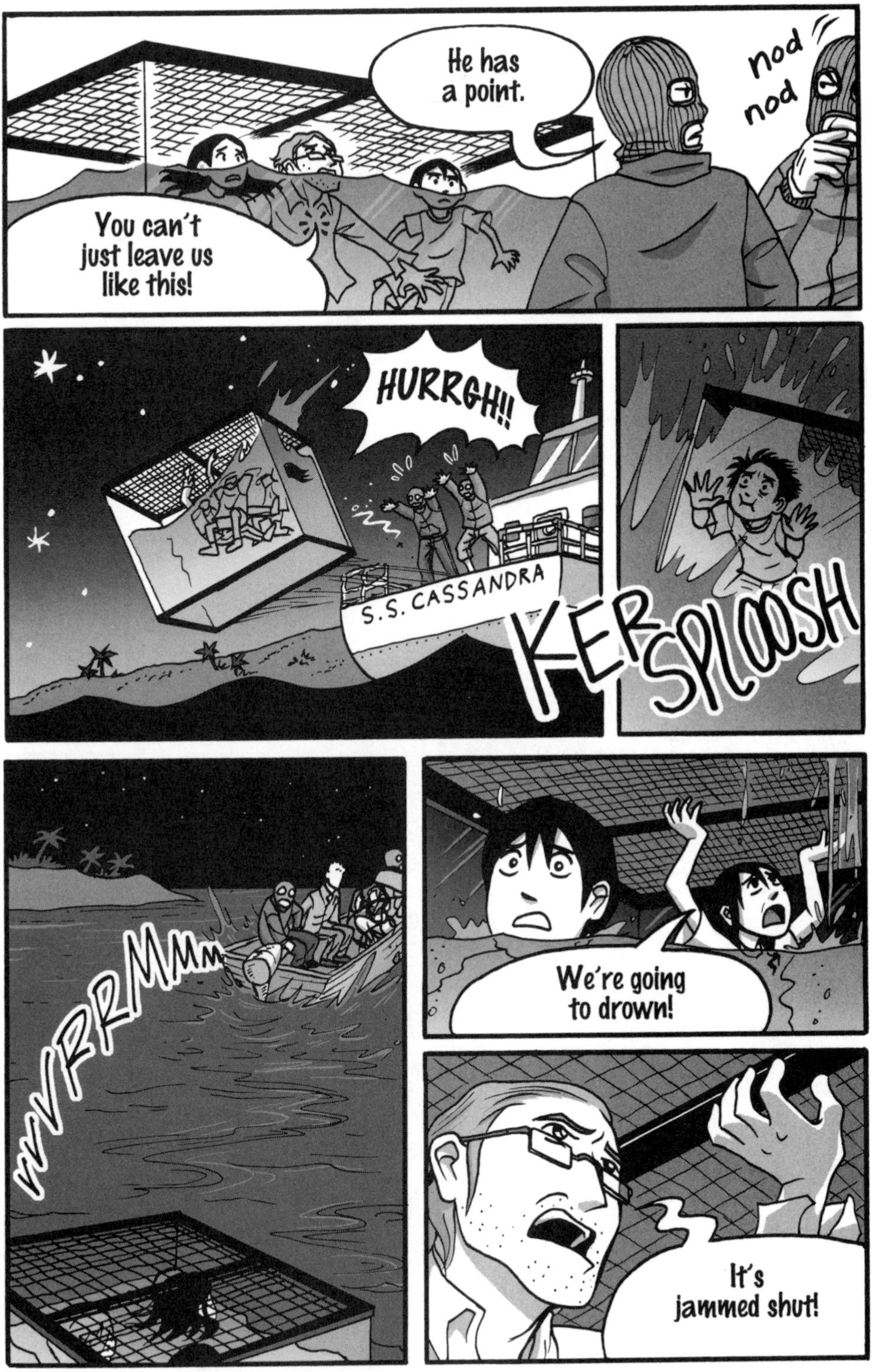
He has a point.
nod nod
You can't just leave us like this!
HURRGH!!
S.S. CASSANDRA
KER SPLOOSH
wwVRRMMmm
We're going to drown!
It's jammed shut!

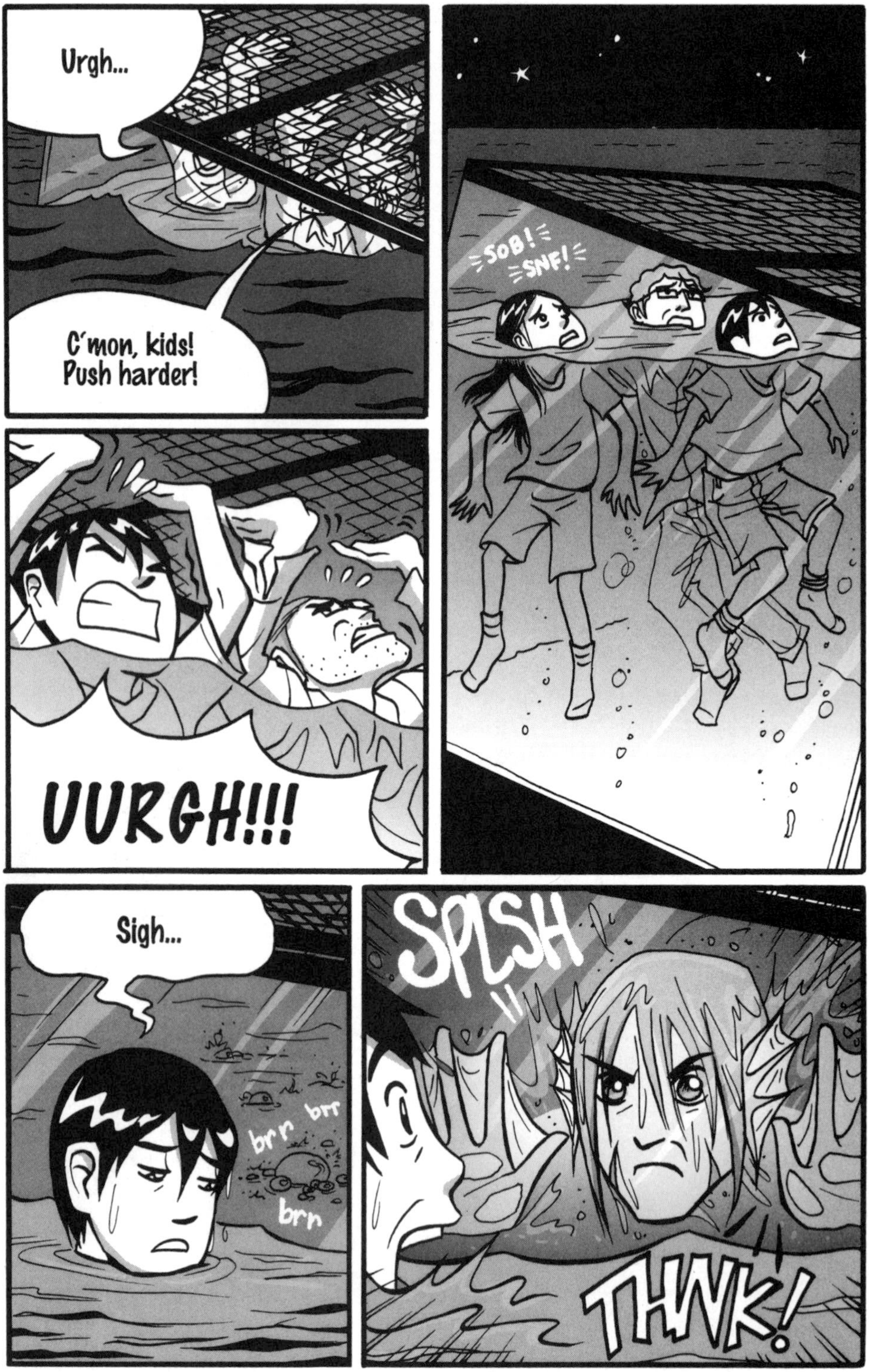
Urgh...
C'mon, kids! Push harder!
SOB!
SNF!
UURGH!!!
Sigh...
brr brr
brn
SPLSH
THNK!

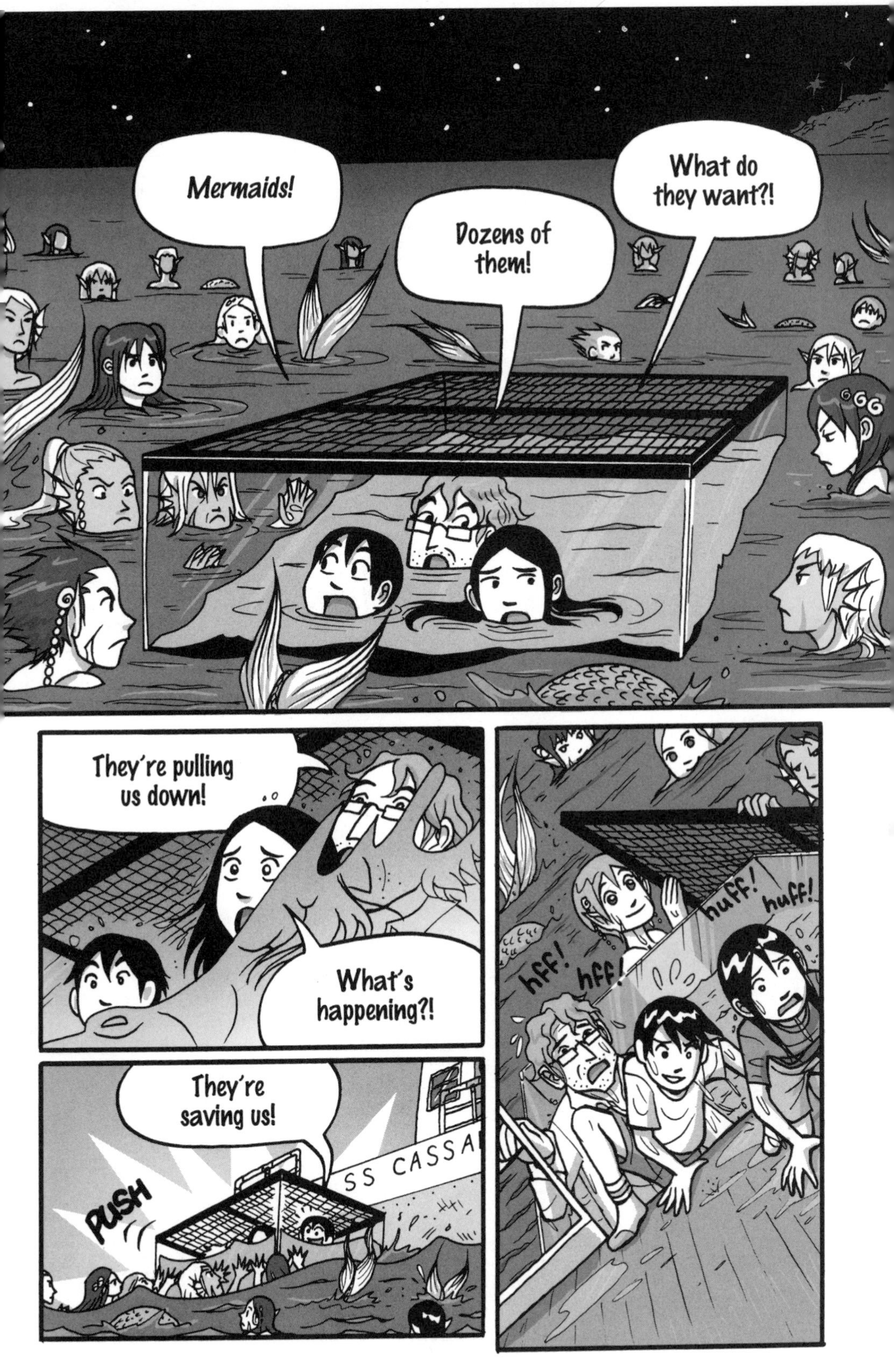

Mermaids!
Dozens of them!
What do they want?!
They're pulling us down!
What's happening?!
They're saving us!
PUSH
SS CASSA
hff!
hff!
huff!
huff!

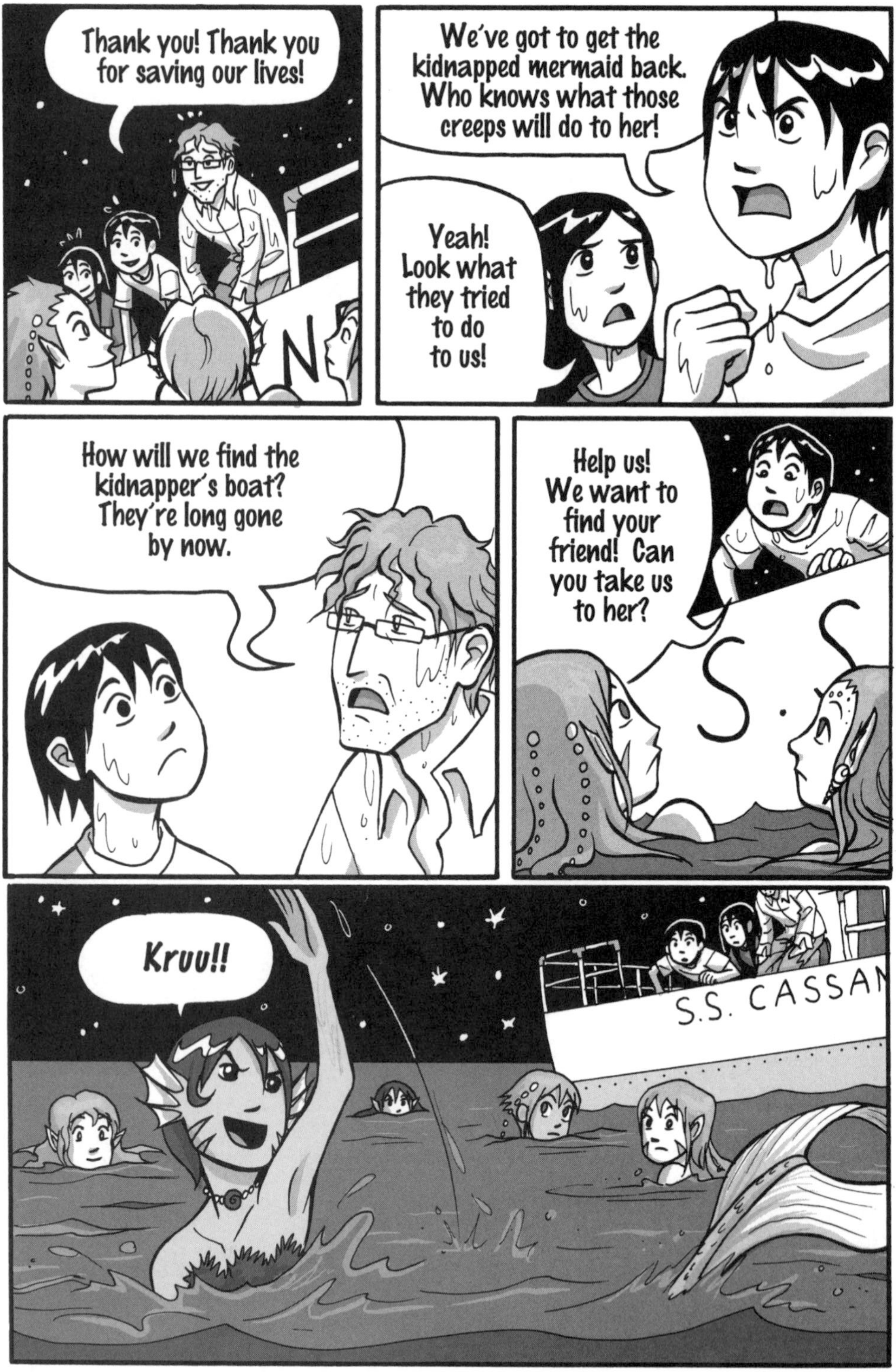
Thank you! Thank you for saving our lives!
We've got to get the kidnapped mermaid back. Who knows what those creeps will do to her!
Yeah! Look what they tried to do to us!
How will we find the kidnapper's boat? They're long gone by now.
Help us! We want to find your friend! Can you take us to her?
S.S
Kruu!!
S.S. CASSAN

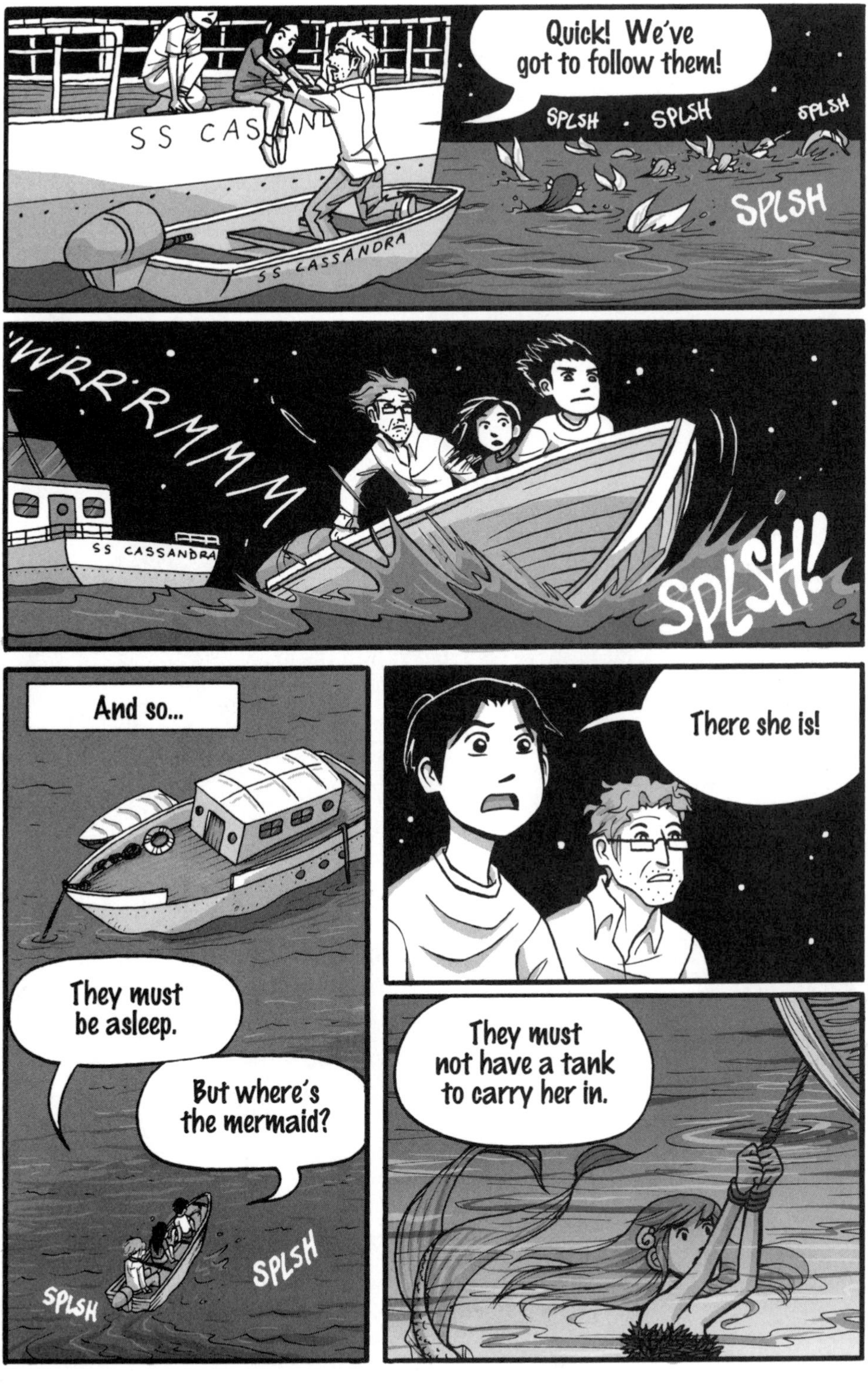
Quick! We've got to follow them!
SS CASSANDRA
SS CASSANDRA
SPLSH
SPLSH
SPLSH
SPLSH
WRRRMMMM
SS CASSANDRA
SPLSH!
And so...
They must be asleep.
But where's the mermaid?
SPLSH
SPLSH
There she is!
They must not have a tank to carry her in.

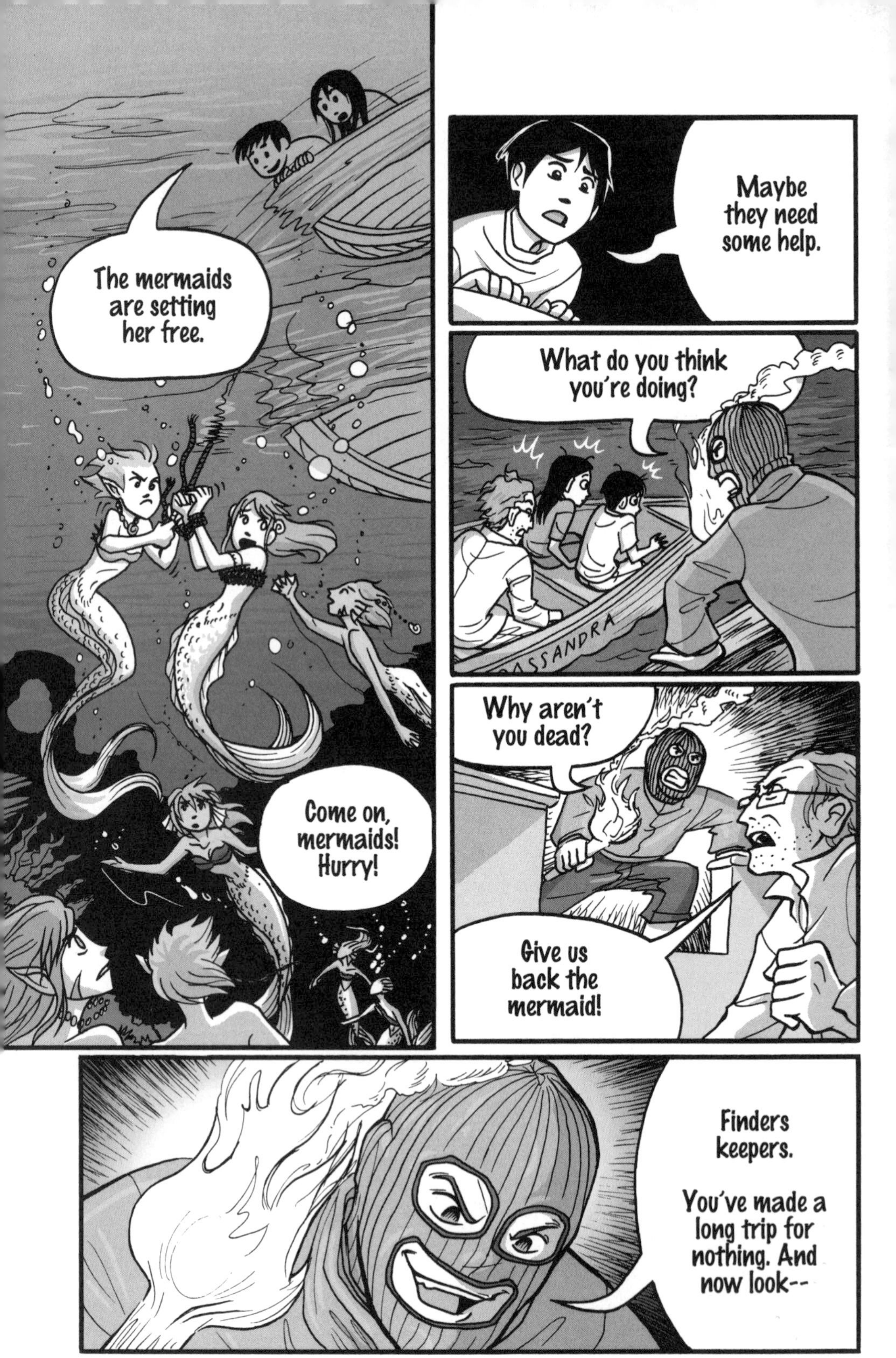
The mermaids are setting her free.
Come on, mermaids! Hurry!
Maybe they need some help.
What do you think you're doing?
CASSANDRA
Why aren't you dead?
Give us back the mermaid!
Finders keepers.
You've made a long trip for nothing. And now look--

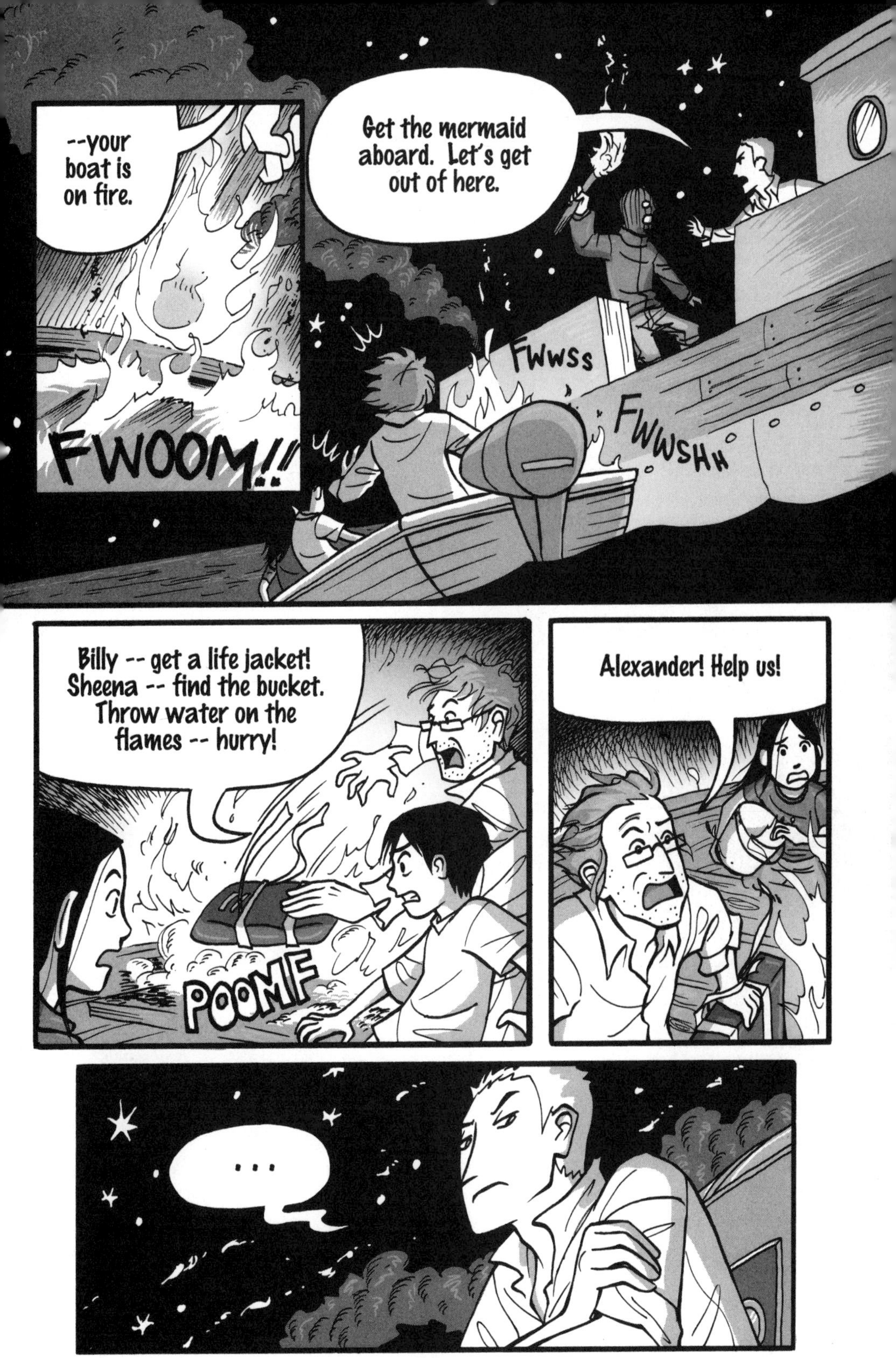
--your boat is on fire.
FWOOM!!
Get the mermaid aboard. Let's get out of here.
FWWSS
FWWSHH
Billy -- get a life jacket! Sheena -- find the bucket. Throw water on the flames -- hurry!
POOMF
Alexander! Help us!
...

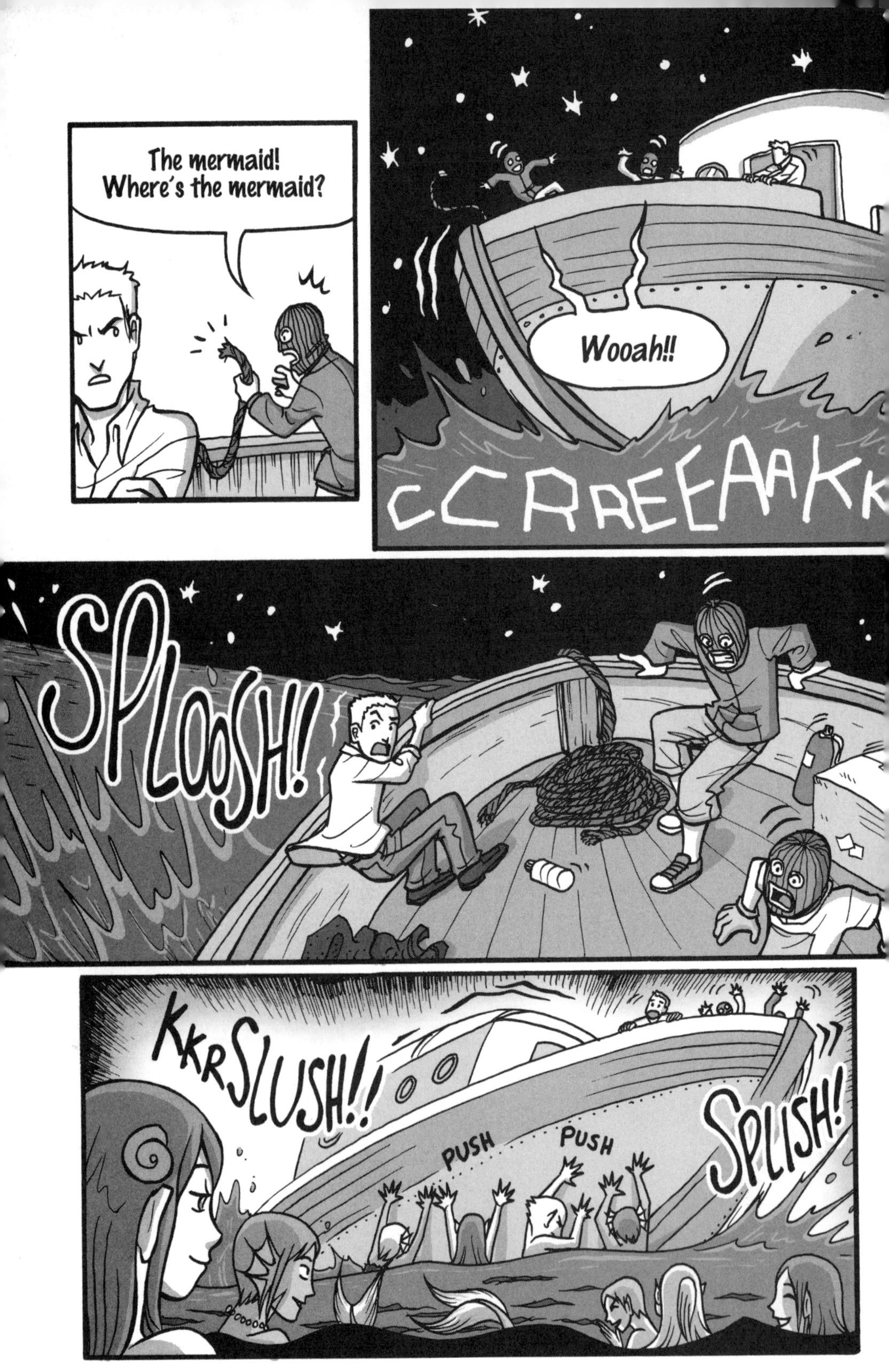

The mermaid! Where's the mermaid?
Wooah!!
CCRREEAAKK
SPLOOSH!
KKRSLUSH!!
PUSH
PUSH
SPLISH!

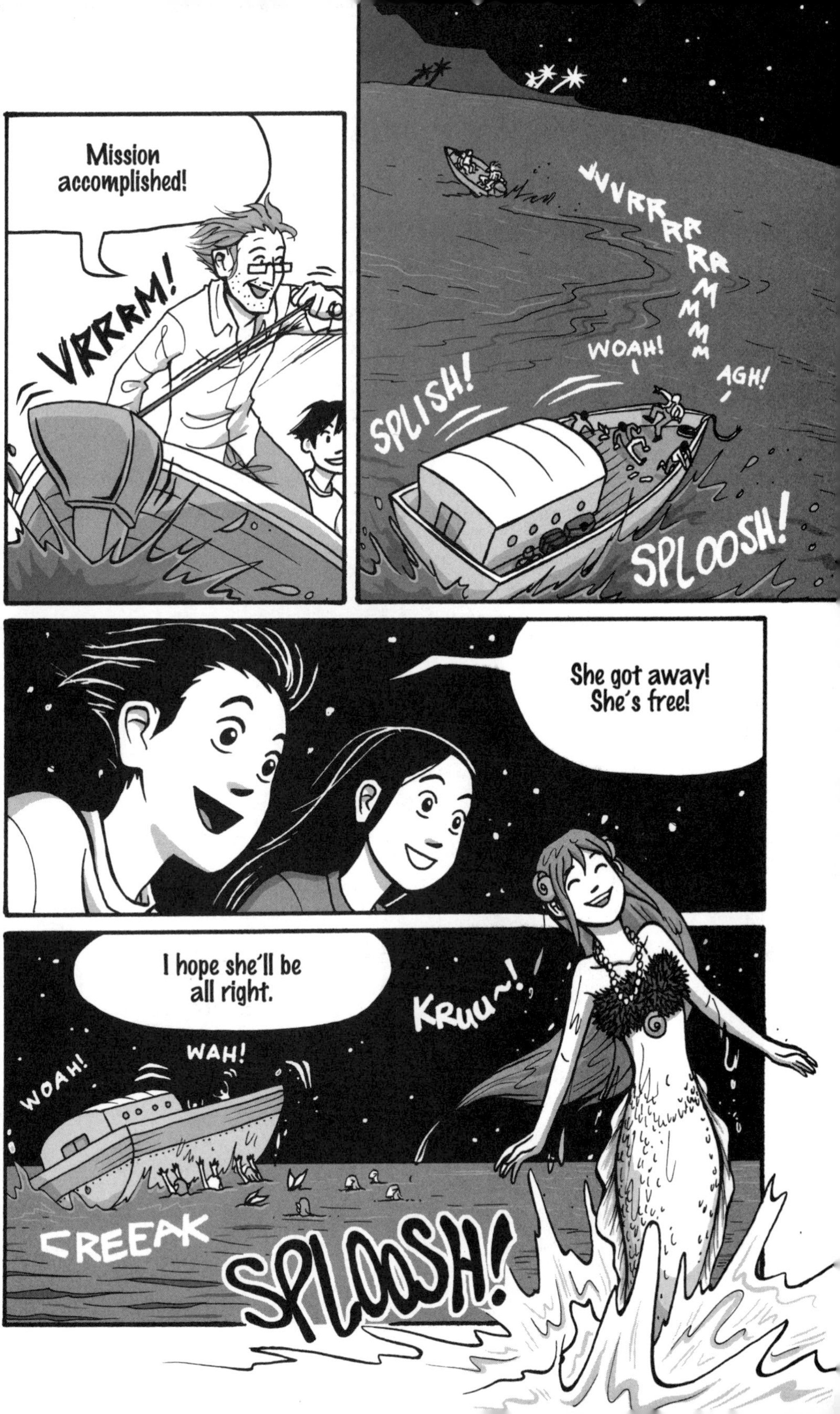
Mission accomplished!
VRRRM!
JVVRRRRRRMMMM
WOAH!
AGH!
SPLISH!
SPLOOSH!
She got away! She's free!
I hope she'll be all right.
KRUU~!
WOAH!
WAH!
CREEAK
SPLOOSH!

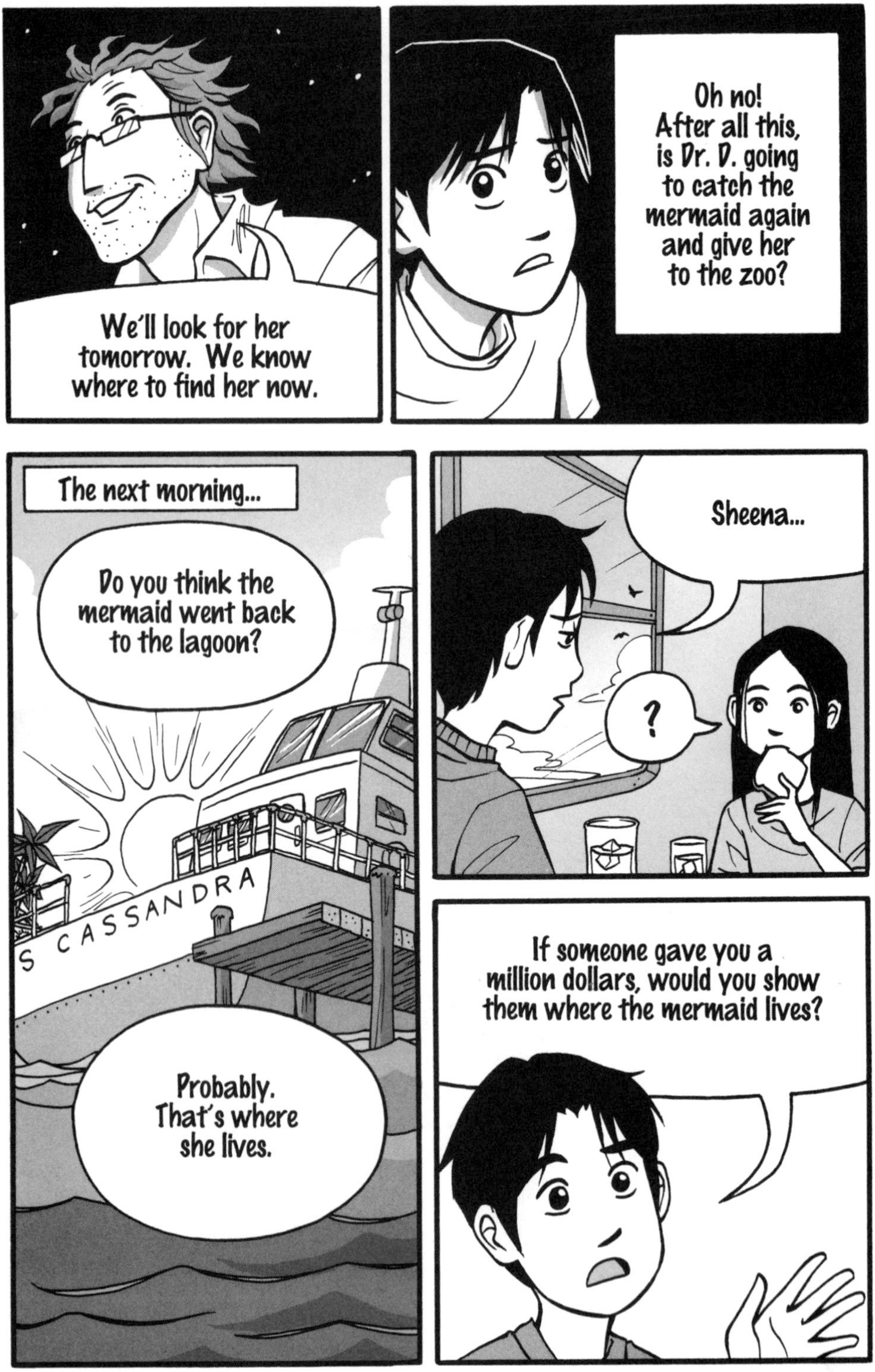
We'll look for her tomorrow. We know where to find her now.
Oh no! After all this, is Dr. D. going to catch the mermaid again and give her to the zoo?
The next morning...
Do you think the mermaid went back to the lagoon?
S CASSANDRA
Probably. That's where she lives.
Sheena...
?
If someone gave you a million dollars, would you show them where the mermaid lives?

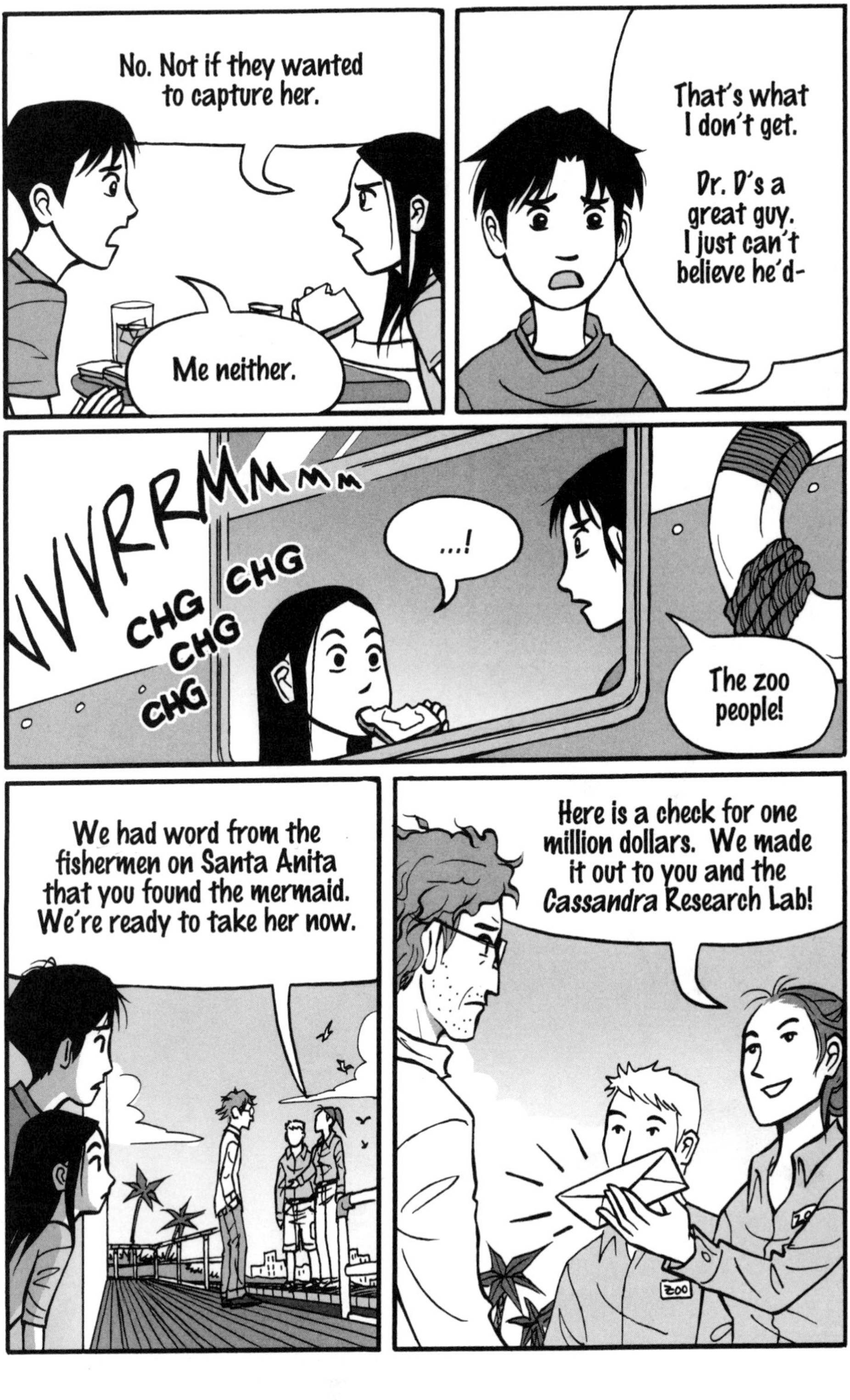
No. Not if they wanted to capture her.
Me neither.
That's what I don't get.
Dr. D's a great guy. I just can't believe he'd-
VVVRRMMMMM
CHG CHG
CHG
CHG
...!
The zoo people!
We had word from the fishermen on Santa Anita that you found the mermaid. We're ready to take her now.
Here is a check for one million dollars. We made it out to you and the *Cassandra* Research Lab!
ZOO

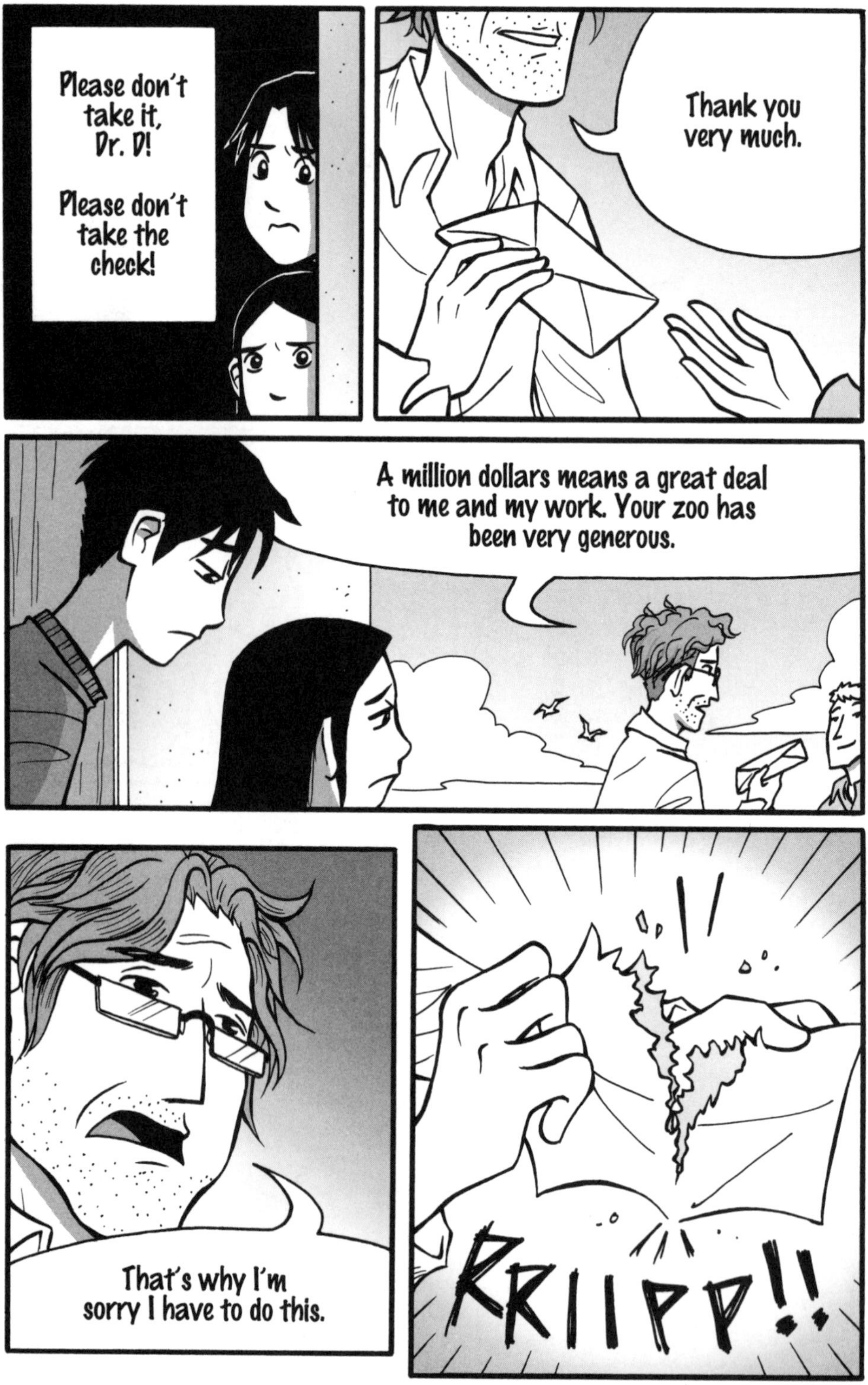
Please don't take it, Dr. D!
Please don't take the check!
Thank you very much.
A million dollars means a great deal to me and my work. Your zoo has been very generous.
That's why I'm sorry I have to do this.
KRIIPP!!

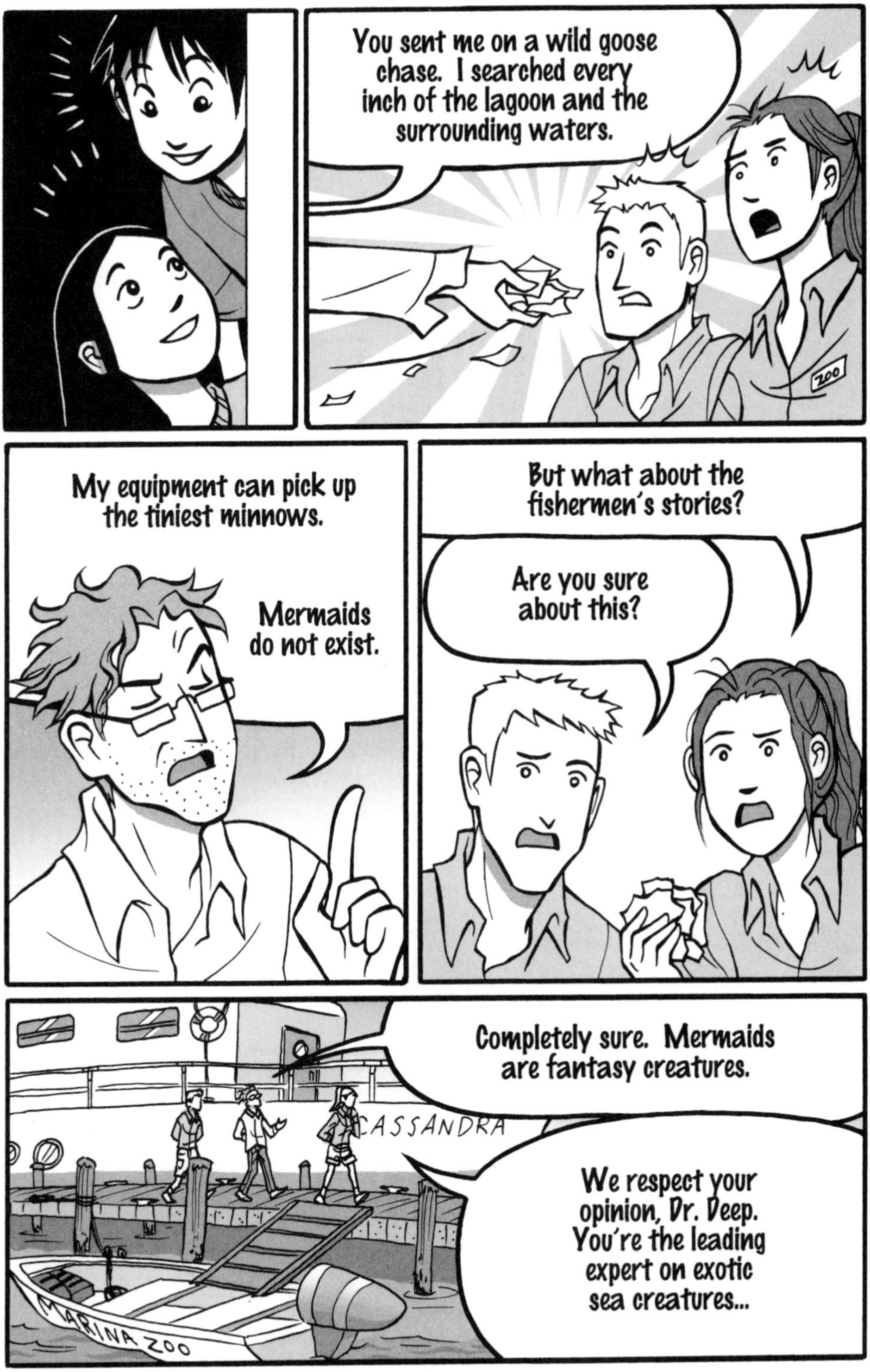
You sent me on a wild goose chase. I searched every inch of the lagoon and the surrounding waters.
ZOO
My equipment can pick up the tiniest minnows.
Mermaids do not exist.
But what about the fishermen's stories?
Are you sure about this?
Completely sure. Mermaids are fantasy creatures.
CASSANDRA
We respect your opinion, Dr. Deep. You're the leading expert on exotic sea creatures...
MARINA ZOO

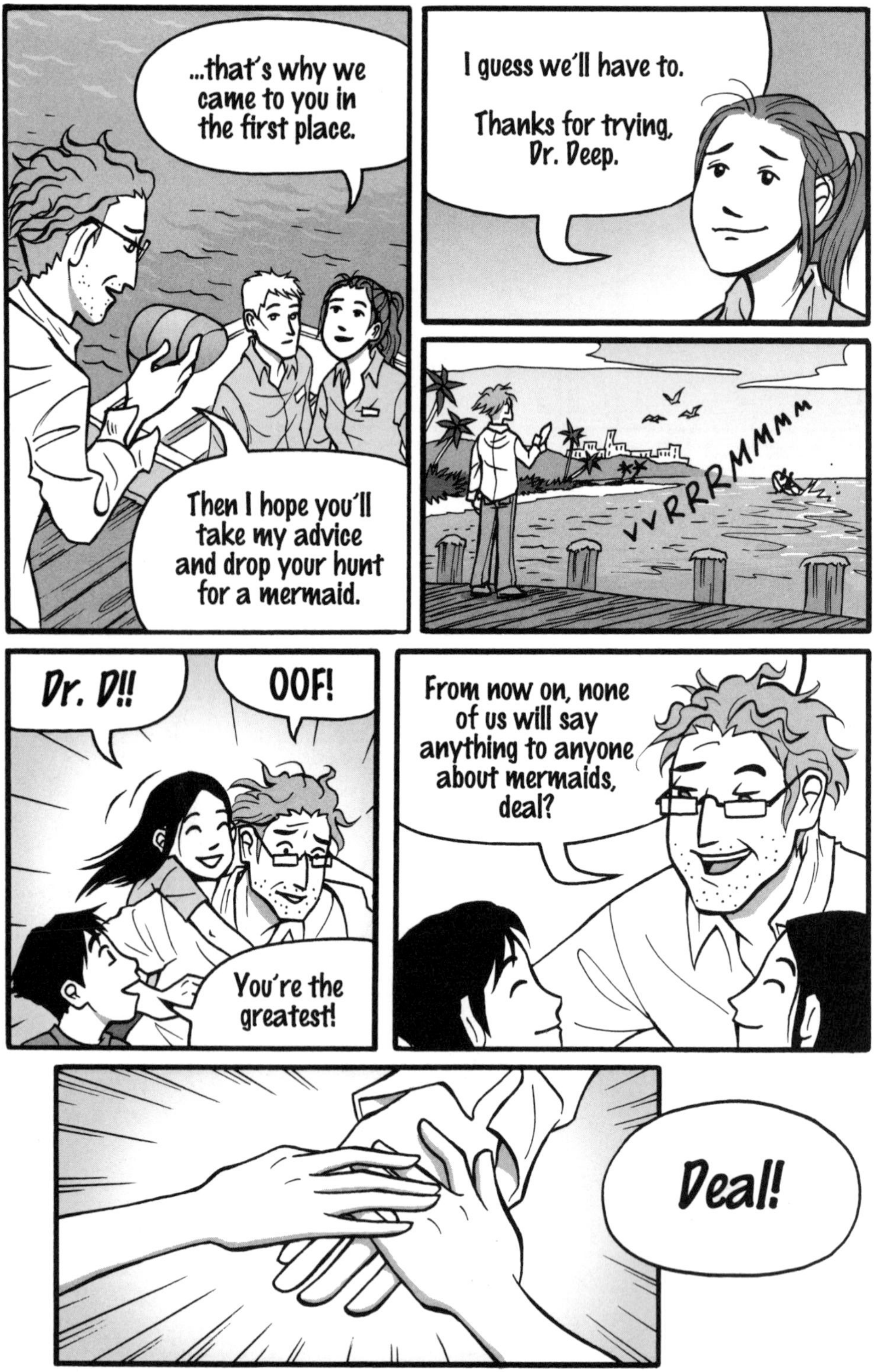
...that's why we came to you in the first place.
Then I hope you'll take my advice and drop your hunt for a mermaid.
I guess we'll have to.
Thanks for trying, Dr. Deep.
VVRRRMMMMM
Dr. D!!
OOF!
You're the greatest!
From now on, none of us will say anything to anyone about mermaids, deal?
Deal!

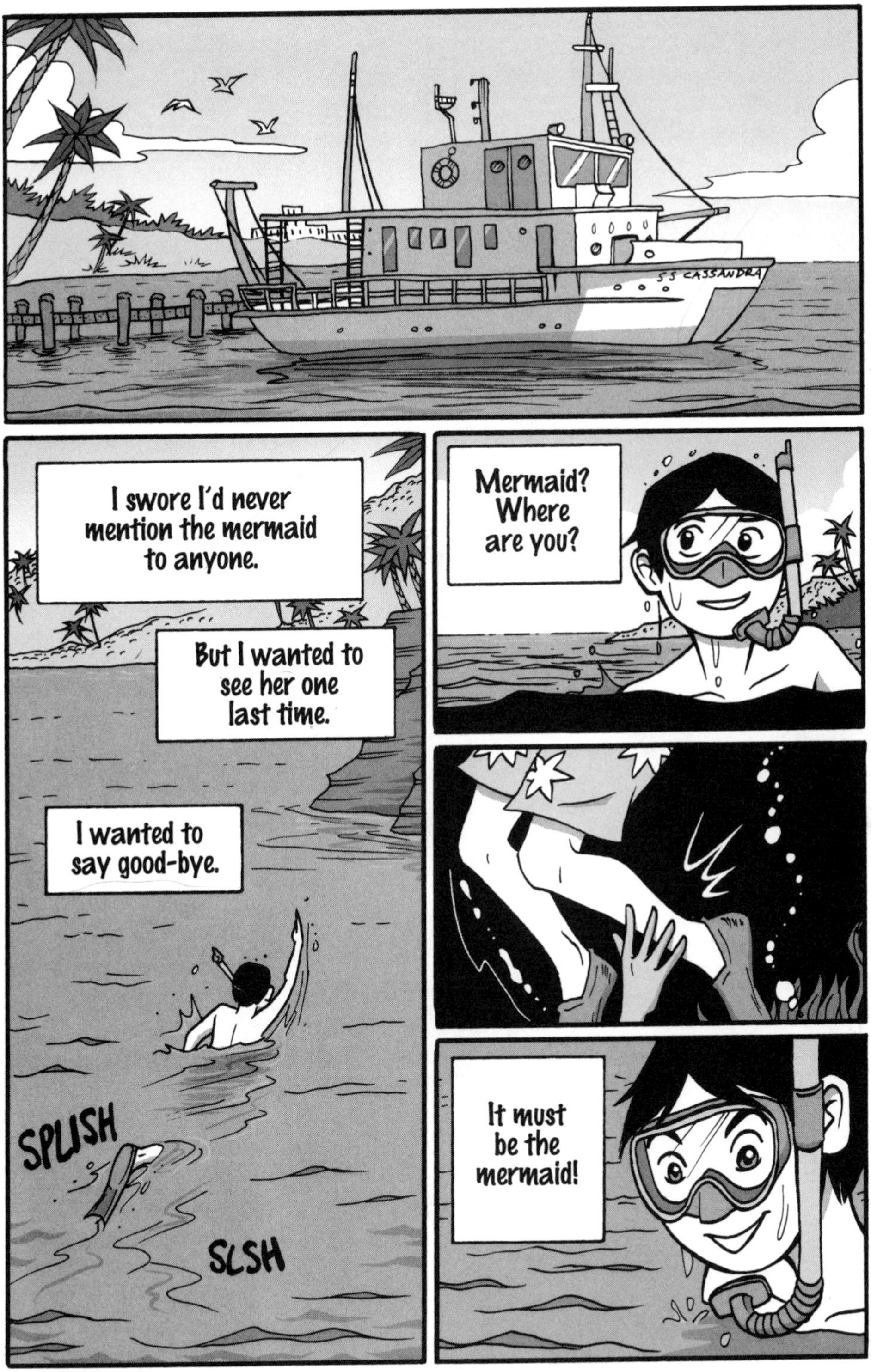
S.S. CASSANDRA
I swore I'd never mention the mermaid to anyone.
But I wanted to see her one last time.
I wanted to say good-bye.
SPLISH
SLSH
Mermaid? Where are you?
It must be the mermaid!

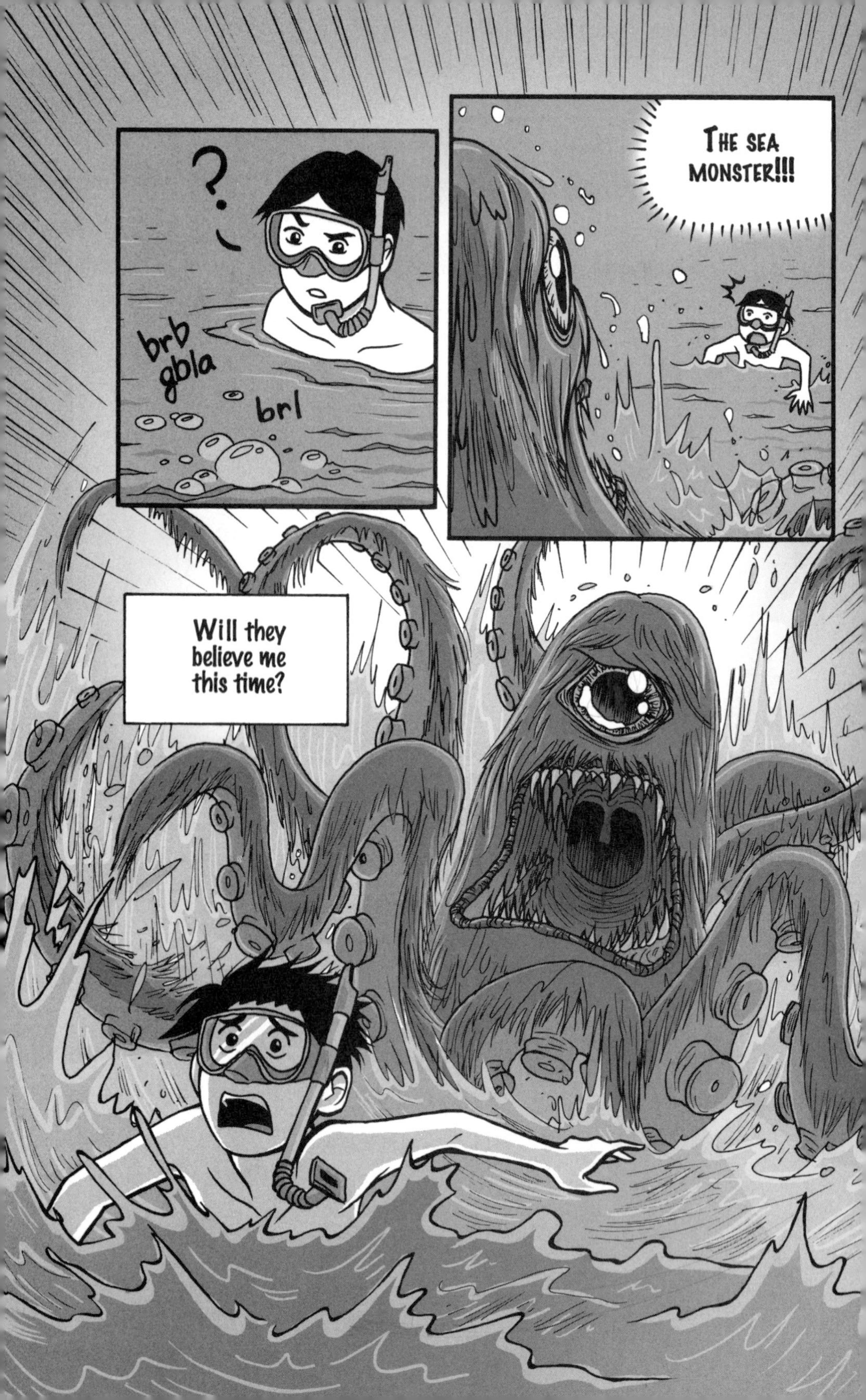
?
brb gbla
brl
THE SEA MONSTER!!!
Will they believe me this time?

MEET THE ARTIST

Jill Thompson

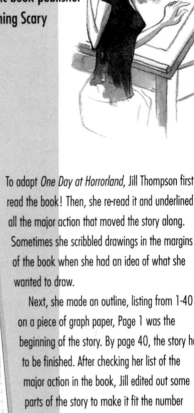

Jill Thompson has illustrated books for nearly every comic book publisher in the United States. She is the creator of the award-winning Scary Godmother series and lives in Chicago, Illinois.

1 on the way in the car
2 lost - Scary sign for land
3 parking lot / buses
4 Car Explosion
5 ticket booth - kids beg - LS Werewolf village
6 in WV - Split Parents kids - wolf
7 - no pinching sign - run to Doom slide - get on / warning
8 start sliding - sliding sliding out
9 - out - wait wait wait no Clay - look on other side. go back
10 take slide together - fall fall fall
11 - out - Clay. - to the House of Mirrors
12 go in - reflections - lost.
13 giggle where are U. - See them - all separated
14 walls move - squeezed - scream
15 floor drop - Okay - Next. Can u die? Only once
16 - Black Flowers - no pinch
17 - doors shut
18 can't breathe - door opened kids disheveled
19 run out - Have you seen our parents. - they left.
20 Wander for hours. - Alligator pond
21 express worries - Hands Push. Scream
22 hands on shoulders - Mom & Dad! I want to go home.
23 Strange never heard of park. enjoy ride it's your last!
24 in coffin. - coffin shuts
25 - in coffins float. vulture in sky - Spiders - Start 2 scream/cough
26 scream hot sun, ankles itch. Complain to Booth. I hate this place
27 Open. blink - horrible. Alive. Padlock gate. locked in
28 all booths closed - no one leaves
29 - backed up - horrors come hundreds.
30 Horrorland Hidden Camera! What? Cameras
31 - new cars in lot - yellow door
32 - Welcome to Horrorland Challenge. This is real
33 - Run you have 56 seconds. big gorilla thing / dad grabs / to run
34 2 birds - Dad attacked by creature
35 lizards, - carried away.
36 - three survivors - kids cry - mistake
37 - Monster Channel - back to pond now jump in or push.
38 - Pinch her - monsters run, family run
39 - get in bus. here they come no one escapes. squeal out.
40 hours hours. Safe. Horror on bus. OH no! What do you

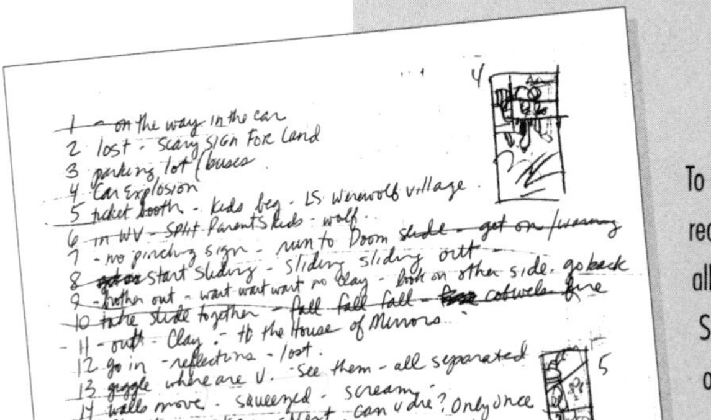

Outline

To adapt *One Day at Horrorland*, Jill Thompson first read the book! Then, she re-read it and underlined all the major action that moved the story along. Sometimes she scribbled drawings in the margins of the book when she had an idea of what she wanted to draw.

Next, she made an outline, listing from 1-40 on a piece of graph paper, Page 1 was the beginning of the story. By page 40, the story had to be finished. After checking her list of the major action in the book, Jill edited out some parts of the story to make it fit the number of pages she had to work with.

Jill then drew small sketches called thumbnails to give herself an idea of how the action on each page would appear to the reader. Next she drew the story lightly in pencil on pages of two-ply Bristol board. At this stage, she also put the lettering on the pages by hand and drew the word balloons. Finally, she used india drawing ink and a Deleter brand manga pen set to finish the drawings and the lettering. After the ink dried, she erased any pencil lines that remained on the board. This is called cleaning up the page. Jill still does all of her drawing and lettering by hand on actual paperboard, but she's also learning how to do the lettering on her computer.

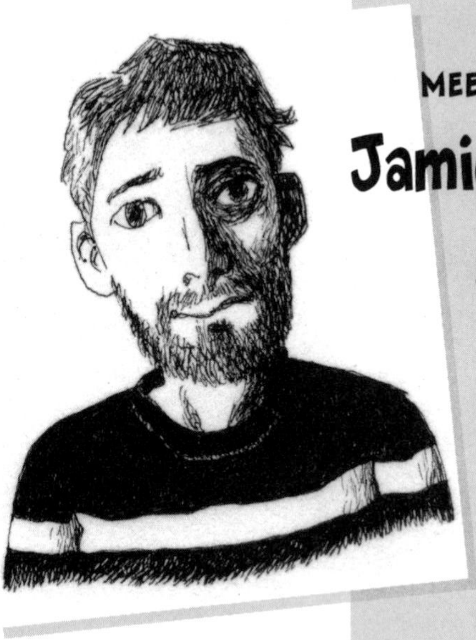

MEET THE ARTIST

Jamie Tolagson

Jamie Tolagson lives in Victoria, British Columbia, Canada. He's been drawing comics for as long as he can remember. He still draws them the same way he did when he was a kid: with a pencil, pen, and paper. Jamie thinks it's more fun to draw on paper than on a computer, though sometimes he does use a computer to add gray tones to his work.

Jamie draws miniature versions of all his comics before he draws the full-sized versions. That way he can read the comic before anyone else to see if it's going the way he wants it to.

When he draws the full-sized comic, he first uses a # 2 pencil to sketch in what is happening on the pages; then he finishes the drawings with a fine-tipped ink pen. That's the part that takes up the most time. Normally, Jamie works a "size up," which means that he draws the pages twice as big as they will appear in the published comic. But for *A Shocker on Shock Street*, he decided to work at actual size, because it's closer to the size Jamie liked to draw at when he was a kid. Art school taught him to draw BIGGER, but he thinks it's fun to draw small, too—that way he can carry the drawing around and work on it anywhere: at the kitchen table, on the bus, wherever.

Jamie found working on this story to be a lot of fun. As he put it, "It's not often that I get to draw page after page of ghouls, ghosts, worms, skeletons, and giant salivating insects."

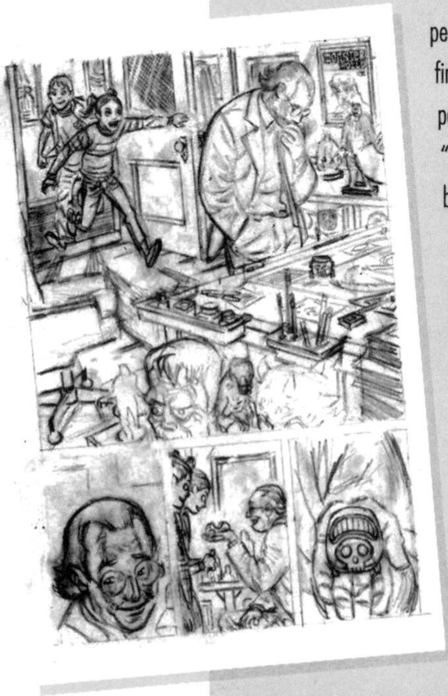

Penciled page

MEET THE ARTIST

Amy Kim Ganter

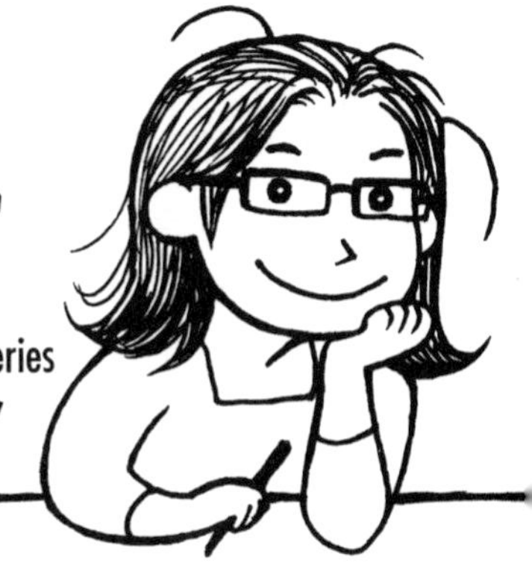

Amy Kim Ganter is the creator of Sorcerers & Secretaries, a manga series published by Tokyopop, as well as the webcomic "Reman Mythology." She has also contributed to the acclaimed *Flight* anthology. Amy lives in Alhambra, California.

Amy read *Deep Trouble*, highlighted her favorite moments, and wrote the script for the comic adaptation at the same time.

Once the script was set, she drew layouts. These are rough sketches, drawn two pages per 8½ x 11 sheet of paper (**A**).

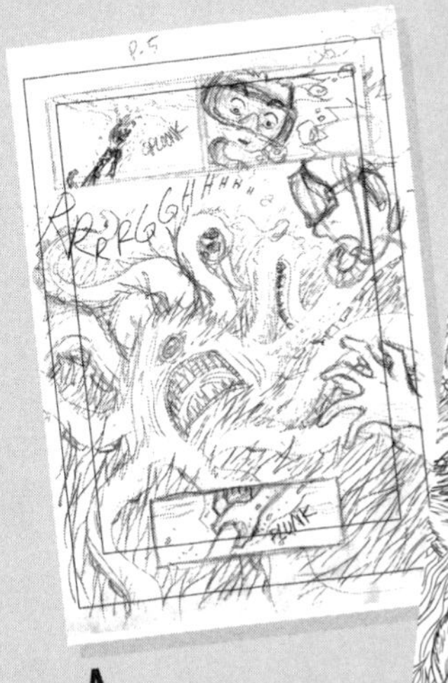
SPLOONK
PLUNK

A

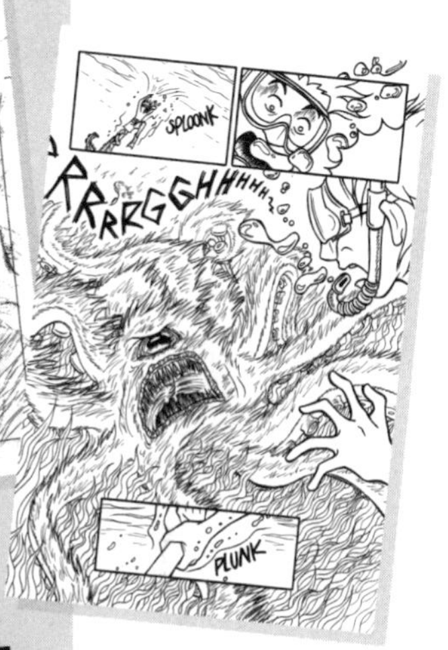
SPLOONK
PLUNK

B

After the sketches were approved, it was time to ink and tone! She scanned in the layouts, increased the size on the computer so they fit one per 9 x 12 sheet of bristol paper, then printed out the layouts in light blue ink. She drew the linework directly on these bristol printouts using Micron pens. Her inks tend to look like something from a coloring book. See how much meaner the monster looks now? (**B**)

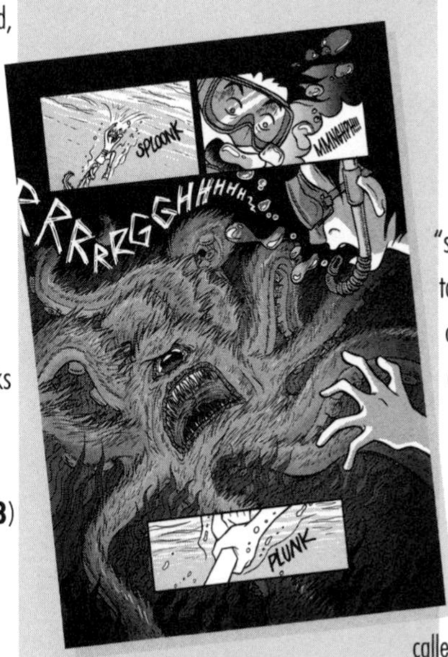
SPLOONK
PLUNK

C

Now the artwork was ready for "special effects" known as gray-scaled tones, which Amy does with the computer program Photoshop. She also adds in the dialogue, which she had already typed in the computer and the sound effects, which she draws by hand. (**C**) Multiply this process 46 times and you have a cool Goosebumps Graphix story called *Deep Trouble*!

MORE GHOULISH TALES TO COME!

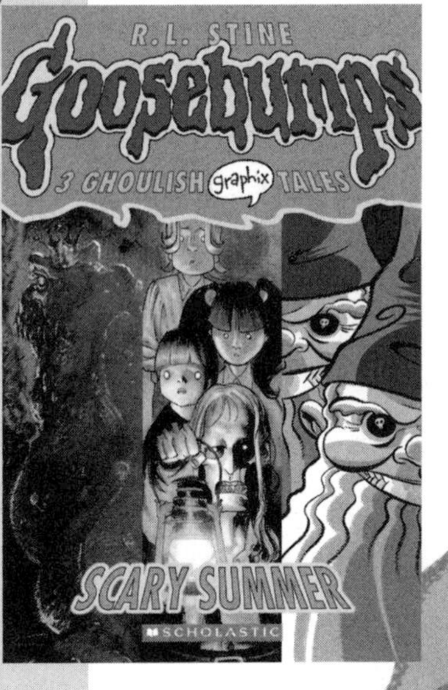
R.L. STINE
Goosebumps
3 GHOULISH graphix TALES
SCARY SUMMER
SCHOLASTIC

Wish that summer would never end? Not *THIS* summer!

Sandy beaches, tidal pools, shoreline caves . . . ghosts! A brother and sister's seaside vacation turns spooky at ***Ghost Beach*** by **Ted Naifeh**, creator of the creepy Courtney Crumrin series.

Someone's creeping through the garden, whispering nasty things, smashing melons, and squashing tomatoes, but those funky lawn ornaments can't move . . . right? **Dean Haspiel**, a veteran of Batman and Justice League comics and the acclaimed artist on *The Quitter*, knows just how to portray ***The Revenge of the Lawn Gnomes***.

In his comic series like The Bakers and Plastic Man, **Kyle Baker** proves he's one funny artist. The perfect guy to draw a story about a summer camp where it's all fun and games and everybody's happy. Too happy . . . That's why one young girl is out to uncover ***The Horror at Camp Jellyjam.***

AVAILABLE IN JULY 2007

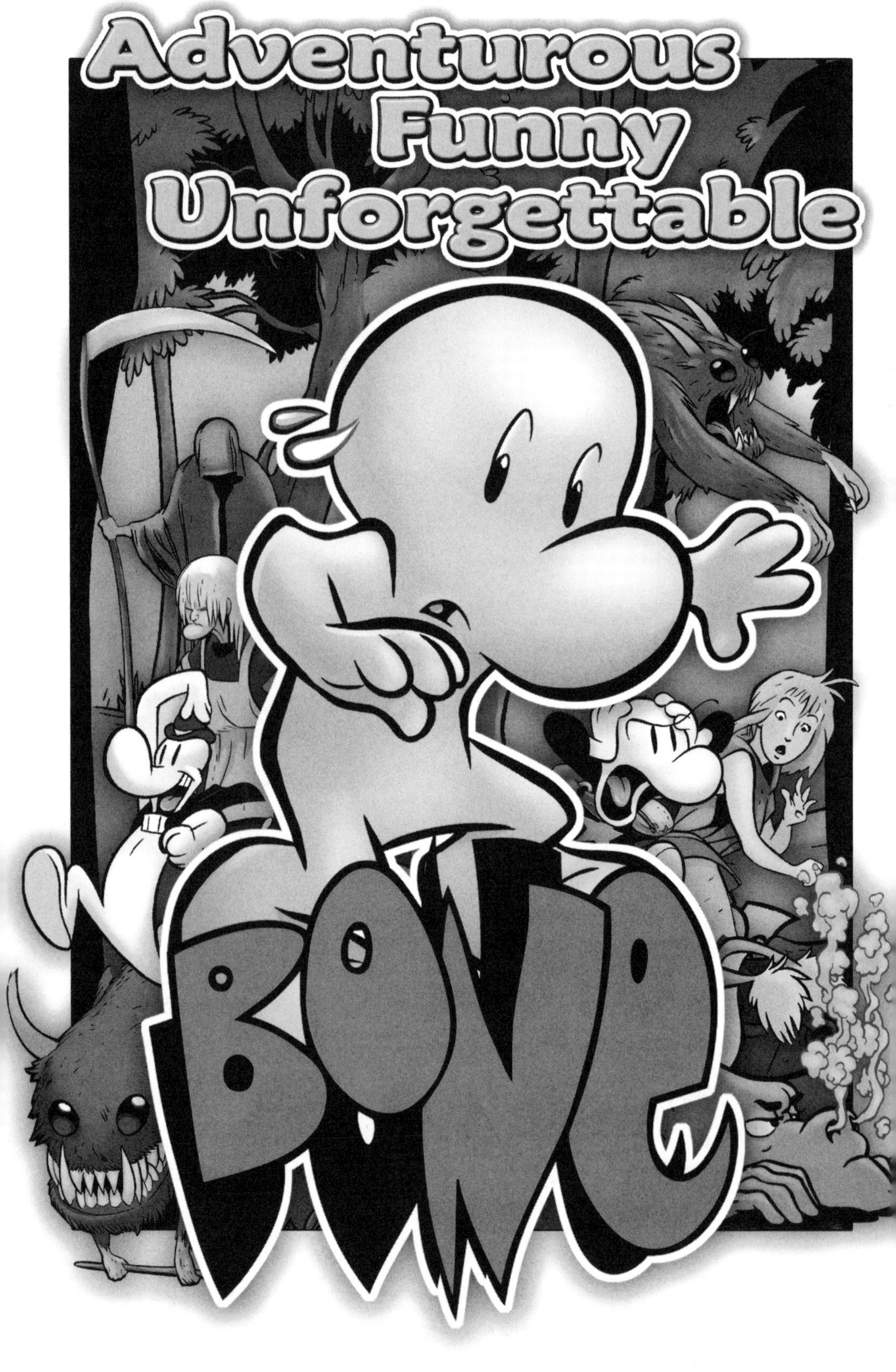
Adventurous
Funny
Unforgettable
BONE